the gambler

the
g a m b l e r

CHRISTINE DWYER HICKEY

**NEW
ISLAND**

the gambler
published 2006
by New Island
2 Brookside
Dundrum Road
Dublin 14
www.newisland.ie

Original edition published 1996 by Marino Books

The author has asserted her moral rights.

ISBN 1 905494 10 6

British Library Cataloguing in Publication Data. A CIP catalogue record for this book is available from the British Library.

Printed in the UK by CPD, Ebbw Vale, Wales

New Island received financial assistance from
The Arts Council (An Chomhairle Ealaíon), Dublin, Ireland.

10 9 8 7 6 5 4 3 2 1

In memory of my father

CONTENTS

PROLOGUE

There is a bed made up in the corner for the nights he is too drunk to walk. Looking down at it now he knows last night must have been one such; the pillow folded the way he likes it, the blankets frowning on the floor. And his shoes? Always he remembers to take off his shoes. This amazes him each time. The things he has remembered to do without remembering the act of doing them. The whiskey bottle for example, with the cork replaced. And the glass, an extra one and clean, for when he wakes. He has seen his wife do such things over and over: the baby's bottle near to hand to silence that first cry, the table set the night before to facilitate the morning rush. Does she, he wonders, remember doing them at all? Or does it seem to her, as it seems to him, to have been attended to by someone else? Someone unknown? And his coat he notes too, there draped over the shoulders of the chair. All this seen to. And by him. Who else would ever enter this room? He feels his upper arms; yes, sore again. Who else would cross the door where the last flight narrows to the top? And where wall to wall, he has staggered the blows, this arm, now that. Now this one again.

Somewhere, a mile above him, is a ceiling. And another mile below, an undressed floor. The gaps between the planks of wood run under and away from his feet like spikes. So he is standing.

The first thing to do is find the day; the next his place within it. Even after the shutters have been unfolded, the difference will be minimal; it is a room that daylight does not impress.

He has a feeling it may be Sunday. When he has opened the shutters, he can be sure. And he will get around to that. In a moment. He will get around to it. Any minute now.

He reminds himself of what he will see then: an early morning worshipper, perhaps, or a struggling cyclist leaving the night shift behind. Otherwise the vista of the quays to his left will be unperturbed; no clutter of traffic to worry its course. No distractions; grey stone and soft water. Easy on the eye. Yes, easy.

And bald steps leading to the Four Courts and the vacant black arcades. On the pediment above they will stand: wisdom, authority: statues of the righteous sort. And more to the centre there will be Moses. He can depend on that. In the middle with his tablets of the law, there will always be Moses. He will find him there. In a minute.

The river will stretch out slowly through the city. It will skip between them like a favourite child. And they watching over it, with a supervisory eye. Moses on the one side. His well behaved family silent and serene beside him. And downriver a little and across the way, at the first brick of Wood Quay, the first tip of its wide and ancient smile. Looking down from the top of the house, a man wanting or half-wanting to satisfy a vague curiosity as to the day he is now living through.

Standing at the shutters now, he waits before unfolding them. His busybody ear has started up already, sensitive to every sound. It tries to establish a reality that he could really do without. His ear straining, struggling, defiant as it always is. Picking up sounds from downstairs first; the busy-lipped whistles and the mulatto of muffled conversations. And then the clearer sequence; one, two, three chairs being pulled from table-tops, back down along a clean, unworried floor. The bottles are all that remain now, the giggling crated bottles, hoisted up from the cellar and ready for unloading. Only the silent tasks are left. The rubbing up of shines and polishing of light into the dull bar-room. Taps and mirrors, brass rails and brass trims. And a chorus-line extravaganza of glasses, all shapes and all sizes. To brighten the interior. To keep away the dark. To push it back and up the narrow stairs, confine it to the uppermost floor.

His ear is satisfied. It moves on now to the noises from the street outside. Too loud, too busy for Sunday. Perhaps he has been mistaken all along? Yet it sounds too busy for any day at all.

There are footsteps marching, marching. There are flimsy childish cries and thicker ones calling out. And music. Is that music?

He leaves the shutters for the moment and walks across to the only other piece of furniture in the room. The chair, long ago carried from the bar downstairs. He drags it across the bare floor, his coat-tail swinging as he goes. His ear makes too much of the grating noise and the emphasis of his game leg: tip, then tip, then tip again. He places the chair before the window and walks back. The bottle . . .

The bottle he lifts slowly and with both hands he transports it to the window. He returns for the glass. This time one hand will do. Now he is ready. He lifts the steel latch away and sets it carefully to one side. Then he folds the shutters into themselves. The windows are drizzle-damp. He sits down on the chair and settles himself so that he can feel there is the same amount of seat space all around him. Now he is balanced. The number ten plays peep-o in his mind. Why ten? Did he borrow ten bob from someone last night? Did a horse number ten come in for him or more likely fall miserably out? Is it the tenth of the month? The tenth month then? October?

The noise from the street is louder now and his ear is at its keenest. Sifting through the sounds. Bands, footsteps. What else? Horses. Hooves of horses, jangling harness, tinkling reins. And ten. The number ten. He is married ten years. Is that it? He has been ten years the proprietor of this house. He will never be more than ten years here; in a fortnight it will belong to somebody else, become somebody else's timepiece. The eldest son? That child is ten. The same age as his marriage; younger by just four months. He closes his eyes. Here now is the month. November. After that the Christmas one? December.

He sets the glass between his knees and waits before he reaches down for the bottle. Not yet. Not ready yet. He looks out through the window. He is losing his day.

At first he thinks he is looking down on Smithfield Market, row after row of cobbled stones. Gentle bulges, smoothly black. There is a sense of movement, his movement, flying lowly, slowly, across the stones, like a bird about to land. He can feel himself reel. But then he realises. No. Hats. These are hard hats bustling along. It is not he who is moving; it is the hats. His balance is restored.

Now soldiers coming ranks-full and uneven; a privet hedge trimmed by a madman. High low. Medium slow. Some are way lower than others. And these are gliding. Gliding midgets? No. Pushed along in a chair that moves. Wheels, not legs. Wheelchairs. That's it. And one or two more – much taller than the rest – growing upwards, shoulders narrowing. Heads as small as fists. Deformed? Wait, no. He sees – these are children, children dressed in khaki and perched on top of shoulders. Boy soldiers. Fathers' shoulders. Hup, two, three . . . passing, passed, gone. Gone past.

Now the women coming, apple ladies from the Pillar and fine

12

suburban ladies and where now are all the ladies going, where . . .?

He reaches down to the floor and his hands like a jib crane bring the bottle up to him. And he says to himself, 'Three hands would be handy.' Three or maybe four. He wonders which to put on the neck of the bottle, which should be used to pull? He closes his eyes. The cork gives itself easily to his hand. Another thing remembered – loosen the cork in preparation. No, two hands would do after all, with such forethought, such planning. He draws the bottle back like an arrow to the bow and watches jerks of whiskey lose the way. There, it's there – the mouth of the glass. No, there . . . look . . . He shifts the jib crane a little to the left. Now. Now it knows where it's aiming. Or almost. The problem is getting it to stop. He steers the jib crane back over to the right, where, confused, it feeds the floorboards. With the heart of the run. Best Jameson run. He'll have to break the heart of the run. He pulls it up . . . Now. Now the dribbling has stopped.

There is shadow along the quays outside. A twilight background. The uniforms, too, are sombre. And the faces? The faces stained by the drizzling rain are darkened by it, as a pavement might be. And yet there is a colour snatching out to get him. Snarling out from the twilight. Colour, vicious colour. Red. Slashing crossways over the crowd of shivering flags; Union Jacks. Union Jacks? The small sense of time he has acquired goes tumbling away from him. Union Jacks? Is that not strange? Could that be right? And such a lot of red now blotting on to the shadows. Fribbles of it, spilling over, all-staining red. Poppies. Ah yes. Poppies, running in the wash. Insistent in their frailty.

His two hands grasp the glass and draw it up towards his mouth. But too far a journey. Too much to expect from it, one little glass. He leans to greet it. They meet, the glass and his mouth, at a midway point. A compromise. They reach each other and he sucks it up sharp. Shivering whiskey he sucks it in, feeling its sting. There now. He hasn't lost too much. Just a little to his knees, his chin and, dropping on his neck, a sprinkle. Now the glass has become more manageable, lifting up and allowing him to drain it. It hits his chest. Yes, it's Sunday.

This time the refill goes without incident and the glass comes up to him; no trouble at all. Almost steady, almost there. And he about to do his part, when he stops. What's that?

Straight across the way from him, where Chancery Place gives way to the bridge, his eye is attracted by an umbrella. But a particular umbrella. And a greatcoat too. But cut with unusual style. He will still notice such things; particular umbrellas, unusual style. He will still notice noticing them. The umbrella has a low-spanned dome, like a flower almost, sleek and shaped and standing out from the crowd of others. Foreign. It is a foreign umbrella, just as the greatcoat is, with its considered cut. It begins to move towards the bridge. Coming across? He feels it may be coming across to him. He waits to see. But then it stops. A crowd of boys have interfered with its path and the umbrella lifts for a moment so that the face beneath it can see. And be seen. He knows that face.

It looks up towards him as though it can see. But not into here. Not this far, it can't. For he has checked this room from every street angle and has loved it for its kind invisibility. The face looks blindly and then a changed mind takes it back to the corner of Chancery Place. Where alone it moves away from the crowd.

Now drink again . . . His ear nudges him with the slurp sounds that he makes. He shuts it off. Yes, there was a time. A time when such a sound would have brought him pleasure, like glass and bottle kissing in a darkened room or the band outside haunting itself with a brass funereal march. There was a time.

Down towards the sleeping markets and the pill of the Bradogue; secret river, the figure is almost out of sight now. He sees it disappear down the aisle. The aisle? Ah yes. That was the last time, alone then too, despite the marriage service just complete and his sister's trail of wedding gown skirting by his side. His sister Kate. Somehow he had managed to be alone then too. His sister's bridegroom. Well now, well.

He looks up and across the sky. He looks up until he finds Moses. Their eyes meet; there you are. Yes, they say to each other. That's it. Now we have it. Armistice Day. Ten years since Armistice Day. There's your ten for you. I have mine and you have yours. Ten years.

He fills the glass again. He's going to need it. There will be gutter squabbles, he thinks, before this Sunday is done.

I

THE IRISH HOUSE: NOVEMBER 1928

ONE

Maude looked out the window. Down on the back terrace the evening starlings had already gathered, and Henry still not up out of bed. She watched under the sunlight, the twitch and tic of their chunky backs the colour of spilt petroleum or the sunpecked jet of a widow's gown, blue and glossy green and purple shot in silk. They no longer looked like a simple congregation of birds. Now they looked like . . . Well, what did it matter what they looked like! They were birds just the same. And besides, the twilight and the winter sun, with its certain dazzle and its heat turned off. So bright today, all the same, hard to believe it would soon be over. Another day gone, and Henry . . .

A late night it had been, yes. But really . . . Staying in bed until this hour. She had never come across such a fondness for the bed. Why, Pat Cleary would have had a week's work . . . She checked herself. No. That wasn't fair. How many times did she have to be reminded? Her first husband and her second were two different men and should *not* be compared. Not under any circumstances. Not in any way whatsoever. And yet . . .

Ten years after Pat's death and eight years into her second marriage, she found them both sometimes, side by side in her head, fidgeting with the final preparations. One might be fixing a bow tie perhaps, while the other's finger swept flecks from his straightened back shoulder. And there would be other gestures too, deliberate, like the twitch and pat of cuff links being settled

19

(for on these occasions evening wear of the strictest formality was always worn by both gentlemen) or the dry discreet clearing of a manly throat. And sometimes too, she would note (although not so deliberate) the involuntary movement of a chin tilting into a suitably dignified angle or an eyebrow rummaging for the spot most likely to manifest intelligence. Whichever way was chosen, each one prepared himself in his own peculiar way, as if both were to be judged. But only one could be chosen and by her, for whatever the issue of the moment might be.

And if, for example, it happened to concern hard work or indeed, the style and grace of a turn or two on the dancefloor, she could see Pat then, turn a smug and childish grin on Henry and he sulk with disappointment. And if on the other hand . . . it were something else, (*that* something else), Henry would be in the superior position and the tears would dance up bright in Pat's clean and ageless eyes.

Maude walked back to the bureau. There was Kate's Christmas letter; there was Kate's Christmas photograph peeping from its slit. She had hardly looked at either yet, checking only to see if this time an address had been included. Perhaps this time? Oh surely this time? But no, there was nothing. No clue except the postmark. New York again, but another district this time. She followed the circle of letters on the righthand corner of the envelope. M-a-s-p-e-t-. She strained her eyes. What? 'a'? Yes. Maspeta? No not an 'a'. 'h'? Is it 'h'? Yes. 'h'. Maspeth. That was it. Never heard of it. Where in the name of . . . ? Another district or suburb of New York, she supposed. Oh why couldn't Kate trust her? Just once. One time out of ten? Her only sister, after all.

'It's like being dead,' she told herself then in the mirror. 'As if I'm dead. And looking down on my sister, knowing her life, her circumstances, and her knowing nothing about me.'

Absolutely . . . nothing. And year after year, telling me about it all, having to learn a little more, become a little more familiar with it all: Samuel, the children, the fashions, the music. Her coloured friend with the face as big and bright as a black moon. (Kate said). The food, the traffic, the view from the east-side bridge at sunset. The this, the that. Telling me all the news (except of course, where to find her) and never being able to as much as ask a question. Subways? Do you mean actually *under* the ground? Twenty minutes? It took you twenty minutes to drive three blocks? Really! What length would that be now, say compared with Grafton Street?

Or never being able to tell her things either. Never being able to tell her a blasted . . .

Maude sat down. Although she's getting the newspapers. She must be. She knew when poor Pat died and about the birth of little Patrice, about the marriage to Henry too. All these things that can be newspaper found. Read by any stranger's eyes. But the other things, personal: Patrice being such a lovely little singer, this new house that Henry loves and that I haven't yet quite come to. My Lincoln-green coat that I'm not so sure about . . . too fitted or too young, or too both. I know so much of her life and she knows nothing of mine. No nothing.

And look, they're *still* forwarding the letters from Kilmainham for goodness sake. She doesn't even know I've moved.

Maude looked at her old address, the lines drawn through its details, cancelled out, her old life.

She guesses though. Look up there: 'If not at this address please forward.'

She slid the photograph out and studied the back of it. It was a different size this time, slightly smaller than usual. She hadn't got a frame to fit it. She would have to get one tomorrow when nt into town. Only then would she look at it. When it could be set up alongside the nine others that were kept on a shelf in her dressing-room. Only then, when she could compare, look for clues, for changes from last year, the one before that. Right back to the first one. (And none could be as strange as that first one, that was the *most* . . .)

And who are these strangers? she remembered she kept asking herself, every time she had looked at it: who are they? And yet they had both looked just as they had done when she had last seen them just a few months previously. Before they had sneaked away, her sister – her *married* sister – and her husband's driver. But to see them both like that for the first time. Together. Kate sitting down and straightbacked as the chair and him with his hand on her shoulder. His hand. It had been shocking and funny at the same time. But how small the scandal seems now, more than ten years later. Getting smaller each time, each Christmas. Whereas the other things – the differences that start off discreetly – how they've grown. Like the children. The children . . .

How tall now? How tall since last time? Have they changed, looking more like Samuel now or Papa? Can little glimpses of Papa be still seen in her boy, Benjamin? And the girl? What colour is her hair? It looked fair the last time. But dark the time before. Little Maudie. Little *me*. And what about Samuel? Is he still the same? The one that never seems to change, looking just as he used to do when he held the door of the motor car open as if it was a shield he needed in order to protect himself. Stretching his hand around it to take hers: 'Ma'am'.

And so far there had been nothing in him, not even his good suit, to make her feel he would do other than call her ma'am and doff his hat to her. Just like the old days. Just as always. Were they ever to meet again.

And then Kate, what would she be like? Hair up or down? Has it grown fully from the bob of '24? Oh the shock of that, she'd never forget. And a little bit of envy too. How she would love to be so daring. But Henry would never allow it. He said it made Kate look like a Hun in a helmet.

And her hands, would they rest in her lap so quietly? Or would she have something in them, a rose, a book, another child perhaps? Maudie would be what now? Nine? Benjamin eight.

She tapped the back of her hand gently with the photograph and almost turned it over. But, no. Keep it for tomorrow, give herself all those hours of speculation. Somehow it made her feel closer to them all, as if she had had a say in what they wore or how they stood. 'Maudie, your hair tied back from your face; now good girl, that's better. And look up. You too, Benjamin, up, not down. That's it.' (For she knew Kate would want it frozen in the photograph, a statement made with no ambiguity: neither child had inherited their mother's unfortunate hare lip). 'Over here. Yes, that's right. Should Samuel be wearing that suit, Kate? What do you think?'

Yes. Well, in any case tomorrow she would see for herself. Just as soon as she came home, with her sister's family safely framed and ready to be brought into the privacy of her dressing-room. And it seemed fitting, somehow, that she should keep them there to glance at while she dressed. As when they were girls and Kate would sit with her and nod or shake her head as each new article was held up and spread out for inspection. Sometimes Maude felt sure she could hear the tuts or ahhhs. Or even 'Good heavens, no!' in exclamations from behind her.

There was a knock at the door and Philomena walked in. 'Mr Masterson is asking for you, ma'am,' she said.

'Is he up then, Phil?'

Philomena shrugged just a little. 'He called out to me from his room when I was at the linen press, ma'am.'

'Oh. I see.'

'Has Patrice come home yet?'

'No, not yet. But Miss Bates said she'd walk her up the avenue as soon as they'd finished choir practice. She promised she'd have her back in time for tea. Shouldn't be too long now.'

'Ah, good.'

Maude turned back towards the window. 'Listen to them, Philomena! Such a racket. What are they like at all? You'd wonder what's the matter with them? I mean they have Patrice's bird tables and half the bread in the house besides. A whole terrace to themselves and a row of splendid treetops to sleep in, with an uninterrupted view into the Phoenix Park. What do they want, Philomena? Can you answer me that?'

Both women stopped for a while to listen to the confusion of the birds, a deafening squabble of whistles and clicks, wheezes and warbles. There was, too, about the whole furious arrangement a cantankerous and threatening air.

Then Maude stood up. 'Better go and see what he wants,' she smiled at Philomena and they left the room together.

As if she didn't know.

Maude came in and stood at the end of the bed. 'Henry, aren't you up yet? You really are a disgrace.'

Henry Masterson stretched his arms up over his head and watched his wife search for his dressing gown. 'I was waiting for you,' he said softly.

Maude turned away so that he couldn't see her face. 'What can you mean?'

'Look at me,' he said. She did. And saw him lower one hand

24

to pat a space beside him in the bed.

'Really, Henry, don't be ridiculous, it's mid-afternoon, for goodness sake. And Lotty is coming to tea.'

'Oh God, not Lotty. You certainly know how to kill a fellow's ardour, I must say.'

'Henry, really.'

'I'm sorry Maude, but that Lotty . . . '

'She's bringing her new baby for Patrice to see.'

'Patrice? Oh that's lovely, I must say. And supposing Patrice wants to know who or *where* the papa is?'

'Oh Henry, she won't. Don't be so cruel. It's just a little baby. She calls him Harry, you know.'

'Does she really? How thrilling for him.'

'Yes, it's Henry really, but Lotty says Harry is a much nicer name for a . . .

Henry lifted his eyebrow, 'Yes?'

'*Henry.*'

And he grimaced playfully at her rebuke.

'Besides,' she continued, 'it's the same as your name really.'

'Well, I trust she didn't go to any trouble on my account.'

Henry watched her fuss unnecessarily about the bedroom. At least she hadn't left the room. Was still here, with him. A good sign at any rate. What was she wearing? Ah, yes. Two ribbons on each hip, buttons down the back. More like underwear these modern dresses. Although he was beginning to get used to their convenience. Not that he didn't miss the old way, mind: the slow peeling off, the eye and hook pop of release. And the soft flesh then slightly scarred from a day of long captivity. No, there was no finer way to enhance the slow bubble up and no mistake . . . if one had the time of course. And it certainly took that. These days a fellow could have a head start. Gave her less time to change her mind, too, which could very well happen before the first bodice was down. Now, with what once would pass for underwear being in essence outwear or, as he thought of it himself, the first hurdle being the last, things were a lot easier.

And as for this new length . . . At first he thought it robbed the imagination of too much, while at the same time allowing the other chap a bit too much knowledge of one's private pleasures.

But, well, looking at her there stretching up and over to reach his dressing gown. Yes, looking at her there, it does seem to have been a waste, hiding that ankle, that calf, for so long. The back of her knee . . . now, there's a thought.

'Come here, Maude,' he said again.

'Henry, it's broad daylight.'

But he could see the colour freshen her cheeks and her eyes, he could see moisten a little. And he could hear too the false note of disapproval in her voice.

'It's almost dark,' he said.

'That's just because it's winter. Now come on. Up you get.'

'No. Not unless you come over here first.'

'You know very well what will happen if I do. And . . . and I still have to try on my new gown for the armistice day ball.'

'But that's not for another two days; you've plenty of time yet.'

'No. No I have not. Supposing it doesn't suit?'

'Of course it will suit. Tell you what, why not try it on now?'

'Now? With you here? You must be joking.'

From the neck down, she covered herself with his dressing gown as if she were naked. Another good sign, in his opinion.

'No, no, I promise you. That's the furthest thing from my mind. Try it later, if you prefer. I just want to talk to you, that's all. Tell me all the news. Come.'

'Promise?'

'Of course.'

Cautiously she moved over and sat down on the side of the bed.

'So tell me, how are you?'

'Oh Henry, I'm fine.'

'Good. That's very good. And are you looking forward to Christmas?'

'Oh don't be so foolish.'

'No, no you must answer. We're having a conversation, just as you wished.'

'All right. I suppose I am.'

'Good. And when are you seeing your repulsive little investment man?'

'Oh, didn't I tell you? He telephoned from Antwerp. He is way behind schedule and he won't be in Dublin until February at least. The stock market is positively buzzing, according to his own lights, and he's never been busier. So thank goodness for that. You know how I hate the whole wretched ordeal.'

'Yes, you poor thing.'

'I almost wish I was.'

Henry smiled.

'I had my Christmas letter from Kate,' she said.

'Early as usual?'

'Yes, well, you know Kate. Always ahead of the rush.'

'Still no address?' he asked.

'No. Nothing.'

Henry began to stroke her hand. 'Don't fret over it, my dear. At least you know she's well.'

'Yes but it's so . . . so frustrating.'

He turned the sleeve of her dress up a little. (Oh no, don't say she was going to cry). He continued, 'She knows what she's doing.

And there's really nothing else she can do, you know.'

Henry stroked the inside of her arm, the underside, the chicken breast bit, hidden from the world and white to unlined white.

Except for the veins, those delicate threads, mauve and palest blue. A lick he'd give them soon. A nice long lick.

'She could trust me.'

'Hmmm? Oh I'm sure she does. But . . . Well, Maude, we've spoken about this before. If it ever came out, I mean – if Pakenham were to find her – it would all come out. And you know what that would make her. And her children, darling. Her children.'

'Like Harry, you mean,' she pouted.

'Who's Harry?'

'Lotty's . . . '

'Oh, yes. Well, legally my dear, you know, there would really be no difference and what chance would her children have then? Even in these modern days there has still been nothing invented to beat respectability, I'm afraid. Without it, well . . . Her children would be just like Lotty's – illegitimate.'

'Don't say that word, Henry, I hate it. Such an ugly word.'

'What? Illegitimate? I'm sorry but there's no prettier way of putting it. Your sister's children and Lotty's . . . well. Although personally I regard the two issues as being entirely different and from what I know of Pakenham don't blame Kate in the least. Perhaps her choice of mate could have been better. I mean, a driver. But it is almost 1929 after all; one must tolerate, it appears.'

'But she married Samuel. She did. Before she had any children.'

Maude put her hand up to her face. And here come the tears, groaned Henry silently.

'But she was still married to Pakenham. She still is. In the eyes of the law she's a bigamist. A very serious crime. For herself *and* Samuel; they'd both be put in prison, you know. It's safer for everyone if she keeps her whereabouts a secret. You must understand.'

'Yes, Henry. It's just that. Well, I have no family now. I haven't seen my sister for ten years. And as for my brother . . . '

'Now I won't have you reproach yourself on his account. You know you really have done all you could possibly do for him.'

'Have I, though?

'Oh Maude, please. He was given a bottle factory and a public house. Handed to him, without him having to lift as much as . . . as his hat. He's just one of those people who are destined to make a botch of everything they behold, I'm afraid. First the bottleries and now he has to sell the Irish House, I mean, really. The wonder is he managed to hold on to it this long. I suspect we have Bart Tully to thank for that. You know, I met his poor wife in the village the other day and she tells me Bart is never home, practically runs the place on his own. Your brother rarely deigns to set foot in the place unless he's in need of a drink or a nip from the till. What else can you do? You've bought him the lease on his new house. You're paying for his eldest child's education. Unless of course, you want to give him this house too? My car. Or here, what about my suits? Why not give him the lot?'

'Yes, but his wife, his children. I never see his children. My own nephews.'

'I know how you feel, Maude, but come now. Forgive me, but Greta or her children, well, they're hardly suitable companions for Patrice now. Are they?

'I –'

'I don't mean to be as hard as I must sound. But it's for your own good. You do understand, darling?'

'I do. Really I do. Henry?'

'Yes, my dear.'

'Has anyone ever called you Harry?'

He smiled to acknowledge her little joke. She smiled back through the tears.

And there really was such a lot of them. Where do they keep them all? he wondered. Women. What little canalway system have they got inside their head. Or breasts? Maybe that was it? The reason they were so soft, so full. Teardrops stored inside ready to be released at any given moment. Still one thing, he realised: tears, at least, required comfort. Which could be the first step to . . .

'Don't cry, my dear. Come here to me now. Come on.' Tenderly he took her head between his hands and drew her face to his. 'Oh my poor, poor darling.' Tenderly he looked at her and then . . . He opened his mouth and with his tongue long and wet shoved it into hers, before he pulled her over and laid her out flat on the bed beneath him.

Henry does it differently. Henry isn't the same. Henry uses his tongue the most, as if it were another hand. He never says he loves her. He seldom speaks. Except to tell her: move this way, move that. Do this, do it this way. Pat always said things, love words, small little senseless things but full of love. Henry bites her, leaving bruises. Leaving marks. He makes her do things she doesn't want to do. Except while she is doing them. He makes her do things she doesn't want to have done. When she thinks about them later. But she isn't thinking now. Bits of pictures stream past her, trying to be thoughts. But they aren't, not really. They're just . . . starlings squirming on the terrace, a gown waiting to be filled. Flowers for the drawing-room, a dinner menu to be decided. And faces, children's faces from the photographs along the shelf, Maudie, Bennie with his gold-rimmed spectacles. Now Lotty's little baby. Now Greta's eldest son. And Patrice. The same, the same. Do they have a look about them all? Are they all in some way marked? In a roomful of children conceived with respectability would they stand out? Born out of wedlock. Illegitimate . . . Patrice . . . What would he think if he knew? What would he say? Patrice. (Patrice? Do you mean to tell me she's a . . . ?

A bit of a thought. But causing no shame. No shame now. Her body won't allow her shame. 'Shh,' it says. No. This is not the time. Later if you must . . . Later there will be shame. All sorts of shame. Later there always is. Like when Henry tears her clothes and she throws them out, too ashamed to answer Philomena when she says, 'Good heavens, how on earth could this have happened?' Shh, her body tells her, this is my time now, one song, one singer, and the pictures float away.

She used to whisper with Pat like children in the dark. But she liked to see his face too, to have just enough light to see it. Hold it, touch it. To kiss its lips on lips on . . . And memorise it. That carved hook behind his ear, so flat, so curved. Resculpted by her hand. Her hand. Her kiss.

She never looks at Henry's face. Once she saw it, once . . . and wondered how she'd gone to bed with a husband and ended up cavorting with the devil.

But Henry makes her forget to care. Henry makes her want more and harder. Say it too: 'Harder. Harder.' Henry makes her legs scream out and gives her another voice too. But not in her throat. Down there instead. Right down there. That nobody can hear but her. No matter how it screeches and sings. No matter how it sobs for more.

And she never utters love words, now. Not to Henry. Because she doesn't care to say things she cannot hear. And she cannot hear because she is too busy listening. To the voice. The secret voice inside her.

So that when she opens her eyes to look around she thinks, who is this man? Isn't that Henry Masterson? What is he doing here? What has any of this got to do with him?

Maude looked out the front bay-window. She could see by the electric lights, coming out white from the drawing-room behind her. And leaking too, from the various windows of the house. Up and down across the driveway, in finely cut slices. There was Miss Bates and Patrice stopping by the taxicab, where Lotty and a driver were wrestling with a bassinet. There was Patrice bouncing impatiently on her heels, and Miss Bates shyly peeping inside, her hand pressing down on the frills and lace tucked like a pastry covering over the baby that was in there somewhere, a baby pie. And here were they all now making their way up the steps that led to the door, where Philomena would be waiting. Yes, she could hear her speak:

'Oh let me see him; let me have him. The dote, the darlin', the little lamb.'

Maude looked out the side bay-window. So there he was. Funking off again. She might have known. She could see him now. Making his way across the terrace and over to the wall where the garden ended. Too far for the light to throw, but if . . . She made visors of her hands against the window pane. Now she could just about make him out, beneath the rows of trees where the silent starlings had at least settled for the night. She could just about see. There . . .

Through the door in the wall, so that he could pass out into the park on the other side, his tall frame stooped low. As a horse might stoop to come out of a stable.

Two

Bart Tully swung himself back and on to his bicycle and watched the deer cross over. He waited for a moment and then, pushing his full weight down onto the pedals, heaved against the tightness of that first rotation and cut towards the line of animals crossing his path. He had his elbows winged and his head bent low to the handlebars and he heard himself cry out in a voice he didn't recognise.

There was a hesitation first, as if the deer couldn't quite understand. Couldn't accept the danger. And for a second Bart thought he would crash right into them. 'Oh move, would ye move! For the love of Jaysus, Mary and bloody Jo – '

He tried to stop. But it was too late. He was travelling downhill at full speed, the pedals were loose; beyond his influence. There was nothing he could do.

Then *bang* like a shot from a gun, they were suddenly gone. A scatter of legs bursting out and away from each other. And he felt himself fly through the sudden empty space they had left behind them.

And they hadn't uttered a sound. Not a whistle. He had always imagined they would squeak or grunt. Or something. Give some demonstration of fear. You'd think in all that panic, there would have been *something*.

Bart circled his bicycle back and watched them stampede away from him. Sorry now he'd done it at all. It hadn't been in the least bit satisfactory. He didn't know what had come over him. Why he should have done such a thing.

He only knew that he had had a sudden compulsion to see them in flight, see their highly strung bodies race resilient, punching through the grey morning air. Had he meant to chase after them? Like a dog. Or maybe it was just to run with them. Run with the herd. Was that it? Race along with them, through them. With them. Like a thread.

They were waiting there, splitting up now, some running towards the horizon and the stag, others taking recklessly to the trees. He could hear their hooves beating off the ground. He wished he could follow them, catch them. Stroke them till they were calm. Share his sandwiches with them, even. But they'd never let you near them. Hated humans really. More than dogs. At least in a way, they respected dogs. But humans? If you touched one of their fawns, the mother would have nothing more to do with it. Would leave it to die. Fancy. Hating humans that much.

He slowed down, leaving the wheels to tire themselves out until, helpless, they came to a shaky stop. Astride the crossbar, Bart, raised on his toes, looked over through the rags and bones of a tabescent forest, to the sky where the stag still stood. Square, the blazon of his antlers clear against the sky; his staghood. Immovable. Was he watching him? Did he know it was Bart who had broken the peace? They had been so placid up to a couple of minutes before. And look at them now. Just look. You'd think he had taken a gun to them.

But he loved the deer. He loved them dearly. He hadn't meant any harm. Why did they have to be so bloody timid anyway? They could have gored and ground him between a couple of them and yet they let him be master. Now why? And another thing and worse, would they remember him? Become afraid. Too afraid to be natural in front of him again. Next time maybe scuttling the minute they saw him? Oh no, that would be awful. Just awful. That would make him the same as every other punter that crossed these gates; an intruder. And he wasn't the same. He just wasn't. He felt the privilege in all this space. It somehow made him feel as if this was his land. His. And the deer, too, somehow his stock. He often found himself making a mental note of things that were not quite right; nothing passed his vigilant eye: 'Must have a word with the gamekeeper about that fallen tree,' or 'That fence needs fixing before it falls. Must speak to Moriarty.' If anyone ever heard him, they'd think . . . But. Well for that one hour, it felt natural. Not batty in the least. When he left Nell in the cottage rented at the bottom of the Knockmaroon Hill and pulled the door after him, he was going to ride or walk his land; whichever he chose. A squire. It always cheered him. Not even the wettest morning could dampen that feeling. That he couldn't look forward to this? Well, it was inconceivable. It would take from his day.

And the morning dictated the tone of his day. Bart preferred mornings, always had. He liked to feel a keenness from the word go. Even as he pushed the bike up ahead of him as if it were a reluctant cow. Hup now hup, hup, along the ruthless hill and under the bridge. He felt a keenness even then. Looking forward to the next hour. The solitude, the dormitory lights from the convent bursting through the darkness. The bit of exercise, the breakfast then; ravenous for it. And the deer. He always loitered a bit to watch the deer. Knew their seasons, their habits by now. Watched their newborn grow bigger and stronger; right up to velveting. Made him feel quite paternal really. Now they might recognise him. Start to fidget as soon as they saw his bicycle come down by the convent wall. Then *scatter*. What a pandemonium that would be. Bringing the nuns out as well as the rangers. So that he would have to move off. Miss it all. Just as the lights came on too. Blinking sleepily one by one, over the thick grey convent wall. He wouldn't be able to concentrate on them now either. Couldn't hang about with all that racket going on. Wouldn't be long before the rangers copped he had something to do with it. So that would be two aspects of pleasure he could lose for his stupidity. In no time at all, the park would become just that, a park. Somewhere to take a short cut through – on the way to. On the way back from. No more. No more Squire Tully.

Bart looked back at the convent. All lights were up now. All secret action going on inside there. How could he be expected to concentrate on them in future as he liked to do? Watching each spark of yellow filling the long narrow windows with light. And imagining what it must be like. What it must be like inside there. Sometimes he could hear the handbell ring from the holy sister's hand. Shaking it up, shaking it down. Come on now girls, time to get up, up, up. And the young ladies. Lifting themselves from bed, stretching arms overhead, so well developed for their ages. Too old to be at school really. And sliding down on to their knees. 'Our Father who art . . . ' Their sleepy heads held in hands designed more for pillow than piety. And then pulling themselves up to sit on the bed end, stretching out leg by leg, pulled stockings long and woollen over their poor pinched knees. Wishing they would go higher. Higher. Up to the icy part, the top of the leg. The thigh. That's what they were wishing. Probably they were. Probably giving a rub too, to coax the heat back into the . . . white, white flesh all the way up there and giving just the slightest wobble on the plumper girls.

How could he enjoy all that, imagine it slowly? With the deer scarpering away from him so frightened, they might hurt themselves. And the nuns peering out through the windows.

36

'What's the matter with the deer? What's going on out there? There's a man, sister. I can see a man. On a bicycle. Somebody call the ranger. Quick now before he gets away.' No. Not much joy in that. He could forget about it, under those conditions. And the rest of his journey then. What would that be like? Full of fear instead of anticipation.

A good strong cycle was what he always enjoyed, all the way through as far as the Hole-In-The-Wall. And breakfast with Mother. A rasher and a chat. He'd be lost without it. Starving by the time he got there. Hungry as a hunter. Nothing like it, then. The smell of relief; to know it's coming your way, on the brink of you. Satisfaction.

Sometimes Mother fried him an egg, flicking the hot grease over it till it grew a skin, like a cheek it'd be then. Looking up from the black of the pan, a small fat pudgy cheek. And then watching the rasher melt into the butter and the butter melt shyly back to it and folding it over in a blanket of fat fresh bread. And dip dip dip into the egg. Then the sup of tea. With the only alcohol he ever touched dribbled in. A drop of Powers to keep away the cold.

Bart felt his stomach rumble. He was hungry. 'There'll be no breakfast today, though,' he said aloud. And then wondered why he had said such a thing?

He reached inside his overcoat pocket and pulled out a packet of sandwiches. Might as well eat them now. There'd be no work today either. Not now there wouldn't be. He shook his head. Why was that again? It didn't make sense. Him missing a day.

And today was a big day. Wasn't it? He was supposed to be there. He *should* be there. And there was to be a party too. Wasn't there? Armistice Day party. Free drink for all with gobs on them, no doubt. The boss would see to that. And not many days left to him now, not many days to stand on this side of the counter anyway. Or to change his long white bib as many times as it took to be free from the porter stains. Fussy to a fault, when it came to aprons, that was. More's the pity he couldn't have been a bit more concerned about the quality of his business. Lost it all. Near enough. The poor chap. And to have been given it so young too. Too young probably, that was it.

Now if Bart had a shop of his own. By God, what he'd do. By Christ, he could make a go of it. Make it throb with prosperity. He could work like ten men, had a great head for figures and more and he had the one asset that was more value than any amount of capital when it came to being a publican: he was a teetotaller.

Still he didn't have the money, so no use. No, none. And at least they'd kept him on. Thanks to the bossman that'd be. So why's this he wouldn't be going to work today?

Bart put one hand on the crossbar of the bicycle and pushed it away, lifting himself up over the saddle as he did. He held on to it then, wheeling it alongside him over to a bench. Yes, there he could eat and still keep an eye on the deer. He sat himself down, the bicycle leaning awkwardly against his arm. Bart patted the saddle. 'We make a very handsome couple,' he said reassuringly.

Now his hands were free. Free to open the sandwiches out on his lap. Thinner bread than Mother's; she cut it thinner. Almost as though she'd shaved it off the loaf, he sometimes thought. And the butter tended towards the centre, rarely making it out as far as the crust. Too quick, that was Nell for you. Did everything a bit too quickly. A bit too smart for her own good. He took a bite. He hated corned beef. The way it greased up on to the roof of his mouth. Seven years of it without a break. He gave up eating it when? After six weeks or so. Threw it to the yard dog mostly or if he wasn't about, let the gulls have a barney out front of the pub.

He had forgotten how disgusting it was. 'Cornered' beef, as she called it. Cornered bloody beef. Which in a way probably made sense, 'I've got you cornered now, me boyo.' He took a bite.

And the sacrifice that went with it. 'I coulda got something cheaper, you know . . . coulda spent the money on meself. But with you working all hours for that – Oh I'd say it, I would, if I could only bring meself.'

Nell hated his boss. Thought him the worst in the world. Which wasn't fair. Poor chap. She hated him because she believed he made Bart work around the clock . . . which wasn't true either. Bart just pretended it was, so he could have his breakfast and his dinner break with Mother and a little nap then in the bed he slept in as a single man. And so he could stay on later in the evening if the bossman had a few over the top, help him sort things out. And he liked to have a cup of tea then, when it was all over and the counter shone again. Listening to the sounds of cup and stirring spoon. Sipping it quietly then while the others hung up their bibs and helped themselves to a pint. Which they were quick enough to do, mark you. But not so quick when it came to escorting the other fella home. Oh no. That was usually left up to you know who. And making a spectacle of the pair of them too, up the quays and singing and dancing as if he was back on the stage, waving his stick at any old passer-by. And frightening them half to death. After spending most of the day with not a word out of him. No, Bart would have to say, he never saw anyone to change personality as much as himself with a few on him. Sure you couldn't let him home on his own. God knows what . . .

But imagine telling that to Nell though. 'I had to walk the chief home because he was scuttled again.' Oh she'd love that all right. Jam on her bread.

Bart took another bite and chewed it loosely as though he

might spit it out at any time. Nell was the best in the world but –

He took another reluctant snipe at it. Her food would poison a rat. Which was one of the reasons he was spending all that time with Mother. But how could he tell her that? Women could be so funny about a chap's mother. He had to let her believe he was working.

And anyway it wasn't just the grub. It was the chat too. Mother took an interest in things. Sport even, or politics. The customers too. Oh yes, especially the customers; she knew them all. As though she'd ever met them. Their kith and kin too:

'How did Tom Alford's son fare out at that interview? Ah did he now? I'm delighted for him. Be sure an' tell him I said, well done now.'

'Oh I will, Mother.'

'Here, is Carabini's brother-in-law still poorly? Ah, go away. Tell him I'm praying for him, night and day.'

'Oh, indeed an' I will, Mother.'

'Did you tell Quinn about the wireless sets in Hogans?'

'Oh I did.'

'Did you tell him to tell his wife you could get one on easy terms? Could have it for the Christmas?'

'Oh I did.'

But of course he never did. You just couldn't, though. Go relaying all her little messages across the bar. They'd be looking at you as if . . . and the most of them was bad enough in anyway without giving them more cause. Without him saying the likes of: 'Mother was just saying that if you've trouble with your chest again, be sure to get a good rub for it with some warm camphorated oil and cover with a flannel vest.' Talk about giving them ammunition. Camphorated oil. And besides the bugger'd probably drink it.

Not that he minded the odd ragging, not Bart Tully. Loved

nothing better than a laugh. Although at times, he felt they took it a bit far. But that's the drink for you. You have to be putting the merriment somewhere. And they couldn't overdo it with each other, too touchy by far the most of them. Be afraid they'd get, or have to throw, a punch.

One thing about the bar life though – it gave Mother an interest. Kept her in touch with things. Ten years already. Ten years since she had to sell her house in Camden Street. A lovely little house too. She never admitted the reason. But Bart knew it was to get him out of a spot. He knew she couldn't have really wanted to move out to a ten-bob cottage on Blackhorse Avenue. It was on account of him, that time, so that he could leave the jeweller's shop with his head held high. Pay for the snuff box that was whipped from under his eye. And they never spoke about it either. Never mentioned a word of it. He never told her how grateful he was. From Camden Street to Blackhorse Avenue. Now *that* was a sacrifice. A real one. And feck you and your cornered beef sandwiches. He threw a detached crust to the ground behind him.

Never said as much as thank you to her. Poor Mother. The subject just never came up. Yet they spoke about near enough everything else. You could talk to Mother. Tell her things. Things you couldn't mention to Nell. No way, you could. Like that time he'd seen the chap exposing himself, for example. Now, Nellie wouldn't even acknowledge that a chap had anything to expose, never mind that he'd go as far as to do it. But Mother? Mother howled the place down when he told her.

'He was *what*?' she insisted he repeat it first. 'He was . . . you know . . . hangin' out. Hangin' out, Mother. Every last bit of him.'

'And what did you say to him?' she asked.

'"Good morning, says I to him, a bit nippy this morning."

And do you know what he says?'

'No. Tell us. What did he say?'

'He said. "Excuse me," says he. "Do you know where the deers do be?" That's what he said.'

Mother laughed for a week over it. Thought it the funniest thing in a long time. 'Do you know?' he sometimes heard her repeating to herself. Or then chuckling quietly. 'Where?' she might ask on its own. Or then again, 'The deers do be,' he'd sometimes hear her say as well.

The harsh dry throat-call of the stag came through his thoughts. 'Ah sure, God love you,' Bart said aloud, 'I know how you feel. Dying for it. Aren't you?' He took another bite from his sandwich. 'Aren't we all?' he asked through bread-muffled breath. 'Still it's all right for you. And you with a harem of them. There's me, with just the one. And three weeks till Christmas.'

And at least your rutting season ends sometime. Unlike the rest of us. Who are susceptible at all times of the day and night.

Though for him, the morning was the worst. Bart closed his eyes. He sometimes felt he nearly once. When he woke up with it at him. And lately? He didn't know what came in to him lately. But . . . it was yesterday wasn't it? He almost. Got off the bike and over to the convent wall; it would have been so easy. So quick. Would have taken him no time at all. And the thoughts of them all in there. He could hear the bell ringing to call them. Clanging steadily. 'Up girls up. Time to get up.' He could see himself for a moment just taking it out and . . . Oh why not? Who'd know? Who would? Who'd ever find out? Just a few quick pulls and . . . But then he reminded himself. Is that what you want to be? One of those perverts that the park has always been a haven to. That'd be lovely all right for Mother to read in the paper. 'Bartholomew Tully, counterhand in the Irish House public bar, was today charged at the District Court for . . . ' (What would they call it? Had it got a legal name?).

When asked by the judge if the defendant had anything to say, he replied: 'Excuse me. Do you know where the deers do be?'

No you couldn't be carrying on like that. Had to take control of yourself. Which is just what he did. Cycling harder than ever till his legs felt the strain, biting his lip till it hurt him enough to cause distraction.

Bart folded his greaseproof paper over and smoothed it at the crease. He folded it again and slipped it back inside his pocket. It was calm in the forest now, the deer beginning to regroup cautiously, concolorous and distant. He reached into his inside pocket and took out the Baby Power bottle. He looked down at the milk squeezed inside. Ridiculous it looked, the bottle, without the usual gold clear liquid. How many times had he told her: 'Nell, there's no need for the bottle of milk. We've plenty of milk inside in the bar. And not a drop of it begrudged to us.' How many times? . . . Sending him off like a schoolboy. No wonder they jeered at him inside. He unscrewed the cap and let the milk roll back over his tongue and down into his throat, enjoying the glugging sound this made more than the taste, which was sweet and warm and slightly tainted. No work today. No. That's right. A long day so with nothing to do.

He smacked his lips and edged the bottle down into his pocket. He'd miss the party and a busy day too. The busiest day yet. And Bart loved it when it was busy. He loved to pause during the rare lulls, pretending to listen to some drunkard's guff and casting his eye over the commotion, trawling for something more interesting to take home with him to Mother. With a glass in one hand, a cloth in the other, stuffing it down and screwing it in until it extracted a shine worthy of inspection. Taking it all in, without appearing to do so. He closed his eyes and smiled at the picture: he could see himself marching up and down behind the counter. Up and down along his long narrow pathway. Could hear his feet thud smartly over the boards and see his hands, reaching out behind him for a bottle of this, a bottle of that. And in front of him then, drawing the dark carved baton with its nips of brass, slowly down. Till a pint took shape beneath it. And his bartime chant:

'Be with you now, right ye be. Will that be it? Will that be all? A squirt of this? Another splash? Rightio. Slate is it, Jack? Only till Friday? Ye sure now? Ye are? There ye go then. Not at all. Thanks very much and . . . Thruppence.'

He liked his job all right. Much better than the jeweller's shop. Which he could scarcely remember now. Except maybe for the view from above, down through the glass and the dark velvet trays with sparkles pinched on in rows. And no chat, no news, no nothing but strange poker faces, Madam or Sir? No friendliness at all. Except for . . . yes, funny that all right, the one friendly face was the one that got him the sack. Well might she have been friendly all right with the best snuffbox in the house tucked into her muff. And him feeling so sorry for her flat nose and short lip too. Still, she did have a kind way about her. For a change. And it's strange how stuffy people get when they're spending a few quid on baubles. As he was only just saying to Mother the other day. The opposite when they're spending it on drink. Want to know you then. Want you to like them. Pals, that's what they want. They get lonely or something. Lonely. What's this she said now back to him? Oh, it was very good. What was it now?

Bart looked up. Was it raining? He blinked. He felt something on his face but . . . ? He held out his hand, full stretch to the fingers. No. No, funny it had felt like there was something. He reached up for his face then and at his touch felt it buckle as if he had broken it. Tears, that's what it was, tears. He was crying. Bart stood up and pulled the bicycle to him again. He would cycle hard, bite his lip till it bled if needs be. Cycle as hard as he could. A distraction. Yes. That's what he needed. He placed one foot on the pedal and with the other gave a little hop. He lifted himself over and instinctively found the saddle beneath him.

He could remember now. Why. Why there'd been no breakfast. Why there would be no work today. And it no longer seemed strange that he should be cycling the way he had come not two hours since. For he was going home. That was it. Back to Nell. He was going home to tell her that Mother had died in the night.

THREE

Mrs Gunne could hardly believe her eyes. Was it? could it be? Could it possibly . . . ?

That woman walking in front of her carrying some sort of a crate with what looked like hens inside. But really, hens. What would she be doing with hens? The idea. Although the young lad with her. He'd be about the right age all right.

The train from Cork was singing in the distance. Reminding her: Mustn't forget Beatrix. Any minute now.

Then she saw the boy turn around to wait for the train to cut into the platform. Why, the spit of Maude's Patrice; it had to be. The same colouring and all. It was like looking at her in knickerbockers. And they'd be about the same age too. It must be. The woman stopped to change the crate over to her other hand. She leaned down to say something to the boy. Ahha. So it was her. That profile, why you'd know it anywhere. And that walk too. You could pick it out from a thousand.

'Greta, Greta dear, is it you? Is it really you?'

Greta swung around and for a moment Herbert thought his mother might faint, so white her face had suddenly fallen. There was a fat woman in a fat hat, all red-faced and laughing at nothing, her hand slapping her breast one minute and then Mother's arm the next. And back and forward as if she was on a rocking horse. Mother didn't look at all pleased. Not in the least. Although her smile was wide and full and: 'Mrs Gunne, how nice to see you,' she said.

But Herbert knew she was lying. She looked sort of sick inside and seemed to be trying to hide the crate behind her back.

'And this must be . . . ?'

'Herbert,' Mother said. 'This is my eldest.'

The fat lady threw her hands up in amazement. 'Mercy me, how like your cousin you are. The spit, the veritable . . . Don't you agree, Greta? Isn't he just the . . . bless him.'

And she brought her hands down around his face, giving it two little slaps before leaving a big wet kiss on one cheek.

Herbert could keep his face quite still, not the flicker of a grimace. But he had to try hard not to wipe his cheek with the back of his hand. He could feel the wetness still, as if he had a leaking face. He wondered would it leave a later stain. Like the one on the ceiling of the second floor. In Father's pub.

He turned away. The train was struggling to a halt. Behind its windows he could see moving shadows. Herbert stood straight as a statue and, keeping his eyes on the one spot, let them come to him, passing him by, one by one. It was almost as if it were the same window and all these different people were taking a quick turn to appear to him in relays. (Out of the way, my turn next . . . Oh hurry along, would you? I want to see Herbert. I've *got* to see Herbert.) All the way down through the carriage and into the next one and the next one too, maybe. And nothing would stop them, right through to the end. Except maybe the lavatory. But Herbert wasn't quite sure about that. Which way it was situated? At the side or in the middle? How much room did it take up? Did it mark the end of each carriage, stopping you from passing, like the piano stool in the tram? And where did the gick go when its water went flush?

Herbert had never been on a train. Except once when he was

a baby. Mother and Father took him to Wicklow and he wore a dress with frillies on and little white booties made of cloth. But that wasn't remembering, that was just looking at the photograph portrait in the box in the end of the wardrobe. In Mother's bedroom.

He watched while the shadows turned into people. Sometimes he saw them stretching up and pulling shapes down from above the window. Other times lifting hats from below and placing them then on top of their heads. A couple of times a face took a dip down to peep outside to the platform, before turning away to gather armfuls together: umbrellas or canes, hats or coats. And parcels. Lots of parcels. There were whistles and gurgles and rumblings and roars. And then . . . It stopped. The train. With one last dry screech. It stopped. It just . . .

Now at the window was a girl. Or a young lady maybe. It was difficult to say. She was dressed like a young lady, but her face was like a girl's. Maybe she was a girl playing dress up. That's what she looked like. A plump face but pretty too. Her hair was almost white and seemed to be made of tubes, three or four fat ones hanging on each shoulder. She was looking at him. Nearly. She was really looking at the crate in his hand. He lowered it to the ground carefully. Now. Now she was looking at him. Up and down and up again. With her mouth squeezing up a little to the side. Then she was gone.

Herbert looked back down the station. It was wonderful. He loved it. Any disappointment he had felt when he first walked in was gone now, blown away. The outside had been so . . . so fancy cake beautiful, and when he had walked inside and found that there was really so very little to admire. Except a huge barn. A huge black barn. And gashes in the centre with stitch marks all up along. As if an operation had been performed. Huge and public.

And nobody to look at really. Just a few. And mostly chaps with peaked caps on, looking so bored and walking so slowly over the same spot. Again and again. Waiting. Train waiting. Waiting to blow their whistles.

But now? Now that the train was here, that had all changed. There were door slams and footsteps and everywhere cries of recognition.

'Oh look, Oh look. There he is. There he is.' The woman jumping up and down behind the railing. And the girl with the feathers and the buckle-bright shoes: 'Yoo-hoo! Yoo hoo?'

(Me Herbert. *You* who?)

Another whistle then came skating above and over the long narrow train tops and up. Up to the rafters above. Where there were pigeons. Looking down and gossiping, nudging each other too. 'The fat one's called Mrs Gunne. And that's Herbert. Oho-oh. He was ten last month gone. His mother doesn't like Mrs Gunne you know-oooh. Why not? Don't know-oooh.'

Behind him he could hear the women carry on as if nothing were happening. As if they were in a garden, all alone. And behind an orchard wall, so high nobody could see them.

'And how are you getting along, Greta, it must be years since . . . '

'Fine, Mrs Gunne, thank you for asking and your . . . '

'And how many have you got now?'

'Four.'

'*Four*? Well I can hardly believe it. Four? Boys or . . . '

'All boys.'

'Oh you poor thing, outnumbered in your own home.'

The fat lady tapped Herbert on the arm. And winked. He winked back and she said a small, 'Oh' first and then turned away to Mother. 'And have I heard correctly? Have you sold the Irish House?'

'Yes, that's right. My husband has sort of retired, to spend more time with his family. A public house, day and night, you know.'

The fat lady didn't seem to mind the crowds or maybe she just didn't notice them. But they were passing and tipping off the three of them all the time. Some said they were sorry or 'Excuse' or 'Beg pardon.' But others seemed annoyed; one even tutted and muttered, 'Something, something, something, stupid something woman.' But she didn't in the least bit notice. Mother did though. The crate kept swaying softly in her hand, from side to side, and the birds were becoming agitated. He could see the tawny flickers through the honeycomb gaps at the side. Waving at him. 'Help. Herbert, help. It's all squashy in here.'

Herbert turned around and faced the two women so that they all formed a circle together. It might be safer this way, make them less noticeable. Or at least more compact. He lifted his crate up again and put it in the centre so that they were all standing around it. Mother's arm must be tired but she wouldn't put her crate down. He touched his then gently with his foot to show her: see, Mother, you can put it down, quite safely. You don't have to hold it till your arm goes dizzy.

'But money, Greta, dear. What will you do for money?' the fat lady sang.

'Oh we're fine on that, thank goodness; there's the garage, you know. We bought one last year; it is doing *so* well.'

'Oh well, now. As long as he doesn't take to dancing again.'

Mrs Gunne laughed her head off at this.

'You should have seen your father dance. "Twinkletoes" we used call him – only don't tell him, will you – when he was a guest at my home. I used to look after him, you know, the dear boy. But Greta, what on earth have you got in them boxes?'

'Oh they're just some chickens for the children.'

'What do you mean? To eat?'

'Oh no, to play with.'

Mother had gone quite pink now and the fat lady was staring at her. Very hard, very hard indeed. Now Herbert knew why she hadn't put the chickens down. She was ashamed of them. Fancy going to all that trouble to write to breeders all over the country and then when you finally got them, instead of being delighted, you were ashamed. Poor old biddies.

'I promised Herbert he could start to breed them. For an interest like, a sort of hobby. For his birthday.'

'Why, how unusual you are, Herbert. And when is your birthday?'

Herbert looked at Mother and then said, 'I can't remember, really.'

'Oh, you funny boy.'

'It's Tuesday,' Greta laughed uneasily.

'Really? Oh well you must allow . . . '

Over her wrist the fat lady pulled a handbag, a thickly ground handle of tortoiseshell hue. She unclasped it; then, clop. And its jaw dropped wide open. There were shiny sweat bobs over her lip. He could see them now while her head was lowered into the bag. And her fingers rummaged down into its teeth and pulled out . . . A money purse.

And all the time Mother was saying: 'No, no really, Mrs Gunne, and I won't allow it . . . couldn't possibly . . . won't hear of it. No, no, no.'

'There now,' she said as if Mother hadn't uttered a word, 'Two whole shillings. What do you think of that then, young man? And in the new coinage too. A flor-in, it's called. Isn't that a nice fishy on the front?'

'Answer Mrs Gunne, Herbert.'

'Yes, ma'am,' he said, 'it's a lovely fishy.'

'You buy something nice for your chickens.'

'Oh no, Mrs Gunne,' Mother started up again.

'Greta, Greta, stop that now will you? Don't spoil my pleasure. There's a good girl.'

'That's very kind of you, Mrs Gunne,' Mother said, quietening down a little. She took a breath then, a rather large one and smiled. 'It's been lovely seeing you again, but I'm afraid we really must be . . . '

'Oh surely not? Won't you wait one moment? I'm meeting Beatrix off the train. She was staying with friends in the country. She lives with me now, you know. Sweet thing.'

And then attempting to see over and through the crowds, up she went on the balls of her feet with her neck jolting out, jolting back again: like Ronnie the Rooster.

'Oh where is she? Where in heavens can she have got . . . ?'

She put one hand down on Herbert's shoulder.

'Your mother used to be her nursemaid, you know, when she worked for me. Beatrix would be only raging if –'

Herbert looked up and saw that a fire had been lit in his mother's cheek. 'Yes,' he heard her say, 'that was how I met your father. He was one of Mrs Gunne's lodgers at the time.'

Now the fire had stretched nimbly over and sparked up on Mrs Gunne's face.

She laughed slyly, though, and said, 'Tell me Greta, will we see you at Maude Masterson's party? Hmmm?' she paused and flicked her hand down through the air. 'Masterson – it sounds strange to say it. Tell me, Greta, what do you think of him?'

'Of whom?'

'Why, Mr Masterson, of course.'

'Oh, he seems very . . . '

'Ah yes, but he's not Pat Cleary, when all is said and done, now. Is he, dear?'

'Indeed.'

'Yes . . . well? *Will* we be seeing you and your dear children at Maude's Christmas party this year? I don't recall seeing you there last year . . . or the one before that come to think. Am I mistaken?'

Mother looked away. 'I was in confinement, as it happens.'

'Oh, dear me, yes. But this year, perhaps. I trust you're not . . .?'

The fat lady nodded her head several small times in little tight circles as if she were looking for something, a bee or a fly that might land on her nose.

'No, Mrs Gunne, I'm not.'

'Oh well, perhaps in that case.'

'I think I may have a previous . . . what date is it again?'

'Why the sixth of January, as usual. Little Christmas. Always the same date. Every single year.'

She drew Herbert towards and then in front of her. 'Come, Herbert, with your young eyes, help me look for Beatrix.'

'But how should I know her, ma'am?' Herbert asked.

'Why, because she's so pretty, child.' Mrs Gunne smiled down on him. 'Golden hair and skin the colour of milk.'

She rubbed Herbert's cheek then with her little finger as though she were testing it. 'His skin is very salla, don't you think, Greta?'

'Sallow, Mrs Gunne? I don't know. Olive I would have said.'

'Oh, but don't get me wrong. It suits him, I must say. I'm not quite sure it flatters his cousin as well. I always think a paler complexion more becoming on a girl. More refined, hmmm? There's nothing will beat the old peaches and cream. Now there's our Beatrix, had to be sent home from India, you know. Where her mother and father are living. The sun was simply too atrocious for her delicate skin. Practically roasted her alive. The lamb.'

She turned back around towards Herbert and stooped one arm over his shoulder to point through a gap in the crowd.

'There she is, Herbert. Can you see her over there? With royal blue coat and fur on the collar. Yes there. There.'

Herbert looked. It was the girl from the train.

'Is *that* her?' he asked.

'Yes, run along, dear, and ask her if she'd like a hand with her bag. Good boy.'

When Herbert ran and stopped and ran and stopped and finally and reluctantly took the last few steps towards Beatrix, Mrs Gunne turned to Greta. She smiled and frowned at the same time.

'Greta, dear, I hope you won't be offended . . . '

'Offended, Mrs Gunne? Why on earth should I be?'

'Well, my dear, it's just that I have heard rumours.'

'You surprise me, Mrs Gunne. I thought you were above that sort of thing.'

'Oh indeed I am, as you very well know. But . . . well if you ever . . . what I mean to say is . . . I'm still up on the South Circular, you know. Still the same house, though I've had it done over from top to toe. You'll hardly recognise it. The kitchen – all electric – so modern, I don't know myself. But as I said, dear me, I am being clumsy. I would be delighted to help you out. Should you need it, my dear. Tell me, are you still a dab hand with a needle and thread?'

'Why, how kind you are, Mrs Gunne, but let me assure you things have never been better.'

'Oh I am pleased. I knew it had to be no more than malicious gossip. I said as much at the time.'

'And as for me still being a dab hand, as you put it, I really don't know, Mrs Gunne. To tell you the truth, I have somebody who does all that sort of thing for me now. Ah so, here are the children. How long did you say it was since Beatrix was in India?'

'Over two years.'

'Two years? And she still hasn't got rid of the sunburn? Oh dear.'

Greta laid the crate down and took a few steps towards Beatrix. 'My dear child, you won't remember me but I remember you. You've hardly changed at all. What a fine lump of a girl you've grown into. And that lovely country complexion . . . '

She kissed Beatrix on each cheek and said, 'Come, Herbert, we really must be going.'

'Can I offer you a lift, Greta dear . . . I've my car waiting outside.'

'How kind, Mrs Gunne, but I have my own, waiting for me.'

And the two women smiled so sweetly at each other that Herbert now thought they were *both* going to be sick.

Herbert wanted to stay. He wanted to stay in the garden with the high orchard wall and the whole world passing along outside. Just Mother and Mrs Gunne and himself. And Beatrix. She was so . . . well really so . . .

Mother was dragging him by the hand. 'Come Herbert, quickly, get out. We must get out before them.'

She sounded frightened. Almost as if she were being chased. As if the fat lady had a gun and was going to shoot them. Herbert longed to look back, to see where they were, what they were doing, if Beatrix was saying anything to her grandmother. He wanted to laugh out loud the more he thought of her, but Mother was far too panicky to tolerate laughter. He would probably get a good clout for himself.

But she was such a funny girl. He never knew girls were funny before. Although he didn't really know many – not any. He would make it his business to from now on. Now that he knew what they were like.

He had started to walk up towards her. Just as the fat lady had told him to. And she knew he was coming. She had been looking at him while he made his way through the crowds. Never taking her eyes off him. Not once. And looking more and more disgusted the nearer he got to her.

'I'm, I'm . . . ' he had started when he finally stood before her. She tutted softly and rolled her eyes upwards. To the pigeons. The squat cosy pigeons.

'Ohooo look at Herbert now. Making an ass of himself. And that's Mrs Gunne's niece; her name is Beatrix; she's a lady child. Playing dress up; look at her big woman's shoo-oes. Ooh ooh.'

'I'm to help you with your bag. Your grandmother said.'

'Oh, did she now?'

Herbert put out his hand for the bag.

'Take that hand away or I shall bite it,' she said.

Herbert withdrew his hand. 'But your grand . . . '

'Why?'

'Why?'

'Yes. I said "Why?" Why did she tell you to help me?'

'I don't . . . '

'Shall I tell you why?'

'I don't mind.'

'Because she's a big fat lazy sow. That's why. A big fat bloody lazy sow. Too lazy to help me herself. And too mean to pay a porter. And I should have a porter. Not a boy. And certainly not one in *knickerbockers*.'

Herbert looked down at the ground. He was humiliated; he wanted to die. Right on the spot. He wanted to throw himself under the train just as the lavatory was going flush. But he wanted to laugh too, to burst out laughing. Fancy calling your grandmother such names. Fancy being so bold. 'I'm sorry I'm not a porter,' he said at last and so sincerely that Beatrix laughed instead of him.

'Don't be sorry,' she said then, changing for a moment. 'It's not your fault.'

Then she narrowed her eyes again and came back to herself, 'If I had my own money. That is if she, the big fat lazy sow, didn't keep stealing my money. My father's money. I should have a porter to carry my luggage. I should have two if I wished it. When I lived in India, I had . . . '

'Does she steal your father's money?'

'She steals the money he sends to me. Never gives me a penny. Starves me to death.'

Herbert looked at her. 'You don't look starved,' he said.

'Well I am, starved, starved, starved. Nothing to eat on the train except one lousy bloody chocolate bar and a bottle of Vimto. One lousy bloody chocolate *arse* bar.'

She had tears in her eyes now. And her mouth had tightened in like a little nut.

'Oh,' Herbert said. 'Oh, I feel so sorry for you.'

But he wished she hadn't said that about the chocolate bar. It made it so much more difficult not to laugh.

'Thank you,' Beatrix then sweetly replied.

And now he would probably never see her again. Mother dragging him away like this, as if with each step she wanted to put more and more of the crowd between them and Beatrix and Mrs Gunne. He wondered: did she speak like that in front of her grandmother. He couldn't wait to tell George. It would make a nice change too, him having something new to share with George. Instead of the other way around. They'd laugh for hours. They might never stop. A chocolate arse bar. Imagine.

The crates were knocking off his knees. One at a time. First the one in his hand. And then the larger one in Mother's. They were taking turns to hit against him. Right on the cuff of his knickerbockers trousers. Ouch, Mother, ouch . . . He didn't want to laugh now. Although he felt somehow that those awful knickerbockers might well deserve it. And why did Mother have to be such a fusspot anyway every time they went outdoors. Always having to be dressed up. Knickerbockers. So old-fashioned. And they were for small boys anyway. Not for him. He would tell Mother. Out straight. Mother, he would say, I'm not . . . any more . . . knickerbockers. He would tell her soon. Or some time.

They were outside now. Out through the door where the columns stood thickly and Mother pulling at him still. 'Over here,' she whispered urgently. 'Over . . . '

But why, he was going to ask her. Why are we hiding? Why are you so afraid? But Mother hated questions at the best of times. And he had so many, he would surely only get away with one. Two at the most. No, one. The mood she was in. He would have to choose.

Why were they pressed in against this wall hiding behind that group of porters, watching Mrs Gunne and Beatrix walk out and get into their car? And why . . . Why had Mother told all those lies about the chickens being for the children? Why, Mother would kill you if you even looked at them. She only let Herbert feed them because he was her eldest. Her 'head of sense'. And the garage? What garage? There was a huge yard at the back of their house and a shed and stables that were supposed to be for motor cars once. When they bought the house last year. When Aunt Maude bought the house for them last year – but he wasn't supposed to know that. That was something George had found out. But Mother kept chickens in it now instead. Rows and rows of them. She said motor cars were like himself, in the clouds and driven by fairies.

And as for Aunt Maude and her Christmas party? Why, they never went. Not that he could remember. They were never invited. Not that he could recall. And there were no photographs to help him to either. He could check later. With George. Yes that's what they would do, when Mother went over to see Mr Milinski, the egg man. They would go rooting. Together.

Through the slitted back window of the car, he could see Beatrix's hair tubes wiggle and Mrs Gunne's hat flounce as it crossed over and up the dark hillway that strung the two hospitals together. The one on the bottom where Harvey the Jarvey went when he broke his leg. And the one on the top, that Mother always pointed to when they passed, saying: 'Do you see that place, Herbert? Do you see it now? Take heed. That's where I'll end my days. That's where he'll drive me. And you'll all be pushing the cart. Till I'm left frothing at the mouth and staring out through those bars like a monkey gone demented.'

They moved away from the wall and slowly came out from behind the group of porters. Mother was calmer now. She waited till they could see the motor car disappear out of sight. Then she spoke:

'The bloody woman . . . that fat old bitch. That's all she is. Come along, Herbert, be careful with that cage. And as for that Beatrix one? Little dumpling, dressed up like a dog's dinner. Ridiculous, she looked. Hurry on, Herbert. What has you dawdling?'

Herbert was looking up the hillway on the other side of the road. That car. That was Mrs Gunne's car. Mrs Gunne and Beatrix inside it. They had pulled in to watch them. Himself and Mother walking away from the station. And no car of their own. Nothing. Nobody waiting to drive them away from their lie. She knew, all the time she had known. Yes, she was a fat old mean old sow. She knew and she still had to be sure to enjoy it. Poor Mother . . . She'd die, she'd just . . .

Herbert ran up alongside his mother as they came to the sweep that led to the bridge. They turned. Thank goodness. Their backs now safely to the hill with the car hiding beneath the shadows. Mother wouldn't have to know.

'No taste. No taste whatsoever. When she asked about your father, I should have said . . . '

But she didn't say what she should have said. She wasn't speaking to Herbert anyway, not really. She was just giving out to herself, reconstructing the conversation, experimenting with the whole meeting in retrospect. And so rude. So rude to Beatrix, now that she'd given herself a second chance. 'Hello, Beatrix, still stuffing your fat face with cheap broken biscuits? And how is your dear mother? Does she still have a smell off her that'd trip you up?'

Going on and on. Herbert was embarrassed in case people thought it was him she was so cross with. He smiled vaguely so no one could suspect him of being the cause of her anger. And when she pulled his arm occasionally to hurry him along, he acted as if it didn't hurt. It didn't bother him at all. Then she stopped and sighed contentedly.

'We'll take the tram, that's what we'll do. Yes.'

She looked down at him then. 'And what has you grinning like a half-wit?'

'Nothing, Mother.'

Herbert looked down at her hand. It was opening out in front of him.

'Give me your money, then.'

'What do you mean?' he asked the hand.

'You know very well what I mean. We'll pay for the tram with the money she gave you. And well she might. She still owes me the best part of a month's wages. The miserable old . . . '

'I . . . I . . . '

'What? What? Where is it?'

'I gave it to Beatrix,' he said at last.

'You what?'

'I had to do it, Mother,' he cried out, 'she was starving to death. And besides it was stolen money. The fat lady stole it. I couldn't have accepted it anyway.'

When he felt her hand come down on the back of his neck, he was glad she was such a fusspot really, all suits and hats for the smallest outing. And gloves. He was glad she was wearing her winter gloves.

FOUR

Greta was thinking about hands. Sitting at the kitchen table where, from the corner of her eye, she could see enough bills to wallpaper the bedrooms and the hall. And the henhouse too probably. And all she could think about were hands. She was trying to remember what they used to look like, used to *do*. For they weren't always like this. And they didn't always do the things they do now. Once they were . . . ? Well, other hands.

Those sunny days in Clare Street, working in Aunt Florence's shop, for example. They made things then. Things that would last, things you could look at, admire. She guided them across the cloth, through a series of movements and they transformed it into something desired. Paid for. Appreciated. And nothing for her hands to concern themselves with but cloth. The touch of it, clean and fresh, bright scissor blades crunching through. And the silver shreds of holding pins pierced round, about and under. And then the cotton threads flying through in small even nips under her fingers white and lean. So neat. Ah those days. And nights too . . . that was the time she was working at night as a waitress. In the Gresham Hotel. Things going so well; she had *two* jobs then, days with Aunt Florence. And evenings, twice maybe three times a week:

Hands measuring the distance between rows of silver then, tipping the fractions into place. Placing triplets of glasses, stem first, at each setting. And nothing could be blemished; all must be kept as clean as . . . hands covered in white gloves, those were hers. They served things then. Slices and spoonfuls. And gravy lavished down over the bumps. And the smells coming up to her, discretion, warmth. Succulence.

And then there were the later times, working as Kate's maid, oh yes, what about those? Hands doing little or nothing at all then. Except slipping in and out of gloves for day, for evening, for day again. And staying dry anyway. Always dry. Except for hair baths once or twice a week, her own or maybe Kate's.

Greta worked the oatmeal and vinegar together with the back of a wooden spoon until it came out a paste. And: 'Just look at them now,' she complained to her youngest child, sitting in a box by the door. She stretched her hands out and then brought them back down before dipping them into the mixture and coating them over as if they were herrings about to be fried. Then she sat down and rested her wrists against the side of the table so that the hands stood side by side, erect as two little puppets. She waited for them to dry.

'Now as for my mother's hands . . . ' she began and then stopped. Had hers become as bad as that? Almost? Or worse? Surely not worse? For lately it seemed to Greta that no matter which light she put under, her life with all its aspects, it looked the same. After all these years, all this *trouble*: she really was no better off than her mother. There had been moments – of course there had been moments – that would have been far superior to anything Mother may have experienced. Her London days – (think of those) – why Mother would never have been able to imagine the like, Mayfair and Hafton House and 'Madame' relying on her for every little thing, totally dependent on her until disgrace had sent her packing. And back home again.

And then there had been Kate's house. Being part of the 'Cleary set' – remember that? – and brought everywhere in motor cars. To race meetings and socials and at-homes. And a ball. Once there'd even been a ball (when Kate's husband Pakenham was away and couldn't object). Like part of the family she was then. Most people wouldn't even dream that she was a maid, assuming her to be a relative or a friend. She had been set up for life there and then just like that – she had tripped herself up and headfirst fell, going all the way down, not stopping until she hit rock bottom. All the way down to Mrs Gunne's household. Disgrace again. Greta blew out a word on a sigh, 'Men.'

Aunt Florence's shop, Hafton House, Kate's, yes. Always the same thing. Always the same disgrace. Still what were they now but past moments? Gone forever. They could only stay alive in her head as long as she let them. And these days she wasn't so sure she wanted to keep them nurtured anyway, wasn't so sure she wouldn't just as soon leave them to starve. To die. For what was the point now? She had let them all go. Just let them slip through the fingers of these hands. That had managed to look even worse than Mother's.

And yes – as she had come to think in recent days – it wasn't just the hands that were worse either. There were other things too. For one, her mother had at least had the sense to confine herself to two children and, another thing, her father was rarely if ever drunk. He might not have been the cleanest man ever to be called a Christian but at least he spoke to his children, played with them even. On Sundays.

'My mother,' she told the baby, 'a stupid clot of a woman. You should have seen her. With fingernails always dirty and the dinner slopped out at you from a spoon crusted with yesterday's mash. My mother – who used to scratch herself like a dog and anywhere she liked too and had the vilest smell of . . . of dishwater and fish water and God knows what other water off her. Or off her greasy pinny – it didn't matter which – as one could not exist without the other. My mother, who used to clean her gob with the corner of the tea-cloth and put bits of raw tripe into her mouth while she prepared the dinner. And eat out of the pot too. Or off the pot lid, standing at the end of the table while we all sat. Well. My mother, who all my life I swore I'd be the complete and utter opposite to and who is now, by the way, the envy of my life, was at least – at the very least, able to hold her head up when she went out. And never had to crawl to anyone. *And* she had a new coat on her back every single Christmas. Which is more than I'll be able to say this year. Not a stitch. Unless you can count that thing.'

Greta nodded over towards the hat she had earlier thrown into the box to keep the baby amused.

It was a present. From her Aunt Florence. It had arrived at the door in a beautiful box with the name of Aunt Florence's dress shop on the side. A beautiful *big* box. Greta had marvelled at the strength of the postman to be able to lift such a monstrosity so easily up on to the table. She was full of admiration (until she realised that he intended lingering for a chat, that was). Out the door she thought he'd never . . . out the door so she could just let herself fly at it. That beautiful, beautiful box, the *size* of it. A tip, that's what he'd been expecting. And wouldn't you know? A Christmas drink too, most probably. A nice drop of whiskey for himself. Well he had his arse. That's what he had.

And while he spoke of the weather and the shops and the price of this and that, she rummaged through the drawers and up through the back lanes and alleyways of the kitchen dresser to where old jars and tin boxes loitered, half forgotten. And muttering replies only as was necessary: 'Indeed now,' and 'Sure there you are,' and 'Oh don't be talkin' to me,' and 'I declare I just don't know . . . '

And all the time imagining the contents of the box. Whatever would Aunt Florence have packed inside? A goose perhaps? All bald and prickly. Or a beef? A spiced one, not a screed of fat on it, russet and lean. And a jar of preserved fruit squeezed in tight together and pressing their faces out through the glass in dismay. Apricots, oh apricots. Imagine the like. And maybe one of Florence's rich cakes weighted with figs and sultanas and such dark secret things. With the whiff of foreign liquor breathing out from it. 'Have you been drinking?' she'd ask it crossly later on, to give the boys a laugh.

And the postman still gassing away, about the new coinage now. Everybody was talking about the new coinage now. She was sick to the death of it.

And why should she care? Money was money, wasn't it? she had snapped at him over her shoulder, and hard enough to get whether it had a queen or a pig for a crest.

'Well,' he'd answered, 'you're dead right there, Missus. But . . . meself now . . . I had to laugh when I seen the pig on the ha'penny all the same. A pig? Did you ever? And what does that say to the world about the Free State, can you tell me that now, Missus?' Greta made no reply.

'Will I tell you? No respect for their money. That's what it says. Pigs in the kitchen and pigs on the ha'pence.'

'Is that right now?'

'And there's another thing . . . they hold a competition for the best design for our new money. *Our* money mind. Our independent money. And who do you think wins?'

'I haven't a notion,' Greta said, turning around to face him at last with a jar in her hands.

'An Englishman. Now. What do you think of that? Years of struggle and bloodshed and we're *still* lettin' them tell us what to do. Still makin' our decisions for us.'

'Imagine that now.'

She began to twist at the lid of the jar. It was the one she kept hidden from Him, in case he took a mind to go for a dip. Which was all the more likely these days, since he'd gone and sold his own reservoir.

A smile cheered the postman's face when he heard the lid softly release itself. He continued: 'Though now, I have to say, I like the idea of the hens and chicks on the penny.' He gave a little chuckle. 'Ah yes, now that's a nice one all right. On account, they say, that it's the coin most used for the women and children and their pleasure must be catered for. Sure God love them all the same. That's what the judge of the competition said in anyway. And here. It should suit you too, with a yard full of birds outside.'

Greta looked down into the jar. There was silver bits and copper bits, and bits struck out in nickel. She pecked at a copper one and lifted it out. 'Ah ha,' she said and handed it to him. He didn't look in the least impressed. But what did she care? And what did he expect in anyway, from the woman of the house? A half-a-crown? It got rid of him quick enough, all the same. Off out the door with him and his shiny yellow penny. And now and at last, she could be alone with the box.

But Greta couldn't believe it when she opened the lid. *Hats*. That's what there was. That's *all* there was. No goose, no fruit, no envelope of money. Just hats: a thick peaked cap for Herbert, a brown velveteen one for George, a sailor's cap for Danny and a baby's bonnet for Charles. And for her? A turban. A beautiful turban hat, yes . . . in satin and lamé with a large cabochon brooch of tarnished silver stuck through its side. But . . . ? She picked the hat up into her hands and rummaged through its rucks, then she plucked the insides of the other hats, one by one. *Nothing*. Finally she gouged the tissue insides of the box out onto the table. And the only thing she found was a card: 'Merry Christmas - Florence'.

Merry Christmas? Merry Christmas? And after Greta had written to her telling of her plight. How that waster had been forced to sell the pub in order to pay off their – no his – debts.

(For what fun had she ever had running up debts?) And this is what she gets for her cry for help. A turban hat? And where in the hell was she supposed to wear it? Out to feed the bloody chickens?

No doubt it had been the product of a changed mind, too. Which added to the insult. A reject. 'Oh, it looked different on paper, Miss McNeice. I don't think, really I don't, now that I see it, that it's quite what I had in mind. I mean to say . . . I don't think it's quite . . . Well, *me*.' How many times had Greta heard that story before when she worked for Aunt Florence? Every season had its box of 'not quite me after alls'. Every season had its box of changed notions.

You'd think she would have sent a few bob. Something for the children at least. And she had been the last hope. Been depending on her for some sort of a Christmas. All the sales I got for her in my time. All the money I made for her. Around the clock I worked. Around the clock and back again. Sundays too, without a twitch. And this is what she gives me. Oh yes and won't we be the grand sight on Christmas day, won't we just? At morning service, there we'll be – all in our skin and nips, but at least we'll have the finest hats for the top of our heads. 'Well, many happy returns, Aunt Florence,' Greta had said before pulling the brooch back out through the cloth and flinging the turban hat in at the baby, who at least received it with open arms and a gurgle of appreciation. And was now, an hour later still occupied with it, or rather the taste and munch of its thick spongy rim.

Greta tapped the back of one hand gently. Not yet dried,

another few minutes yet. And oh to have them as white as before. But no matter what she did, greasing them before and after, giving them a thorough drying for themselves then rubbing in glycerine, lemon juice and eau de Cologne, they *still* came up looking like skinned rabbits. Those damned chickens. Why she had ever started them in the first place? They'd have her pecked to a pulp before the spring came. Her poor hands, ruined. Ruined for life. At least, though, she'd held on to her figure. Well, to the street eye anyway. Inside her clothes it was all puckers and scars and mackerel brindled skin from being stretched by babies bullying for space. But a decent bit of cloth and who could tell? And it was as well to have a figure, in case she'd ever need it.

'Huh,' she laughed out loud, 'chance'd be a fine one.'

She turned to the baby, 'I say . . . chance'd be . . . '

She had noticed Mrs Gunne checking it over all the same, to see if she'd been padded out by motherhood. Or worse, shrivelled up from hard times. Only raging she'd be that it was still as trim as ever. Raging. But that was about all. All else had gone downhill, inch by inch, her hair, her skin. Her teeth were all right though . . . still could smile. If she had anything to smile about, that is.

She looked at the baby. But he could smile all right, he never stopped.

'Oh well you might grin, my bucko. Like your brothers before you. Maybe the first one had cause. But you . . . ? God knows where we'll all be by the time you've sense. God knows what shack we'll be living in by then.'

If anyone had told her ten years ago it would all end like this: four children, a useless fool for a husband and nothing. Except ten pullets that cost her £5 which she had to borrow from Aunt Florence, plus the initial expense of setting up. And a cockerel that might or might not. (What she'd do if they didn't show profit . . .) Still no point in worrying about that yet. Hadn't she another two years to think about that. The one thing old Milinski forgot to mention of course, it would be two years before you could call a penny a profit. Him with his fancy ideas: 'No motors? no garage? no money? So what's wrong with chickens? A good living to be made from the chicken. And you never go hungry. Always a little something in the larder. And I can tell you everything you need to know. There's nothing about chickens that I don't know already. Trust me, I know what I'm saying . . . '

In the meantime, with the pub gone the way of the bottle factories, it would be no time at all before he'd be hanging around the house and under her feet, as soon as whatever little was left when he paid off his debts was well and truly squandered. And all resources dried up too. That useless family of his. How she had ever allowed herself to have got mixed up with them. Tight-fisted to the last. And money to burn. To boot.

Greta spoke to the baby again. 'And don't get me wrong,' she told him. 'I understand Maude not wishing to be responsible for the general wellbeing of every bookmaker and publican in the city. Or not wishing to finance any more willy-nilly schemes, the theatrical agency, the garage, the typewriting machines. (Oh God, would you ever forget those typewriting machines?)

'But she could give something to me. Yes me. After all we – No, you. You and your brothers. Well you're the only living relatives she's got, beside her own daughter, your cousin. And her sister Kate. Wherever she may be. And that one had plenty of it too, I don't mind telling you. I suppose she took it away with her or maybe left it behind for Maude, as if she hadn't enough of it already. If Pat Cleary were alive, he'd see us all right. I know he would. But that lanky streak of misery Maude's married to now . . . I suppose he's behind her. Keeping all the hay for his own barn.

'Think they're great too, no doubt, paying for Herbert's education, right up to university. University, I ask you? When he could be bringing money in. Well they can stuff that for a start. And getting us this house, for the want of a better word. The state of it. Making sure it's slap bang in the middle of these . . . these slums. Pulling any chance my children may have had right out from under their feet. Right out from under them. And fat lot of good Herbert's fancy schooling when he has to come home of an evening and live amongst guttersnipes. Thank God Mrs Gunne didn't ask where I was living now. That's all I've got to say. Thank God. She mightn't have known we moved at all. Yes, Mrs Gunne. That . . . '

A week later and Greta was still smarting from the encounter with Mrs Gunne. Seven days on and she still was haunted by the voice inside her head prompting and scolding her with 'What you should have said was . . . 'And 'Why didn't you just say . . . ?' It was beginning to get on her nerves. If she had to stage one more imaginary meeting where she put Mrs Gunne through one more humiliating experience or indeed insulted Beatrix beety root one more time . . . well, she'd go off her rocker. That was all about it. She'd had enough. Of Mrs Gunne. And her granddaughter. And not being invited to Maude's Christmas party? She had about enough of that too. She didn't care. She just didn't give two –

Across the yard, she could see her husband, coming in through the twilight, with young Danny up in his arms and talking down to him, as if the child could make sense of it all. Was he drunk? Greta wondered. No? Well, he was standing anyway. His hat was on straight. And there was no doubt about it, he had a fondness for that child. For whatever reason he had chosen to love him, just as he had chosen to ignore the others.

And he had, in fairness to him now, looked at Herbert once.

The night he was born. Greta shyly holding the baby out to him had said, 'A boy.' And – 'Ah', he had politely answered, glancing down at the infant. 'Very nice. Very nice indeed.' To her knowledge he never looked at him again unless it was completely unavoidable, that is, if somebody drew his attention to the lad. 'Herbert's getting big,' or 'That's a clever lad,' something like that. Or if the boy spoke to him, which was rare enough these days, thank goodness. How awful it used be having to watch a small child be humiliated by unrequited love or admiration, or whatever the hell it is that small boys yearn for from grown men. With Herbert she had thought it was because he was not . . . Well, there was a possibility that he might not . . . Well, all right then, he wasn't, couldn't have been, the father of the child. Although it had never been mentioned or discussed between them, it was always there, a silent subject. A silence that Greta appreciated, as it happened. No questions asked at all. And when the child was born well outside the limits of respectability, he had never as much as raised an eyebrow. It was as though he believed babies only took five months to grow. It had warmed her to him then, she remembered. Thinking so much more of him for it. Vowing even while the shock of the birth was still raw in her, to have another baby as quickly as possible. To have a son of their own. His own. A gift.

Then George was born and no doubt in anyone's mind as to who the father was. And Greta had felt sure it would be different. She held the baby out to her husband and said, this time with pride: 'A son.' And the father looked down at the small face and said. 'Ahh . . . yes very nice. Very nice indeed.' And the only difference George's arrival made to his life, was that he now had two children to be ignored instead of one.

But with Danny it had been different. The minute he saw him, she could tell. And she hadn't even bothered to hold the baby up, just left the little roll lying beside her. Hardly even glancing at her husband until . . . He leaned down and peered into the baby's face. And then he lifted it up. Up out of the covers and into his arms. Greta had nearly fallen out of the bed with the shock. And there was nothing particular in Danny that she could see, no extra spark, no extra expression to merit this attention. But whatever it was, it was something in the child, not the man. For when the latest baby came he reverted to his usual indifference. Hadn't even bothered to come in to see him at all. Not even an 'Ah yes, very nice'. And now Charles was almost a year. And she hadn't noticed his father look near him yet. Not that she could recall. But Danny? Well. Danny was welcome to him. And his love. And pity the child for having to put up with it. A complaint she never had to suffer from herself. In all honesty and recollection.

Still that was the price of respectability. And she had always known there'd be a price. She just hadn't expected it to be such a long-term arrangement. A whole lifetime of disappointment.

And yet it had once seemed worth it. No more than the slightest risk, so much to gain, so little to lose. A miracle was in the making and she didn't care or think of repayments. A miracle: a respectable woman, after all. Marrying into a family she had once been in service to. Well off and a career for her husband too, all laid out and waiting. An entire bottle-factory at his disposal and a public house too. Not too bad at all. And him hardly more than a lad. And him who had started out with wanting no more than a pair of dancing shoes, a cane and a collapsible hat for his tools of trade. She couldn't really complain. Hadn't she gotten away with her biggest disgrace to date? A pregnancy out of wedlock. And she'd had a proper wedding too. Small but elegant and what with being fitted up by Aunt Florence, no one could really be sure is she or isn't she? Except Mrs Gunne of course, who would swear it whether she was or not. To Mrs Gunne's mind every wedding was a military wedding (except of course, her own. And her 'dear sweet' Marguerite's).

Not that Greta minded people knowing that part of the scandal. As long as they believed the father and the groom were one and the same. And Mrs Gunne had always had that doubt. But now? Now after seeing Maude's child and mine, two cousins and looking so much like each other. It's probably been keeping her awake at nights wondering how we managed it, her precious lodger and the lady's maid. And the two children so unusual looking too. She'd have to believe they were blood relatives now. It's almost as if . . . Yes, hard to believe they were not. How it must confuse her tiny mind. And what a stroke of luck for me. And Herbert too. Not so awkward for him now, being so unlike his brothers.

Outside, she could hear the little boy's giggles sharpen to near-hysteria and raised herself up off the chair a little to see: yes, just as she thought, they were playing horsies again. The father running along by the yard wall and bouncing the boy in his arms as if they were jockey and mount. Reliving some race doubtless, he must have won a few bob. Not that she'd see a toss of it. Not on your nellie. And he'd better not keep the child out in that cold much longer, not with his chest. He'd better not.

They had moved over towards the stable and there was silence again. Nearly time to start the tea. She would wait for the two boys to come back from Mr Milinski's and hope to goodness that this new rooster didn't prove to be another dud.

Greta stood up and moved towards the basin at the other end of the table. With her right hand looking diseased, she lifted it up and over to the simmering kettle. There she filled the basin half way up and added in cold water to thin the robust burst of steam into slighter wisps. She refilled the kettle and set it again on top of the stove. Then she tested the water with a wary fingertip. Yes, just right. She looked beside her. All ready? Nice soft towel and then the mixture of lemon and glycerine to finish the job. She could feel her hands begin to irritate and lifted them up to have one last look before plunging them down into the soothing water below. 'Oh those bloody chickens. May God forgive them . . . ' and then turning to the baby: 'Wish me luck.' She lowered her hands.

But the door opened before they had reached the water, slamming against the wall with a loud bash. Oh that door, that door. How many times must she tell them? A cold evening wind barged suddenly into the room.

'Will you mind the bab – ' she began, turning to scold Herbert and George. But it wasn't her children she saw standing in the doorway. It was two other children. Two strangers. A boy and a girl. The girl had a cloak with a collar of fur and a muff in her hand that was its match. And the boy? The boy was dressed in a tailored suit and his eyes looked through a small pair of gold-rimmed spectacles. They were staring rudely at her hands. They made her feel ashamed. It was as though it was she who was intruding. And who were they anyway? Who did they belong to? One of his cronies no doubt . . . Coming in here as if they owned the place, who did they think they were?

'Would you mind telling . . . ?' she began and then stopped. A shadow had risen up behind the two children. Now a protective hand was laid on either of their inside shoulders.

'Oh my God,' Greta said in a whisper, 'oh my God I don't believe it.'

'Hello, Greta,' she heard Samuel's shy voice say.

Greta stared at him for a moment or so and then: 'Kate . . . ?' she asked. And he shook his head slowly.

But she needn't have asked him at all. She already knew. One look at his face and she just knew. She lifted her hands to her face in shock and looked down at the children. Kate? Kate's children . . . ? The poor little . . .

They were looking back up at her, their heads cocked to one side. Clear-eyed and curious, and seeming only interested in the trail of oatflakes dropping now in scales, from cheek to chin and all the way down, sticking like sores to Greta's chest.

FIVE

We came to Dublin a week after Mama died. She died towards the end of November and by the time the month had turned we were on a ship pulling out of New York harbour. But we hadn't set out to go to Dublin then. We were supposed to be going to Liverpool. Papa had to tend to things, he said, business things. Whatever they were, I couldn't say. I knew Mama's attorney was in Liverpool, so I guess it had something to do with him. Anyway, it all had to do with our future. I could tell that much at least.

When we were up on deck and longing for Papa to leave us – so we could forget our mourning for a moment and be, just like everybody else, excited – I remember him mentioning something to Adeline about Dublin and Aunt Maude. And I listened, as I always did when I heard her name (on account of it being just like mine). As if anything that concerned her, concerned me and all the other Maudes all over the world too probably (except I didn't know any others). It was as if we – my Aunt and I – were one and the same and it were to my mind inevitable that I would grow into that tilted and serene profile daydreaming out an unseen window in the side of an old photograph Mama had kept on her bedside table. With that dome of carefully arranged hair, rich and smooth as melting chocolate to the spoon, something I would somehow acquire in the future, in exchange for the sparsely knitted curls I knew to be my own.

'I'm going to have to tell her,' Papa was saying. And Adeline, nodding carefully, started to cry again, just as she had started every time she had looked at one or the other of us for the previous few days.

'I don't think I should go in person though,' he continued. 'No, I don't think so . . . That would hardly be wise.'

And Adeline moved her head again, this time from side to side.

'Perhaps I'll write from Liverpool?' Adeline's head went back to nodding then until Papa said, 'Although not to tell her in person,' – and it changed direction again. 'Oh what am I to do? What am I . . . ?' he implored finally, rubbing his forehead into the heel of his hand.

But Adeline didn't answer him. She just kept on moving her head in accordance with whatever Papa was saying, up and down if he seemed decided on something or from side to side if he did not. For she knew, I suppose, he wasn't really talking to her. He was thinking out loud, fumbling sort of, the way he had been doing lately. As though he had awoken in the middle of the night in a strange house and was trying to find his way to the nearest light switch.

I turned away then back towards the city, grasping the Woolworth building firmly in my eye. When the opportunity came, I wanted to be first to shout: 'There it is. There it is. I saw it first.'

For even though Benny was one whole year, two whole months and two days younger than me, he always seemed to be first. He was even first to see Mama lying in the coffin. But right now he had his shoulders bent over the balustrade and I could see his head dangle and peer all the way down to where the ship spouted laundry-bright spittle out through the side of its mouth and back into the water. As long as he stayed intent on this operation, I had a chance. I could be first, this time.

Behind me, I could still hear Papa fretting to himself: 'I'll send the box, though, that's what I'll do. I'll make sure it gets there two weeks after the letter. Would two weeks be enough? No. Perhaps I'll tell her about the box in the letter and then send it; what? Two weeks wouldn't give her enough time to absorb the shock. Maybe three. Would three be enough? On the other hand it might console her were I to send it sooner. Who can tell? Yes, anyway, we'll see. I can't make my mind up just now.'

And at last I heard Adeline speak, 'Yes,' she said, 'We'll see. We'll see. That's what we'll do. We'll just wait and see.'

It was almost as though she was going to be there with us.

The ship gave a long gruff cough then, so rude and sudden that we all jumped and a man in uniform called up and down the deck for visitors to disembark. Adeline hugged me first, then Benny, then me again. And I had a feeling I might never see her again so I kissed her face somewhere near the lips where it had run a little purple. Like a big black grape that had begun to soften. Then Papa walked with her to the gangplank and as soon as we saw the crowd gobble up their heads, we became again our everyday selves.

'It's the Woolworth building,' I yelled. Benny was jumping and waving at people down below and attempting to grab out at the explosion of ticker tape, sprouting all about us from the dockside to the deck. He answered me like it just didn't matter: 'I know, I already saw it.'

(No you did not. I saw it first. Did not. It's mine. It *is* not; it is not.)

And I knew I was being a baby but it was mine. Benny wanted it for no reason other than to be first. But I had a reason. A real one.

I wanted it for my own, because Mama and I had stood at the

bottom of it on that last day that we went out together. It was the day she posted her Christmas letter to Aunt Maude and we had streetcar-hopped all over Manhattan until Mama found a place she liked enough to hand over the envelope. Malspeth, I think it was called. And we went downtown then and first we saw Times Square and then we saw the Woolworth building and lots more besides, in between and later. But it was the Woolworth building I liked the best. Standing looking up and up and trying to figure where the tip of it would end. And all those strange designs in terracotta lace, looking so delicate and yet somehow so mean. And wondering, the two of us, how it all stayed together, all the way up. And if it would make a rainstorm come, poking a hole in the bottom of a cloud and irritating the sky like that by sticking into its skin. Like a stone in your boot or a button on a too-tight skirt. Wondering until our necks got sore and Mama said, 'Let's take a peep inside.'

And that was scary for a minute, trying not to get noticed. But nice then too. All glass specks on the ceiling and bronze bits shaping out of the walls. And a portrait too of Mr Woolworth's face melted into the cornice as if he were part of the building, as if the building were his body. And fast legs cutting past us from every corner while we stayed perfectly still. Yes that was all very nice. But not as nice as being outside and wondering together, just the two of us. Wondering about the sky.

But now on board ship with the skyline all still and spread obligingly out, like the best grade girls at school assembly, now it seemed silly for one or the other of us to claim it, as it was the most obvious building in sight. And so we stopped and picked on other landmarks to argue about. (It's a hundred-and-fifty-one feet high. It is not, it's a *thousand* and fifty feet high; it is not. It was given us by the Irish government. It was not. It was the French

80

Government. Irish. French. Irish. Fr . . .)

Then Papa came back and we were silent again. And more than a little ashamed. And determined, both of us, not to enjoy ourselves for one more second. Not one more second ever, as long as we lived. Until we were all in heaven together again. Together again with Mama.

We loved the ship, though. Its bright halls and elaborate tables. Its deckchairs managing to pull warmth from the December sun. And those round-eyed windows that supervised the antics of the sea, day and night. No matter which colour it was wearing, no matter which way it moved. The ship was called the *Celtic* and Papa said it was one of the 'Atlantic greyhounds'. Which made us feel proud and say to each other 'Oh . . . one of *those*, one of those *greyhounds*.' He said it had a sister ship too, called the *Cedric*. And Benny called me Cedric then for a day or two until he forgot and went back to calling me Maudie or pan face or string bean. Or other names he was always thinking of and then forgetting. Just as I was getting used to them.

Everybody on board was so kind to us and speaking to us in a church-hushed voice, and that made us feel obliged to behave sadly all the time. And we were sad, of course we were. But sometimes, just sometimes, it would slip away from us and on those empty winter decks it would suddenly let us loose: the sound of our boot-thuds startling the wooden floors and our screeches of laughter tumbling overboard like crumbs to the wind and the sea. And the escort of low flying birds forever on our trail.

Papa's sadness never let him loose, though. And he always looked worried. Like he was squabbling with himself. I knew it had to do with this decision about Aunt Maude and telling her about Mama, and how and when he should do it. And the box. I knew it had something to do with Mama's box of letters. He had kept it with him in his cabin on the whole voyage, not minding how much room it took over. Or how many times we had to step across or around it. And he had it wrapped so many times that it looked sort of careless, like a bundle of old clothes. He was always touching it too, especially at night after dinner when his eyes would get a little cloudy and his speech a little slow. 'That's your Mama's life with me,' he would say more than once, while he struggled into his bunk. 'That's her life in America. It's all there. She's in there. Every little bit of her.'

And Benny hated when he said that. He would scowl and look as if he wanted to kick the box to pieces. But he didn't understand. Papa didn't mean that she was all squeezed up inside there. He meant her letters, of course. The letters she wrote to Aunt Maude but never mailed. One for every week since she had left Dublin. There were as many letters as weeks in ten years. And not one had been put in the mail. Not ever. I started to count them in my head one night while going to sleep and then just when I had an answer I remembered the Christmas letters. Those were sent and would have to be subtracted. But I fell asleep before I could complete the calculation. And the next morning I couldn't remember what to subtract them from. After that, whenever I couldn't sleep, I always started over counting the letters. But I never reached as far as that number again. I always seemed to fall asleep first. So I never knew for certain.

I bet Papa knew, though. He held on to that box dearly. Even that night on Calf's Rock – where our voyage ended so abruptly – he had it clutched to his chest. That was the night the ship crashed and we all got thrown out of our bunks and landed on the floor in the dark. That night when we were huddled together on the curling velvet seating of the saloon smoke-room with glasses and ornaments strewn on the floor and smashed glass panels pointing long sharp accusing fingers at each other. And the captain came in to tell us that we were off the coast of Ireland, ashore on Calf's Rock and we were near the lighthouse and would be moved by tenders to Queenstown where we could spend the rest of the night until tomorrow when we could go by rail to Dublin and then on to Liverpool. That night his worries seemed to ease a little when I heard him say: 'Well, if that's not a sign, I don't know what is. If that's not a sign. Queenstown. Who would believe it? Full circle. We've come full circle. Queenstown. That's that then. I'll tell her in person. Now that I'm here. That's what I'll do. I'll hand it over in person.'

And he patted the box as if to say, 'All right, all right, everything's goin' to be all right.' It was the way he might have patted Mama's shoulder or mine. Or Benny's too. When we were feeling lonely or upset. Or in need of his kind hand on our shoulder.

He let out a sigh then, long and loud so that everybody turned to look. It sounded as if someone had let all the bad air out of him. And he smiled out at the darkness as if he were saying thank you to the sea. Thank you for having made his mind up for him.

He looked calmer after that. And even joined in with the singing, which started up as soon as everybody realised that it wasn't going to be another *Titanic* after all. 'Pack up Your Troubles' and then a little later, when we were being lifted down into the tenders and moving thickly over the black water with its broken tips of sly silver light guiding us in, 'Goodbyee Goodbyee' to the people still aboard and queueing for their turn. And we could hear their reply: 'Goodbyee Good-byee', singing after us until it grew too faint and we could only hear the slap of the waves beneath us then and the shivering hum that kept on bouncing out through our rat-a-tat teeth.

It was Christmas time in 1928 by the time we got to Dublin and I loved it from that first moment. To me it was just like a toytown, a whole city that could fit into one or two neighbourhoods, so that you never had to keep worrying about what was across the bay or where the building blocks might end and the grass begin. And the bridges were short and compact and it was good to feel in proportion to things. Benny didn't like it so much though; he liked things to be big. As in New York. Although he may have just said that to contradict me. He was always doing that, pretending not to like things just because I did.

We moved into a hotel in the town, small on the outside, I guess, but once you got inside . . . And so many rooms that were just for eating in, we thought, Benny and I, that the Irish were very greedy indeed. There were even eating rooms in the basement, a grill room and an oyster bar. On the ground floor there was a restaurant and a tea lounge. On the first floor, a coffee room and a banqueting room. There was also an orchestra playing at different times in different rooms, in the restaurant sometimes and other times in the tea lounge. We liked the tea lounge best, with its squat wicker chairs and its palm trees growing out of dumpy brass tubs. And hats and gloves moving to the sounds of conversation and the gentle sound of string music swaying always in the background. It had a panelled ceiling too and a partition of dark wood and frosted glass that Benny climbed up on once to take a peek over and caught a waiter eating a fancy, in one guilty mouthful. Or so he said.

We liked the hotel and thought of it as a sort of doll's house, with so many rooms to explore and look over and an elevator too, where we played Guess the Oyster. This was a game we took to playing when Papa left us for three days and went to Liverpool. We would stay in the elevator and, as passengers came and went, we had to guess who was and who wasn't going to go to the oyster bar. This involved following the suspect right to the door just in case he or she should go into the grill room instead. Benny always won. He could take one look and yell, 'Oyster'. And he was almost always right. These Betcha games were essential to us; we used them to make decisions: settle our disputes. We just couldn't seem to agree on anything so the outcome of a game would be the judge. Particularly during that time when Papa was away.

No one in the hotel was supposed to know that we were left alone all night. Papa had ordered supper in our room for us and we had to be sure to be there to receive it. And he had told the management that he was out on business during the day, and would be at business dinners for two nights. So we were supposed to say the same if anybody asked us: 'Oh, he's just gone to a meeting,' or 'Oh, he's just gone out to a business dinner.'

I was so scared every time a knock came at our room, the heat pumping up on my face until I thought it would burst. And Benny *still* wanting to play Betcha.

'OK. Guess. Which one, Big Nose or Bobby Long Tooth?'

'I don't know. Benny, stop it.'

'Ah come on now. Betcha it's Big Nose.'

'Benny, open the door. *Open* it.'

'It's Big Nose. Betcha it's Big Nose.'

'Open it.'

'Not till you betcha.'

'OK, then, it's Long Tooth.'

'We sneak out after supper if you're wrong?'

'Yes, yes, all right; just open the *door*, Benny.'

'Cross your eyes and hope to die?'

'OK.'

'Cross them. Are you crossing them?'

'Yes, yes.'

'Ah ha, I told you, I won, I won.'

And then he would go yelling and hopping out from behind the door, while the porter with the nose like a salami would stand there waiting to be told where to put our supper.

But I left Benny to deal with all that; he was so much better at it, saying, 'Oh what a shame, you just missed him,' or 'He'll be back in a little while, you can just leave it there,' (like it was really true). His favourite one was, 'I'm afraid he's not available; he's in the . . . ' and then pretending to be all embarrassed he would put his hand over his mouth and say, 'Ahem, ahem'. Meaning he was in the bathroom, I suppose. Finally he would hand over one of the tips Papa had left in the drawer lined up in a queue: Tuesday morning, Tuesday night, Wednesday morning, Wednesday night. Thursday afternoon.

'He said I should give you this.'

'Thank you, Sir.'

'Oh no, thank *you*, Sir.'

And Papa had warned us not to leave the hotel in the evenings. But Benny always wanted to. I always wanted not to. And that was usually why we had the games in the first place, because the winner got to do whatever the winner wanted. Which meant we nearly always went out.

I liked it, though, when we did. The lights were sort of nearer, easier to see. The shop windows too, you could get at them and stay there too, if you liked, without being shoved out of the way. The florist's shop had holly wreaths just like at home and even in the main shopping avenue, there was a greengrocery store with cart tops outside cobbled over in fruit with green leather holly sprigs hedging the one variety from the next. Imagine having a grocery store on Fifth Avenue? And nobody seemed to be in any kind of hurry; there was hardly any traffic and lots of bicycles and slow sturdy horses pulling slow sturdy wheels.

And you could see the sky.

Benny wasn't so impressed and he kept saying it, too, out loud so that people in the street stared at us. 'Jees, look at that dumb little Christmas tree! Why, back home we got them a million times bigger. Right up to the sky bigger. You call them Christmas lights? Little itty bitty things. Why, in New York the dogs wear those kinda lights round their neck.'

I asked him to stop talking so loud and to stop making his accent so large. He wouldn't, though, because he had seen something like it in a vaudeville show on Brighton Beach and the audience had laughed and laughed and so he thought he was being funny. I didn't though. I knew Mama would hate it if she was listening down, to hear him swagger on so. But he didn't care, he wasn't scared. He was never scared of anything much really. Except, maybe, the uncle with the limp. I think he was really scared of him.

When Papa came back from Liverpool, he had gift boxes and parcels wrapped in bright seals and coloured ribbons. He asked us if we had behaved and of course we said yes. We didn't bother him with the story about the lady with the fox-fur wrap in the elevator nor the gentleman with the toupee in the lobby. I didn't even mention Benny's spectacles and how they had spent the last few days in the drawer, a stranger to his ears. Nor did I tell him about our evening walks up and down Grafton Street. Even though I'd sworn to Benny, I would, I really would, tell about him yelling and boasting and shaming us all. Nor did I tell, in the end, about the music lady in Woolworth's store and how Benny had insisted she play and sing for him, from sheet music he had no intention of buying, just so he could laugh at the way the notes came down her nose and her hands bounced on the keys of the piano, pretending not to be angry. I was going to tell him about Benny climbing up on the tea lounge partition, but I thought I'd best hang on to that one in case I might need it for a trade at some later time. It was always as well to have a trade where Benny was concerned. So Papa said because we were such good children we could open the parcels.

And the room was suddenly filled with great balls of hurly-burly papers all brightly coloured and rolling over the beds and down on the floor. And it was like a miniature Coney Island, same feeling and all. Benny got an engine and a harmonica and a boat you could sail in a lake. I got a jump rope and a tea service. And a very big doll, which just made me sad and miss Mama and I started to cry so hard that I wore myself down into sleep and Papa carried me to bed and I could hear Benny in the background saying, 'I hate girls, they're such stupid babies, always crying and carrying on. I just hate them. Dumb things. Girls. I hate 'em. Cry babes, I just – '

But behind my closed eyes I could remember how nice Mama's brown hair looked when it was being brushed out before she went to bed. How nice you could make it, if you spread it over her shoulders. Like a velvet curtain up on a stage, soft and yet strong and somehow awfully patient too.

The day after Papa's return from Liverpool, we left the hotel for ever and went looking for our relatives. No one said goodbye to us, not even Big Nose or Long Tooth who looked the other way when we tried to catch their eye. And I could remember then how different it had all been not a week before, the sudden rush of livery, arms and legs, closing in on us, and how frightened I had been at the eyeless swoop of cap peaks and smiles. And one long yellow tooth beaming out from all the confusion. But I had nothing to fear now. It was all so different now; this time we carried our bags without help.

And first we took a waggedy tram all down by the river where the distant buildings swerved with the quayside. No two appeared to be identical, all shapes were there, so that as we moved nearer to them, they looked like a row of mixed onlookers of various widths, in and out, curtseying to various heights, up and down.

We got off outside a building that was the strangest I had ever seen. Yet friendly too, unlike the Woolworth building with its rusted bones all knitted together as though it had been skinned. No. This one was much more approachable than that. It had somehow fitted itself snugly on to a corner and, flexing around it, had softened any edges into a curve through which Papa was about to disappear, dragging our luggage, piece by piece, behind him. But not before he had told Benny and me to stay out on the sidewalk and study the building until he came back. We were to tell him what it was all about. A dime would buy the best story.

And there was plenty to study. An elaborately illustrated page in a picture book, that's just what it was like. Above each window and door there was an inset into which a stage scene had been deeply cut. In the largest one there was a group of raised carvings. Men in old-fashioned breeches, all sat around a table. In the next one, there were two holy men climbing a mountain. And then, in another one again, a weeping girl played on a harp that had no strings. Separating each of these scenes from one another were long strips running downwards and divided into boxes. In each box there was either a chair or a dog. Each figure stood out on its own as though it were real; so, too, was each one large enough. It was like a house with no privacy, a house that had been turned inside out. Or at least had its front wall peeled back like the lid from a tin of sardines.

And that wasn't all. Up above, on the brink of the entire building, a crown was fitted on. A crown of wrought iron, from which occasional turrets rose like horns to the sky. Any rare inch of space that had been forgotten was compensated with a purfle of waves or tendrils or tiny crimped frills. And finally, stretched out across the middle was a band which said 'Cleary's' over the smaller door and over the main front window 'The Irish House' in a strange kind of squat lettering that looked as though it had been sat on.

And under the evening sun, the whole confection took on a misty gold and dusted it lightly around itself from crown down to the sidewalk, where our two bewildered heads were looking up.

After a while, when we couldn't figure any story out of it all, the scrawny dogs, the men in breeches and curled wigs, the point in playing an instrument without any strings and reminding ourselves that you couldn't spend a dime in this city anyway, we decided to move through the gap that had earlier taken Papa and to settle ourselves in the dent between the heavy outer door and the other prettier one on the inside.

It was sheltered in here, a small lumber room with our luggage propped softly up against one side and welcome as familiar furniture around us. By now it had grown cold, for small as the river was, it seemed to be splashing iced air over its tidy grey walls aiming at any part of our bodies we might have left exposed. Benny was bored and started up almost at once: 'Huh, call that a river. That's a stream. That's not even a stream, that's a leak.' And so we began hitting out at each other, which kept us occupied and helped us to keep warm.

Each time the door opened we stopped hitting and peeked inside. And each time we could see a little more. First there was a bar counter all along one side and men in unremoved hats sitting high up and drinking from big black glasses and smoking from behind their hands. The next time the door opened there was Papa talking to a man on the other side of the counter. They were leaning toward each other as if they were having a secret. Then the door swung open again and this time it was Papa, telling us we could come inside as long as we were as quiet as mice.

He rushed us in through the doorway and at first I couldn't see a thing, except for Benny's cap collapsing off his head and now there it was hanging down between his two hands. I could see Papa's hand slide our baggage through a gap in the bottom of the bar counter and another hand reach out to pull it away and out of sight. And the sawdust. I could see the piles of sawdust spread over the freckles of the real floor beneath. Which was where I kept my eyes, until Papa said 'It's all right, Maudie, I'm here. You can look up.'

And I lifted my head then just as the man behind the counter put down his bar towel and tipped Papa a nod towards a corner. Papa used the same nod to pass the message on to us, adding in a whisper,

'Remember now, two little . . . ?'

'Mice,' we replied.

We sat under a nook on two short stools each with a cut carved hole in the middle and Benny whispered to me that they were for letting stinkballs out through. And it was awfully hard not to giggle at that but when I looked around I stopped. For now I could tell what was inside here: it was a bucketshop. I knew because Adeline used to tell us that her husband spent every Saturday night in one, drinking and singing, and swearing and breaking the law right into the Lord's Day, she said, and not caring about no thing or no one save enjoying himself.

There didn't seem to be much singing in this bucketshop

though, nor much enjoyment. Just a sometimes mumbling of men's voices in the dusk. Some of them didn't even bother to talk. Just sat alone on the bench by the wall, leaving long spaces between one another.

One or two of them were reading newspapers but others weren't doing anything at all. Just sort of staring. Staring at nothing that I could see. At the other end of the room there were games being played. But in a hushed way, too. A couple of men standing and throwing small black rings at a board with numbers painted on and the whole place was so quiet, you could hear the slaps of rubber when the rings landed and slid back down to the floor. And I was worried then, because Adeline had said that anyone caught in a bucketshop went straight to prison and after that, was put on the next train, the A-train, straight on down to hell.

But then the man behind the bar counter brought us two small glasses of milk and a tiny packet of cookies each. And I wasn't scared any more. When we said, 'Thank you, Sir' he laughed out loud and said to Benny, 'That's a grand pair of specs you've got there.'

And I looked sideways at my brother, for I knew how he hated his spectacles for the comments they invited and I knew how he hated them for themselves. But then the man put Benny's cap back on his head, this time sideways. And I saw him grin upwards. And now he really looked like one of those Brooklyn street-kids he'd been trying so hard to sound like all week.

Papa sat near us, up high at the counter and spoke to the man. His name was Bart. We knew because throughout their conversation we could hear his name being called from different parts of the room. 'Bart, when you're ready,' or 'Sameagain, Bart.'

Sometimes it was just 'Bart' on its own. Everybody seemed to want Bart. Especially Sameagain, who said it three times already.

But Bart didn't seem to hear him. I suppose he was a little deaf and that's why he was leaning so close to Papa while they were speaking. I couldn't really see his face, just his hand with a crumpled cloth beneath its fingers, moving lazily over the same spot, and pausing only now and then whenever he lowered his voice to an even softer whisper. I couldn't see Papa's face either, just the back of his head and his shoulders and down further, round the side of the barstool, behind his knee, the folds of his trousers melting into each other before they all parted to their separate ways down the rest of his leg.

Sameagain was beginning to look a little annoyed. He left his spot on the bench and came on over. From where I was sitting, I could see his face. He was looking Papa over once or twice while he waited for his drink to cook or whatever it was doing boiling up and then simmering down until it was a calm black inkwell. Then he spoke.

'Usedn't you be Samuel?' he asked and the back of Papa's head tilted back. But it was Bart who answered. 'Used to be and still is,' he said. Then Papa shook the man's hand. But I could tell he hadn't recognised him.

'And didn't you . . . ?' the man tried to continue, but again he was interrupted by Bart, this time with a a sudden rush of words. 'Nowww, I hope you're not expecting the slate for this one? New man's not a slate-lover, you know. Oh no, it's for the roof and the roof only in his opinion. Can't give it to you; so there's no point in asking. No, No point at . . . '

The man moved his head slowly towards Bart but he was still speaking to Papa. 'And didn't you used work for Pat, Lord rest him, Cleary?'

'That's right,' Papa said. 'At one time, I did.'

'A sad loss,' Sameagain said, slapping some coins down on to the counter and sliding them over towards Bart, 'a sad loss indeed. You just missed his brother-in-law, you know.' And Papa's head turned and looked towards the door.

'No, no. I don't mean now, about a week ago. Sold the place, so he did. More's the pity. A decent man, a gentleman. Which is more than can be said for – between yourself and meself – the new man. He's a bit of a – '

But down in our little nook, we couldn't hear what the new man was a bit of because Sameagain leaned towards Papa and whispered it.

He came back up talking out loud. 'Oh indeed, indeed,' and with one foot pressing on the brass rail that ran close to the ground and one hand pressed firmly on the bar counter he bounced himself a little as he spoke. 'Married now, you know,' he said.

'Yes, I heard. Four boys,' Papa answered him.

But Sameagain didn't seem to hear him because he just came out and said, 'Four young lads. Did you know that?'

'Yes, Bart here was just telling me.'

'He's a sister lives out in Chapalizard. Married again she did. That'd be Cleary's widda. Ah but sure you'd know her.'

'That's right. I would.'

'The other one fecked off – '

Papa started to speak very quickly now. Almost as quickly as Bart. If Sameagain could understand both of them at the one time, Benny and I could understand neither. It was like they were going to be late for something. Something real important and had to say everything all at once, before they ran out the door. Benny and I stopped munching and looked at each other.

Papa was saying, 'Where does he live now? Did he buy another pub? I must drop up and see him. Tell me, are you from around here yourself?'

And Bart. Bart was saying, 'Chapelizod? Know it well; me own part of the world as it just so happens.' And scared. They both seemed sort of scared.

We could see Sameagain's head move from one to the other and back again and stopping only when Bart asked, 'Same again is it, Harvey? Well?' The man held up his glass and looked at it, still half-full, black from the bottom up and then onwards a thin rinse of cream to the top.

'On the house, of course.' Bart winked and Papa said, 'Here, let me.'

And I could see his elbow moving backwards and his hand disappear down into his pocket.

'Well, that's very dec – ' Sameagain began.

'You go on over and sit yourself down and I'll bring it across in a tick.'

'But I have to tell him where – ' Sameagain said, sounding all disappointed, like the way Benny might do when he's told it's bedtime already.

'Don't you worry about that. I'm takin' him there now as soon as I get me break. Go on, over you go before I change me mind.'

He moved away then, back towards his place by the wall and as he passed me I could hear him mutter to himself: 'On the house? On the house? Well, that's the quare – '

And I stood up then. I just had to. I stood up pretending to fix the end of my coat. I had to see.

And Bart's face was all red and Papa's face was all red and I don't know why, maybe one of them had let out a stinkball through the hole in the stool. But they were embarrassed about something.

Yes sir, they were.

When we came back out nightfall had sneaked down and the river was lying back like a big dog belly-up, enjoying the tickles from the gaslights above. And all along its quaysides, you could see the covered trams transport passengers up-river and down, their faces so sharp against the neat blocks of misted yellow light they might easily have been ink drawings and not real people at all.

We turned the corner then and upwards into the darkness and I didn't know if I loved Dublin so much now, away from the light and the busy streets. Benny and I followed Papa and Bart, a bicycle rolling along between them and their two heads jigging over it in conversation. And I slowed up my step when I saw the covered bridge before us at the top of the hill, feeling myself fill up with dread at the idea of having to pass up under it. Its deep arch held together two sides of a long thin church. The only hint of colour against its ancient black came from the stained-glass windows, that weak blue and red, like old veins with a trickle of thin blood struggling through.

I could see Benny was slowing down too. Sensing the doubt in my step, he too had become afraid. Was he, like me, thinking of a tomb and a woman with a familiar face? Up there under that arch? Her hair wild, a tangled mass of rope. For who would brush it now at the other side of the arch? Who would keep it smooth and trouble-free? (It seemed since she had died that was all I could think about, her hair. It was a worry ever present in my mind).

And now just a few more steps and I knew I would see her. Just a few more steps and she would be there. The silver-backed brush stretched out in her hand. Pleading with me to help her. Not able to stand the way she looked, not one more second. 'Please,' she would cry out to me, only me. 'Please.' And no one would see her, not even Papa. No one would believe me if I tried to explain. Why I could never walk up under that arch. Why I would sooner die.

I stopped then and grabbed Benny by the arm. I was trying to think of a plan the two of us might get away with simply because we were of one mind, for once. But then Bart turned and pointed his bicycle at an angle away from the archway and towards a side alley off the menacing slope of the hill. And we looked at each other, Benny and I, before following behind, with a brisker step and an easier mind.

It seemed like a long walk then to Aunt Greta's; it seemed like a long way from Jury's Hotel. Although later in daylight I would come to know it was a fraction of that first impression that it gave me. I would know it could take no more than ten minutes or thereabouts. But that night? That night in through those narrow streetways where sometimes the houses were short and front doors were stoopless and at ground level, or other times they rose tall into the shadows with laundry lines jutting out from poles out front, the occasional tatter of forgotten clothing left behind to fend alone through the winter night.

And that night, with the lonely voices yelling here and there from no place to no one, and the isolated cry of a baby that seemed to be following us, no matter how many turns we took. And passing people by who looked at us as if we were crazy when we said, 'Good evening,' until we ended by becoming them, with eyes down each time we saw another being whose path we had no choice but to cross. And we had to cross them all: the ragged children carrying milk jugs from a dairy at the corner and wearing rubber boots although the night was dry. And the women with shawls over their heads and arms folded against breasts as if it were the law and to walk any other way would have you put under arrest. And men huddled together against the hot wall of a bakery stealing heat from the furnace on the other side. The mean red eyes of their cigarette tips following us as we moved on past. That night,

I felt as though I was on the longest journey. Much longer than the one that had taken us from New York Harbour to Calf's Rock.

So much longer than that.

And nothing pleased me once we had moved away from the river and the wagging streetcars. Nothing pleased me once we had moved away from the Christmas streets and into the hinterland.

And I thought then, that nothing might please me again. Not ever. Until I saw my cousin, that was. My cousin Herbert. I knew then I would always be pleased by him, at least. The moment I saw him. I just knew it. When all those dark narrow streetways widened in my mind. And Billy the lamplighter brightened the way.

II

THE BLESSED BAMBINO

SIX

Mr and Miss Carabini sat side by side on the Lucan electric tram from city centre to Chapelizod village. And taking pleasure from the sun-brindled river and the sun-softened grass lying flat by its side, they sat in silence. A smile, or a pat from a fatherly hand to a daughterly glove enough for both, with their own private thoughts to contend with, as well as everything else.

Mr Carabini was remembering home, a place called Lucca, situated on the Piana di Lucca, an agricultural plain of the most prosperous sort, in the plush, flush greenery of the surrounding Tuscany. And whereas as a younger man he had thought of it often, now it was hardly at all. Unless, that is, he happened to be aboard the Lucan electric tram when he could not, given the similarity in name, avoid a thought or two slipping homeward across the sea and down along the continent to his father's Lucchese home.

It was a walled town, Lucca. Like Dublin once had been. And over there on the right of him now he could see the reliable walls of the Phoenix Park keep the tram company all along the Chapelizod Road. So there were two reminders now to shake him back to the past. The name on the front of the tram and the wall of the park just beyond his right shoulder.

The Carabinis had lived just outside Lucca, a few steps, no more. At the back eastern gate with a splendid view of the walls which, not more than a century gone, Nottolini had taken upon himself to fill in and top off with a tree-lined roadway for carriages and the like. So that citizens had forgotten all about the Romans and the sweat of slaves well used and worn in the laying of foundations. And the citizens had forgotten all about the merchant families too who had left along the walls their touches here and there over the centuries. The del Carretti, the Guinigi or even the Segromigni. And had come to think of them now as Nottolini's walls. And besides wasn't it he who had turned the bastions into public gardens? And nice to have somewhere to show yourself off on Sunday afternoon. And wasn't it he too who had cleared out that clutter of tenement buildings on the floor of the arena when grandmothers were girls? And nice to wonder what eventually became of those girls, instead of worrying about merchants. Or Romans. And their string of sweating slaves.

But the hills outside remembered, from the lower slopes up. And the vineyards too, all blistered with jewels of velveteen purple. And the orchards and the olive groves. And the wild possessive clematis draped over holm oaks standing side by side with sweet chestnuts and long-limbed pines. The drying barns, too, on all the farmsteads, with their honeycomb bricks laid out to take ventilation from two directions, the *mandolato*. They could remember. They could remember it all. Back to the days of merchants, when horseback or carriage-drawn they would struggle upwards, first beneath, then beside and finally passing them out altogether. Higher and higher, until the ville various had been reached, so positioned to look down on Lucca, up there from their place near the sky. They could remember. The who and the when. If not the why. And further back too, all the way as far as the Romans. They could remember it all as though it were yesterday.

But back at the gate, young Carabini had no memory yet, back in the shade of the Porta Santo Donato. Through which his father every morning strode across the via Santa Giustina to the via Di Poggia where he would stretch open the doors of his barber shop to the heads and chins of the good citizens of Lucca. Except for Mondays, of course, when he would heave an extra hour or more while his liver argued with the backlog of glass after glass of deepest chianti, Sunday sweet.

That was his Papa, Bruno Carabini, who had turned to managing other men's hair, because he himself had none with which to concern himself. Smooth as a melon since twelve years of age, Bruno Carabini: the bald barber of Lucca. But what a set of moustaches that man could keep. Oh yes, he kept the best moustaches in town – *magnifico*. The envy of all. Except for his only child, his son Aldo, who loved them proudly. As he did his Papa. And gratefully too, his Papa and his Papa's moustaches.

And he had such a lot to be grateful for:

His magic for one. For that's where he had learnt it. Or rather how to love it. From Papa. From Papa in that sunless shop of chrome and porcelain and clean sharp smells. What you could do when the hand moved quicker than the eye . . . That's where he had begun to find out. From watching Papa, with his swift manicured hands flying snip snip snip across another crown. And the scissors twitching all about and the comb simultaneous in its rise and fall. And at such a speed, not ever colliding. Not even tipping off each other in passing. Not ever. Not once.

And then slowing down a little until the scissors were calm enough to go plucking up up up nostrils of the blackest kind to root out petrified stowaways cowering in there against the inside walls of caves that always had a twin. Was that, he wondered now, was that why Senor Vecchio had such gapes, like two wondrous mouths up over the tufts of his disobedient moustaches? From Papa's scissors prising them open. '*Avanti, avanti*. I see you in there. I see you.'

Papa's shop – and the flourish of a steaming towel withdrawing from an upturned chin. Hey presto. Or a razor gleaming over the bump in the road on a thin-skinned neck. (How could he do that without ever breaking the skin? How?). And the buffing of nails on fingers spread out like rows of dead men along the arms of the big chair, buff, buff, all round, down up and round again, buff, buff, buff. His elbow moving virtuoso, like a violinist's. What the eye can't see . . .

Papa's fingers – and taking a head between them, as if it were a ball, to guide it gently into a different pose, then . . . off the sable brush would go in flicks across the backs of freshly shorn necks and down a little, breaking the hug of an affectionate collar, to seek and disperse stuck hairs. And – abracadabra – another head of hair growing down there on the floor. And Papa's eyes, steady in their gaze despite the flurry of movement all about him. He hardly seemed to need them, except for watching the eyes of the customers through the mirror, the one in the high chair, the others sitting patiently on the side, as they talked and talked and argued and sang. Sometimes they even sang. That's what he missed now. That's what he missed the most, the talk. How he had loved it once. Why had he stopped? Where had that love gone to?

He had of course, in the beginning, taken it over with him. And using it to a few fellow-countrymen that in his loneliness he had managed to mouse down, as if he were a cat with whiskers. Sunday afternoons, what had they talked about? He could remember the handshakes, the kissed cheeks, the hand clapping his back as he clapped back. The laughter. He could remember the laughter. But the talk? What was it they were saying? What did they *talk* about? He could remember the places: Fredo's restaurant with the blinds pulled down; the Dolphin hotel and English tea in the afternoon. And a picnic. There had been a picnic where he had met his wife. On Dollymount strand with flapping straw hats longing to take to the wind and the ladies' skirts longing to follow. But what the conversation consisted of? Heavens knows. All that noise. And all forgotten.

Was it because he had turned his back on his own language? Was that it? He had been ashamed of it. That was true. Afraid that it would, with all its extravagance, embarrass him in front of this new tongue, strict and unlavish. This English, so always to the point. Afraid it would stop him from developing his new way of talking, of thinking, in words that were not really his own. And now? Now that he had learnt the rules and could at last remember to follow them. Even managing, for the most part, to keep his hands quite still, down by his side or pocket-bound, or at any rate from constant emphatic jigging about. And now that he could converse with seldom hesitation, he found in fact that he seemed to want to less and less. Could that be so? He certainly didn't seem to talk as much as he had once done. Was it because it took half as long to say something in English? Twice as long in Italian. (The facts before the feelings? The feelings before the facts?) Or had he just lost the love for it? Lost heart? Through negligence let it slip from his own hands? Through carelessness made it vanish?

A funny little thing, to spend all those years perfecting a language, a language that your children use as natural, to keep at it and at it, still to this morning adding to his vocabulary with two new daily words. And for what now? Just for what? To sit in silence on the tram with his daughter. In silence.

A shame that. What a shame that was. And she going off to live in another man's house, and not even as this other man's wife. But to take care of his child. And another other man's child as well. Another other man's two childs, children. *Bambini*. Not a word to her. Had he spoken? Not a one.

He would repair that at once. They would speak like he and Papa used to speak. Like friends. Right now. This minute. He turned to his daughter and she turned back to him. And he smiled and patted her hand once again. Finding after all that he couldn't think of a single thing to say. Even for today's new words. He couldn't seem to find a sentence they would fit into. Poor Lucia. Children, he then sighed to himself, can be so difficult to talk to when they grow up. Every story is one already told. God knows how many times. Every joke already heard. When they are small they will listen, even want to listen. Even *beg* to be told. (Tell me the story of . . . Ah please, again. Ah go on. Once more. Just once.)

But when they are older? They make you ashamed for giving them boredom. Make you ashamed. Five years ago I could have told her about the feast of the holy *bambino*, and not a matter if I had told it each Christmas before. Not a matter if I had told her this Christmas already. She has gone from me now. Now that she can make me ashamed for my repetition. There now. He had found a sentence for one of today's words: repetition.

Just after a scut of terraced houses ran into the church of St Mary, a string of Epiphany worshippers came through the sally port, out and about. And Carabini remembered his instructions. Time to get off and look for the village. After the church, Masterson had said. After the . . .

But it had come on him too suddenly, with all his dreaming of conjuring hands and Christmas *bambini*. Mr Carabini felt his hands tremble as he flustered over what to lift first, himself or his box of magic. And at what point he should make indication to the tram to come to a halt. Indication. Ah now, there it was, *numero due*.

Through the village and on past the cottages, the first significant gap showed itself. He checked the name of the house? Yes it was. And the two turned in away from the road where a driveway, lifting upwards, waited. And a little steep for Carabini with his trick box to carry as well and his hat sucking tightly on his head. And Lucia? She had her own bags. So he couldn't ask for help. In former years a car had been sent for him but not today. Today he made his own way. The first time that he had had to notice how near it was to town, how far from the tramstop. He would have organised a taxicab. Had he known.

But a strong girl. His Lucia. And young; it made no matter to her. He could tell. Would she please Masterson, though? Or would he say something. He would have to notice. No doubt about that. But would he say it. 'Wrong daughter,' – or something? Carabini felt his face rush suddenly warm.

'You fat little imbecilic simpleton,' he had said once. That time when the dove released was a corpse and flopped down on to the stage. And Mrs Masterson sitting in the front row, when she was still Signora Cleary. But how was he to know? How? And always he suspected Algie and that Castle fellow of playing a joke. They did so enjoy jokes. But how far would they go? Snap the neck of a dove? No, no, not. Surely not. But angry Masterson, how angry that night. Would he say something like that again? Oh, surely not in front of Lucia? Poor, poor Lucia. Who had hardly a word from her Papa all morning, this last one probably as his little girl.

But it was the wrong daughter. And Mr Masterson could be so very, very particular. When they had run into each other last week on the stairs outside the Italian consulate's office, it was Angelina he had by his side. Pretty Angelina. Bella Angelina. And Masterson had asked how old and what doing? Then he immediately mentioned his wife looking for a governess for her daughter and two other children, relatives, he said they were and would . . .?

And of course Angelina could hardly contain herself. Children? she loved them. Governess? she always wanted to. Mrs Masterson? a wonderful woman. Kind and beautiful and kind and . . .

And Masterson didn't seem too fussed. No references, no probing questions, no mention of previous employment. And Mr Masterson wouldn't consider as much as a call-boy without that. Two interviews, he always insisted, for a boy whose only job was to make a pot of tea and knock at dressing-room doors with calls to curtain up. But for Angelina he had merely smiled and said, 'Why don't you come along with your father to the children's beano on the 6th; you can start then. And mind he doesn't forget his conjuror's box. Mrs Masterson is depending on him.' And shaking one hand, 'Signor Carabini,' and holding momentarily another, 'Signorina,' he had squeezed past them down the stairs and back out into the light of Talbot Street.

And why did he have to make it sound like an insult? Signor and Signorina. Instead of one of respect. Oh, had he noticed that she laughed a little too much? And her eyes? Did he notice their inexcusable shine? Or did he still have an eye for the pretty ones? Not seeing much beyond their looks, not caring either. Oh no. He couldn't allow his little Angelina. Not with that man. Under the same roof. Although marriage may have . . . ? But. Just in case. Remember poor Matilda? Better to be safe. Besides, it would only be a matter of time before she would do something foolish. Be asked to leave. And would he say it then? Calling her into his study, my frightened lamb? Or worse. In public, in front of the other servants and the children? That she loves so much. Would he say it? 'You imbecilic little . . . ' Not to my child. Oh no. Not to mine.

Carabini stopped a moment and had a little gasp. He looked at Lucia waiting for him a stride or two away. Yes, she would be safe here. A clever girl. Nothing foolish to disgrace his name. And Masterson? There would be no sneaking worry about him late in the night making his way to her. No. Not Lucia. Masterson would take one look at her upper lip and its lace of fine black hair. And? Ladies and gentlemen, his lust would be – Pfff – vanished to the night. Oh well, he sighed before starting off again, who would have thought it, eh? Who would believe I would have a daughter to take after my papa?

Carabini gently shook his head and then he caught his daughter's eye looking back out from under the lip of her Christmas hat.

'Why are you laughing?' she softly asked.

'Me? Oh Nothing, *cara*. It's nothing. Just a little bit of life, that's all. Just a little bit of life.'

Lucia, her voice having graced many a wedding in many a one, was rather fond of churches. And she knew most of them by now, from the Star of the Sea in Sandymount, to Arran Quay's SS Peter and Paul. Occasionally she had been called upon to play the organ too, but she hardly preferred that to singing. Singing was a pleasure that she couldn't begin to describe, not even to herself, that sense of freedom that came over her whenever she looked down on the pews. And the rucks of colour laid out like flowerbeds on either side of the aisle with the gentle passage of wedding cloth gushing up the middle. And her solo notes hovering – so that she sometimes thought she could see them – over the bridal heads, following them all the way to the altar where the men would be waiting: best man and groom. Priest and God. She hoped Mrs Masterson wasn't going to be awkward about her singing. Otherwise the position would lose its appeal. It wouldn't do at all if she were expected to give up her singing. Her churches? Oh no.

And sitting now on the edge of a seat in the largest room she had ever been in, she was put in mind of a church. The size of it for one thing, and the height of its ceiling. It must cost a month's wages in coal to keep warm. However, she noted (straightening her hem and aligning it to just below the bulb of her adequate calf), other than size and height, there was little else that was churchlike about this particular room. And there was certainly nothing very churchlike about its present occupants. There were the ladies, for starters. Their looks, just what you'd expect to see in the pictures. And their voices too, like those you'd hear on the BBC wireless, although what they were saying – you wouldn't hear that on the wireless!

Sitting or leaning – you couldn't really call it standing – they were smoking cigarettes, and two of them had their hair cropped to the ear, one of them complaining bitterly about it too, as if everybody else was to blame and she'd been the victim of a countrywide conspiracy:

'Oh you clever thing, Maude,' she was whining. 'You knew all along, didn't you? That it would never last, this shingled business. You might have told me, you know. How I wish I had been as cute as you. And never taken the chop. I mean look at it. Will it ever again? I could kill myself, really I could. It's so unfair. Do you remember? The way it was. The way it used to be? Right down. Right down to my . . . '

'Arse, darling?' the other cropped head lazily suggested and Lucia caught herself steady before a flinch had a chance to betray her shock.

'Yes. All the way down. And further. Now? Now it looks positively ridiculous with this new flouncy look all the rage. It doesn't go at all. I'm dreading this year's dance season. I am. Really. I've a mind to cancel out. Was I such a fool New Year's Eve at the

Plaza? Looked all wrong. It quite spoiled the evening for me. I thought midnight was never . . . Throw me in the fountain now, I thought, put me out of my misery. And it was still only nine o'clock.'

'Plaza, did you say? Were you there?'

'Yes, weren't you?'

'No.'

'Oh? I'm sure I remember talking to you.'

'Perhaps you were. But I wasn't there.'

'Oh.'

'I was supposed to be. And then at the last moment was roped into a thing out in that bloody awful fat woman, what'shername's house in Killiney. Everyone at least a hundred and looking hideous in fancy dress. All ruffles and wrinkles, you know the sort of thing. So bloody tedious I can't tell you. Except for – well, you'll never guess who was there?'

And Lucia lost the conversation then, as it dipped down in a huddle between them. And over there by the fireplace, along with the heat, they kept it to themselves, with all its screeches and squeals and secret little hoppity laughs.

She looked away and thought of the parlour at home. How nice it had looked, New Year's Eve. The fire in its hatch-like grate, full and brave, defying the cold breeze that had come bulging in through the window the instant it had been opened to admit the midnight bells: that any minute would, any minute at all. And candles and greeting cards along the mantelpiece and across the piano and in a perfect line to the front of the oak shelves, tucked either side of the fireplace. All around the room at a certain height, like a balcony of blurred colour peering down through the dimmed lights. Mother with the sweets she had made herself and no two the same, so that each time the plate was offered there would be the giddy laugh of indecision and the playful warnings in the background, Mr Castle and Algie Browne: 'Ah ah, now, not the biggest. I'm watching you . . . greedy, greedy.'

'Ah don't mind him. He has his eye on that himself.'

And Father smiling down at the gentle animation of wine pouring from a height down into its serving jug, the slow tumbling brook of it babbling down, embossing the plush red skin. And then, over on the sideboard, ready and waiting on the tray, the tiny cut glasses filled amber to the tip with *Lacrima Christi*: tear of Christ. All the way from Naples and Father's Aunt Maria. As soon as the bells' first note, they would have it: Golden tears, to salute the new year.

Angelina, laughing, laughing. And Mr Thompson from next door keeping well up. And Father's pals Algie Brown and Charlie Castle: one rubbing gleeful hands together, the other quite still but beaming, looking as if he were ready to burst with delight.

And the goldfish? They had had such a laugh over Angelina's new goldfish. 'And what did you call them?' Algie asked in all politeness. 'Charlie and Algie,' she replied and everyone howled.

'Well, I hope I'm not that fat fella there with the gunner eye. He has a quare look about him.'

'Oh no, Mr Browne,' Angelina reassured him, 'That one's Mr Castle, not you.' And they all howled again. And Mother shook, the way she did when she really let herself laugh, and she had to put the sweets down to wipe her eyes.

As for Christmas dress? Flouncy or sleek? Wool. Plain wool, mustard and black, with just a change of collar for just a change of occasion. And Angelina, still dressed like a child, Mother seeming to forget she was eighteen and a bit. Protecting her no doubt. Keeping her safe behind childish cloth and Cromwell shoes with the larger tab. But still so pretty. Those clothes made her look all the more so, which Mother couldn't seem to see. Angelina laughing, laughing. But it was merry. They were all so merry, rushing out to the street under the chorus of new year bells. Ringing in for miles around, St Michan's and St Paul's, and over the river rolling down to them, John's Lane and St Audoen's with its fine peal of six, beating out from its Norman tower. And brave Smock Alley too, where after emancipation the first proud *Angelus* had dared to call out. And all around them in and out. Happy new year. Happy new year. And: 'How do you say it again, Mr Carabini?'

'*Felice Anno Nuovo*, Mrs Carter.'

'Oh yes, yes, yes, *Felice* ann . . . ?'

'*Nuovo.*'

'Of course, of course, *Nouovo.*'

'*Si Si, Nuovo*. Well done.'

And all the cries then following hers: '*Felice Anno Nuovo*, Mr Carabini.'

'*Felice Anno Nuovo*, Mrs Carabini. Lucia, Angelina.'

'*Felice Anno Nuovo*, Mr Sheedy.' And Father then with the tears bright in his eyes, '*Felice Anno Nuovo*, everybody.'

And just as every year, Mrs Sheedy was first to say it. 'Why Mr Carabini, you're upset. Whatever – ?'

'Oh it's nothing, just the *Lacrima Christi. Lacrima Christi.* Mama quick. Quick, take out the other bottle. To all our friends. Good neighbours and friends. To nineteen twenty-nine. Hello.'

Lucia glanced around. But no friends here. For the past hour and a half Mrs Masterson had been the only one to have acknowledged her presence with the occasional kind glance or a silent 'Are you all right?' mouthed across the other heads, all of which – Lucia noted – were far lower than hers. She certainly was tall for a woman; it's a good job the ceilings were so high after all.

And that she was so rich to be able to afford them. Why, in a house like the Carabinis' she wouldn't be too long developing a hump, always stooping to enter a room. And the tight little stairs going down to the kitchen? Her lovely carriage would be lobbed in two.

And she amused herself then by thinking if what Father had told them about the goldfish rang true for humans too? That they grew only as big as their surroundings and in China where they all swam around in great big ponds, they were quite the giants, more like smoked haddock than the tiny glints flittering nervously in a round glass bowl for Angelina to stare through, trying desperately to restrain herself from overfeeding. And killing them with kindness. Yes . . . and there too were the Carabinis all small in build, small and wide, like the house they lived in. Except for Angelina of course, who was just small and narrow. And come to think of it, remember the cot bed she slept in for years? Until she was about ten or eleven, at any rate. How narrow that was. Well who could tell?

Lucia looked round the room again and up to the plaster-pocked ceiling. Yes, she could very well find herself taking a stretch, now that she was going to live in a pond instead of a bowl. She looked down at her plate and the few remaining crumbs of biscuit cake. But would there be much fear of overfeeding?

Secret now shed, the lady who had passed such a painful New Year's Eve in Killiney stood suddenly back, opening up the group as if she were a gate. The conversation rushed out again for all to hear or not, as they wished. She then knelt down and sat on the floor. On the floor! And with so many beautiful chairs and sofas to choose from. This one hardly stopped talking, and her legs fidgeted uncomfortably about, showing almost all aspects of her white silk stockings. And her language? Her language really was

114

shocking. Lucia had never heard the like. Not even from a man with drink taken. She had felt herself blush more than once this past hour. The most uncomfortable one she could remember to date, in her twenty-odd years on His earth.

One of the ladies drifted away from the group and over to the window where she was now carefully arranging herself on a *chaise-longue*. Like an invalid, a beautiful invalid. And not even having the manners to remove her shoes. Rubbing off the velvet upholstery and scuffing the nap in the wrong direction as if it were a piece of old flannel. She laid her head against a cushion and was combing her hair with her fingers, strand by strand and with much concentration. Sometimes she sighed, lowering her deep lids (painted? were they painted?). But nobody seemed to notice. Or care. Now and then she reached out for a glass which she had left resting on the edge of the *chaise-longue* where it could topple at the slightest interference. And it looked like whiskey too. With boxes of ice inside. Cubes they were called, Lucia knew. Supposing it should fall? What a stain it would leave. Lucia tried to remember the remedy. But Mother always took care of that sort of thing herself, where best furniture was concerned. And besides locked away in the parlour the threat was seldom. Although once there had been the scandal of Algie Browne and the glass of red wine that day after the races. And Mother in a huff for a month of Sundays as if it had been poor Father's fault.

Lucia lifted her teacup to her lips once more and sipped. Cold now. But she didn't mind; it gave her something to do. And besides, where should she put the cup once she had admitted it was empty? Should she walk over to the table by the window, place it down gently and then walk back, with nothing in her hands, no purpose to her being here: no point? Or should she leave it on the mantelpiece perhaps, reaching up to tip the flecked marble with the bottom of the saucer? No, that would mean having to approach the group of ladies. To the right of her? But that was a bookcase and no other cups were laid on it; perhaps it wasn't permitted.

She took another sip and listened to the scurry of hysterical children out on the lawn. Like savages they were. And it was almost dark, but nobody paid them any heed. They must be freezing outside; perhaps that's why they were screeching so much. So wild. Of course they were the poor children Mrs Masterson entertained each year. But what of her own charges? Would they be as wild? And where were they? When would she meet them? It seemed strange no mention had yet been made.

Lucia crossed her legs and squeezed herself in tight. She was dying to go to the toilet. Just bursting. Where was Father? Where could he have got to? He shouldn't have left her alone this long. Not here. Not like this. All on her own.

The door opened then and a group of men, led by Mr Masterson, came through. She looked up. No. She looked away again without disappointment, never really having expected her father to be amongst them. They headed away from the ladies towards the opposite end of the room, one or two older gentlemen pausing on the way to acknowledge the female presence. The company began to settle down, accepting thick glasses of apricot-coloured liquid from Masterson, who was passing them along the conveyor belt of gentlemen's hands, reaching out. And all the time keeping up a topic that had come through the door with them. It had something to do with politics. Or perhaps it was to do with sport. No wait. It was both. A bit of both. They were discussing the proposed motor-racing rally to take place next summer.

'Well, Masterson, I don't know,' a man at the back was saying, 'I mean it is progress. Motor racing is a modern sport. And like all things modern, we'll just have to put up with it.'

'Put up with it? Is that what you believe? Tell me, Darby, where's this you are from? Dundalk, is it not?'

'That's right. Dundalk. And before you say it, I know. Far from the Phoenix Park so I won't have to put up with the noise and the crowds and dirt left behind. But all the same, Henry – '

'I wasn't going to say that. I wanted to ask you, merely ask you, if you have any idea how much this blasted farce is going to cost? Any idea at all? No? Well I'll tell you, shall I? Twelve thousand. *Twelve thousand* pounds. And now, one second, don't interrupt me now, just for one second. Can you think of anything else one could spend a few thousand on?'

'Well, of course, put like that, Masterson, there are several – '

'Like a fire brigade?'

'A what?'

'A fire brigade. Oh correct me if I'm wrong, but I believe Dundalk to be lacking in a fire brigade? A notion just a little too modern for our *Saorstát* government, would you say?'

Lucia almost laughed the way he said *Saorstát*. He took the word as if it were a great boiled sweet and rolled it inside his mouth and over his tongue. *Saorstát*: a boiled sweet and with a very nasty taste, too, judging by the face on him.

'Yes, well, as it happens you're right there, Masterson,' the man from Dundalk began again. 'The last one was sold for scrap and there has been nothing since. Yes, I take your point. I'm afraid you have me there. I was expecting you to come up with something more obvious, tuberculosed children or some such thing.'

'Aha, and it's a good job then. We are to have our progress in the Phoenix Park and not in Dundalk?'

'It is?'

'Well, what if one of these fellows should have a collision? What? Set fire to himself? They'd be pretty much lost in Dundalk, waiting for street urchins to fetch their pails of water.'

The men all chuckled, the two seated at the front lagging just a little behind, as if waiting for a lead. These two were in constant agreement with Masterson. Every word. 'Indeed, quite so, Mr Masterson,' one of them kept saying. 'And you have it there, never a truer . . . ' was what the other one preferred. And Lucia could see they lacked the independence of the other gentlemen, beholden somehow to Masterson's approval. Theatre people, most probably. Or perhaps they were just hoping to be – there did appear to be an underlying sense of rivalry between them. Perhaps one had yet to be chosen, asked here today to carry out the interview so that the noise of children would be bearable. Two birds, one stone. And none of his precious time wasted. Were they magicians, she wondered, from the Irish Artistes Agency? The one that shared the stairs with the Italian Consulate's office, where Father and Angelina had met Masterson last week. An agency that was known for its magicians and conjurers. Its novelty acts. Its 'something differents'. Was that why Masterson had offered Angelina the job so hurriedly, embarrassed to have been caught by Father, looking for magicians when he had just a few days previous said that they were quite out of mode? And that Father would have to go at the end of the season. Promising that the moment . . . the very moment . . . he would be the first. Informed post haste, by king's messenger, he swore it. And Father coming home to tell them this, all puffed up by it as if it were a compliment. 'Mr Masterson, he say to me. He say the very moment . . . '

Lucia did not care for Mr Masterson. Not in the least little bit. For she could imagine days when Father was allowed to sit along that privileged row and to laugh at Mr Masterson's jokes and say – 'Indeed, indeed. Never a truer . . . ' But now that Father's hands had dried up and trembled disobediently, he couldn't be trusted into the inner circle. He could only be trusted to trick for the children. And probably only used today because Jaffe was otherwise engaged. If there was one thing she knew about the Mastersons it was this: they always went for the best. And Father? Father was no longer the best.

Lucia took a hurried glance towards the group of men. Only Masterson was moving, before them, up and down, stopping sometimes to make a point with a raised hand or to twist himself round on his heel before returning along the track he had chosen for himself. There were six or seven gentlemen in all, Lucia couldn't be sure unless she looked directly at them. Which she would never dream of doing. But she could see Mr Masterson, though, his long thin shadow struggling to keep up with him in the lamplight. And thinking to herself how funny it was that a fat man like her father could move so quickly, while a thin one like Mr Masterson had such a slow crawling step. That lifted. Like a spider.

The matter of her bladder was becoming more urgent by the second. Now what would she do? She looked around. The two groups at the two ends of the room were preoccupied. Engrossed with whatever it was that was going on in their particular circle. No one was looking her way. The door was slightly ajar. Perhaps she could just . . .

Outside now in the enormous hall, her feet, across the chequered floor, made a patter towards a group of older ladies seated in a circle. And all as plain as crows except for one, who on a leather chair sat, the largest and most talkative and offering the only alternative to grey and navy blue with a peach-and-silver ensemble that emphasised her all the more. Lucia tried to look as if she knew where she was going, smiling a little just in case they might give her recognition and worried, should they do so, that she had forgotten their names. (Mrs Masterson had introduced her to them earlier.) But all she could remember was where they were from, not who they were. There was that woman from the Cottage Hospital For Little Children, and the other one from the Dublin Country Air Association. The Protestant Orphan Society and the Albert Home for Aged Protestants also had a representative. She wondered if she had the nerve to ask them where the lavatory was; she even rehearsed her query in her head. But then she found herself passing by without having uttered a word. Too late now, she thought, and too timid to retreat. She kept on walking, the waft of their conversation thinning out behind her.

'Oh now, I knew them all. Going back a long time. I don't mind telling you.'

'Is that so now?'

'Oh yes. Pat Cleary, you know, a very close friend of mine. We were like – '

'I believe he was – '

'Oh, a gentleman altogether. Why I don't mind telling – '

'And you know, I've always wondered if it was true that . . . ?'

Lucia found a door, half-open at the other side of the hall. She peeped inside. 'Oh Father, there you – ' She stopped. He had his back to her, seated at the far end of a long gleaming dining table. Down on the floor a little girl was gazing up at him, listening so intently to every word that Lucia just couldn't interrupt. He was telling her the story of the Christmas *bambino*. He sounded so . . . well, so foreign. Just as he used to do when she was a little girl herself. When he was relaxed and happy and off his guard with her, as he was now with this child at his feet.

'Through the streets,' he was saying, 'through the narrow streets and across the wide squares, they carry him, a baby Jesus so beautiful in gold and jewels and all that is precious. With everybody singing and one person carrying in a basket the invitations sent to the blessed *bambino*, that he might come and visit their sick children. And to each house, he is brought, rich or poor, slum or grand villa while the crowds follow behind waiting outside for the holy *bambino* to bless the home of the sick child . . . ' He paused and lifted his hand. 'Now you going to ask me, if I know any child that he make better?' Lucia could see the crown of the little girl move eagerly up and down. 'Me,' her father said and she could hear him slap his chest as she had heard him a thousand times before. 'Yes, me. When I was thisa size . . . ' he raised two fingers of his hand to find an unlikely size of about two inches.

'That small?' she heard the child ask.

'Oh yes, I never eat a thing, not a mouthful. I so sad with no Mama, you see. The angels took her away and leave me behind.'

'Oh, you poor Mr Carabini.'

'Oh no, not poor. Not now. Look at me now.' His hand slapped again, this time on his stomach, and Lucia knew, although she could not see him, that he was blowing out the cheeks of his face to make them appear fatter and more ruddy than they already were. The little girl laughed. 'The Christmas *bambino*, he make me fat. He make me too fat now.' And the little girl laughed again.

'My wife, my wife she say to me, "Oh, why your Papa ever put that invitation into the holy *bambino*'s basket? One day you go and burst. Pufff. All over the house." You know what she calls me? *Ciccione*. That's what she calls me.'

'What does it mean?'

'Oh, Fatty. It means Fatty,' he said carelessly and, delighted, the child squealed back up at him.

Lucia rapped gently on the door. 'Father?'

He turned around. 'Ah Lucia. Come, come, come.'

But Lucia stepped back out behind the door so that Carabini

was forced to come into the hall, to leave the child behind him.

'Lucia? Why don't you come meet Patrice? You must – '

'Not now, Father. I have to go, you see.'

'Go? What do you mean go?'

'To the . . . ' she pursed her lips discreetly, ' . . . you know.'

Carabini looked at her for a moment and then 'Ahh . . . to the . . . ? Ahh. Yes, yes of course,' he understood.

'But where, Father? Where is it?'

'Oh, I do not know, *cara*, up the stairs perhaps? I see ladies go up the stairs. Up and down. Up and down. Every time I come to this house, it's all they do. Up and . . . '

'Oh, but I don't like to. It could be anywhere up there. And besides it might not be allowed. I mean, there might be a different one for . . . '

Carabini thought for a moment. 'Wait, I know. Go ask in the kitchen. Yes, do that. The Philomena is very nice. You don't have to be shy with her. She tell you. She tell you where you should go.'

'Yes, all right.'

'Then you come back?'

'Yes, Father, I'll be straight back.'

'Meet Patrice?'

'Meet Patrice.'

'Lucia?'

'Yes, Father?'

'Everything is going to be all right. Is it not?'

'Yes, Father, I'm sure it is.' Lucia touched him lightly on the arm before walking the way he had pointed her.

There were two sinks in the kitchen, as deep as baths. And each one full of cups and plates of best china as careless as a rockery in arrangement. Half-eaten cakes, piled up shamelessly on silver trays on the table. Such a waste. Such a disgraceful waste of good food. Near the pantry door, a woman was sitting, her head bent forward and her breast moving slowly up and down. Her hands were tucked together in the lap of her white pinny. Sleeping. How could she with all this hullabaloo? Lucia frowned. Ohhh, still no sign of a toilet.

She walked back out through to the hall and passed along the bottom of the stairs, taking another turn into an alcove. The ceiling dipped. Lucia squinted. Near the end was a tuck for old raincoats and wellington boots. They were made apparent by an unshaded bulb which gave that dirty sort of half-glow you might expect to find in a garden shed. She moved a few steps on. And at last, the frosted window of that door at the end of the corridor. It had to be. It was.

Inside, she closed her eyes with relief and then snapped them open again. The door? Had she? Yes. It was all right, she could see the bolt was shut. There was somebody outside. Oh no. Don't say they were going to wait for her to finish? They would hear the toilet flush. And she would have to come out red as a beetroot, and apologetic. Who could it be? One of the gentlemen? It would have to be, if the ladies used upstairs. Oh why couldn't she have just asked one of those charity women or given the maid in the kitchen a wake-up shake? You'd think in a vast house like this the smallest corner would afford some privacy. Perhaps, though, they didn't want to use the toilet; perhaps they were just coming to fetch a coat from the dip under the stairs? She would wait a moment or two. Then she heard voices, two voices. A woman's and a man's. She couldn't make out what they were saying, but the man's voice she felt sure she could recognise. Was it? Was it Henry Masterson's?

Lucia lifted herself away from the lavatory seat and brought her clothing together again. She could feel the beat of her heart travelling up through the glands in her neck and a guilty sweat leak cold through her skin. Oh no, not him. Not him, of all people. Had it been anyone else. The thoughts of coming out to his sneer. But the voices stopped then. Had they gone?

She took a step forward and peeped through the curtain gaps at the glass of the door. No, still there. There was a shape, just one, like the silhouette of a strange animal, almost zoological in form. It was a man and a woman, joined together in an embrace. A lengthy one. The right hand side of the shape was lean and tall and had bent itself down to meet the other side, reaching upwards. Reaching a long way upwards. Lucia heard her own gentle gasp and in the mirror caught sight of her eyes widen. It was him all right. That was his frame, his long arms: his hands at the end of them. Touching her, feeling her, touching on, squeezing on, what could only be her . . . her . . .

Oh, what sort of a place was this at all? That father had so thoughtlessly brought her to? What sort of people?

Lucia closed her eyes and then opened them again. Yes. She had been right first time. The woman was short. Far too short to be Mrs Masterson.

SEVEN

When Lucia Carabini first saw John Henry curve his way up the gallery steps of St Augustine and St John's, she felt nothing stronger than a glimmer of amusement. He had, it would seem, climbed all this way up to pay her a single compliment:

'Seldom have I heard Schubert so beautifully served.'

'Thank you, you're very kind.'

She was pleased, but not overcome, being used to compliments of this sort. Usually they were withheld until she was on the steps outside, and then expressed with no more fuss than a hand pressed in passing on her arm. A keen faced bride-to-be might ask to engage her for the coming nuptials, or a hopeful mother, small boy in tow, might suggest that her son be considered for the choir. Any other comment or compliment received up to now had been from parishioners or visiting clergymen. But she was certain of this, he was no parishioner. He had hardly acquired that tan from the sun that shone down on the denizens of St Nicholas Within.

It was the first time anybody had actually taken the trouble unnecessarily to brave the spiral stairs that seemed, when viewed from their very first step, a flimsy prospect extending right through the roof to the sky outside and offered no guarantee of safe delivery.

'The serpent to heaven,' the choristers called it. And even they, she noted, were cautious enough whenever they had to negotiate ascent. And even warier on the way back down, keeping a shrewd distance between one another and postponing the giggles they had accumulated throughout the service until they had safely landed and were free of the wrought-iron monster.

Yet the stranger had risked them and was now about to do so again, concluding the interview with a slight bow of his head and an apologetic, 'I just felt I had to mention it.' And he departed as suddenly as he had arrived, his step clang slow and unvaried all the way down in a perfect four-time beat.

She had returned at once to arranging her sheet music back into its case and, having no reason to presume she would ever see him again, thought no more about the matter.

Had she been quizzed about his appearance in the next hour or so, she would have been able to report he was a gent from tip to toe. His teeth were exceptional, film star calibre, no less. He was tall enough to have had difficulty with the steps but not so tall as to avoid being dwarfed by the church organ which rose gauntly behind him as he delivered his little remark. Had she been asked about him a week or so later, his features would already have started to lose their distinction. By the end of a month, she might not even be able to recollect a single thing about him. He would be a smudge in the grounds of her memory. However, she would recall that he was one of the best-looking men she had ever set eyes on. But she hardly saw that as being any of her business. She had long since given up considering handsome men as being something with which to concern herself. She knew her limitations, and such men did not come within that narrow range.

The Sundays ran into each other, one, two, three, and each one saw him return. Although he never again faced the gallery steps, he was always there, part of the congregation and seated at the centre aisle just a few rows up from the door, so that from the point of view of the gallery, his would be the first pew to be revealed. Between the statue of St Augustine and that of St

Monica, between the first station of the cross on the left wall, Jesus Meets His Mother, and the last station of the cross on the opposite wall, Jesus Is Nailed to the Cross, he was there. And she couldn't help noticing that throughout her solo, his head would turn just a little to the side and then turn back again to face the altar. Several times this occurred, as though he were engaged in a gentle struggle between his instinct and his sense of propriety. As though he were trying not to look back up at her.

He did manage it just the same, when the Mass had drawn to an end and the head tops poured outside, his face showing for a second in an upward glance before realigning with the rest of the crowns and passing under the gallery and out of sight.

On a wet Tuesday night in late January, she stood in the vestibule watching through the doorway the squally showers scat and patter against the pavement. She clenched her fists inside the pockets of her macintosh coat and thought of her mother. There was no way Mother would ever have allowed her to come out without an umbrella. And no hat either. What would Mother think if she could see her now? But it wasn't her fault. She hadn't meant to come out so unprepared. She just hadn't been able to find her things in the cloakroom, that's all. And she had left them there last Sunday, she was sure of it. But they had disappeared, the victims of a merciless tidy-up. And she couldn't find Philomena either to ask her if she knew where they were. And she couldn't find Mrs Masterson, although she wouldn't have liked to ask her anyway. They could be anywhere. In any of the rooms, in any of the cupboards. She hadn't the time to look for them. The house was too big. The house was too big.

She walked out to the steps and looked across the street; it was gushing. Under the row of lamplights the rain showed clearly its intention not to let up until every drop was shed. Just how much she missed living at home came to her now with dismay. Lucia wished she were young enough to sit on the step and cry.

She thought about going back inside but she had been last to leave, staying back to tidy up after choir practice. The church was empty now and dark. She had made it so herself. Pushing the last switch up and frightening herself half to death, she had hurried away from the rows of saintly shapes, locking the door behind her. The caretaker wouldn't be due for at least another hour. Nobody inside but the Blessed Sacrament and He'd hardly have the loan of an umbrella. There was nothing to do but make a dash for it. And just about to raise her music case over her head to do so, when she saw a man pass along the railings outside and pause. He looked at her and then before she knew it, he had climbed the steps to be at her side. It was him.

'Hello,' he began. 'You're the soloist, aren't you?'

'Yes, that's right.'

'Filthy night, isn't it?' he frowned under the shade of his umbrella. 'Pitchforks, wouldn't you agree?'

Lucia looked up at the sky. 'Yes, I would.'

'I can't help noticing you're without an umbrella.'

'Oh. Yes, it was foolish of me. But I'll be fine. I don't mind the rain. I like it, really.'

'Oh, yes. I do too. But then I can afford to. I'm not a singer.'

Lucia nodded.

'May I get you a cab?'

Lucia thought of the price of a cab and hoped it hadn't shown on her face. 'Oh no. No, I prefer to take the tram,' she said.

'I see.' He looked away from her for a moment and then turned to her again.

'Look; I know you'll think me forward but would you mind if I were to accompany you to the tram stop? It would at least give you some shelter.' He lowered his umbrella slightly. 'Might save your voice.'

Lucia didn't know what to say so she said nothing.

'Well, if you'd prefer not to. But please, will you at least take the umbrella?'

'Oh I couldn't possibly – '

'Well, does that mean you will allow me to walk with you?' He smiled shyly at her.

Lucia found herself returning the smile. 'Yes. All right,' she said, 'if you're sure you don't mind.'

They took to the street and the passing traffic whispered through the dark lining of rainwater underwheel. He said, 'And which tram will you take?'

'The Lucan tram. I'm going to Chapelizod.'

'Ah, Chapelizod – the Phoenix Park?'

'Yes, that's right.'

They came along High Street and the rain drummed softly on the outer dome of their umbrella. He took her elbow as they crossed the road.

'You have so many beautiful churches in this city. You'll probably think it silly of me but I . . . I have this thing for churches.' He laughed softly at himself.

'Oh no. Not at all. I'm fond of them myself.'

They faced Lord Edward Street and the rain took a spiteful turn, flushing suddenly onto them so that he had to drop the umbrella a fraction. She felt its ceiling rub against her head.

'This is a very wide street.'

'We can go this way,' she said, and they crossed back over again and down Fishamble Street.

It was quieter here, a narrow street with high houses that shouldered the brunt of the weather. The water made sikes and

129

gullets as it rolled downhill, nuzzling into the kerb. No wind, no sudden spouts, just a steady mizzle.

'It's easing off,' she observed, stretching her hand out beyond the confines of the umbrella and withdrawing it again just as quickly. 'Well, almost – '

Her gloves were too short. Mother would never have allowed them in this weather. The veins on her wrist sprang up with the icy slap of rainwater. She was surprised at how cold it was out there.

He spoke, 'I see you have your own corner of the Vatican in St John's.'

'The shrine, you mean? Our Lady of Good Counsel; yes.'

'It's very ornate.'

'I sometimes think a little too ornate,' she said.

He stopped and looked down at her. 'Really? I wanted to say that myself. But I didn't like to be rude. It is a little fancy, isn't it – for a church of its size, I mean.'

They walked on again and now they were out on Wood Quay. She could feel her stockings slide a little in her shoes. She could smell him, now. A touch away. Cologne and something else, a man's smell. But not like Father's. Father's was onions and red wine and pomade. And black tobacco too, when Mother would allow it. This was another bouquet altogether. His coatsleeve rubbed against her mackintosh and she changed her step a little to avoid it. 'Now, there's another place that's pretty fancy, I must say.'

She followed his nod up the quay.

'That pub on the corner. The Irish House, I believe it's called; a most unusual spectacle.'

Lucia smiled. 'The woman I work for . . . she used to own that.'

'Really?'

'Or her husband did. He died.'

'I'm sorry.'

'Oh, I didn't know him. Anyway, it was a long time ago. She married again. Her brother took over but I believe he had to sell it.'

'Wasn't cut out for the publican's life?'

'No, he was a dancer.'

'Ahh.'

They came to the end of the quay and the rain dropped to an easier pace. 'And what do you do for this lady? Do you teach her music?'

'Oh no. I'm a governess, I suppose. For her little girl.'

'And do you enjoy your work?'

'Oh, yes; she's a well behaved child. Musical too, which gives us a common interest. It's an easy job, I must say, for the moment anyway.'

'Oh? Are you expecting it to get more difficult?'

'Well, busier anyway. There will be two more children to look after soon, from America. Relatives. They're moving in soon, I'm told. I don't know exactly when.'

'You'll have your hands full then.'

'Yes,' she laughed, 'I suppose I will.'

There was silence between them for a while until they came along by the Franciscan church of Adam's and Eve's. 'Another church,' he laughed. 'Would you recommend it?'

'Yes. But it's not my favourite.'

'Tell me then, which is?'

'St Paul's is nice. I mean I like it. It's very simple in its way. It's back along down there. Down past the Four Courts. You can't see it from here.'

But they looked anyway, across and down the river together and he nodded. 'I must pay it a visit.'

And she felt her heart bob down a little. (Did he mean he wouldn't be coming to St John's next week?).

'Some day during the week,' he concluded, 'perhaps during my lunch hour . . . ' and she felt her heart bob back into place.

'Do you mind me asking: are you a foreigner?' She spoke and then regretted it. It had sounded so rude. 'It's just that you don't seem to know the city very well . . . and − '

'I suppose I am. I'm English.'

'Oh I didn't mean − '

'That's all right. I'm even foreign in England, I've worked abroad most of my life.'

'Will you stay here long?'

'I think so, I work here now. Just down the quay in Lever Brothers. You know, the Sunlight Chambers.'

'Oh yes, I do.'

'"Where the sun don't ever shine," as the head clerk tells us every time the address is mentioned.'

She smiled.

'I like Dublin, I would have to say.' He slowed up and looked carefully at her. 'Although it can get a little lonely. I've never been very good at making new acquaintances, I'm afraid.'

'Yes,' she said, 'Yes, I think I know what you mean.'

She wondered what it would be like to take his arm, to slip her hand inside his pocket. What would she find there, a few bits of change, the stub of a forgotten tram ticket, his fingers curled into a nest?

'Would you . . . would you like to get out of the rain for a bit. I mean, there's a hotel just up the road, The Clarence, perhaps you know it?'

He was looking at her nervously. 'It's a very respectable place. We could have coffee, if . . . if it wouldn't be too much of a bore for you, that is.'

'Well, I'm expected. I mean – '

'Yes, of course. I do apologise. It was presumptuous of me to have asked. What must you think? I'm . . . I'm awfully sorry.'

'Oh, no. No, not at all,' she said. 'As long as I'm not too late. Coffee would be nice. And it is, as you said, a very respectable place.' And she fell in with his step, trying not to think of what Mother would say. Or the look of horror that might whiten her face.

There was a fire burning somewhere in among the panelled wood and the sconce lights curling from the walls. Her coat hung next to his on a stand dripping together, the two of them, softly on to the floor or the umbrella bucket, where she could pick out his from the knot of other crooks. There was a tray brought to the table and a white lacy pinny stretching out behind it. A long-nosed coffee pot peered snootily at her from over the range of cups and saucers and the plate of cherry-dotted biscuits. Lucia nursed the lump in her throat and tried not to look at the pot. Would he expect her to pour, to lift it up and guide it to his coffee cup? To ask him how many lumps? One or two? And then to go back again and pick up the plate: a biscuit perhaps? And to chat as if this were all normal to her, sitting at a table with a handsome man? Here in the Clarence Hotel. Would he expect all that, and what would he think when it all collapsed hopelessly into her lap? She glanced at a woman across the way, handling all the accoutrements with ease, smiling at her companion as she passed him a freshly filled cup. She was sorry now that she had agreed to come in. Sorry now she would have to disappoint and shame him.

'You're shivering,' he said. 'Isn't it a funny thing, you don't notice just how cold it is until you come into the heat. Why don't I pour?'

And she watched while his hands took care of everything, upturning the coffee cups, lifting the pot, and the cream-jug there, so small in his hand, so frail: like a little silver bird. 'Now,' he said, when at last it was all over, 'I didn't make too bad a fist of it, did I?'

And he told her a story then that she could hardly hear, about some country he'd been in when he was a boy. And the sound of piano notes glistening out through a window, down to a sweltering square where he had stopped his game to welcome them. It had been like a feeling, he said, of falling unexpectedly in love.

Outside again on the quays, they crossed for the bridge, her damp coat clinging to her like another skin. A man and a woman passed them by. They nodded to each other, couple to couple. The same, she thought, they think we're the same. She looked down at the river, simmering softly under the rain and listened to his breathing, closer now, and the taste of coffee, his or hers, lounging on the air around them.

They stood at the tram stop and now that they were facing each other she wanted to fix her hair. She wanted to tighten her belt into her waist too, so that he could see her improved figure since leaving Mother's second helpings behind. She wanted to disappear up a laneway then and dab a little something behind her ears. That American scent that Mrs Masterson had passed on to her after she had decided it was too young for her own use. She wanted the tram to stay away and leave them here forever. Yet she wanted tomorrow to come, quickly, so that she could practise pouring tea, or coffee, or anything at all, once it came from a heavy silver pot. Just in case he should ever, they should ever. Just in case there was ever another time.

'You love music very much, don't you?' he asked.

'Yes, yes I do.'

'Anything in particular?'

'Oh, opera, I would have to say.'

'Opera? Have you a favourite?'

'Yes I do. *La Tosca*.'

'Ah yes . . . *La Tosca*. What's your favourite aria? No don't tell me – I'll guess.'

'"Vissi d'arte",' they said together and then they both laughed.

'"Vissi d'arte",' he repeated, looking down at her and nodding gently.

When the tram came in sight he looked at her for a moment and then he seemed to shake himself. 'Oh my goodness,' he said, 'I haven't even introduced myself. You must think me an oaf. I'm John Henry, by the way.' He held out his hand and she looked at it for a moment before returning hers.

'I'm Lucia Carabini.'

'Then you too are a foreigner?'

'Yes. I suppose in a way I am.'

'We are two foreigners in a strange city.'

It sounded so nice she didn't want to correct him. She didn't want to say that she had been born here, had lived here all her life. Two foreigners.

'Some people call me Lucy. You may if you – '

'Lucy? why on earth would I want to do that. Lucia is such a beautiful name.'

The tram had stopped beside them now. The tram was waiting. If he were going to say something, he would have to do it now, while an old lady fumbled with an umbrella and the conductor helped her safely to the ground. 'May I?' he asked, 'Next Sunday? Next Sunday after Mass?'

'I . . . I don't know.'

'May I telephone you then? Are you on the telephone?'

'Yes, but I can't remember the number.'

The conductor bounced back up on to the platform. He was standing looking at them.

Lucia put her hand on the bar.

'Is it in the directory?' He stretched his arm out fully, extending the umbrella for her benefit as she climbed on to the tram.

'I'm sure it's in the directory.'

'Yes. Yes, what name?'

'Masterson. Henry Masterson. Or Maude.'

'Or Maude?'

He placed one foot on the platform and looked up at her, the umbrella still in part between them. 'Goodnight, Lucia,' he said.

Lucia nodded and turned away.

When she got back to the house, there was no voice to say, 'Lucia, Lucia, you're soaked to the skin. Take off those wet things and into the bath.'

When she crossed the hallway and climbed the stairs, there was no voice behind to follow and say, 'What madness is this, to keep you out half the night? Get straight into bed and I bring you something hot.'

When she got to her room there was no one to talk to. No one to answer when she said, 'I met this man, you see, a foreigner like me.' Nobody spoke. No voice at all.

She remembered his smell now as she filled up the bath, she remembered his touch as she took off her clothes. She held her elbow as he had done, whenever they had crossed a road, she held it to see if had it melted in his hand. It was still there. She looked in the mirror and whispered to herself. 'Lucia, what a beautiful name. What a beautiful voice.' She looked in the mirror and a voice answered her then. 'Lucia,' it asked, 'why is your hair stuck like wet moss onto your head? And those tiny drops over your lip, how did they catch in the dark hair that grows there?'

The altar boys were crisp in linen, three on each side. The altar in between was coral reef. It would snap and crumble in your hand.

His hat was a bowler. Strong and black. It would have drummed leather in the inside to hold its shape.

The shrine of Our Lady of Good Counsel was behind a cage with angels stuck on the top like dolls on the highest shelf of a toyshop. The tiles behind the cage were flecked with painted gold.

His hat lay on the seat behind him. His back was straight. His head was bowed.

The tall candles spat and sparkled behind the cage. The short candles whimpered. Grouped together in a brass cusp, in a brass basket. On long brass legs. They whimpered.

Her voice felt shy inside her throat. The organ introduced it. She pushed it out; she gave it courage. Her voice began.

His fingers pushed his hat to one side and he sat down beside it.

The priest raised his hands, he parted them towards the congregation. The surplices flocked. Brown-gowned Augustinians shifted like ghosts between the marble pillars. St Augustine's sad eyes and long narrow nose stayed perfectly still. The priest brought his hands back together again. She sang. She closed her eyes and she was standing at an open window. She closed her eyes and there was a piazza laid out beneath her. Her notes fell softly, glistening down. She opened her eyes.

His head moved a little to the side, then back towards the altar. His head moved again. She could almost see his profile. He was trying not to look up at her. He was trying very hard.

III

Bread and the Circus

EIGHT

Herbert could remember when houses were different. Different houses on different streets: avenues and roads, a terrace and a green. And a crescent once too, where the houses stood round in a semicircle as if waiting to do an Irish reel. There were houses to consider and houses to dismiss. There were ones to move into and ones to move out of. He could remember, too, when there was a choice, of where to live and what type of house to live in. When hand-in-hand with Mother he crossed that many rooms and climbed that many stairs he sometimes mixed them up in his head so they all became as one. A mishmash house with every kind of stairwell and every colour wall. With windows that winked or looked surprised. And a hall door too, covered all over in brass knockers, each a slightly different shape, like a face full of sores.

When this happened he had to press his memory very hard indeed to distinguish one house from the next. Which was it now where I fell down the stairs and which was the very first front door that closed solid behind me on my first day to school? And the granite steps that led to a door – another one this time it was and yellow? Where's this that was now with Mother sitting on them crying in a temper, a typewritten letter flapping from her hand? And 'Ohhh,' saying 'Ooohhh, I could kill him with these hands' (meaning Father, he supposed). And the furniture laid out like a babbie house display. All over the lawn and shattering the gravelled driveway, a heavy kitchen dresser, looking about ready to collapse without a kitchen wall behind it for support.

Some houses had more than one set of stairs, going down as well as up, roosting on their kitchens. Kept tucked in at the bottom, behind. And making it a secret room that only some could share. But these were long-ago kitchens, the latest ones were easier to find. Like now: the first room to be entered. By all and sundry. Mother said, 'Like chimps up in the zoo, we are, the world and his wife gawking on while we're having our tea.'

And Herbert always thought she was exaggerating. Usually it was just the odd rap at the door, and what choice did people who came calling have? Was it their fault that they had no front door? For this was half a house, the first half a house they had ever lived in. It used to be a whole one, until Father got the idea to let the upstairs front and it meant no sitting-room and no dining-room and one bedroom less. And no hallway, and no front door. But Mother was allowed to keep the rent and it must have been an awful lot for Father always said, each time she asked for money, 'Haven't you got your rent?' before he walked out the door. The back one that is, that led to the big yard outside.

But today Mother was right: it really was a case of the world and his wife coming to watch them have their tea. There never was such a number of adults in the kitchen, that he could remember. There was Aunt Maude's second husband, and Aunt Maude herself and Bart from the pub. And Mother and Father. And the Samuel man. Herbert was the only child left among them. The others had been sent away and he had been kept behind to be part of the adult secret. One that kept on changing. Every other minute. Herbert was very bored. But not as bored as Father, who said nothing at all and looked across the room, out through the window, as if he were sleeping with his eyes open.

Father liked windows, though, Herbert knew from long ago.

And long-ago houses. Father always preferred the windows.

When it came to looking for a new house, it was Herbert who went with Mother. Once or maybe twice, before Father might come along. But sometimes he wouldn't bother at all until moving-in day. Herbert thought this was a very strange way of going on, not caring in the least what your new house might look like. Or where it might be. He would much prefer to know his house first before it became a home. He was glad Mother took him with her.

Except for the times when she went to see the really grand houses (like the one they used live in when Herbert was born); he hated that. Making her voice grand to match them. Coloured houses by the sea. Or stern ones out Ballsbridge way. At first, Herbert used to get all excited, believing that they might really be going to live there. But after a while he knew it was just a silly waste of time because they always ended up with a much smaller house. In a much more ordinary place. And he couldn't enjoy himself, not the way Mother seemed to do. He was afraid they would be caught out pretending to be richer than they really were. With Mother saying 'I'll be in touch,' as if she really meant it.

It was much better when the houses started to get smaller because that meant they were to be taken seriously. He was happy then, standing at the doorstep with Mother and listening to the first sound of the bell-pull running through an empty house. With her doing a last minute tidy-up of hats and gloves and a tug maybe at a jacket hem to stretch the creases straight. And all the time her eyes flicking over the front of the house, the windows and the garden, trying to take in as much as they could before the door was pulled open.

And inside then, his opinion was asked. On everything. For Mother would look at every little thing. All about. Touching everything she saw. And sticking her nose into presses and drawers as if she were looking for something. A missing scissors or a spool of thread. If there were sofas, Mother would sit down and test them softly, bouncedy bounce. If there were tables she would skate her hand over them, making sure they were really as smooth as they were pretending to be. And as for chimney pots, she always looked up them, checking if they were suitable for Father Christmas, Herbert used to believe. Although he knew now that he was practically grown that it must have been for something else. And there was always a man there with them, a different one for each house, and he always made a smile before opening doors to rooms, in a way that made you expect a surprise inside, a different one each time.

'What do you think, Herb? Suitable or not? What do you think, hmmm?' Mother would ask him when she had finished her inspection. Or if the man with the smile should turn his back she would sometimes pull a face or whisper a disapproving word.

'A bit shabby,' she said once of a house near the humped-back bridge, down by the canal (an all-brown house it had been with a peculiar smell and stuffed birds staring out from behind glass cases). He was glad that turned out to be a house to dismiss. Some houses were furnished and some were bare. But after the house with the granite steps where their furniture was all laid out on the lawn, Mother said it was 'as easy get one furnished as not and why throw away good money dragging your bits from Billy to Jack and never knowing whether they'd go with the rooms or fit for that matter and supposing they didn't then having to put them into storage which cost a pretty penny whichever way you looked at it and . . . ' So they sold their own furniture. Except for the dresser, which Mother couldn't be without. And the piano, too, they'd kept for a while. But then Mother said it was an old nuisance and hardly worth the cost of carriage. And so they sold that as well.

After that they never did seem to find another house that had a piano already there and waiting.

But Father, when he came, only looked out the windows. The room didn't seem to matter to him; it was just something you crossed over to get to the windows and what lay outside. There was a garden once in Terenure and a tree with rusty leaves and a pathway to an empty clothesline. At the bottom near the little shed. For two whole years that became Herbert's garden and the shed his secret house. And George's too. For two whole years. And a bit. They made mud cakes and sold them to each other, a penny for the chocolatey ones and one and thruppence for the ones with currants stuck inside. And there was a wooden door that led into the laneway at the back where sometimes you might see a motor car. Or meet a neighbour. 'Good morning, Herbert. Good morning Mrs . . . ?' She gave him tea and grown-up sandwiches and he sat deep into her sofa with the cabbage roses on, his feet just reaching the cliff edge where the frill began its drop. Down all the way to the floor.

Mother was happy then. Happy with her big round stomach and Georgie Porgie Puddin' an' Pie resting on her hip. There were shops down the road, with peaked canvassed caps jutting out over them in stripes of blue and white for one, and another had red ones that you could look up through to see how the sky had pinkened. See them from beneath just as the fruit did, all neat and snuggled side by side, tomatoes in their satin skins. And peaches that looked like babies' bums with just a lick of suede. And even the doors along the shop rows wore pyjamas. That was how swanky it was. Down the shops in Terenure. You could go on your holidays there, it was so nice. If you didn't live there already, that was.

There was a nursemaid too and a woman who did. She cleaned

145

the house. So Mother could lie down in the afternoon, her feet denting a pillow at the other end of the bed and the coverlet all lacy-white beneath her. As if she were lying on snow.

It was a big house too and Father had a motor car that bulged in the front. Like Mother did. It was a big house, with the kitchen underneath and bars on the window of the scullery room. And when Herbert asked the woman who did what they were for she said they were to keep her in, stop her from sneaking out home too early. Herbert ate in the kitchen and Georgie Porgie too. Grown-ups ate upstairs. But mostly it was just Mother alone because Father forgot to come home from work. 'A queer fish,' the nursemaid called him to the woman that did. And Herbert looked next time at the shops where the fish lay slimy and dead on trays of white tin with blue trimmed on. And most of them were queer. But none looked anything like Father. There were no chickens to be fed then, so Mother lay down in the afternoons and in the evenings she had her dinner and then she lay down again. That was the house in Terenure. Big enough to be always alone. The shed for him, the dining-room and bedroom for Mother. And for Father, the big black motor car where he sat to read the newspaper. Although there were plenty of places to read indoors.

Now there was nowhere to be alone. No shed either, and if you dared to open the henhouse they'd tell, screech and yell. And telltale tattlers every one of them. Then Mother would give you a good clip on the ear for yourself. Once on a Saturday night he had been sent down to Father's pub to give him a note that Mother had written and when he opened the door it was the very same thing, that sudden explosion of screeches and yaks. That's what the henhouse was like, a public house. Herbert hated the hens, always drunk and pecking at each other. And their babies too, pretending to be cute, when they weren't really; they were no more than cannibals, trying to eat each other and making their little brothers and sisters bleed. They were cruel, little chickens. Cruel like the men in the pub, the way they were always laughing at each other and at poor old Bart, imitating his walk. And calling him Molly Tully. But always behind his back, sucking up to him up front, though, in case they got barred. At least the chickens weren't hypocrites, at least they did it to each other's faces. Or beaks.

George hated the chickens too, although he didn't always. Once he loved them and wanted to know all about them. He said they worked like a factory inside, the yolk first and then the shell fitted on later and growing into an egg growing and dropping down all the funnels until squeeze and . . . *plop*, out they came. Herbert said he didn't believe him and so George said he would prove it and he opened a hen up to see how it worked. Then Father larruped him. With a belt they'd never even seen. A big wide one with a buckle on. And Herbert cried and cried. But George didn't cry; he stayed perfectly quiet while his skin broke and cracked under the buckle. And Mother cried too and threw herself between them. 'Leave him alone. Leave him alone.' And father stopped and looked up and asked her, as if he'd only just that minute seen her, 'What do you want?' with his voice all hushed. And she said 'I want you to leave him alone.' Then he said, 'Well, what did you bloody well tell me for, then?'

And that was the last time Herbert called George a liar. He would believe every word out of his mouth for the rest of his life. Even if it was the biggest lulu that had ever been invented. And that was the first time Herbert hated Father, because he knew. He knew he didn't care two hoots about the hens or about how the egg might grow. He just wanted to hit George. To hit him with a belt no one had ever even seen before. Because the drink had turned sour in his stomach, Mother said later on. That was the house in New Street. With no front door. That was the house where you could never be alone.

And just as well there was no woman who cleaned this house, because the kitchen was always full. And besides now, Mother was the woman who cleaned the house, the woman who did. But at least she had no bars on the window. And could go out if she wanted. To the henhouse. Or somewhere.

And the house in New Street was getting smaller all the time. Cousins in the kitchen. And queer sort of cousins, queer clothes and queer accents. And not even the same religion. Catholic cousins, they said they were. And Mother said they were spinning yarns and not to mind them a bit. But the Samuel man said yes it was true and then Mother said, 'Well I've heard it all now, indeed and I have,' and she sat down then. Right in the middle of making dinner.

And they went to Mass where they spoke in Latin. And every time they met a priest, they curtsied, as if he were the King. And they wouldn't eat meat on Friday, so Mother had to do them an egg. 'Will I do you an egg?' she asked when the girl cousin said, 'We can't eat that, Aunt Greta; it's Friday,' to the stuffed liver on the plate. And the boy cousin said, 'We don't eat guts, anyhow.' And Mother wasn't a bit pleased.

But George thought it was very funny. And got a great kick out of it all. Asking them silly questions like what do Catholics eat for their breakfast. and which way do Catholics go to the toilet. He didn't seem the least bit interested in America, or Americans and how they did things. Just Catholics. And in anyway he had lots of friends he could ask, if he wanted. But he preferred to question the cousins. And Mother told him to be quiet and not be going on about it to everyone and the whole street too. Mother

148

was ashamed of them, Herbert had supposed.

And a curtain in the bedroom to divide the girl cousin from the rest. It reminded Herbert now, of the secret shed. All makeup, sort of. But pretending wasn't fun, if you had to do it all the time. Cousins all over the house. And another curtain; but this one you couldn't see. This one was invisible, hanging down between them all, to divide the Protestant cousins from the Catholic ones, peeping slyly at each other through the gaps.

Cousins in the kitchen. And the Samuel man. And not even sure if they were cousins now at all. First they were – Aunt Kate's children. But now that was changing, with the grown-ups discussing who they should be to the world outside. Discussing who they should be behind their backs. Now when they came back, they wouldn't be cousins any more. Now they would be strangers. Strangers in the kitchen. And why was Bart Tully here in anyway? What had it all got to do with him? It seemed to Herbert that the only grown-ups who were missing were Harvey the Jarvey and Mr Milinski. If Bart Tully had something to do with it, why couldn't Mr Milinski? Herbert liked Bart Tully. But he much preferred Mr Milinski.

Aunt Maude was crying but she didn't make any noise. Not the way Mother cried. When Mother cried you knew all about it but Herbert could bet that most of the people in the room didn't even know Aunt Maude was crying, unless they happened, like him, to be staring at the shadow of her face under the cover of her big-brimmed hat. She had her hand pressed down on the top of an umbrella so he couldn't really see the handle, but the ferrule was shaped like two stumpy brown feet and there they were beside Aunt Maude's ones, which were much longer and leaner and were shod in green soft leather with marbled buttons, three apiece. He pretended to scratch his ankle so that he could see the handle of the umbrella. It was a negro's head and Aunt Maude's hand like a Chinaman's hat over it. A negro with a Chinaman's hat. It didn't make sense. Her clothes, though, were so very pretty and made a lot of sense, just two colours, green and cream and matching each other here and there all over her. Right up to the underside of her hat-brim. He could see Mother eye them more than once.

And poor old Mother caught at her worst, in her henhouse dress. She was probably fretting about that more than the secret. About Aunt Kate and the cousins and the Samuel man and all. In between going on about upstairs being closed off because she had just had the carpets cleaned and had to wait until they were dried before they could walk on them again. She said it too many times, Herbert thought; everyone must know it was a lie. Mother always did that when she was fibbing, said it too many times. Over and over. And what would happen if the schoolmaster should come back from the country early and give the door a good slam for itself? What would Mother say then? That there were burglars in the house? And the police would have to be called and they would be found out and . . . Oh why did Mother have to say so much in anyway? Why did they always have to be in a fix? And there she was now going on about it again: 'What a shame we can't have tea upstairs. If only I'd known you were going to call, I would have postponed the cleaning. I wonder would they be dry yet? Hardly, I suppose.' Herbert squirmed.

Aunt Maude, on the other hand, said very little. Just now and then. Usually it was: 'The children, we must think of the children,' or something like that. The third time, she said it so softly that no one else heard.

Aunt Maude's second husband had plenty to say, though, and he stood while everybody else sat. He had it all sorted out he said: the children would come to live with them; it would be safer.

And Herbert felt a rush of gladness then. The curtain could come down and the girl cousin who followed him everywhere would leave him in peace. And the boy one too, taking George away from him, and always starting fights and showing off with his picture-palace voice. He would be gone. And they could have the house to themselves again. But would Mother be pleased?

Herbert knew the Samuel man had saved Christmas, giving Mother money and the Burwoods wireless that he had bought for them. Would that have to go too? *Children's Playhour* was for babies but there were jokes and funny sketches that he and Mother listened to when the others were in bed. And Father had gone out. And he loved the big band sound and the way the Samuel man had showed them how to dance to it. On Christmas night. When even Father joined in. And Father liked the Samuel man, Herbert could tell, and had been in better form since they all arrived. And in the evenings the two men went out walking together and he always came home too, and just a little tight. But not too much. And late at night you could hear them talk in the kitchen about this and that and probably Father's books that had travelled from libraries all over the city. One by one and under his coat until he had a library of his own. Which was nice for Father but not for the rest of them. They couldn't go to any library because of the books Father never returned from long ago or the ones he'd taken when he couldn't borrow any more. Once Herbert had tried to join and brought a card back all signed and ready, but the librarian refused him because of books borrowed in 1921 that had never been returned. 1921, when he was only three. It wasn't fair. And Herbert had felt very ashamed and couldn't even bear to read anything from Father's library now for the times he turned a page and saw the different stamps, Kevin's Street or Rathmines. Or even the National Library, telling him in their perfect coin-shaped prissy way that his father was a thief. 'Herbert, I think you ought to know: your father stole me. Now what do you think of *that*?'

And the Samuel man had promised them a panto next week. All the children. And Mother too. They could wear their hats, she said, the beautiful ones that Aunt Florence had so kindly sent for Christmas. Would that all be forgotten now? But that was what grown-ups were always at, promising then unpromising again. Except for Father, who never promised anything at all.

Now if the cousins were taken away, Samuel would hardly bother with the panto. Not now, he wouldn't. And Herbert missed the panto in his heart, even though he had never even been to one and wasn't quite sure what it was.

But then he heard Samuel say he didn't want to be separated from the children. And then Aunt Maude's second husband said, 'I see.' And Aunt Maude turned around to look up at him, so that Herbert could see the other side of her hat, like a grassy slope leading down to her back. Weeeeee. And Aunt Maude's second husband looked back at her, taking a fed-up breath before he continued, 'We could find something for you, I suppose, so that you could live in. I prefer to do my own driving, of course – but a handyman, or something . . . '

And Herbert thought Aunt Maude must want the children very badly, want them as a pair, and couldn't stop wanting them, just like maybe she had wanted her shoes the first time she had spotted them in the shop window, all shod soft in green and buttons marbled down the side, three apiece. But the Samuel man said no. He was too used now to being his own boss. Thank you all the same. No thanks.

And everything became unsettled again. And there was silence for a while, as if something terrible had been said. Until Bart Tully broke it with: 'I enjoyed that cup of tea, Greta. Would you mind if I – ?' And Herbert sensed in each grown-up mind another plan being rooted out of the clay while Bart helped himself to another drop from the pot.

Herbert listened to the afternoon bells from the cathedral going bong bong on and on and he wondered where the other children had gone to. To spend the money Aunt Maude had given them. And nothing left for him. Why hadn't she told them to bring something back for him? Or given him a penny for later on. Was it because she was paying for his school, had spent enough on him already? But he never asked her to pay for his school, any old school would have done him. He would much prefer to have a penny of his own. And it wasn't all that great either, going to a different school from George, not getting to know the other chaps around the place the way George did ('Hey George, Howiye George. Alrigh' Georgie?'), every time they went out. And having to stand waiting with his hands in his pockets while George stopped to have a chat here and there along the way, as if he were the Dean of St Patrick's. Or the Lord Mayor. Or someone.

Aunt Maude had never even asked him how he was going along at his school, didn't seem in the least bit concerned about how her money was being spent. Now, this afternoon, when he had something to tell her. Something definite, the annual essay prize, out of all the other boys in his class, including the one above, including the one below. She hadn't even found the time to say, 'Well, Herbert how are you going along at school?'

And she'd kissed all the other children. Even the baby. But she'd hardly said hello to him. He could play chess with her too, if she liked. Aunt Maude was a champion chess player. And Herbert's master said he could be too, with practice. But he hadn't got anyone to practise with outside school. And he didn't want to join a club where he wouldn't know any of the other chaps. George thought chess clubs were for sissies and much preferred his boxing club, standing on a handkerchief spread out flat, his feet never moving, while his body went, boi-oing, boi-oing from side to side, like the roly-poly man Danny got for Christmas. And his fists looking huge in fat padded gloves. A punch in the nose straight out from the elbow, that was the way he liked to finish a game, not waiting for hours to move a little doll and whisper, 'Checkmate'. But Herbert liked chess, no matter what his brother said. He much preferred it to punching a nose and the blood squirting out, feeling it burst. He wouldn't like that, no matter how fat his fist was.

Herbert's master knew of Aunt Maude. And her chess playing. He said she was a fine lady. A fine lady champion. He said Herbert was a lucky fellow and that he wouldn't mind having an auntie just like her. He wouldn't mind it at all.

Herbert wondered what it might be like to get a kiss off her. Would there be a smell of lavender or June roses and would the brim of her hat tip off your nose when she bent down to your face? Perhaps Mother might mention the prize, just fit it in passing. He did hope so. Then he could go 'Oh Mother . . . *please.*' And look away all bashful. So no one would think he was a big-headed buffoon.

The others would be stuffing themselves by now. What would they have bought? Paralysed puddin' for Danny because he liked saying the name more than the taste and he would probably try for a swap then the minute he got it. Peggy's leg for George and something else. A liquorice pipe. Or maybe they'd have enough for a few peashooters, pea-shooting passers-by all the way home. And a bag of large sticky mixed, aniseed balls or black slit bullseyes. And first unclump them from each other, next lick off the shreds of brown skin stuck on to them. Then suck. Suck them away to slivers, to nothing. Which was what he had. Nothing. Made stay to hear a secret they couldn't even make up their minds about. And nothing to keep him going. Not even a mention of his essay prize.

And where were they now, the other children? In Patrick's Park with the bell peals behind them, from playground to railings and out to the road? And why couldn't he be there with them? George might forget to hold Danny's hand and a van could come along, like the one that did in Hubie Punch, tossing him up till he fell on his head. Crack.

And what was the point of him being here at all, when they were only giving him half a secret? And if they had wanted him to be part of it, just so he could lie for them to the other children, why didn't they sort out the lie first and then tell him, instead of chopping and changing and swapping funny looks, each time they mentioned someone called Pakenham. And glancing slyly at him as if it had something to do with him. As if something about it was his fault. Or as if he cared.

Father didn't care either, he could tell, now walking over towards the window and staring out through it, the way he did. What was he looking at? Aunt Maude's motor car, Herbert supposed. And he wouldn't mind having a good look at it himself, with its long keen nose and silver-starred wheels needing more than a glimpse to appreciate all it had to show.

Aunt Maude's second husband lit a cigar and the room filled up with smelly socks, so that for a minute Herbert thought Harvey the Jarvey had sneaked in. Then Aunt Maude's second husband spoke again: 'Well,' he said, 'I suppose, given the fact that Pakenham is in India, the children are for the moment safe. We have no reason to suppose he will return. He'd hardly have the nerve. It's just if he ever got wind . . . well, we're talking about money and trouble. Two things he's more than partial to, by all accounts. Enough of both to lure him back in any case. And you know, the first place he'll make for is the Irish House, you can be damned sure of that. Anyone there would be more than pleased to give him this address. Before you'd know it, Greta, you'd be opening your front door to find him on the step.'

'That's what you think,' Herbert said to himself. 'We haven't got a front door,' while Aunt Maude's second husband paused for a slow suck of his cigar before resuming:

'Now, if you're not prepared to allow the children to come and live with us, then it's my view that the safest course would be to move you out of Dublin altogether. You should really go back to America. I can't see any other way around it, I'm afraid. Naturally, we would be prepared to pay for your pass - '

Aunt Maude moved quickly in her seat. 'Oh no, Henry, I couldn't bear it . . . please.'

He blew a cloud around his head and said nothing. He looked at the cloud instead of Aunt Maude. And now she, at last, was taking her turn to speak for the first time this afternoon:

'I mean for the moment, as long as we all agree, and get the children to agree, not to tell any strangers. Samuel could have married someone else. Why not? The fact that the children are . . . are Catholics.' She stopped for a moment and looked at Mother. 'Did you know that, Greta?'

Mother nodded and Bart Tully said, 'Oh now, same as meself and sure what does it matter? Isn't it the same God? Aren't we all Irish now? The Colonel's Lady and Judy O'Grady, sisters under the skin.' He laughed and Aunt Maude's second husband sent him such a look down through the end of his cigar.

'Yes indeed,' Aunt Maude continued. 'What I mean is, he could just as easily be . . . be someone else's widower. Who's to know the difference? What I say is, send the children to Catholic schools;

let them be seen to practise their religion. I'm presuming, Sam, that's what Kate would have wanted?'

Samuel stared down at the floor and said, 'Yes. Oh, yes.'

Aunt Maude's second husband blew smoke out again and said, 'I will admit, it gives, at a remove, a bit of cover for them. Makes it more difficult to identify them, if you know what I mean. But all the same . . .'

'Yes,' the Samuel man said, 'that's what we thought too.'

Aunt Maude wriggled forward in her chair and leaned towards Samuel. 'Do you mean Kate was really . . . ?' she asked him.

'We married as Catholics. Lived as Catholics. It gave a protection, you see, made us part of another world. We never officially converted, just sort of passed ourselves off. But Kate, well in the end she found comfort, became a Catholic, in every way, you could say.'

'Good God,' Aunt Maude's second husband said. 'And didn't anybody look for proof, documentation, some such thing?'

'We had the rebellion to get us off the hook, all records destroyed. Besides, it's not the sort of thing that people tend to lie about, is it? The children were baptised. Whatever about us, they are, you see, Catholics.'

'Yes, but how did you manage to pull it off? I always thought it was a supposed to be a very complicated, elaborate sort of – '

'You read up on it. Go to a few weddings, funerals, baptismals, whatever, pick up the ways. I found it easy enough. I've come across more complicated ones, I can tell you.'

'Ah yes, so you have. Samuel. So you have. You were born into the Jewish faith, I'm told. And what next eh? Are you going to have a bash at Hinduism, what?' Aunt Maude's second husband smirked around his cigar.

'I'll consider it,' Samuel said, 'but I had rather fancied rowing in with your lot for a bit first.'

'Did you indeed?' and the smirk dropped off his face.

Over by the window Father gave a little laugh. Although nobody else seemed to think it was in the least bit funny.

There was a lull then until Aunt Maude spoke again. 'They only have to keep their mother's name a secret, that's all. And in the unlikelihood that Pakenham should return and decide to look for them – all right, I agree, the first place he will go to is the pub – but Bart can veer him away. Can't you, Bart?'

'Oh yes, Ma'am. You just leave it up to me. I'll see to him all right, send him flying after a flock of wild geese.'

'Which will give us time to . . . '

'Think of something else?' Bart suggested keenly.

'There now. Who can prove a thing? Please, Henry? Surely?'

'Eh,' Bart raised his hand to interrupt her, 'Just one thing, one small thing – before we go any further.'

'Yes, Bart?'

'I haven't a clue what he looks like. Wouldn't know him if . . . if he crawled out from under that table.'

'Oh yes. Of course, Of course. Greta? do you have – ?'

'Quick, Herbert,' Mother said, 'the box in my room.'

Herbert slid down from the chair and went away to fetch the box.

'And don't open it,' he could hear Mother call out behind him.

When he came back into the kitchen Aunt Maude had perked up considerably, Samuel having just declared his intention of staying in Dublin, come what may. She was smiling now gratefully to herself. But Aunt Maude's second husband wasn't smiling at all. He was looking at his watch as though he wanted to leave. He said, 'I see. Well, if you've made up your mind on that, and you won't come to live with us – I trust you have sufficient – '

'We'll be all right for the moment. I've arranged to sell all I own in America and have it transferred. I'll just need a bit of time to sort – '

Aunt Maude interrupted him, 'Samuel, if there is anything you need, anything at all. I don't care how much – Please let me know. I would be only too pleased. You will let me know?'

And Herbert saw Mother go all red and annoyed with her. 'Well, I like that, I must say,' face on her, smouldering away into the box of photographs. But the Samuel man said, 'No thank you, all the same. We'll be all right. Thank you. We'll manage.'

Mother passed a photograph to Bart Tully. 'I'm afraid I don't have one of him on his own.

And from the corner of his eye Herbert saw her mouth move into shapes that seemed to mean, 'Their wedding photo.' And Bart nodding knowingly, accepted the photograph, keeping it close to his chest.

Aunt Maude's second husband threw the end of his cigar into the fireplace and said, 'Well, in that case, it's really up to Greta, I suppose.'

And Bart said, 'Lantern of the divine!' with his face gone all funny.

Aunt Maude said, 'What's the matter, Bart? Do you know him?'

'No,' Bart answered, 'but I know her. I mean, I know somebody else in the picture. What I mean is there's someone I've seen before.'

'Yes,' Father said, turning around to him, 'So you have.'

And everybody looked at Bart and at Father, looking at each other without saying a word.

Mother still hadn't answered whether she minded them staying. So that Herbert saw the bedroom curtain drop a little and could feel his legs stretch out again in his own bed and reminded himself

that the panto would just be one night whereas sharing your bed . . .
well, now that could be for ever and the girl cousin following
behind him? That could be his shadow for years and years and . . .

Then Mother said, 'Of course, of course, they can stay here
until they're sorted. They can stay as long as they want.' And the
curtain went up again, now twice as thick and twice as high as
before.

Herbert was really fed up now, Herbert could scream. And
wondering when Danny would stop wetting the bed. And why he
always seemed to come over to his side to do it before sliding back
to his own dry patch. And then Bart Tully said 'Well . . . ' and
everybody looked at him, and waited. But he didn't say anything
else. Just 'Well,' again before slipping the photograph into his
inside pocket.

Herbert stood up and walked over to the window. Half-past
four and the secret still to be sorted. It was almost dark out there
in the yard. He stood beside Father and looked out the window.
Oh, a fine motor car, a real automobile. Like something out of a
magazine or that you might see at the pictures. Oh, a dazzler it
was, from bonnet to boot. He looked up sideways to show Father
his appreciation and share it maybe with him, a little. But Father
didn't seem to notice. Then Herbert looked at the car again. There
was someone inside it. A little girl, it looked like. Yes, a little girl.
So that's what Father had been looking at all along. Herbert
guessed it must be his cousin Patrice. The one that was supposed
to look like him. And she did. In a strange sort of way. Why had
they not brought her in, he wondered? Would she be like Beatrix
Bumbury? Would she be funny? He would love to see her up close.
To speak to her. And should he ask Mother if he could take her
some jam bun?

'Yes,' Aunt Maude's second husband said. 'A splendid idea.

Send them to a Catholic school, let them be seen to be such, and no one will guess. It's worked out well as it happens. Stay here until you're on your feet and then . . . '

'I would just like to say . . . ' Samuel began, 'I would just like to say to Maude that I want you to see as much of the children as you wish and perhaps they could stay with you occasionally, to give Greta a break. I have something in mind that may mean spending time apart from them initially, so if you liked . . . if it wouldn't be too much trouble . . . '

'Oh Samuel,' Aunt Maude said, 'Thank you so much. Thank you so – '

'Well then, all seems settled for the moment.' Aunt Maude's second husband announced his intention of leaving by reaching for his hat and looking at his wife in a certain way. 'At least we know the tenor and the tone of the whole thing. And as long as Pakenham stays in India I don't see why everything – '

But then Father spoke. 'Ah, but he hasn't,' he said.

And Mother said, 'What can you mean? What are you talking about?'

'I saw him, a few weeks gone by, outside the pub on Poppy Day.'

'Are you certain?' Aunt Maude asked, with her eyes opened wide.

'Yes. It was him. He's here all right.'

Behind them the adults exploded with questions but Father had no more to say. He just looked out at the girl in the car and then back at Herbert and out again, where he kept his eyes till the panic subsided and the secret took on yet another glow.

NINE

Mrs Abingdon lifted each end of her fox-fur tie by a head, stunned and small. She wagged them playfully at each other and the wee boy smiled. He was looking at her from the coil of his father's arms and over the wall of his camel-haired shoulder. And planted down on the step below her – so that she was almost at eye level with the child – the two put her in mind of a dandified St Anthony with the child ever-smiling in his arms. There was an older lad too, standing next to them, busy with his boot and swiping it off the step edge as if it were full of mud. Not wishing to exclude him, she stooped a little, wagging the foxes' heads again. But he remained unimpressed, turning a disdainful back on her so that he was now facing the same way as his father, out towards the course. She returned her attention to the younger boy, this time plucking him softly on his cheek. 'And aren't you the fine fellow?' she put to him then.

She heard the father speak and her hand became shy, withdrawing from the baby-soft face and back into the fold of her arms.

His was a well-spoken voice, although it fell a little gruff, from the side of his mouth down off his shoulder, to the big boy at his side.

'George . . . ' he began. There was no reply. After a pause, he resumed. 'George, are you sure? Are you sure about this now? You didn't just pick it for the name? Now, did you, boy?'

162

But the boy remained silent. The father's voice was slightly agitated. 'Would you mind telling me now, if it's not too much trouble, what makes you so certain?'

'*Le Souvenir*,' the boy snapped finally, before sitting down on the concrete step, so cutting himself off from further discussion. 'Well,' the man spoke again, this time as if to himself, 'it certainly is a queer class of a name, a child's fancy: I would have thought.'

The boy's profile showed for a moment, the merest flush of put-upon heat brightening his cheeks. 'I think it's a stupid name,' he complained into the gloom of coat hems and trouser ends that had started to thicken around him. 'I think it's just stupid.'

'Go down and check the starting prices. Go on,' the father said.

'I've checked them already.'

'Well, check them again.'

And the scowling boy reluctantly obeyed, his feet heavy as lead, going down the concrete stairs.

From the step above, Maureen Abingdon watched the drop of his crown now ducking down into the darkness.

And what a surly specimen he was, such a puss on him. She looked quickly down at her racecard.

But what could they mean? *Le Souvenir? Le Souvenir?* She didn't remember a horse called *Le Souvenir*. And surely he wasn't allowing the child to bet in any case? And what was that about? 'A child's fancy'? A perfectly sensible name *Le Souvenir* – why should it be a child's choice in particular? Oh, which horse could they be talking about? Which one? But her eyes seemed to be having difficulty identifying the letters in each name, unable to formulate them into words. So there was nothing they would pick out or accept, other than a series of columns and sections in various widths. Like wrought-iron tracery going up or down the pages, railings

163

and brackets: meander, meander. Or maybe verandah style, across at the top. And all very pretty but what use if she couldn't read them, couldn't understand nor the head nor the tail of them?

It's all the excitement, she decided. Me, losing my senses. One of these days I'm going to give myself a turn, such a turn. And die right here. I'll die right here on the turf.

She looked back up again across the pats and bellies of hat crowns and caps undulating beneath her. All the way down through the cigarette smoke and the blooms of exhaled winter breaths.

Her mind? Had it gone blank again? She tried to remember. What's this she had backed herself? Was it – ? No. Well, how much did she put on it then? What was her stake? She searched through her mind. But there was nothing inside. Blank. What race was this? The Maiden Hurdle? Or was that the last one? The New Year Steeplechase then? Blank. As blank as that course out there, with its dull cabbage-green and its toothless fence rambling round it. Aimless . . . aimless. Wandering. Aimless. Unable to keep anything in. Was it Rath? Rath something? Was that the name of her bet?

The child reached out to her and without thinking, she offered him her finger. He made a determined grab and in keen short pulls began playing with it, pausing now and then to study the squeezed suede tip he had trapped in his grasp.

'Doon it again,' he said. 'Doon it again.' He was looking at the fox-fur sprawled drunkenly down over her shoulders. It was as if he were holding her finger as hostage until she obliged him again. 'Is this what you want?' she asked him with her eyes. 'Is it this?'

And with her free hand, she picked up the claw of the fox and pretended to scratch the plump crescent of his arm. He squealed and his eyes lit bright to hers.

'There's a grand big chap,' she said to him. 'And that's a very swanky-looking cap you have there. Did you get that for Christmas? Sure, aren't you a great man altogether!'

The child was stretching her finger backways, through the material of her glove. He tipped off the bulge of her wedding ring, nervously, as if it might burn him. 'Yes,' she gooed at him, making no particular sense. 'Now, do you see? Now.'

And ten other little hands she'd known before his, grappling with her finger like this, ten other sets of little fingers grubbed around hers. And truth be known, she'd forgotten which was which. Forgotten to watch them grow. Like the letters of a moment ago, laid out on the page, she knew they were there, knew what they meant to say but the difficulty was in identifying one from the other, in really seeing them each for each. Children from both ends of the line. And all the stages in between. Going up and down like a merry-go-round. Children who were adults, children who were mothers. (And a father too, come spring.) And always one at every station, or so it had seemed. Always someone in the crib and someone to dress for communion or confirmation. Always someone to get a job for. Or someone to see up the aisle – which reminded her like a slap in the face (Sadie. Dear God, Oh Sadie.) It had all gone by so quickly too, up and down, round and round. It was as if it had been the one child all along, never ten of them. Never that many. And one left only now. One baby. Her little Theresa, her last little flower. Her very last one (although she'd said that twice before). But now? Now at forty-five, surely to God there were no more surprises in store? Indeed and not, unless by the Holy Ghost. For Tom? Poor Tom. Well suffice it to say the days of self-control were well gone by. The poor man hardly had the strength for to hold a cup. Never mind for anything else.

She was biting her bottom lip and could tell by the boy's face that he had noticed. And with his own milk tooth nibbling a pleat into the lower of his lips, he was staring at her now with an expression of worry, comical in his clear child eyes. Imitating her, he was, picking it up from her. Knowing, of course, just as she did: Maureen Abingdon was in trouble again. And sweet mercy of divine Jesus let me win this day and I promise to you on the life of my last-born child, I'll never again. Just as soon as my debts are . . . As soon as I've . . . Let me watch her. With a calmed eye. Let me consider her with a peaceful mind. Help me now in my hour of . . . Just the once. Just one more time. Dear Mother of God, I humbly beseech . . . Intervene on my . . .

(And Sadie. Suffering Christ, how am I ever to face Sadie!).

She unscrewed and pulled her finger away from the little hand. 'Doon it again,' he said to her, this time a little peeved. Then the father's voice came on sudden, startling her into a vague sense of embarrassment.

'You're not to be annoying the lady, Daniel,' he said.

'Och good heavens no. Not at all,' she reassured the back of his neck and the peek of his nose when it half turned around to acknowledge her. 'You're a good boy, aren't you? A dote, God bless you. I've a boy called Daniel too. Much bigger than you but I bet he's not half as good.' She addressed the child but was really speaking to the father.

'You're not too bad, I suppose,' the man replied, following her example in conversing through his son. 'If I could just get you to stay still long enough for me to get at my glasses and maybe have a look at what's going on down there. What's causing the delay.'

'Oh, would you? Would you like me to?' she offered and with the gentlest of nudges the barrier between them had been broken. The man turned around then, his arm entwined with thin black straps and childish limbs. 'That's very kind of you, ma'am, thank you indeed.'

'Oh, but you're welcome, I'm sure.'

The boy came easily to her and she bounced him once or twice on the crook of her arm. He was heavier than he looked. Longer too. Good gracious. Quite a weight to be carrying around all afternoon. A ton of it.

And it seemed to her that any sighting of them so far saw the child being carried, the father carrying. First coming from the gentlemen's room, then later stopped by a fruit stall, she had noticed them and it had been the same thing. And even at the previous race, from her position further up at the very back of the stand, she had spotted the wee tassel on the boy's cap bobbing up at her through the crowds. Never left him down at all. And he should be well able to walk. Unless? No, sure look at the sturdy legs on him.

How old are you?' she demanded goodhumouredly.

'Oh I'm a very big boy,' came the sensible reply.

'You certainly are,' she murmured, wondering why on earth she just couldn't set him down beside her. (Baby my eye, the lump).

And she had met the man before. Now that he'd shown his face, she felt sure she could recognise him. From Leopardstown was it? No, the Park, she was certain. Nearly certain. Hadn't she spoken to him once or twice? For that was the thing about racing: it obliterated all call for formality; no introductions were necessary. You could speak to people you had never properly met nor would ever be likely to meet again. You could speak to people you'd be afraid to talk to elsewhere or otherwise. A common bond that's what it was. No social niceties needed, no names.

He had a cane with him the time of their conversation. A cane and a straw hat. Summer. Summertime. Yes. Down at the rails. It must have been the Park so, that awkward angle impossible to judge from the stand. She always liked to be down there, right at the post. Judge for herself. He was most likely of the same opinion.

A well dressed young man she had thought, at the time. Not very tall but a way about him, just the same. 'Well that's that then,' he had cheerfully announced to her (for there was no one else about), pressing the bookie's docket between his palms like a piece of new dough. 'Beaten by a complete outsider. In a common canter, if you don't mind,' and he flicked the crumpled ball to the ground. A cheerful gesture the way he had handled it and a careless chirp to his voice too.

But she understood his inner dismay (her loss too, it had been) and answered him: 'Yes – ah but in fairness now, up to the last furlong, well, he did run with plenty of dash. He just hadn't got the stay,' she concluded with a sad little shake of her head.

'How right you are,' he had replied, and they moved together back towards the bookies' stands and the spent scattered dockets tipping off their feet. And as fellow punters they had strolled along then, consoling each other with reminders of past glories and future possibilities, so that within a few steps the horse had been exonerated; it was all a silly misunderstanding of sorts. And between them they had stretched out the disappointment so thinly that you could hardly see it at all. It had been all very pleasant, the subject taking care of itself, taking the responsibility away from them. Yes an easy chat, just the type you might have with a stranger. Then she had stopped, giving light indication that it was time to part company (after all they had just reached the parade ring). And realising the necessity of being alone through those delicate moments before the next race, she knew there would be no question of his taking offence, as they would doubtless be of one mind on this matter. 'Well, good luck to you in anyway, whichever way you throw.'

'And yourself, ma'am.' He had raised his hat and away with them then to their separate tasks. She could remember now discussing form with him and the card for the rest of the meeting. Both disagreeing on prospective winners and yet influencing each other's choice without intention. She'd changed her bet, she well recalled. Had he? She hoped not, for she had won on his deliberation. He had brought her luck. Three winning tickets she had to claim before the afternoon had done with her. Yes, he had saved her skin and rightly so. Could he again? Today? Should she ask him, just in passing, mind, 'Do you fancy anything yourself for the next one?' And what about the one after that? The next meeting then? Or what about the dogs? ('Are you a greyhound man yourself, sir? Dogs, horses, cats?') If they would; any old luck would do.

He was wearing a green felt hat, though. Green for grief. And three of them in the group – misfortune. But then, bad luck or not, he had seen her right last summer. God knows which way she would have been had she not run into him, hadn't grazed off his luck in passing. And putting her in a position to prepare for Tom's homecoming from hospital.

She had been able to pay off money owed for a start. Pay it off so that she could borrow again, a leg of lamb and a trifle you could bounce on. He'd hardly touched a thing, hardly noticed a thing either, just his own bed upstairs, tucked into the wall and his bolster arched the way he liked it. And a pipe – that was the homecoming present – a cherrywood pipe from Kapp and Peterson's, fondled but unlit to this very day. Although he loved it, she could tell. He just wasn't able. And she had made good all over the rest of the house too, able now to fill in the household gaps she had plucked bald while he was away. That's what her winnings had done for her: given her back the glass cabinet ornaments before he had a chance to miss them. It could happen. It could just happen, just like that. She'd had a feeling about it all that week. And supposing? Supposing some day he should say, I want to go downstairs again, down to the parlour; make me a bed by the window bay. Towards the end that's what they often do, she'd seen it before. Heard it, too, of others, strangers now dead. He might like to lie with his head on the big thick arm of their velvet-brushed sofa with the light coming in behind and his mother's glass cabinet beside him. As he might have done, long ago, a small boy, out of sorts. His little treasures, tiny cups and christening spoons and a diminutive selection from the world. A Swiss chalet, a white Roman arch, and a statuette of the Liberty lady, torch held high and crown spiked to the speckled stars on the dark lining paper behind her.

At least she'd not touched the cabinet this time – though apart from that there was no shortage of vacancies about the room – but the cabinet was leading a full and busy life and long may it continue to do so. If only she could. And if not? The parlour door would have to be locked again. against the children saying, 'Mother? where's the . . . and the . . . and the big brass clock?' And Sadie's wedding dress. Two shillings a week. Why hadn't she just put it into the Post Office herself? Couldn't she just as easily have popped in on her lunch hour? Couldn't she have paid it off week by week in the shop? Sadie, sinless Sadie. How could I ever expect her to understand?

The little boy was fingering her earbob. With a clever eye he considered the mechanics involved. She shook her head and he started, waiting for a few seconds until the earbob calmed itself and he dared resume his inspection.

Why had I not stayed free? I was free, for six months (and longer). And he was responsible, this child's father, this man there in front of me, this stranger. He'd given me my freedom. Money in my hand. And I had held on to it too, the relief after all the worry, all the novenas, hadn't been easily surrendered: not this time. My lesson learnt, or so I thought.

The child was growing sleepy. He was fingering the corner of her collar the way he most probably did the corner of his pillow, just before nodding off. His small head, heavy with sleep, began to rock gently down towards her fur-covered shoulder. She shifted her arm a little so that he easily dropped. Let him have a little rest for himself, let him enjoy his peace of mind: the poor child was exhausted.

Mrs Abingdon closed her eyes and tried to remember the moment she had lapsed. Back to that first evening, when she had found herself slipping out after she had put the smaller ones to bed. (Women's sodality she'd said was where she was intended). Had she meant it at the time? It felt as if she had. Until she came up near the church that was, and seemed unable to join the trickle up the steps and in behind the columns, into the shadows. Unable to conceive of her fingertips dipping primly into the font and criss-cross from forehead to shoulders and back again. Unable to bear the thought of the peace and the quiet. And the whispering words nagging softly, through the rows of women down on their knees.

She'd walked on past, right past, hoping there would be no one who would spot her, no voice to recognise and call her back. Then turning at the nearest corner, her heart as breezy as a lover's beating, she cut back down to Dorset Street. And there a tram she found herself seated on and all surprised sort of, like it had nothing to do with her. As if someone had put her there unbeknownst to herself, innocent as this baby in her arms.

All the way up New Street and Clanbrassil. Hacking over the bridge with a bounce and a sway and on up widely then for Harold's Cross to where the slip of a park splits the road to Kimmage. On to the left. Where soon they tucked up, the tram, herself and the scatter of occupants alone or perhaps as a conniving pair. Fawn coats maybe or dustcoats grey or beige. And newspapers folded onto laps, with eyes near to burning a hole through the print of name after name of dogs. So that's where they must be going then? Well who would have thought it, *me* on the same tram as all of these peculiarities. And wonders never cease now do they? With all of us going, together and going. Here's all of us going to the track. To the dogs.

She opened her eyes. The older boy had returned. He was standing facing her, looking intently at her face. She felt herself redden. How long had he been there? The little get. Had her mouth been moving the way it sometimes did when her mind was busy and alone? Was he looking at her as if she were half mad, or was he just wondering what she was doing with his little brother up in her arms? He turned away and she closed her eyes again.

She'd won a bundle too that night at the dogs, laughing to herself on the way home, seeing her face through the tram window sniggering into itself, into its dark reflective blur. And then back to 'Mother, what kept you? Where in the name of – ? Worried, we were, up the wall.' And then next time she'd won again and then again the next, and it seemed as if it might never stop, this luck, this fluency of luck. She had no worries at all now. For the first time in years she saw a clear run-up to Christmas. All accounts settled now, spanking slates clean and waiting up and down Drumcondra. ('And good morning to *you*, Mrs Abingdon.') With a Christmas box presented to her from every shop: conserves, fruit cake, a sunny mound of country butter and enough stout candles to blaze up the house at every window, like a carnival on the street. Open smiles and eyes unaverted, looking straight into hers. And never served by an assistant now, always by the one whose name was over the shopfront, those familiar with her taste for the odd extravagance, the seasonal treat. Only the best. Best beef, best cut, best piece, best customer: only the best. And presented, each item over the counter top, with that extra bit of enthusiasm now that it had been generally ascertained that payment would no longer be such an unlikely event.

She could have stopped then. She should have. Why hadn't she?

Too comfortable she'd been, that's what it was. It had begun to irritate her like a rash: that feeling of endless comfort. She had to go back for more. More what? Money? No, not money. She had always had a weakness for the few bob, true, liked to spend it, and foolishly too. But it was something else that made her greedy, something else she wanted more of. Or to see . . . She wanted to see. What? How far she could push it? Perhaps. She didn't know, she just didn't know. Oh why hadn't she turned to the drink instead? An easier life and half the worry. At least she would pass out sometime, have some moments of peace, of quiet.

She looked at the man, his mouth still and firm under the shelf of binoculars, sleek and protruding. He'd hardly remember her now. Young men like him never remembered middle-aged women like her. She looked down at the older boy (his son?), now dragging a race-card from his corduroy pocket. Could she see a family resemblance? Yes, facially anyhow. But in manner? The father was well-spoken, whereas that young lad, well he had a street accent and his demeanour too was sort of . . . rough. Although they had a look of each other, all three. A nephew maybe or cousin? Poor relation brought along to assist? With what though, the youngster or the horses? For there he was now with a pencil in hand jotting down marks beside the next race layout. He had notes all over his race-card. His very own race-card, a line drawn from the name of the relevant horse out to the column where she could see all sorts of squiggles and sums had been written in. Why the little old Granpa. How old could he be? Proper little half-pint. The cheek, the laughable cheek, really. And the way he spoke to his father, a disgrace.

She settled the cap cautiously on to Daniel's head and looked beyond him to the course below. She would have a good view from here and was just beginning to regret it. She wished she was back up at the very top step, where she had safely passed the last couple of races and where – even if she had dared to look – she could hardly have seen a thing. She had felt though, the silence of the first few minutes of the race filling thickly in her ear, the rare silence of a crowd deep in concentration, more exhilarating than a thousand cheers, moving her more than any operatic aria could ever attempt to do. A silence you could almost hear. And then bit by bit it had become unsettled, with the voices breaking out again. And she had heard the name of her horse drop with countless others throughout the crowd, as each spectator plucked out his own concern. And one eagle-eyed man, right beside her, had been covering the scurry as it progressed. That had been the last race, the latest disappointment.

Then she had been able to keep her eyes down on the shoes in pairs around hers, the tanned and the black ones, the ones that were shining and well-cared for and those that had never known a lick of polish. And all the time, she had imagined the horses' progress to the sound of her neighbour's voice, with the name of her horse coming more regularly throughout what had otherwise sounded to her like a muffled prayer. She had been deaf to everything except that one name. And more regularly again, she had heard him repeat it, as he roused himself with the horses galloping hooves, heading home at last: And into the straight.

But then up there on the highest step, she couldn't bear to wait, to see. She couldn't bear to face it. She had turned away, keeping her back to the action, watching instead the sea, the just discernible sea, through the slit-gap that kept separated, concrete and corrugated iron. Dirty as dishwater, but something to watch just the same. It had been somewhere to put her eyes. Rath . . . ? Drin. Rathdrin. Yes that was one name. And another – Count Dracula, (that had been hers). Yes that had been it. And for a while she had thought, she had really believed. This would be it. She had seen him in her head, flatter for a space then gain another bit. She had pictured his deft shift into third berth and her heart had stopped. She was going to, he was going to . . . And make good for Sadie. And make good for them all.

She had felt her eyes close then and her own voice come out of her, soft at first and urgent then, more urgent with repetition: 'Come on. Come on, Count Dracula. Come on. Come on the Count. Come on!' And then suddenly he was gone. Not mentioned again. It was another horse's name then beating triumphantly from the mouths of chosen punters. It was another horse that had scathed past the winning post. Leaving her voice crying out at nothing. It was as if he'd never even existed. As if she had imagined him all along.

Perhaps this time. Perhaps this race. What had she backed this time? Welsh Star. But she was far away from the sea, this time. She was far away from the back of the stand. And it would be difficult to avert her eyes packed into this crowd, with a sleeping child up in her arms. She would have to watch. Welsh Star – 4/1 – which would give her – ? She tried to calculate but nothing happened.

And there was poor Tom (if only he knew) up in bed and not suspecting a thing. Always too quiet by far. Mrs Hendron would never have a chance to get herself into this fix, slipping off to Baldoyle on New Year's Day, or taking nightly excursions to the dog track (the idea). Not Mrs Hendron. Not with the husband she had. She clucked when he crowed. Nice woman, though. She had been asking after him too. Only this morning, she had asked, 'How is he, Mrs Abingdon? How is he at all?' Grey in the face, Mrs Hendron. Grey like the sea out Baldoyle way.

She was feeling the weight of the child now. He was starting to burn her arm. When would the father turn around and take him back? How long more would she be expected to oblige?

'They seem to be having trouble settling. Ballybracken it looks like. Now wait. Welsh Star too, is on the fidget.' Mrs Abingdon felt herself start, the father had spoken.

For a moment she wasn't sure who he was talking to. Was it her? The older boy perhaps? But no, he was too far down, his hands holding up the cheeks of his face while the heel of his boot tapped sullenly against the riser of the step. (Oh. It's me, it's me. It must be me). She must answer.

'Welsh Star did you say? Wouldn't you know, my lad.' She smiled apologetically as the man turned around and reached out for the child. She passed him back gently. 'Thank you, Ma'am.'

'Oh my pleasure indeed.'

'He's dozed off,' she said softly.

The man nuzzled the child into position on his shoulders, edging with his chin, the small cap back into place.

'I didn't see it was yourself there,' he said to her then, reaching unsuccessfully for the brim of his hat over the bulk of the boy in his arms. 'Oh sure you've your hands full indeed,' and thinking to herself, baby my eye, the lump.

'Do you see that course out there?'

'Yes?'

'Well, if I didn't keep this fellow here practically tied to me, that's where he'd be. It's happened before, you know; out there winging his way. Gone in a flash.'

And she blushed bright red; it was as if he had read her disapproval.

'Sure you can't take your eye off them for a second,' she mumbled.

'And tell me, ma'am, are you having any luck so far?' the man asked, turning the conversation back to the relevant.

'Well, no. Not exactly. Not today. And what about yourself?'

'Oh we're rubbing along all right. The first one pecked on us, shot the jockey out of the saddle. We had the last two winners all right.'

'Oh well done. And this one? What have you?'

'Suziewusie.'

'Ah, isn't that out of . . . ?'

'*Le Souvenir.*'

'Yes. *Le Souvenir.* But a daring bet just the same.'

'I suppose,' the man replied.

'Still, it's all for a bit of fun,' she lied.

'Indeed, ma'am it is,' he lied back.

'Well now, Suziewusie; what an amusing name.'

The man nodded gravely and down near his knee she could see the older boy look up and scowl at her. Right into her face. And, oh, a thoroughgoing cur if ever, a thoroughgoing blackguard! Wouldn't you just love to . . . What he wanted now was a good kick in the backside, a good toe up the . . . Yes. Teach him some manners for himself. That's what he wanted.

But then she reminded herself she had enough on her plate without working herself up over the manners of a stranger's child. For what was he to her, after all? She'd probably never see him again. He was someone else's problem. Thank God, he'd never be hers. They'd have their work cut out for them all the same. And a big fellow too, he was going to be, big and bold as a . . .

'Yes,' she repeated, 'a most amusing name,' and smiled one last time as the father turned away from her.

She kept the smile on her face for a bit then, easing it down slowly to a contented little grin and holding it steady while she soothed the fox-fur bristles into place. It was no more than a flicker now, one for lips that might be humming or thinking of some pleasantry, past or yet to come. A contented sort of countenance, all in all, serene and motherly her face, a pleasant easy sight, beneath her greying hair and the mound of her purple velvet hat.

But inside her heart was screaming at her and her hands were shaking in their gloves. Any second now . . . any second. She squeezed the race-card into a roll and closed her ears to the sounds around her while the horses below jigged into position. All about her footsteps were gathering and there was that tightness in the air, like a cord drawing the talk and pulling it through the crowd. Soon there would be silence again. Soon she would be able to hear it. It was a cold day. It was supposed to be a cold day but inside her coat it felt like July.

The man shifted the boy's weight a little in his arms. The child jerked suddenly awake. He looked frightened for a moment, as though he might start to cry. And then he saw her. He reached out, stretching himself to the fur about her neck. Frisky after his little nap, he wanted to play again. He wanted her finger back in his grip. With all his small heart he wanted her attention. She looked away from him and down to her feet. They had called the 'Off'.

TEN

After the third race-meeting in a row Greta began to get suspicious, after the fifth she could no longer contain herself: 'Why are you taking him with you?' she demanded. 'Why?'

Her husband, daubing the bridge of his leather tan shoes with three little dots of muculent cream, looked up for a moment and said, 'Why shouldn't I? He is my son.' He lowered one foot and brought up the other, now playing the brush across and back in swings of varying lengths and sideways down, shorter and sharp. For a few seconds more, the only sound in the kitchen was the smart military shuffle of bristle on leather.

'Isn't he?' he concluded, curving his voice just a little to the right.

Greta swung away from him and made for the scullery. She could see little Maudie peering up at her as she marched by. 'What?' she asked the child, crossly, 'What? What's up with you?'

'Why nothing, Aunt Greta.'

In the quiet of the scullery she waited for the heat to leave her face. It was dark in here at least, and private. How could he have said such a thing? In front of the children. How could he have been so low? He was nothing more than a vicious, a dirty vicious . . . She stood at the door and her frantic hand beckoned to George ('Comehere, comehere, come*here* before I box your ears').

George looked over at his father. He was occupied. Replenishing the tin with all its paraphernalia. Down into the old biscuit box, in a series of feeble clashes, one by one behind each other they obediently dropped, polish and beeswax, lotions and creams. He was replacing the lid on the tin box now and easing it down at every corner. There was a much bigger box waiting on the floor beside him – a ditty-crate made of wood – brushes, soft or coarse with a selection of buffer clothes set to rest at the front and just enough space left for the tin box to make a nook of its own. There was enough stored in there for one of them to set up outside the Shelbourne as a shoeblack. George watched his father carefully lift and then lower into the crate the box that had the Highlander with rosies on his cheeks, lying flat out as if he'd been mitted. He tried to remember his joke this morning that had put his cousins in stitches: Highlander with the rosies on his cheeks. Which ones? Look up his skirt and you'll see. It didn't seem all that funny now.

The door clicked shut. His father would be gone to gather his racing props, coat, hat, binoculars, the *Irish Field* and such other reading material as might be deemed necessary. His money, as George, after countless attempts to discover the hiding-place at home, now knew, would have to be collected from the Irish House *en route*, from a winking Bart Tully. A key behind the seltzer bottles to a cupboard under the counter and a heavy black box. And an envelope with a sum jotted down the front which grew longer each time they called. And in dainty stitches at each side, plus signs or minus, depending on which way the wind had blown. He hurried through to his mother. She was stooping down to him; her urgent whisper bounced off his face. 'Why is he bringing you with him? Why?' George shrugged his shoulders up and she caught hold of them before they had time to drop down again. 'Why? I'm asking you, George. I'm warning you now: you'd better tell me.'

'I don't know.'

'I thought you wanted to go to your club this morning. And

this afternoon off to play skee ball with your Aunt Maude and your cousins?'

'I do. I mean – '

'And back to her house then for the night. Her huge big house. George, you've always wanted to see it. Maudie's birthday tea. Can you imagine the feast there'll be, the . . . ?'

'I know, I know. Mother, I know.' He was shouting at her now.

'*George.*'

George looked down at his feet. 'I'd much rather go to the boxing club,' he whispered.

'Well, why don't you then?'

'Why don't you ask him?' he said.

'Because he won't tell me. You heard him.'

'No. Not him. Him.' And she followed her son's upward glance toward the ceiling.

'Who do you mean? God? Don't you dare your impudence with me or I'll – '

'Oh Mother, *no*. I mean –' And he looked upwards again this time pushing his eyebrows to their uppermost limits. '*Him*. Him upstairs.'

Greta thought for a moment. 'Not the . . . ?'

George nodded and breaking from her grip, burst out: 'It's all his fault. He's the one to blame. He told me to keep me mouth shut and then he goes and blabs himself. He's a big liar, that's what he is. A big fat . . . ' The door outside clicked open again and George stumbled back out into the kitchen and away from his mother.

While she was considering just what her son could mean, she heard her husband raise his voice to her. 'I'm taking him too,' he said And she knew he meant Danny.

'He's not well,' she began, ' A cold on him . . . his chest.'

But a slammed back door had cut her off before she had time to finish.

Outside in the kitchen she could hear the niggle of young Maude's knitting needles and Herbert flicking over pages one by one, too swiftly for him to be taking anything in. Nobody spoke and even Benny was keeping stim, no more than the slightest whistle to prove he hadn't noticed a thing. And that made a pleasant change too; ever since he'd been to see *The Jazz Singer* he'd had them driven simple, song, word and deed. It was like living under the same roof as that Al – whatever his bloody name was. There would be no need for her to go and see it at all now, not at this rate. (Not that she was ever likely to be brought, of course.) She knew the whole thing off by heart and inside. 'Oh Herbert,' she remembered, in a spurt, 'the hens, the hens. I'm after forgetting all about the . . . Quick now, quick.'

'I've already fed them, Mother,' he answered.

'Oh. Good boy. That's my good boy.'

She stayed where she was for a few minutes more and then came suddenly striding through to the kitchen, disengaging her pinny.

'Herbert,' she said, without looking at him. 'I'll be back in a moment. Keep an eye on the children until your Aunt Maude arrives.'

'But, Mother?' he said, 'Do I have to go? I'd rather stay here, you know, and wait for George. Mother, please.'

Greta looked at him for a moment as if trying to make up her mind but then she heard Maudie's determined little voice, 'If Herbert's not going then I'm not going either.'

Greta looked at Herbert. 'You're going,' she said.

'Oh, Mother.'

But she had walked on by.

And behind her all the young heads turned to watch her unbolt the secret door behind the long velvet drape that nobody was supposed to know about, especially Aunt Maude. They listened to the sound of her step on the back kitchen stairs, going up. First brisk and determined, then a little slower as they reached the top. The schoolmaster. She could only be going up to see the schoolmaster.

'What on earth could she want with him?' Benny asked Herbert with his eyes all agog.

'How should I know?'

'Wanna know what I think?'

'What?'

He stood up and bending a little at one knee stretched his arms out full span. 'We aint seen nothin' yet,' and he wagged his fingers and rolled his eyes gleefully, 'That's what I think.'

Herbert looked away and down. And with a determined lick, primed his thumb to lift yet another page of his book.

And that was how Mother learnt about George and his numerical flair (as the schoolmaster would put it). That was how she learnt that he had a knack most uncanny. While down in the kitchen Herbert's heart went clapperclawing inside his chest and trying not to notice questions from the boy cousin's mouth, or worse ones, more probing, from the girl cousin's eyes, with her ankles going swing-swong-swing under the dangle of wool growing down from her elbows.

Herbert was afraid of Mother and the full story. A half a story would never leave her satisfied. ('I'm not leaving here till I'm satisfied,' was what she always said). She'd keep at it and at it until all the bits were in and the picture was complete. That was

Mother's way. Herbert was afraid of what might happen then. The trouble there'd be, the murder. But when he thought about it more, he realised that this time it would be very difficult to gather, the full story. Not every bit of it. And not from the schoolmaster in anyway, because if he told her all, he'd come out looking the worst. Next to look bad would be Father (who probably didn't have it all either), next Herbert (for not telling Mother in the first place). Last of all George. Because he was always in trouble anyway and that's what happened to boys who were always in trouble anyway – people got used to it. Didn't make such a fuss. Whereas Herbert? Someone like Herbert could cause such a to-do for the slightest misdemeanour. Like that time he'd forgotten to hand in his home tasks and had fallen down by three on his monthly marks. You'd think he had shot the headmaster or something, the scene Mother had caused.

But no matter how difficult it would prove to be, Mother would have her full story just the same. Where would she get it? If Father didn't know and the Master didn't tell, it left only George and Herbert. And they wouldn't tell either. Herbert had promised not to stag, nor would he. And he knew the story better than anyone. Every inch of it. Which meant, now that he came to think of it, that he would probably be put second to the schoolmaster in the line of fire. Or maybe before him even. For he knew more than one side. (And Mother always said there were two sides to . . .) Although this time she was wrong, There were more than two. And it was Herbert who knew all the facts just as they had fallen out. Because George had told him. And nobody could tell a story like George could. And it was an awfully good story too, so that Herbert had remembered every jot of it. Bits even George had forgotten, for when he had asked him to repeat it, he kept on leaving things out – just little things but important to the story.

So that Herbert had to keep on pulling him up (No, no, *no*. You skipped the bit about . . . And don't forget the . . .) till George got fed up and said, 'Tell it to yourself, then, if you know it so bloody well.'

And so Herbert did, going over it inside his head, like the first time he heard it, just like then. Only better now, because he could dawdle with the details as he liked and look behind and over and even under the events and the people involved, their past and their present. So that by the time he had finished, he had made the story his own. Like looking through a window it was, or high up at a picture screen from your hiding place in the dark.

Osmond Whyte disapproved of drink. He despised all tobacco consumption too, whether through pipes or cigars, or even in dark fragrant pinches snuffed up the nose. Cigarettes he firmly dismissed as being for those with nothing better to do with their hands, like cornerboys or American women. And as for the frequenting of theatres or picture palaces, he considered that to be a form of gluttony quite unnecessary to the wellbeing of healthy minds except, of course, for those who might find themselves to be severely malnourished where the imagination was concerned.

He was apt to give the boys in his class a speech against these and other vices at the oddest of times, right in the middle of scripture or mathematics even. And once the rivers of South America had started him off (for reasons unknown to all but himself) to such an extent that George had thought he might burst open on the spot, leaving little bits of himself all over the wall. His speeches seemed to make him itch too, and scratch himself as his objections intensified, so he was a sight to behold with the eyes ripe in his head and the words spit hopping from his mouth and his fingernails fussing all over the itchy bits every other second.

Parents at home thought all was going as it should do in the daily business of education and had no inkling of these frequent and spontaneous outbursts. And because it was much better than learning mathematics or the rivers of South America or matching dates to battles you couldn't give a fig about, there were no squealers in the class to put them right. And besides, Mr Whyte despised squealers, which was considered to be one of his better points. And could cut them to the quick too, while a shiver of glee slithered through the classroom. And every boy's back sitting soldier-straight without having to be told to stop slouching or lolling or hunching over like old women sniffing for ha'pence on the ground. And every boy's mind keen with a similar ambition: to be the first to re-enact the afternoon's performance, to catch a word, a detail missed by the other chaps.

When Norman Cocks went up to tell on George with his face all prissy and pink and his feet moving in smug little steps and said, 'Sir, my mother said I should tell you,' and here he lowered his face a little to the Master's and his eye peeped out to the back of the second row, 'that George' (here he lowered his voice as if everybody didn't know which George it was or what he had said) 'called me . . . called me . . . '

'Called you what, boy? Speak up, won't you? There will be no whispers in this classroom.'

And Norman from behind a breath inhaled long and sharp came out with:

'Cock a rooshy piss and snots

Norman's cock's come out in spots.'

And only Norman Cocks would be stupid enough to repeat such a thing to the schoolmaster.

'Excuse me for repeating, Sir, but Mother said it would be all right,' (and here he lowered his eyes, little girlie-shy) 'seeing as how it wasn't me that really said it in the first place but really him, and Mother said – '

And it looked like George would really be in for it now (bad language being worse than picture palaces and theatres and only slightly better than tobacco smoke and snuff) with the Master's face blown back in horror, first saying, 'I beg your pardon, Cocks, but has your mother recently enrolled as a pupil in this classroom? Point her out to me, there's a good fellow. I should like to greet her.'

'No, sir, I mean, she's not here, sir.'

'Not here? Not here? Then tell me, Cocks, why should I care in the least what Mother says? She has nothing to do with me. Have you ever known me to give a hang about any person outside this room?'

'No, sir.'

'Demote yourself to row D.'

And Norman turned to go back to his place to gather his books and take them humbly with him to lowest rank in the room. But that wasn't all. The Master hadn't even begun. He then stood up and raising his hand in a familiar signal, 'Boys,' he began, 'what do we hate?'

'*Squealers, sir.*'

'And boys, what do we call them?'

'*Pigs, sir.*'

'And tell me what do they sound like, boys?'

And the classroom filled up with farmyard sounds, oinks and squeaks and a whistle too, from Ernest Algar with the slitty eyes and the spacious face who didn't really understand what was going on but could whistle like a silver flute and did any time that noise was called for. And moo calls too and a baaing lamb which had nothing to do really with squealing either but added nicely to the rustic atmosphere. And behind they followed Norman Cocks all the way back to his bench and a little smile pressed into his face as if they all couldn't see the tears stand out like diamonds in his eyes.

'Now, Cocks, is that what you want to sound like?'

Cocks shook his head.

'Come again, boy I didn't quite – ?' and he sliced his hand behind his ear in a salute.

'No, sir.'

'How glad I am to hear it. There will be no squealers in my classroom. Not ever. All that goes on behind these walls is a matter for its Master and its servants. Have I made myself clear, gentlemen?'

'*Yes, sir.*'

In the afternoons Mr Whyte popped often out, 'for a short breath of air while the weather holds firm'. Sometimes he would return in quite good form and might even pass a bag of sweeties around. Or make a joke or two, but nothing too hilarious, just the type that would make the boys go 'haahaaahaaa' altogether in one long high note rather than the sort that would have them slumped over their desks, helpless with laughter. But mostly he came back with the look of the devil on his face and an oration boiling in his mouth, just waiting for a chance to escape. George reckoned he'd probably been out counting pubs again and had noticed one or two new ones to add to his list. Because when he came back in this black mood, they always seemed to be hot in his mind. And when he got on to the subject of drink, there were never any jokes, nor calls for a farmyard chorus. Nor would there be any excuse for as much as the slightest smirk from any face. It was a subject as grave as death: 'The Drink'.

And he knew the name of every public house in the vicinity and further into every part of the city, so that there was nowhere for a public house to hide. And would name them off one by one, alphabetically to illustrate his point: there were more public houses in this city than churches and there were more starving children than not. When he hit on the name of a public house that a boy knew his father to frequent, there would before him grow a blushing face looking up from the benches until one by one, the rows flushed into bloom, like the rose beds up the Botanic Gardens.

He had taken a particular dislike to George, on account of his father being a publican, and quoted something from the Bible (incorrectly as Herbert was able to later point out) to demonstrate how contemptible the man who had publican branded on his heart. Worse even than the blackguards that frequented these places were the blackguards that sold for profit ('And a mighty profit, boys, too, let it be known') alcoholic beverages to men, who in their weakness hand over money meant for food for the children. And all for the gain and wealth of the heathen publican and his self-centred grasping family. With their greedy children and fat wives who might as well be grizzly bears with the amount of fur they wore on their backs.

When he reached this particular section of the speech George made it his business to outstare him with the most brazen face he could muster, refusing to be humiliated. Because he knew it was nonsense and more to the point he knew the schoolmaster, who was after all their lodger, must *know* it was nonsense. If they were so well off they'd hardly need a lodger in the first place nor would they have to keep a squad of chickens in their shed. And as for Mother? What fur did she own, except one very slight trim around a hat she no longer even wore, a hat that Charlie cuddled on his way to sleep. And the other boys in the class, too, all of them knew his mother and her furless back. All of them knew his family yet they would choose to believe the Master over the facts. Swallowing all his innuendoes and turning sly-eyed to show their disdain for the ostentation of George and his swaggering brothers. And were not going to be fooled by his hand-me-down suit either or the fact that they had 'blind stew' the night he had taken Tubridy back to supper. (Just a decoy, they now said. Hadn't Tubridy seen whole sides of beef hanging in the pantry?) And the cheek of him, anyway, tucking into school buns and corporation milk, when everybody knew the chickens they kept in the barn were to roast at a whim whenever supper might be a little late or the boys felt peckish after they'd been to the swimming pond in Tara Street kept at a steady 70° during the cold spell for their very own comfort. Probably arranged by his aunt, too, with a motor car the length of the street or his father with shoes hand stitched by twenty-two nigger slaves. And the biggest proof of all, as Norman Cocks with his face ready to burst with information pointed out, he had *American* cousins. *Now.*

And to think they all used to think he was a sound sort of a fellow. Georgie Rockefeller, the publican's son.

And George was no longer the hail-fellow-well-met that he used to be. Every day brought its scraps and fisticuffs with mothers pounding on the back door, presenting sons and laying out their injuries like patterns on linoleum rolls.

George began to hate school. George began to hate everything, except for Saturday mornings when he could go to his club. And the punchbag was no longer just a punchbag then, it became known to him as 'Whyte-shite's face' and hanging there to be beaten black and blue as if it really was the schoolmaster. (Herbert always thought he should have been grateful to it, because he reckoned that's what had made him the best junior boxer in the club, punching Whyte-shite's face to a pulp).

In the evenings they would dream of revenge on Mr Whyte and every other swine in the classroom. George said he was going to become a Catholic too, which would chuck them all. Catholics had respect for money, at least, and knew how to suck up to its owners. And they might have sins that were hard to fathom but being rich wasn't one of them. (George, in his anger and desire for revenge, seemed to forget at times that it was all made-up anyway and there were no riches to speak of. Besides in a matter of weeks when Father would sell the pub, they would really be hard-up with the same, if not less, income than everybody else). But Herbert didn't bother to put him right, not just yet, George's schooldays being, after all, lonely enough without depriving him of his imaginary position.

And yet much as George hated the schoolmaster, he had to admit to the occasional kindness on his part. Like the time he had bought a pair of boots for Crawford Wilson and had left them on his desk, insisting his nephew had gone back to America without them and would take a bigger size in any case by the time the Free State postal services managed to see them safely across the sea. Or the Christmas he had claimed a one-pound note had fallen from the pocket of Chester Kane and ordered him to take it home to his mother at once. When everyone knew the Kanes were as poor as Job's turkey and had probably never even seen a ten-shilling note, never mind one worth a pound.

Neither could his disdain for the school inspector or Canon Turf by any means go unappreciated. Or that look of aching boredom as if his whole face had a stitch in it when it was his turn to take Sunday School. And of course, finally, there was the fact that he seldom biffed a boy (except for George, whom until recently he had biffed quite a lot).

Although it was a while now since George's backside had felt the wrath of Mr Whyte's strap. It was also a while since Mr Whyte had slipped out into the firm-holding weather for his breath of fresh air. These two facts were connected, George had been able to report. It was because he sent George out instead. Not to count the names of pubs or publicans, indeed. Nor to follow their prosperous wives and children about on fat shopping expeditions. No. It was to go to the betting shops for him. ('Yes, yes. The turf accountants, the racing shop, the bookies, the bukies, call it what you will,' George had responded when Herbert had cried out, '*What?*')

George was the biggest boy in the class. He was also the cleverest. Quick off the mark, he could hold his own. Such qualities as made for an ideal messenger were his. And George was quite pleased to do the job; a penny a trip was not to be sneezed at, a wing in your pocket to lighten your path. And besides wasn't it an opportunity to have a good wander about the city streets? This had always been something of an ambition of his and it had not, due to Mother's devoted vigilance, had much opportunity for realisation. Until now.

There were six betting shops in all on George's rota, which meant he need only visit any one of them once a week. As Mr Whyte took care of the Saturday bets himself, it also meant that George started his rota in a different shop each week. Thus a pattern was avoided and as no proprietor could object to these 'random' visits, awkward questions were unlikely to arise. Mr Whyte drew a map of each route for George and before he left the classroom, the relevant diagram would be slipped into his hand. Soon George didn't need any map at all and would saunter about the streets and quays of Dublin as if he owned them, bidding good mornings all over the place like a proper grown-up man. And at his ease too, once the deadline of the race had been met, taking his time on the way back to school to enjoy the scenery and welcoming over the days, its gradual transformation from strange to familiar. With that constant replenishment of city detail to keep him from ever getting bored: the smell of rashers and eggs soaring out from the Brazen Head while he tucked himself in through the narrower lanes in case somebody from Father's pub might spot him; the smell from the Quaker's shop in George's Street, foreign and thick: Brazil or Kenya roasted, beans, coffee beans squeezed together beneath glass rows, like a slick collection of rabbit gick. There was the Jewman's shop with duck loaves and bagels and barrels of cucumbers like pickled green mickies. And the smell of burnt feathers from chickens inside following him like a dog up the street. And the high smell from the Liffey and the low smell from James's Gate, all musty and sly. There were sunny days and rainy days and when the ice grew its first coat over St Michael's Hill, there was scuttling to be done. There were the smooth Guinness barges and nervous North Quay trams returning home from adventures out Lucan way or Chapelizod or even Stoney-batter. There were hayloaded carts all yellow and fat, messily piled like tossed fair hair. And neater arrangements too, of cabbage triangles up on carts that could somehow hold them steady. There were tall bread-vans and trim milk floats. There were buxom big cars with the passenger sat in the back talking through a tube to the driver sat in the front. And lorries and traps, cabs and brown brakes. And a hearselike conveyance, long and black, for transporting nuns down Whitefriar street, the windows all caged and the white of their wimples winking out from the darkness inside. It would give you the willies, George said, just looking at them. It would make you stop in your tracks until they had passed.

There was the lavender man on Grafton Street and the crazy lady who sang on Chancery Corner and who asked him for a kiss one time. There were girls in smooth hats and girls in rags and up near Smithfield there were the stick-armed drovers, and the 'cow-up' farmers wearing two long coats apiece, one for the money and one for the rain. And wide brown hats all limp at the brim and leggings that flapped when they walked. Their country accents he took home with him, also the spit on his hand before striking a bargain soon adapted by them all, until Mother had yelled, 'Where did you pick up that *filthy* habit?' And they felt it was best to stop.

He said he'd seen G. H. Elliott, the Chocolate-Coloured Coon, falling out of a pub, and Herbert believed him. He said he'd seen the Hai-Yung family hair-raising on Dame Street, and Herbert had his doubts. So he closed his eyes and could see for himself, their straight black hair and long narrow eyes, bouncing and spinning and contorting on wires (or each other) down the steps of City Hall, where father had broken his foot so long ago.

George brought home so much with him, had so much knowledge, that he became an endless source of information. If you wanted to know what each theatre had to offer, which picture was showing where, you could ask George. If you wondered how many down-on-their-lucks had spent the night in the Back Lane charity shelter, with war medals fastened to their tattered suits by greasy ribbons, George could tell you. He knew where the tinkers would bate the tar out of each other on Thursday afternoons. He knew when the fifty-shillings tailor took a half-holiday. And every shop on O'Connell Street, too: Elverys, Lemons, Albert Coates, the piano tuner. Where to buy poplin or Irish linen, where to buy fishheads a penny a bag. He knew that Liquafruit would cure anything with a cough in it. Or that HP sauce was the sauce for all Christmas.

There was so much to see, so much to report that for those first few autumn weeks, he hardly bothered with the essence of his errand. It hardly mattered to him, the why or what for.

Although he did love the betting shops, where old cigarette ends yielded under your feet and the phlegm stood out like cameo brooches against the sawdust's grip. And the men pronounced the horses' names arseways, which always used to make him laugh. Although, he said, you could tell just the same they knew what they were talking about. And the bookmaker climbing up on to his box to announce first the odds and then later the probable results, all proud as an undertaker in his top hat and tails, observing the formalities just as he would if he were on a racecourse. And the hush like in chapel with the occasional cough breaking through and the concentration holding heavy while the cigarette smoke swirled dizzily about.

He never bothered to look at the note slipped into his pocket, except sometimes in passing as he handed it over to the clerk, he might see a few figures, an elaborate name or two, a sum of money and signed at the bottom the unchanging line:

and kindly oblige,

O. E. Whyte.

George would then hand over the money (reserving a penny for himself as Mr Whyte had advised him to do) and then before going home would jot down the winners of previous races at other venues. He was to collect any moneys due from the previous day too, which he would have been quite pleased to do. Except there were never any. And here was the thing: George couldn't help noticing, the one unusual characteristic about this whole adventure: Mr Whyte couldn't back a winner to save his life. George couldn't understand his enthusiasm for something he seemed to be so bad at. George would never get himself into a state of excitement, for example, over Latin verbs. It just didn't make sense, this squandering of time, not to mention money.

As the weeks went by he found this bothered him more and more. He took to eavesdropping more intently in the various betting shops, listening to the old men talk and even the young men who spoke like old men anyway, and it seemed to him that it wasn't quite so much the game of chance he had always believed it to be. There seemed to be a knack. A knowledge, if you like, that could be acquired and used to assist you. So why hadn't Mr Whyte acquired it? Why did his horse seem to be the only one that never made it home? George thought he ought to be ashamed of himself. And sometimes even found himself ashamed on his behalf.

Then one day in early November, George, making his way down to Usher's Quay, felt his head rush suddenly inside. Something had changed. He wasn't quite sure what, except he felt he'd never get to the betting shop quickly enough and that there was more noise inside him than out there on the streets.

And into Buckley's then where the clerk who read his note couldn't care in the least if he should be at school or delivering milk or delivering babies up in the Coombe, for that matter. Or if his mother knew he was there or who Osmond Whyte was to him. And who always gave him a bullseye to suck while he waited around. Although he had never uttered a word to George, never: not a please, not a thank you, not a dickie bird.

And up to the counter waiting his turn, and a man behind him saying, 'There ye are, son,' and George replying, as was his custom to do, 'Here I am, mister.' The man at the counter held out his hand for the note with Mr Whyte's instructions on and George stood for a minute and then turned away. He found himself walking back to the window where the newspaper sheets hung like curtains and he looked down the names and he knew, he just knew. He took the money Mr Whyte had given him and separating it from the note, handed it over to the man behind the counter (this time he included the penny he was to keep for himself) and he said, 'Mother's Pride, please.' And the man with the bullseyes looked at him for a while until George continued 'In the . . . in the a quarter past two at Naas. Please.'

Then the man with the bullseyes popped himself one and reclining it to the side of his face like a boil on a bum, spoke his first words to George: 'Do you want to get a docket?' And George said, 'A docket? Oh yes. A docket,' and went back over to the shelf at the side. He stood himself beside a tram conductor with a shiny new face until the conductor stopped and looked at him saying, 'I suppose you're lookin' for a tip?' and George said, 'Oh no thanks, I only want to know how you . . . '

The tram conductor showed him and George said, 'Thanks, mister,' and went back with the docket and laid it on the counter. And waited.

He got no bullseye that day, and the clerk would never offer him one again. He had risked his precious penny and Mr Whyte's strap searing his backside should his own choice come in. But it was George's horse that came home first. He heard its name called out and they all turned to look at him. 'Ten-to-one,' he heard them mutter to each other as the door shut fast behind him.

He ran all the way back up the quay and all the way straight past Father's pub, forgetting to care in the least if he was caught or if he was spotted. He sprinted St Michael's Hill and down by Werburgh chapel and past St. Patrick's Park. But this time he noticed nothing. This time the streets were empty. Just a stream of colours running past his head, brown and grey and a bit of green as well. As if he were running through an empty field. Not a thing could he remember until he reached the school yard and saw the classroom window. Where Mr Whyte was waiting.

And George to this day couldn't tell how he had known it was that particular horse, whether he had guessed, or whether he had heard the name mentioned before, perhaps in Moore's shop on Bachelor's Walk. Or maybe even in Coffey's on Charlotte Street, where they argued the toss more than most. Or how he knew the horse had the right weight and the right staying power. He said it just happened.

And that was how George discovered what made his blood spice up with fear and joy. Like learning to swim, he said it was, thinking you'd be forever slapping at the water, satisfied enough just to keep your head above it, when suddenly without warning you found yourself skimming through it, in a smooth Australian crawl, and you knew you could never go back to splashing again.

How Father found out nobody knew. Perhaps a chance remark in the barber's shop or in the bookies maybe. Or perhaps down through his window at the top of The Irish House, he spotted one day, George hurrying along the quay, and recognised in his purposeful gait a kindred spirit.

However, one thing was suddenly clear, George's life would never be his own again. George's life belonged to Father. There would be no more visits to Mr Milinski's kitchen to drink thick sugary tea and hear his dirty stories, no more skits out on the street or down in Patrick's Park. And if Herbert wanted to tease a chase out of the barman in Ryan's pub, rushing through one door and out through the other, he would have to do it alone. And all these losses made the days long for Herbert but only one thing played on his mind, the knowledge that his brother would never again throw a punch in the ring of his boxing-club. From now on, any fighting would be out of necessity and not out of pleasure. Such things were left behind now. Such things were just bits of what made up George's past. Now that he was Father's property.

And at first George had fought this sudden attention, whingeing if he had to go to a race meeting and grudgingly answering Father's endless stream of questions. And nobody could say for certain when their relationship began to change, if not exactly into a friendship, then into a need for each other's company.

So they moved in a brace, father and son, heads bent over the table together or disappearing out the yard gate, into the winter air, while Herbert watched after them, wondering what time the last race would be run and calculating in his head how long their homeward journey might take.

ELEVEN

Maude usually invited Mr Hansley from the Guaranty Trust Company of New York to dinner in the first week after Christmas. The trust had its headquarters at 140 Broadway and branch offices in London, Paris, Brussels, Liverpool, Havre and Antwerp. She was the terminus of Hansley's European tour and her dinner served as a sort of farewell and good riddance, to send him safely back across the Atlantic sea and out of her hair. As he seemingly 'popped over' especially to see her, and, as he liked to remind her, went to endless trouble on her behalf (indeed, she could hardly deny, in the last ten years he had managed to make a considerable amount of money for her) inviting him to her home was the least she could do. Or at any rate, there didn't seem to be a polite way of avoiding it.

And managing to fit him in before the busy dance season really got under way, she always saw to it that dinner was particularly good so that Henry might be persuaded, if she promised to excuse him early enough, to join them. As Henry loathed Americans almost as much as he loathed financial discourse, this was rather a feat on her behalf and she sometimes wondered if she held this dinner just to see if, after all this time, she could still charm Henry into contradicting his pleasure, which was not an option he would favour in the normal course of events.

Henry was right, of course. Mr Hansley, the 'investment man', was a monumental bore when on the subject of what she ought and ought not to do with her investments for the coming year. Indeed despite her annual resolve to defy and countermand him, he always managed to browbeat her into submission, so that before she knew where she was she would find herself agreeing with him and would see her pen skirting along the bottom lines of long sheaves of narrow paper she had scarcely had the energy to read. However, once steered away from finances to general chitchat from New York City, Mr Hansley could be quite entertaining. At least she had always found him so. Henry, however, had not. He said he was like a fat old dowager, a Rhode Island Red mother hen whose suit was only marginally louder than himself. This wasn't at all fair. Henry held the preconception that all Americans were loud and brash (he had the unfortunate tendency to judge entire nations on acquaintances made on the vaudeville stage). But Mr Hansley could hardly be accused of being loud. There was something dainty in the way he delivered his newsy little titbits and discreet disclosures on American taste, dress and manners, his quiet, respectful tone nearly driving poor Henry to distraction.

'As if anyone could possibly be interested in the slightest what the blasted Americans consider to be good taste. Talk about a contradiction in terms. And all that tittletattle. Doesn't the fool realise that for gossip to be in the slightest way effective, one should at least be acquainted with its subjects? Really, it's intolerable!'

What Henry hated most about Mr Hansley, however, was his use of the phrase, 'with all 'doo respect'. He used it either to precede the tritest of statements or as an introduction to the most arrogant, opinionated declaration imaginable, which always managed to sound like an insult, and left one with the feeling that there really was no respect 'doo' or intended in the first place.

Although Maude suspected it wasn't really the: 'With all doo respect, ma'am, may I say your flower arrangements are perfectly lovely?' that Henry found most irritating, it was more likely to be the, 'With all doo respect, sir, the age gap between yourself and your wife is considerable. In my experience this can cause a problem in the declining years. I sure hope this won't be the case with you two lovely people.'

By the time Mr Hansley had finally departed, Henry would be livid, undressing himself in a tantrum and throwing his clothes and his threats all over the bedroom floor.

'By God, I'll strangle the fool next year, I will. I'll strangle him or his fat backside will feel the print of my boot, all the way down the stairs and out the hall door. And did you see the way he was guzzling at the port? Hmm? Did you? Just because he lives in a country that is so barbaric they have to prohibit it. I'll thrash him within an inch of his pathetic little life. You see if I don't. Never. Do you hear me, Maude? Never ask me again. Or I'll not be responsible for my actions. Heed me now. This time I mean it.'

She could see Henry's point with regard to Mr Hansley; she could even laugh at it, for despite his temper Henry could really be most amusing about the whole evening and had successfully recounted it at many a subsequent dinner table.

From her own point of view, she had always felt these conversations on New York had helped her to keep, somehow, more in touch with Kate, to picture her as being part of each little scene Mr Hansley so described, painting each meticulous stroke with a detail brush, well dipped in treacle. Or maple syrup, as they would say over there.

But now there was no Kate. Now there was no reason to interest herself in social scraps from New York City. And she was finding these bleak February evenings arduous enough without having to face the ordeal of playing hostess to someone she didn't particularly care for. Mr Hansley was running a month behind schedule and she knew he must be anxious to return to New York to put into practice the instructions he had so keenly received from his European clients. And so she had come up with an excuse of sorts, on the suggestion and assistance of her solicitor, which meant this year Henry, at least, would be spared the pain of dining with him. It was a brittle enough excuse, a badly spun yarn but she just couldn't bear the thoughts of his society, of any society, now that there was this secret grief demanding to be nursed and carried about with her, a constant companion, hidden somewhere on her person or in her handbag. Keeping it always on the inside, there was nothing for her to do but live on, like an adulteress who has lost her lover or the mother of a institutionalised child who has recently passed away. Accepting no invitation, issuing none, excusing herself without an excuse meant her despondency had sometimes been taken for lack of interest or even rudeness; but she didn't care, she just didn't care.

Nor did she mind whether Mr Hansley chose to believe her or not. So long as he pretended to.

Maude tapped lightly on the inner glass pane of Findlater and Sons, solicitors. As she entered, Mr Hansley was already rising from his chair. His hand, followed firstly by his outstretched arm and secondly by himself, made toward her. Her hand responding, stretched out, so that they met half-way.

'Mrs Masterson,' he said, 'I cannot tell you what a pleasure it is to see you again.'

'Mr Hansley.'

Their hands parted company. 'I'm so sorry to hear your daughter has been unwell.'

'Thank you.'

He pulled a chair and guided it neatly towards her. Maude prepared the skirt of her coat before accepting his offer. 'I trust it's nothing . . . ?'

'Oh no. No. She is almost recovered.'

She sat down and behind her, felt him give the back of the chair an unnecessary little jolt. She steadied herself.

'I'm glad to hear it.'

With the sincerest of smiles, he took himself to the opposite side of the table and found his own chair. When he was seated she saw that he was looking intently at her; she felt she was expected to continue.

'However, we have been keeping rather quiet during her convalescence which is, as I explained in my note, the reason we haven't been doing any entertaining, I hope you don't . . . '

Under the dip of her hat, she lowered her face away from him. Pulling the gloves from her hands, she arranged them a little too fussily into her handbag. She hoped he hadn't noticed the colour rising on her cheeks. She was glad Mr Findlater was out, although he knew the reason for her lie – he helped her fabricate it, after all. She still would find the retelling of it an embarrassment in his presence.

'With all doo respect, ma'am, the lack of one of your fine dinners will do me no harm at all,' said Mr Hansley, patting his stomach reproachfully. 'No harm at all.'

He pulled a portfolio from a bundle at his side and dropped it open. 'She's with her nurse at the moment,' Maude continued.

'Is she, indeed?'

He let the flimsy sheets collide and collapse to either side until he found the pages he required: 'Ah ha.' His hand flattened them into place.

'A terribly nice girl. Her name is Lucia.'

Mr Hansley looked back up at her.

'Yes, I was saying to Mr Findlater earlier on how glad I was it's not the influenza that Mrs Masterson's little girl has caught. Now that *would* be a worry. It's taken its toll in the States, you know. Oh yes. Quite an epidemic, we've had. People dying all over the place. Like flies in the Fall.'

'Yes,' Maude said, 'yes. I've heard.' And she felt herself blush again.

Mr Hansley cracked open a silver cigarette case and said, 'I've changed from gold, you know,' as if he expected her to remember.

'You did?'

'Oh yes. Gold cigarette cases are considered *passé* now in New York, almost vulgar in fact. So I gave mine away. To my servant. Different initials of course, but what the heck? Gold is gold, just the same. You don't mind if – ?'

'Not at all. Would you mind if I – ?

'Why certainly not, Mrs Masterson. I didn't realise you smoked.'

'Oh just lately, you know. My husband isn't at all pleased.'She smiled apologetically.

He leaned towards her, his thumb jerking a flame into life, and then drew it respectfully towards her face.

She nodded her thanks.

'Modern women eh?' he winked. 'You know, it used to be quite acceptable in New York for ladies to smoke. My mother, I recall, had the occasional one, socially, of course. But now? Well now, it's really only those from the lower classes, you know.'

'Oh really?'

They blew their separate clouds into the air and each drew to hand an ashtray, a marble bowl for Mr Hansley, a cut-glass plate for Maude.

The afternoon pushed slowly along.

She listened to the noise from the street outside, increase, decrease, increase again. She watched the girls from the office across the street move busily about when a large bald man walked in through the door or visit each other's desks and chatter as soon as he walked back out again. She smoked too many cigarettes; her face felt numb.

Mr Hansley she noticed sometimes, seeing his eyes bright with enthusiasm for his subject. And sometimes she even remembered to contribute a remark or two. She could hear his words, the little jokes that punctuated them; she could see him sit back and then sit forward again as their tone dictated. She could hear him answer questions she didn't always remember asking.

'To answer your question, Mrs Masterson, and a very good question too, if I may say - '

She retained some of his information. She knew for example, that on 1 January, four billion dollars were distributed to owners of shares of stock in American corporations and the holders of American corporation bonds.

'Four *billion* dollars, as we speak, Mrs Masterson, are being counted by investors. Now can you imagine that?'

'Indeed, no.'

'Well, it's true, you know.'

'Oh I'm quite sure.'

She heard him speak of percentages and as he rattled them off, saw him tug at his shirt cuffs, as if, like the school cheat in the examination hall, he had tucked them up there, for his own sly use: 'Production of manufactured goods has increased by nearly 178 per cent in the past 26 years, horsepower capacity by 256 per cent.'

'Good heavens, where will it all end?'

'That's just it, Mrs Masterson. That's just what I'm trying to tell you: it *won't*.'

As if she were blind, he told her how he saw things, over and over: 'The way I see it ma'am, there are three steps when it comes to prosperity, Step 1: make money. Step 2: save it. Step 3: invest it wisely. In order to do that, ma'am, you must take the best advice possible. And that is where I come in.'

Towards the end of the proceedings she forced herself out of inertia to honour the promise she had made to herself following last year's meeting.

'I'm very happy with your advice, Mr Hansley, indeed I am. But you know, this year, I have a feeling – no not exactly a feeling – what I mean is, although I by no means want to relinquish my American interests, I would very much like to invest something in the Irish stock market. After all, we have a new country here and I have lived here all my life and besides, I am Ir – '

'The Irish stock market?' Mr Hansley blinked and looked away as though he were trying not to show his hurt. After a moment he returned his attention to her.

'You do mean, the . . . *Irish* Stock Market?'

'Well, yes.'

'I see. Is this the reason you wish to retain some of your funds this year? Your note said – and I have it here in front of me – you would like to cash in one thousand dollars worth of your securities. If you don't mind my asking?'

'Oh no. No. That's, that's another matter. I just want to increase my flow. I mean, I've had some unexpected expenses recently.'

'Of course, that's your own affair.'

'Of course.'

There was a long silence before he resumed. 'Mrs Masterson,' he said at last, 'your late husband, if I may say it, was a very astute man. A very a-stute man. Would you agree with me there, ma'am?'

'Yes. Mr Hansley. Yes I would.'

'Well, I will just ask you, with all doo respect, to think of the growth industry in the United States during the past thirty years.'

He paused and Maude realised he meant her to think of it now. She tried to make her eyes look busy.

'Yes, Mr Hansley?'

'Is there any reason to suppose the country will go otherwise than forward during the years ahead?'

'Well, no. I suppose.'

'Well, there now.'

He patted the desktop and his laugh was tolerant.

'By all means, have a little interest in the Irish stock market. I'll give you the name of a good local man – but for fun, I would respectfully suggest. After all your husband, your late husband, meant for you to be looked after. And your daughter? Well, we've got to think of that fine little girl. You have her future to consider. Have you not?'

'I have a lot of futures to consider,' she muttered.

'I beg your pardon, ma'am?'

'Nothing, Mr Hansley.'

He nodded, pulled another cigarette from the case to his mouth and then slid a sheaf of papers across the desk to her. He passed her a gold speckled pen.

She watched her signature take shape beneath the curl of her hand. She turned a page and watched it again. She saw Mr Hansley's finger alight on the page before her, like a fat white fly, landing on a dotted line she had overlooked. She hesitated and then signed again.

'Are you sure I can't take you out to tea? A drink? Or something?'

'I'm afraid I have another appointment. Thank you all the same.'

She rose to go. 'Oh before you go, I brought you this little gift from Antwerp, I do hope you like it.'

'Why, thank you, Mr Hansley, how kind.'

'Compliments of the season and all that. A little late, but there you are.'

Maude took the box and held it in her hand. Perfume again, no doubt. Just like every year. The same bottled scent for each of his female clients. She wondered what he bought for the men?

'Now you keep that little Lucia warm and fat. She'll be on her feet in no time.'

'Patrice.'

'I beg your pardon, ma'am?'

'Her name is Patrice.'

'Oh.'

'Well, goodbye, Mr Hansley.'

'Until next year, Mrs Masterson. I'll be in touch.'

He stood up but didn't leave his place to see her to the door. Nor did he offer her his hand. They were, after all, both now occupied, shuffling and rearranging the documents she had just signed into neat little bundles across the top of Mr Findlater's desk.

When she came out onto the street, she thought the clock at Weirs must be slow and checked her own watch bracelet. No. It was almost four o'clock. She had a few minutes yet. Could she really have been in there for only an hour? She walked up Grafton Street and came to the Green. So shaded inside there under the arch. So quiet. A nice bench there would be and a twilight lake with ducks glazing over their own serene shadows. She looked back down Grafton Street with its shopfront windows beginning to take light. All those windows. All those people. She remembered then what was ahead of her and nervously searched through the crowd for a familiar shape; there wasn't one. There wasn't even a face she could pick out of all the movement. Just hats and coats, front and back, flickering over a street that was getting ready for its night shift. It would be dark soon. They would be closing the gates of the Green. She would have to hurry. She turned her back then and looking left and right, tucked her handbag to her chest and hurried across the road into St Stephen's Green.

On a quiet bench, in a dusky light, with modest winter foliage shy against the darkening sky, she sits. An occasional bicycle cutting through, an occasional workman homeward bound. Or a messenger boy trying to make up time, puffing from behind a basket as high as himself. The inquisitive lights from the Shelbourne Hotel peering over the treetops and Mr Hansley's gift sitting like a kitten on her lap. Its crisp coloured paper and wide stiff bow. She lifts it for a moment and then lays it by her side. She lifts it again and this time slides it under the bench, where she will be sure to forget it.

In the distance, she sees the man approach. Coming from the left across the expanse of grass. She turns her head away to the right. There is the bridge, solid and bare, shrugging in the centre up towards the half-light. The outline of two women intrude suddenly on to it, rising over its bump and diminishing then as they descend it. Their step quickens as they make for the flat ground. She watches them walk away from her.

From the corner of her eye, she sees his frame grow larger, stronger. And his leg lifts to take him over the iron scalloped border and on to the pathway. She keeps her head turned towards the women. They are, arm to arm, linked to each other, heads bobbing in conversation, sisters. They look like sisters. They have the same walk, the same carriage. One does the laughing, the other the talking. Did they have any idea, any idea at all, of how lucky they were? How unbearably lucky?

The gravel has taken his steps now so that she can hear them, coming clearly to her. Coming out of the silence, his steps. But slower too. He has slowed them down as he nears her. There is another sound clicking alongside them, the ferrule of an umbrella or the butt of a walking cane. He will be beside her soon.

She can no longer hear the women. She can barely see them now. One dim shadow they make, melting into the bushes, disappearing through a fold in the thick wall of the privet hedges on the far side of the lake. Out of sight now, they are gone.

He stands beside her for a moment before she hears him speak.

'Good evening,' he says.

Uninvited, he takes a seat beside her.

'You're looking well,' he says. 'As beautiful as ever.'

'What do you want?'

'Only what is mine, by right.'

'You have no right.'

'Ahh, but you know that's not true.'

'Morally, you have no – '

'Morally? Are you trying to make me laugh?'

'Say what you have to say and go.'

'I have suffered,' he says. 'I deserve something.'

'Money, you mean?'

'Yes, unless you can think of anything else. Some other way to compensate me.'

He lays his hand on her shoulder. 'I hold all the cards, you see. And you know, I just can't seem to make up my mind. Can't quite decide just exactly what it is I want.'

'Take your hand off me; take it away.'

He slides his hand downwards to her breast and leaves it there a moment. 'I hold all the cards,' he says again. 'You have no choice but to give me what I want.' She reaches for his wrist and pulls his hand away from her.

'You have no choice,' he whispers, leaning towards her ear. 'You have *no* choice.'

She feels his breath rub itself against her neck.

'Have you no decency,' she asks him, 'no decency at all?'

'No.' He laughs suddenly as if her question has surprised him.

He caresses the gravel with the tip of his umbrella, spreading it gently into a circle until there is a bald patch among the stones.

'Now let us examine these cards,' he says. 'All the cards. Your sister was a bigamist. The Jewman too.'

'Samuel, you mean?'

'The Jewman,' he corrects her before continuing. 'I would not hesitate to expose him, to prosecute if needs be. I feel it would be my duty.'

'But what about her children?'

'What about them? They would learn to live with it. They seem sturdy enough to me.'

'What do you mean "to you"?'

'Oh, I've seen them. I see them quite a lot, you know. I do hope you lock up the silver with that pair in your house. They say kleptomania runs through the blood, which is another card in my favour. And, besides, I feel they should be told. Told all about their mother. That she was a thief. A bigamist *and* a thief. Oh, Maude, I cannot tell you what a burden it has been to carry all this knowledge about with me, all these years. It would really be quite a relief to be rid of it all. Quite a relief.'

He looks down at her and grips softly the nub of her knee. 'But I do hope you don't feel I've neglected you, my dear. That I have been ignoring you, your little secrets. Because if you do, let me assure you, I have a place right here in my heart for them. That child of yours, for example, well, what can I say, except how unlike Pat Cleary she is – how remarkably unlike . . .

'I don't know what you mean.'

'Oh come, my dear; of course you do; of course you do.'

She crosses her legs to stop them from shaking. She slots her hands between her knees. She holds herself down as best she can but the shaking is still there; it will not stop. It is too strong for her. It will not allow her to run away before the gates are closed. And where is the keeper's whistle? she wonders, where is the keeper's uniform, telling them it's time to go. The gates will be locked. The gates will be locked.

'Maude?' she hears him speak again.

She makes no reply.

'Maude,' he repeats, this time his voice a little firmer. 'Or do I mean Mrs Masterson?'

Now at last she turns to look at him. 'Yes, Mr Pakenham,' she answers him. 'Mrs Masterson is what you mean.'

TWELVE

When Bart unbolted the front door the Dancer was already standing there, cats and dogs and him soaked to the skin. He had his back to Bart, leaning against the wall and looking out at the morning traffic or something over there on the far side of the river. His collar was up and scuffed to his ears and he had no hat on his head. He must have left it down somewhere or had it stolen on him again.

'What in the name of – ? You're like a drownded – '

Nervous Bart stepped outside and glanced sideways up the quay. 'Have you been here long?' he asked.

The Dancer shrugged.

'The bossman'll be in any minute. We're not open for nearly another hour. You know what he's like.'

Bart picked up the rain-sprayed milk bottles. He swiped water streels down the neck and off the torso of each one and then gave them a final drying rub on the side of his apron before snuggling one under each arm. The other two bottles he collared between his forefingers and thumbs. 'A great idea, this bottled milk,' he said, 'd'you not think?' He stepped back into the doorway and waited until his friend turned around. Shook-looking he was, the colour of the grey sky behind him and the grey rain squirting out of it. 'Come on,' he said resignedly, 'A quick one, mind you. And *one*. I have to clean the front bar yet.'

And so the Dancer followed the barman, slipping behind his

jaunty steps and taking their lead into the gloom of the unlit room. 'Can't you pull open the shutters?' he asked, noticing suddenly the shapes of bar furniture around him. He had the feeling they were men, silent men, seated at tables and along the bar, their eyes peering at him. And he was frightened by the fact that he knew the room was empty, frightened even more by the endless possibilities of a wayward mind in a darkened room.

'Hold on,' Bart said, 'Just stop right where you are. Now don't budge.'

Bart laid the milk bottles down on the counter and came back for the Dancer. He guided him by the elbow and the Dancer followed until he felt a tall stool block his way. Picking his spot then with his hand on its seat while the wet from his shoes mulched the sawdust on the floor beneath his feet, he waited for Bart to turn on the lights and extinguish the crowd of staring drinkers. The smell of polish from the back bar flew aggressively up his nose. He preferred to swallow it down than risk a cough.

'Hurry it up, Bart, would you?'

'Christ, you must be in a bad way.'

Bart pulled up the hatch at the counter and stooped himself down and under it. On the other side he sprang back up and made his way to the light-switch panel where he played with nipples one by one, until he had just enough electric light to see by. He pulled a glass from the line behind him and from an undershelf a bottle of whiskey. He looked at the Dancer's face and changed his mind. He put the glass back into place and this time reached for a cup, one with a good strong handle on it. He filled the cup half-way and slid it across the counter. 'Now,' he said, 'Get that into you.'

The Dancer looked at the cup and shoved his hands down into his pockets. 'Go on,' Bart urged him. 'You look as if you could do with it.' The Dancer took his hands out of his pockets and laid them on the counter. Again, he looked at Bart.

'What's wrong with you – ?' Bart began and then stopped, finally realising that the delay was due to his presence. The man wanted privacy. 'I'll be back in a minute,' he said.

He went into the kitchen and over to the door. Up on his toes he peered at the yard outside. No sign of him yet, the bockidy-arsed oul bastard. If he caught a customer before opening on the premises, there'd be blue murder. The sack too, most probably. The sack. A man getting sacked once in his lifetime was one thing. But twice? He'd have to shift the Dancer before the boss came back, that much was certain. And no use waiting till he heard the car pull up outside either. A last-minute runner would clearly be out of the question, the condition he was in.

In the silence of the house, Bart heard easily the sound of the cup meeting the counter. He must be finished; he'd hardly have left it out of his hand with as much as a drop left. Probably had trouble enough lifting it in the first place. Bart hurried back in, adopting his barman's whistle by way of a warning.

'Feeling better now?' he asked in a cheery sort of 'Here's your hat now what's your hurry' tone.

The Dancer looked slowly up at him.

'Ah Jaysus,' Bart began. 'You can't be serious. I'll be out on me ear.'

But he took the cup anyway and filled it again. He plucked the cloth from the side of his apron and mopped up from the counter the drops of whiskey which had spilled the first time around.

'I should get you one with two handles on it,' he said.

He was tempted to reach over and mop up the drops that had dribbled onto the Dancer's coat too. But he didn't like to reveal he had noticed those.

The Dancer struggled with the cup for a moment and then caught it with his lip. He kept it there until it was drained and pushed it back across the table. 'I'll be back in a minute,' he said.

Bart watched him hurry towards the door of the gents lavatory and shook his head gently. When the long dry sounds of keck and retch came out into the bar he held on to his own stomach. 'Oh God,' he muttered to himself, 'I'm not able for it.'

He looked up at the clock. This could go on all morning. He'd seen it before, many a time. Thinking they'd never get it into themselves quick enough, to hawk it all back up again. How the hell was he ever going to get rid of him now? A Baby Power. That's what he'd do: see if he could send him off with a Baby Power. For a half an hour or so, or until opening time at least. But then supposing he *did* come back at opening time and the matter of his slate still to be settled? And he'd assured the boss it would be cleared up as soon as the Dancer came in. Had even made an excuse up on his behalf about a race meeting over in England. But he was skint. Bart knew it from the empty envelope inside the black box that was supposed to hold his racing kitty. Oh, he'd hardly put the hammer on me again? Nellie'll have me guts –

The door opened again and the Dancer walked slowly through.

Bart put the Baby Power on the counter and looked at him sadly.

'Why do you do it to yourself?' he asked.

'Because I like it.'

He grinned at Bart and reached into his inside pocket. 'I've got something for you. A letter.'

'For me? What kind of a letter?'

Bart took the envelope into his hand and examined it. 'I don't know anybody in Liverpool,' he said.

'You do now.'

'Why did it go to your address?'

'Open it and see.'

The Dancer picked up the Baby Power and edged it down carefully into his pocket. 'Thanks, Bart,' he said, 'I'll see you later.'

He walked out the back way, through the bar and into kitchen.

'Here. Where do you think you're goin'?' Bart called out after him.

'It's all right,' he shouted back, 'I think I know the way.'

It was the afternoon by the time Bart could get away from work and the rain had stopped a long time since. The sun had dried out the ground and the walls along New Street were well aired when he rolled his bicycle around its corner. He swung his leg over the crossbar and was about to turn under the archway that led to the Dancer's yard when he stopped. There was a ladder blocking his way and an old kitchen stool with brushes stretched out across a paint-daubed rag that might have been used as a vest one time. He saw Samuel come out from under with a paint pot hanging from his hand.

'Mr Tully, sir,' he said, 'And how are you?'

Bart leaned the bicycle against the wall and pulled the clips away from his ankles. 'I don't know, Samuel,' he said. 'I just don't know.' He shook each leg out and stamped his feet on the ground.

Samuel laughed, 'Had a bit of a shock, I gather.'

'A bit of a one?'

Samuel put the pot onto the ground and took the sides of the ladder into his hands. He climbed up until he had reached the edge of the arch. 'Pass me up that pot there, Bart, like a good man.'

'This one? Right. This one.'

Bart stretched up with the pot held out to Samuel. His arms felt weak. Even his arms.

'I nearly came off the bike twice, on the way,' he said. 'I don't mind telling you, me nerves are in tatters. What am I to do, Samuel?'

'How do you mean?'

Samuel dipped the brush into the pot and it came back up thick and luscious. He scraped the excess off the side and lifted the brush to the stone wall. He carefully trawled its nib down and inside the outlines he had earlier drawn.

'I mean, what am I to do?'

'Spend it, I suppose.'

'But sure I can't spend it. It's not mine to spend.'

'She left it to you. Of course it's yours.'

'Yes. But what about *you*? What about the chislers?'

'She left them something, too. And a bit of something for the boys inside. They all have a few bob to look forward to when they come of age.'

'What about *you*, Sam?'

Samuel's feet came two rungs downwards and he pointed to a smaller brush he had left at the end of the ladder.

'I didn't want anything, Bart. She knew that.'

'But . . . but that's ridiculous. Now, Sam, if you don't mind me saying. That . . . that's just all me arse.'

Samuel laughed, 'Bart,' he said, 'I'm surprised to hear you use such language.'

'Well, I wouldn't, normally.'

Samuel took the small brush from Bart and climbed the ladder once more. He squinted one eye as the brush made a slow approach into the narrower tips of the letter W.

'Ah come on, Sam,' Bart wailed up at him from the street below. 'Will you at least talk to me, for the love of Jaysus.'

'Jaysus?' joked Samuel. 'Who's he?'

He listened to the sounds of distress coming softly from Bart below. Tuts and pants and sharp little sighs. It was spoiling his concentration.

'Ah relax, Bart, would you? You should be delighted with yourself.'

'Relax? Relax? I've had the scutters all morning. I've never been in such a state in all me – Could hardly change the barrels. I'll get the sack, that's what'll happen to me.'

'Sure you hardly need to worry about that now,' Samuel smiled.

'It's not funny. It's not – '

Samuel sighed and came back down. He laid the brushes across the top of the paint pot and lifted it over to the wall at the side. He cleared the stool and sat himself down. Out of his pocket he pulled his tobacco pouch. His fingertips sifted and rolled until a cigarette appeared in his hand. He held it out to Bart.

Bart shook his head. 'No. No. I won't. Me stomach. I'd be sick. I couldn't.'

Samuel nodded and took the cigarette himself, lit it and sat back against the wall, plucking tobacco fibres away from his tongue.

'Now listen to me, Bart,' he began, but stopped then to pull on the cigarette again.

'Ah I'm listening, I'm listening.'

'She wanted you to have that money. I never wanted her for her money when she was alive. I don't want it now. That was always understood between us. She had enough of that from that other bastard. To be honest, I didn't even know she'd made a will. I didn't think anyone would ever benefit from it. But I'm glad you have it, really I am. I wish you all the best with it.'

'Ah, but why me?'

'Now, I think you know the answer to that yourself.'

'All right, I do. But there was no need for that much. It doesn't deserve that much. I left her alone with a snuff box and she fecked it; I'm not saying she didn't. But it wasn't worth *that*.'

'It cost you your job.'

Bart nodded painfully. It looked like he was ready to burst into tears.

'And you could have described her more fully to the police. Could have got her caught if you wanted.'

'Well . . . '

'Look, Bart, stealing was a weakness of hers at one time. Something she used to do . . . to . . . to console herself, I suppose. Once we got to America that all stopped. But she never stopped feeling ashamed of it. Accept the money and she's clear. Free of it. That's how I see it, anyway. That's probably how she saw it, too.'

Bart shifted his feet uncomfortably about; he furrowed his forehead with his fingertips. 'But – ' he began.

'That's an end to it, Bart.'

Bart looked up at the arch.

'What are you doing?' he asked.

'Painting the name of our new business over the premises.'

'You're startin' a business?'

'That's right.'

'With . . . with himself?'

'With himself.'

'Well, all as I have to say to that is the best of luck to you and don't forget to tie your bootlace,' Samuel laughed. 'He's not the worst, not a bad oul skin, really.'

'Ah sure I know that, Samuel. I *know* that.'

'Anyway, we'll see.'

Samuel stood up. 'I've taken most of his money from him. He won't be doing much drinking.'

Bart pursed his lips. 'That's what you think.'

Samuel made for the ladder again, 'Well congratulations anyway, Bart, and I mean it. I hope you believe that.'

'Thanks very much.'

'What'll you do with it?'

'Do with it? I'll have to explain it to Nellie first.'

'Don't you worry your head about Nellie. She'll get used to the idea quick enough. Why don't you buy yourself a little pub? You could make a go of that.'

Bart laughed dismissively. 'I'd better go inside and see Greta first.'

Samuel looked down at him. 'I wouldn't do that just now, Bart. I don't think she'll be exactly thrilled to see you, if you know what I mean.'

'That bad?'

'Worse. We had to put her to bed.'

Bart folded the ends of his trousers and clipped them into his ankle. He pulled the bicycle towards him.

'I'll come back, will I, when things have cooled down?'

'Yes,' Samuel said. 'You do that. But Bart . . . '

'Yes?'

'Do me a favour and don't give him any money. Give Greta a few bob if you like, but not him?'

'Ah, Samuel, I mean to say, give him his bread and his cheese. He was always good to me.'

'I understand that.'

'But he's bust.'

'And that's the way I want him to stay. For the moment anyway or at least until he starts to get his mind right.'

Bart lingered for a while, watching Samuel fatten the letters with crimson paint. 'What sort of business is it?' he asked.

'Why, motors, Bart,' Samuel answered him, 'What else?'

Bart settled the bicycle under him then and guided it on to the road.

'Where are you off to now?' Samuel asked him.

'I haven't a clue, Samuel,' he replied. 'I haven't a fuckin' clue.'

IV

BROOKLYN HEIGHTS: 1928

Thirteen

It was some sort of an excursion they were on, seated on top of a motor bus, the old-fashioned type like Papa used to have, with the roof rolled back and the sky close enough to scrape. Right up at the front they were, with everyone behind them in the best of spirits, going 'Oooh and ahhh,' and clapping whenever another spectacle occurred. Kate joined in each time, gasping and applauding and gasping again. And although the feeling of astonishment stayed with her throughout, she couldn't seem to remember just what it was that she had found so spectacular not a moment since. The instant it was over, it was forgotten, until the next one occurred and she heard herself cry out again.

For the past few minutes things appeared to have quietened down. She could hear the other passengers fidget with sweet papers and bottles, and talk quietly amongst themselves. One or two got up to stretch their legs, walking softly up the aisle as though afraid their feet might burst through the floor.

Kate looked down. The road was narrow, the flatlands it cut through uneventful, except for the grass growth to either side, blonde and emerald green rolling away in tufts, whispering gently to each other on the breeze. There was nothing to see for miles and miles. Kate sat back and relaxed. 'Isn't this fun?' She smiled at Samuel and leaning her head against his shoulder closed her eyes to rest for a while.

She felt Samuel nudge her, 'A drink?' he said. 'Would you like a drink?'

'Oh yes, it's so warm. Dry as sand I am. Dry as dust.' But after several grabs and sways, she still couldn't seem to get the glass to stay steady in her hand. 'The road is very bumpy here,' she laughed. Samuel held his hand behind her head and lifted the glass to her lips and she wrapped her fingers around his wrist until she could feel the water soothe and quench her thirst.

'Don't you find it bumpy?'

'Yes,' he said, 'It's a bumpy road.'

Samuel took the glass back and Kate looked ahead. She could see the landscape was beginning to change. The grass had all but disappeared and in its place there was something growing. What now, she wondered. What would they have come up with now?

They were clutches of something, dark in colour and flecked with occasional green. She raised herself a little in her seat and leaned down over the front window, straining her eyes to see. What were they? Mushrooms? Some sort of stones? Or flowers maybe? Were they flowers?

But on closer inspection she recognised them as tiny trees, not saplings. She could see now they were fully and perfectly formed – but trees. Real trees. Whatever would they think of next? How could they have managed to grow them that small?

'Look, Samuel,' she said, 'up ahead, tiny trees. Aren't they realistic? It's like a midget forest.'

Samuel put his arms around her. He was trying to hold her. But she didn't want to be hugged. She wanted to stand, to stand up and see the trees. She could feel his face against her neck, 'Not now, Samuel. Not in front of all these strangers. And anyway I want to see them. I want to look at the little trees.'

The bus slowed up alongside them and Kate bent herself over the window to get a better view.

'Careful there,' Samuel warned.

She began pointing down. 'Look,' she said, 'Those are Gravenstein, and there, that's the wealthy Baldwin. And over there, the winter banana and yellow transparent apple tree. And look, real apples on the branches. The size of peas they must be. And yes, that's the Italian prune and that one there, that one there must be the Bing cherry tree.'

Samuel laughed. 'I didn't know you knew so much about trees.'

'No,' she said, puzzled, 'No, neither did I.'

The bus staggered and Kate felt herself drop back into her seat and roll over to one side. Her eyes fell on the window panes across the aisle, which seemed to be decorated with a light trim of snow. But how could that be, when it was so warm? So summertime warm? Was it another attraction? A novelty perhaps?

And what strange windowpanes for a motorbus anyway. Like house windows, more like. A bedroom. They were just like the windows of her bedroom. And there was Adeline standing in front of them. Adeline, black as molasses. 'You're black as molasses there, with that frosty window behind you.'

'That I am,' Adeline smiled. 'That I am.'

'I can't stop now. I'm on a journey, an excursion. With Samuel.'

'Of course you are, honey.'

'I'll tell you all about later, shall I?'

'Yes, you do that.'

'Adeline? Where did you think they got snow at this time of the year?' But the bus took off again before she could hear Adeline's reply.

They turned on to a left bend in the road and she reached for Samuel's hand. 'Oh my God, Samuel – ' and she could feel her voice fill up with tears. The beauty of it. The strange beauty. 'How could they do that?'

'I don't know,' he said, 'I just can't imagine.'

There was a structure built across the horizon, like a series of caves reaching high and solid. There were huge loops made throughout in even rows, gaps that looked as if they had been melted into the great facade. In each one there was a statue of a man or a woman but so enormous. How could the sculptors have managed to attain such a perfect shape? They must have had to climb all over them like ants. It must have taken them years and years . . . Smooth and white and reclining to one side, they had their backs to the motorbus, as though they were looking out over something. A thick plumage of wings grew in a pair from each curved back. But they seemed to be made of something else, not stone or porcelain. Not any sort of alabaster, but actual plumage. Thick wads of natural feather. Kate thought she had never seen anything so clever. Down on the roadside, a man was standing looking up at the huge display. A normal sized man, tall but not unnaturally so, he had long blue-grey hair that grew well down his back and he wore a winter coat falling down to his ankles. How could he? In this heat? The poor man must be ready to drop. He raised his hand and pointed up. Look, his finger pointed. Now look. He turned his hand gracefully, elaborately slow, and his fingers were long and quite beautiful too. Round and round he danced them above his head, pausing now and then to stretch and freeze his fingers for a moment before continuing again. It was as if his hand were a dove. And yet, when he raised it higher towards the statues, it seemed to lack any significance. Against their enormity, it looked like nothing, hardly more than a fluttering speck of dust. The man looked up at her and he bowed his head slowly. Look – his eyes asked hers – why don't you look?

'Look,' she repeated to Samuel. 'Look. They're . . . they're alive. They're actually alive.'

The statues had begun to move. And now they were not statues at all. Now they were men and women, naked and smooth. Giants resting in the afternoon heat. They turned around, one by one and gave a careless wave and a soft hurried smile before returning to their view. And then they were still again. The merest flounce on a wing as it turned away with them was the only movement now.

'Alive. Samuel. Alive. Oh it must be some sort of a mechanical trick, Samuel. It's like Steeplechase Park without the crowds, without the noise. What a shame we didn't bring the children. Could you imagine their delight, they would just love to have . . . ' The motorbus stopped then and she rocked a little with it before turning to see Adeline smiling again. 'You should have seen them, Adie. Like angels, they were but so big. So unbelievably big. How I wish the children had been with us. Such a sight, I never did. Are you listening to me, Adeline? Can you hear me, Adeline? Can you hear me?'

'I can hear you. You're shouting. You should try to rest now. Stop that shouting.'

'Oh but how can I help it, Adeline? How can I?'

There was a sudden lurch and they were off again. The bus seemed to rear up before careering off downhill, picking up speed as it moved. They drove on but Kate wanted to look back, to look back at the statues. She turned around and could see them now from the other side of the caves. And alive again, they were laughing at her and shooing her on playfully with their huge hands. They were moving so slowly and the bus was going so very quickly, too quickly, she felt.

'Samuel,' she began, 'we're going far too quickly. There'll be an accident if the driver doesn't . . . '

She turned to him, clinging to his arm. 'Why are we going so quickly? Tell him to stop, can't you? Tell him to stop.'

There was the sea. It was the sea the creatures had been looking down at, the sea they had been watching over all the time. The motorbus was going faster now. Faster and faster towards the sea. A grey troubled sea. Just like it had always been. And cold, would it not be too cold? 'Oh Samuel, I'm afraid now. Are we? Are we going in?'

'It's part of the excursion,' he said. 'Don't worry.'

She squeezed tighter on his arm and said, 'Oh Samuel, I'm afraid now.'

But it wasn't all true, a little part of her was thrilled too, like on Coney Island when you scream with terror and delight all mixed up. You want it to stop but you can't bear it to stop. You want it, she heard herself cry out. They were going in.

'I'll close my eyes. Tell me when we go under; tell me if there's anything awful. I'm not going to look. I'm not. I'm not. Oh Samuel.'

They pierced the skin of the sea. The glimpse she got of it before she closed her eyes showed it puckered and . . . aged since she saw it last. Aged.

They moved down but now the speed had gone. And all was slow again. Slow, down and down. Moving so slowly, as the giants' hands had done. Samuel's fingers slipping a little away from hers now that they were wet. But it was so easy to breathe now and not cold at all. And she could hear herself whisper to him, 'Is it all right? Is it all right? Can I open my eyes now? Samuel? What will it be like if I open my eyes?'

'It will be beautiful,' he said. She opened her eyes and it was.

It's the small things that are precious, the smell of onions on my hands, the stroll down Montague Street with a shopping bag fat at my side. Tomay toes, sweet potatoes, honeycured ham. The sugar-coated chruscik *cookies I have bought from Mr Koskta's shop, I will leave at the top, so that when I turn into Hicks Street I can take a nibble, feeling them crunch and melt into a sweetness that in all this time has never lost its strangeness.*

You cannot know what a pleasure it is for me to prepare a meal, to sweep a floor or to spread a counterpane over the bed where we have been together the night before, Samuel and I. And later then to hear him whistle on the stairs, letting me know he is home with his news of the other world across the East River or further out into the farther reaches of this Long Island.

When the children are asleep we sit and talk, late into the night. There is always so much to say, some change since last he has been to a place, some new event occurring or threatening to occur. Always something. I have my own tales too, from the kindergarten on Joralemon Street where I work five mornings a week: who it was I met that day, in which shop, on which street. And there are other things besides, our life together, our friends, the children. There is always some new plan to be discussed.

I like the sound of my own voice now. I like to hear it improve with time, with practice. My harelip presents a challenge to me now instead of a shame. I can even say it now: 'Harelip.' I can even write it down without feeling any pain. I have taken speech classes in the past; some day perhaps, I may take surgery. That is what is so great about these Americans; no matter how bad something may seem, they will always find some way to improve it. They know how to make the best of the worst, they know how to face it.

In the mornings when he takes me tea, I wait for him to go out and I cross to the window. I look down on the recession of trees on my street, on Willow Street and behind that again on Columbia Heights. Across the brownstone houses, tall and terracotta coloured, and the rooftops rising and dipping, each to its own design. And it all reminds me of a giant Italian garden, russet-coloured earthenware with the green protruding, wherever it can find a space to grow. I watch the heads of the longshoremen and the skip and hop of school children making their along the bluestone pavement below. And I think to myself. I am happy. I am happy. I am . . . happy.

There is a view of Manhattan across the river and people rave about it at sunrise, at sunset, at night when the lights pop and wobble on the water. There is a huge bridge that connects us to that world over there. It is longer than you could ever believe possible. It is like some great creature that has surfaced from the sea, its carcass like an untiled roof from head to toe, its spine playing host to an endless python of crawling automobiles. And along its deck, pedestrians like so many insects pick their way across. I cross it, too, from time to time and feel Manhattan scream and laugh in my face. It is funny and it is frightening. It is like being a small child at a carnival, some vast distorted playground only bearable if a trusted grown-up is at hand, into whose coat you can bury your face from time to time, when being overwhelmed loses its pleasure.

I cross back again, glad to be home amongst the alianthus trees and the squirrels that run at your feet come the fall. Sometimes I think I have already died. In that long narrow room suspended above the North Circular Road. I cannot remember the downstairs rooms, you see, or the staircase that connects it to the bottom floor. In my mind it will always be midair, a bird that is unable to land. And there I am with the closed lids of all those windows around me. Those windows I have blackened against the world. And I have starved myself to death, as I had meant to do all that time ago, when I was besotted with unhappiness and shame. Beneath my bed there is a box, full of trinkets I have stolen, symbols of other people's happiness, other people's lives. My breath is almost done when a whisper comes through the keyhole to me. I get up and go to it and open the door. A familiar hand takes me safely through it. And I am here in Brooklyn Heights watching Samuel turn the corner into Orange Street with the smell of onions strong on my hands. And I am happy.

Kate put down the pen and looked up at the window. It was snowing. The first this season. Always so special, that first wondrous fall.

'Adie,' she called out, 'come quickly; it's snowing.'

From the kitchen she could hear Adeline complain to herself.

'Snowing! Well, Lord, but that's all I need, and me with no galoshes, no weatherproofs. I'll get d'influenza next. That's what's gonna happen. Next me.' Kate smiled to herself and called out again, 'Do you know what I love about this country, Adeline? Do you?'

Adeline continued to grumble quietly to herself.

'The seasons. That's what I love.'

'So you say every time another one comes around.'

'Well it's true. At least here you always know where you are. There's no apathy; never an indifferent day.'

'In the winter you freeze, in the summer you sweat. That's all I know.'

Kate picked up the pen again but Adeline walked into the room before she had time to put it to use.

'There's a protest goin' on outside Hickson's hardware,' she announced.

'What sort of a protest?'

'On account of them sellin' alcoholic appurtenance.'

'Oh Adeline, what do you mean?'

235

'You know, highball glasses, cocktail shakers, all that stuff.'

'The anti-saloon league are at it again, you mean?'

'Seems like a waste of time to me. Nobody I know pays no attention to the Volstead Act. Except maybe you and Mr Samuel. 32,000 bucketshops in Manhattan alone, I've heard it said. Like to see the mayor that can clean that up. Like to see him re-elected if he tried.'

Kate laughed and bent her head towards her letter again. But Adeline was still standing behind her. She hadn't finished yet.

'Tell the truth now, Kate. Didn't you ever?'

'Didn't I ever what, Adeline?'

'You know. Didn't you ever take just the teeniest drop? Just to keep out the cold?'

'No, Adeline, you know I did not.'

'You that against it?'

'No. I just don't break any rules, no matter how foolish they may seem. That way I don't draw any attention to myself.'

'Attention? You? Don't make me laugh.'

'Adeline, I have to finish this letter tonight. I promised Maudie we could go to Manhattan tomorrow to post it.'

'Know somethin', Kate?'

'Mmm?'

'You sure have a mind like a maze. The maziest mind I ever did meet.'

'Thank you, Adeline.'

'That were no compliment.'

I am to cook Christmas dinner for eight people this year. The children, Samuel and myself, Ida Phillips from the apartment downstairs, Mr Kennedy from the kindergarten, Miss Cummins from my Ladies Literary Club and Father Donnigan from the Church of St Charles

Borromeo, where we were married. Adeline is going on about it all being too much for me, how I'll never be able to manage on my own. All that trouble, all that preparation. But she is only raging because she won't be here. She has promised to spend Christmas with her sister out in Flatbush and will miss all the fun. Besides the flu epidemic has closed the kindergarten down and it probably won't reopen until well after the holiday, so I will have plenty of time to prepare.

I sometimes wonder what I used to do with all my time, sitting around waiting for it to pass. Waiting for other people to make decisions for me: what I should wear, what I should eat, where I should go. What an eternity it must have been, all those hours between rising and sleeping. And rising again.

On Christmas day I will serve first, minted grapefruit. Then roast turkey, mashed potatoes, giblet gravy, Brussels sprouts with chestnuts. And on the side, raw celery and cranberry jelly and white grape and almond salad. On the silver servers I bought with last month's salary, I will lay my plum pudding, already cooked and lovingly swathed in muslin, like a mummy's head now hidden in the dark and doing whatever it is that Christmas puddings do in secret, to ripen themselves for consumption. On the smaller silver salver I will offer raisins and nuts and sweet small clementine oranges. And to drink? Coffee and milk, I'm afraid. Unimaginable to you, I know, but you get used to it. And besides, having no alcohol to do it for them, people tend to come out of themselves all the sooner.

These guests are our friends in the main. We try to keep to ourselves. At least we used to in the past. But in America it is not always that easy. The Americans always seem to be ready to take a step toward you, while we, on the other hand, are more likely to be stepping back. I believe them to be the most hospitable race in the world and one is often put in mind of a small boy standing on the doorstep of newly arrived neighbours, hardly able to contain himself with excitement and blurting

237

out in all spontaneity the moment the door opens 'Hi, my name is Jimmy; wanna be best friends?'

After dinner we will exchange gifts, small and often homemade. Then we will have a singsong with Ida Phillips playing on the piano. She knows them all, from Schubert's 'Hark, Hark, The Lark' to her own particular favourite, 'Ida – Sweet As Apple Cida', raising her small hand to her bosom every time the word 'Ida' occurs and finishing with a flourish on, 'Ida, that's meeeeee'.

The 'me' lasts as long as it takes for her hands to run the keyboard at least four times. Father Donnigan plays as well, tin-pan alley mostly or else sentimental Irish airs. Last year, when it was Miss Cummins's turn to play hostess, he did a blackface sketch and danced the Charleston for us. The children are laughing about it still.

They are all quiet people, kind and unlikely to pry. We have all here, I suppose, our own past, our own secrets. But the present is what we are living through, the present is our mainstay.

'I don't have my galoshes; nobody told me it was going to turn out this way. Nobody said nothin' to me about snow.' Adeline had come back into the room and was standing now with hands on hips scolding the weather for its lack of consideration.

'Never mind. You can borrow mine.'

'Huhh. They'd hardly do my toes, never mind my feet. Fine sight I'd make.'

'Well, Samuel will drive you home then.'

'I can't go expecting Mr Samuel to take me home and him only back from work.'

'He won't mind.'

'I know he don't mind. But I do. Supposin' he leaves the automobile and walks home? He'd have to walk all the way back to the garage, take out the automobile again, drive all the way back here for me, take me all the way to my house, then take the automobile back to the garage. And then walk all the way home again. No, it wouldn't be right. Expectin' so much from a good man. A good man can get fed up with bein' good, let me tell you. Working all days working all hours. A good man deserves some consideration. That's my opinion. That's what I say.'

Adeline's husband has run off on her again and she hates going home to an empty apartment. She is searching through the snow for a reason to stay. I can see her face through the window, which when happy shines like a big black moon, all dented and furrowed with worry and looking like a cushion that the cat's just stepped off. I think I'll tell her to invite her sister to spend Christmas with us. Then I will have ten people instead of eight, and one at least to help me.

Samuel bought his fourth car last month, a beautiful Oakland sedan. He has spent the last few weeks overhauling and perfecting it. And now it is – perfect. He has a new garage too, on Atlantic Avenue, with space enough for five or six cars and a glass cubicle in the corner for an office and a telephone as well. He employs three men to chauffeur his cars. And you might think he hasn't made much advancement in the past ten years, coming to America to do the job he did at home. But these are his cars and he is the one referred to as Boss. Each day for him is a whistle-stop tour of the world. He knows the Scandinavians out Bayridge way and the Germans in Yorkville too. He has been to Italy in Bensonhurst (where they have exact replicas of towns in Sicily, would you believe?) and Italy elsewhere in Greenwich Village, the Bronx and just about anywhere there are Italian families enough to make up the slightest congregation. The Poles in Humboldt Street all know him by sight and the Russian Orthodox too, from around St Stanislaus church with its five copper domes bulging from the top. He has travelled with them all, eaten with them too. He has heard all points of view (except maybe those of the impenetrable Chinese, who probably don't even divulge that kind of information to each other). From Coney Island beach to Little Shore Bay, and all the boroughs in between but Brooklyn especially, inside and out and every inch of its two-hundred-mile shoreline. And you wouldn't find a man more content in his job than Samuel is now. He wanted to employ Adeline's husband to drive the new Oakland. He even had him fitted out in a chauffeur's uniform. But he never showed for work. Not even the first day. And nobody knows where he is now. On Christmas day we will drive the new sedan to Mass. I wonder would there be room enough for Adeline and her sister? I must ask Samuel. He won't mind. But I will ask him anyway. We consult each other about everything, you see. Equal partners, that's how we work things. Equal partners, that's what we've always been. Right from the very start.

When Samuel and Kate first came to America they had between them two hundred and fifty pounds. Half of this was the sum of Samuel's savings and in 1918 made for a respectable enough amount. Of course, it could have been even more respectable but when Kate suggested they could take as much as they needed from her father's settlement, Samuel had lowered his head and said simply, 'I want us to be equal partners.' And so she transferred her funds to a firm of solicitors in Liverpool, promised herself she would never think of them again and withdrew the exact same amount as that contained within her partner's pocket. And thus equally provided for, they started off on their new life together.

They spent the voyage revising their past and by the time they reached America they were a Roman Catholic couple, engaged to be married (or already married, as the need might arise); the man a mechanic, the woman a nursery-school teacher. They booked into a small middle-class hotel off 42nd Street and looked for a way to begin.

Kate didn't love New York City, not the way Samuel seemed to do. But she didn't hate it either; she simply found it irksome. A spoilt child prone to tantrums, screeching and kicking at every corner and jolting her at the elbow every time she wanted to take the time to relish a delicate moment. A brat she had somehow been forced to take along on what was supposed to have been a romantic picnic for two. She was really interested then only in the cords and strings of her new relationship and the warm fresh feeling that it gave her.

Samuel was more practical. He knew they needed a home, they needed work, and – as he reminded her every time they lay in bed together – they needed a priest.

Every morning Samuel would go out into the city in search of work and Kate would wait for him to return. She never left the room without him, preferring instead to stay and prepare for his return. She might take a bath or fix her hair, sit by the window and glance through the newspaper or down to the street observing the great rush of America going frantically about its daily business. She liked to tidy the room then, paying particular attention to Samuel's things and taking pleasure in the accidental intimacies she might come across. The sight of his shoes next to hers by the wall, the tangle of her stocking across his coat on the chair. A strand of her hair on his pillow or the stain of pomade on hers. She liked being with him. But she also liked being apart from him and looking forward to being with him again. She liked too, those first few moments of shyness between them when he returned and later strolling through the streets on his arm to a diner he would have chosen earlier on, a dollar a plate. He was careful with their money and she liked that too, the novelty of such caution bringing her a strange sense of security. They would sit then, opposite each other, testing new food and afterwards she would watch him smoke and listen to him speak. She enjoyed every word, without paying too much attention to the content. What mattered to her most was the sound of his voice and the fact that he spoke to her. And besides she didn't mind what he worked at or where they lived. Whatever Samuel wanted was fine by her.

As the days went on and each new plan passed them by, she began to notice that Samuel was fretting. None of the jobs seemed to appeal to him. There were plenty of them and plenty of interviews but none seemed to take his fancy. And she noticed too that he appeared to have forgotten any notion of working with motor cars. It was the more elusive and rarer posts he chose to follow now, Wall Street banks, stockbrokers' offices or real estate agencies. None of the accommodation met with his approval. Either it was too expensive or if affordable seemed to be in neighbourhoods he considered to be beneath them. It surprised and even amused her to discover how fussy he was.

One morning about a fortnight after their arrival, Kate sat up in bed reading aloud from the situations-vacant column. The more immediate jobs were the more menial but she read them anyway because they sounded so unusual. 'Turkish bath attendants, cigar counterhands, pool-hall waiters, bookmaking assistants on Brighton Beach . . . '

'Is that what you want me to be?' he asked her sadly through the shaving mirror, 'A bookmaker's tout?'

'I want you to be whatever you want to be,' she paused, 'No, I want you to be what you are . . . a mechanic.'

'A driver, you mean. A servant.'

She hadn't meant to hurt him but she had. She could see it in his mouth, even from behind the curls of shaving soap and the careful cut and flick of his wrist. And she knew then he wasn't being fussy on his own account. It was because of her. He was trying to be good enough for her.

She woke in the night and Samuel was sitting by the window smoking a cigarette. The light from the street outside showed the back of his head slightly bowed and a hunch at his shoulders. He was looking at the floor.

'Aren't you coming back to bed?' she asked him. Samuel didn't answer her. And she felt then the first sudden twitch of marital discord. It was a feeling that came too close to rejection, a feeling she didn't ever want to experience again.

She knew then it was time to break out of the cocoon. Time to do what he had wanted all along: to work as equal partners.

The next morning when Samuel went out Kate searched through yesterday's newspaper. She could remember seeing an advertisement for a house in a place called Brooklyn Heights. Was it yesterday? Or the day before? She knew the house was out of their range but the description of the area had caught her fancy. Left, right, she scanned each page until she found it. She stretched across the bed and pulled the map of the city towards her. Before leaving each day Samuel would mark his destination on it with a cross, so that she could see where and how long he might be. He had gone to look at an apartment on the north of Central Park and then on to an employment agency in Madison Avenue. She searched for today's marks. Yes, she should have plenty of time. He'd hardly be back before late afternoon. She dropped the map on to the floor. All those crosses spreading across it. It was beginning to look like the plan of a cemetery.

Down in the lobby she waited for a long time before making a move. She thought about going back upstairs and forgetting the whole idea but then she remembered the smart of his silence the night before and forced herself to be brave. She peeped through the door and slowly pushed herself out on to the steps. She waited until she found a gap in the crowd into which she could insert herself. Into the fray, then, she nervously moved.

At Grand Central Station she began to relax a little. She sat on a bench and looked around her. There were whistles and flags and barrel-vaulted shells sucking trains out of the city. She was in the right place at least. Here there would be a way out. All she had to do now was find it. She looked up at an enormous timetable flicking destinations on and off the wall but her eye couldn't seem to keep up with all its activity. Where on earth could Brooklyn Heights be?

A porter was kind to her: 'You don't sound Irish,' he said.

'I am,' she insisted.

He was a fellow-countryman who had been ten years in the 'United States of America', as he, giving it full title, constantly referred to it. He seemed to want to prove this to her and so listed off its sights, its dangers and delights. He kept her talking for what seemed like a very long time, then he took her outside and introduced her to the statues over the entrance, Mercury, Hercules and Minerva. He took her back inside and walked her around the main concourse pointing out the signs of the zodiac on the ceilings. He showed her the floors and asked her to guess what they were made of.

'I have no idea,' she said.

'Go on,' he insisted. 'You'll never guess.'

'All right, I never will. You tell me then.'

'Why, Italian *bottocino* and Tennessee marble of course.'

'Of course,' she laughed.

He asked her then to guess the diameter of the station clock. After several of her suggestions had been rejected, he announced: 'Thirteen feet. Now would you credit that? That's how they build things here in the United States of America, that's how they do things: *big*.'

At last he took her to the subway and after she gave him the money he bought a ticket for her. He then helped her on to the train and told her what stop to get off at. 'More English, I would have thought,' he said ensuring that he said the last word just as the doors snapped shut and she was unable to reply.

At Clarke Street she found her feet and followed those in the know to the stairs that ascended and the daylight outside. All morning she walked through streets named after trees or fruit or one-time dignitaries who had left their mark. She passed tall brownstone houses where women congregated on the steps and took the time to say hello to her. She passed grander houses with only one bell each and hired maids fussing at door accoutrements until their brass sang out to passers-by. She took coffee in a tiny shop where the waitress stared kindly at her nose and asked, 'Does that hurt?' in a way that made Kate laugh. She came back outside and found a park with a garden inside specially designed for the blind. So she closed her eyes and pretended. And yes, it all smelled differently then.

On Sydney Street she saw an old priest standing on the steps of a church and muttering to himself, deep in conversation with some person only visible to himself. She stood at the railings and watched a small boy nervously approach him.

'Excuse me, Father, but Sister Theresa, she'd like to know if we can come over for confessionals in ten minutes.'

The priest looked at the boy for a long time and then asked him who he was.

'Why it's me, Father. Tim; you know me. I'm an altar boy.'

'Tim? I didn't recognise you. Have you got bigger?'

'No, Father.'

'Smaller, then?'

'No, Father.'

'Oh. Tell Sister . . . ?'

'Theresa, Father. Sister Theresa.'

'Yes. Well, tell her baptismals are on Sunday.'

'No, Father, confession. She wants confession.'

'Why, what has she done?'

'I dunno, Father.'

The priest raised his hands and waved the boy impatiently away. 'Confessionals are in ten minutes. Sister Theresa ought to know that by now.'

Kate smiled to herself. She had found her priest.

She moved away, her hand following the railings, touching their curls and complications until she came into Columbia Heights. She looked up at the rooftops. Some were mansard, some were curbed, others were lobbed off flat at the top. There were clouds above them and birds landing and departing at their chimney pots. She heard the whistle-boats nearby and followed their curr around to the back of the houses. There was an esplanade with benches and a parkway with a small playground. She saw New York from the other side, looking small and neat. Compact almost. The river set a distance between her and it. She found this distance pleasing. There were people strolling, some with dogs, others behind baby carriages. Some looked rich, others poor but nobody looked afraid.

She looked at the back of the houses. They had long narrow gardens and pretty painted fences. They had a view over the river and balconies to appreciate it with. Some had roof gardens too with ironwork furniture and greenery in sprigs or fat little shrubberies. On the way back down her eye was attracted by a figure in a top window. An old man, probably as old as the priest she'd seen earlier, holding a pair of field glasses up to his face. What was he looking at? The view, the river? That bridge down there? She didn't know which. But she would find out, she told herself, some day, she would.

She made her way back to Clarke Street and saw a large detached house with plenty of windows and shingled painted wood. There was a sign over the door that read, 'Vacancies' and a large black woman standing on the porch, flicking stray leaves from the end of a broom back out on to the lawn. She looked up at Kate and smiled. 'Lovely day,' she said.

'Lovely day.' Kate smiled back at her.

These few words delighted Kate: it was the first time she had ever spoken to a black person.

She found her way to the subway station and this time bought her own ticket.

When she got back to the hotel, Samuel was waiting. He jumped up from the end of the bed where he had been sitting.

'Kate? Where were you? I've been worried sick. I was just about to call the manager. You shouldn't have gone out like that all alone. I didn't know what to think. How could you, Kate?'

'I've found it, Samuel,' she said. 'I've found it.'

'Found what?'

'The place. I've found the place, the church. I've even found the priest.'

'What are you talking about?'

She dragged a suitcase from the top of the wardrobe and flung it on the bed.

'Come on, now. Quickly, we haven't got all day.'

She moved over to the drawers and began dragging clothes out and piling them into the open mouth of the suitcase.

'Kate, will you please explain.'

'I will, I will. On the way there.'

She opened the wardrobe door and began pulling clothes into her arms.

'Although Samuel . . . ' she began.

'What?'

'I'm afraid I didn't find you a job. You're going to have to do that yourself.'

We have been five years here on Orange Street. Five years come the spring. I've been looking out the window at the snow thickening outside and remembering our first days here. Our first home in Clarke Street. And then that place on Hicks Street, where we lived two years. Another year on Cranberry before we came here. This is the biggest apartment we've had so far. Two top floors. Three bedrooms, a sitting-room and a dining-room besides. A kitchen as big as any I have seen, our own bathroom. And a garret room where I can paint, when I get the time. There are other people in this house. 'Ida sweet as Apple Cida' on the first floor and in the basement three or four young women. I don't know the exact number because they all look the same. They wear short skirts and short hair and every time you pass the hallway one or the other of them (or is it the same one?) has her ear pinned to the telephone talking in the shorthand language, understandable to no one but themselves. They work in the city as stenographers. Or 'stenogs' as they say themselves. They play jazz records on their gramophone all weekend long. And when young men call to take them out, they sit in their cars and sound the horn until the door opens and down the steps then a stenog will merrily skip. Adeline prays for them, the neighbours complain about them. Samuel and I rather like them.

Some day, Samuel says we will own our house. Perhaps one of those on Columbia Heights where I saw that old man the first time I came here. I can sit in the window then, just as he used to do, and stare at the Brooklyn Bridge through my field glasses. He built it himself you know, an accident forcing him to continue from a bath chair and carry out his instructions with the aid of his binoculars and a willing wife to carry messages to and fro. And twenty years later, when I first saw him, he was still looking out. Had he, I wonder, grown senile like poor old Father Bradshaw? (It was he who married us all those years ago, bless his kind and absent mind.) Or was he just checking to see if it had all been worthwhile. I hope he found it so. He is dead now, two years ago. And I still miss him, still feel a little surprised when I pass and see an empty space, and a lace curtain settled over the spot where he once watched.

When we move to our new house, we will have a drawing-room and a vestibule and a host of other useless rooms besides. So that when I am old and bedridden I probably won't even remember what the half of them look like. But Samuel wants his own house. And whatever Samuel wants is fine by me.

I will keep, though, a soft spot always for our first home together in that rooming-house on Clarke Street. Where we shared a bathroom with countless others and always waiting for the time to be right to tiptoe to it across the corridor. And where we discovered our dear friend Adeline. I look up at that house each time I pass and there is our old window and the verandah where first I watched autumn coming over Brooklyn Heights, efficiently, keenly. Leaves swiftly falling, rufously, crimsonly clear. Never once stopping, until the job was done and the trees stripped bare. And I came to know for the first time why it was they called it the fall. And not some meaningless name like autumn.

'He's here. He's here. Mr Samuel is here. I see him talking on the street to Mr Geisson from down the block. I'll go get his supper.'

'No that's all right, Adeline; I'll do it now in a minute.'

'But you gotta finish your letter.'

'I won't be long.'

'He'll be hungry. And cold.'

'Yes I know, Adeline. I'm just . . . '

Kate looked at Adeline's large reflection through the window. 'Oh Adeline,' she said, 'I don't suppose I could ask you a favour?'

'You can ask, I suppose.'

'Would you mind staying tonight? I thought we might take a stroll after supper. You might look after the children, if you didn't mind too much.'

'No I don't mind at all. I mean, I'd be glad to oblige.'

'Oh good.'

'Supposin' he don't want to go?'

'Oh he will; he likes to stretch his legs after being cooped in a car all day.'

'You sure?'

'Yes, of course, I'm sure. I want to show him some Christmas toys for the children. We can go window-shopping.'

'For the children? In that case . . . '

'Tell you what. Why don't you go and make up a bed for yourself in Maudie's room. Before she goes to sleep?'

'A bed? Yes. Yes that's what I'll do. I might tell her a story.'

'Yes, she'll like that. Might help her to sleep. I'm sure she's far too excited about tomorrow to close her eyes.'

Samuel's whistle came up the stairs and the two women turned to watch the door open.

'Good evening, Mr Samuel.'

'Good evening, Adeline.'

'You hungry?'

'Yes. Yes I am.'

He took off his hat and looking over at Kate, brushed the snow flakes away from the brim.

'Hello, Samuel.'

'Hello.' He took a step towards her and then he stopped. 'You're looking very flushed, Kate,' he said. 'I hope you're not coming down with something. Are you feeling all right?'

Kate stood up to greet him and lifted her face to his kiss.

'It's snowing,' she smiled.

V

SCHADENFREUDE

FOURTEEN

Spring saw the chicks arrive in their hundreds and cover the floor of the barn in yeeking yellow balls of cotton. Each morning, when Aunt Greta put on her henhouse dress, Danny and I went in with her to adore them. When I looked down, I would feel myself swell up with love. I wanted to embrace them. And not just one or two of them either, I wanted to embrace them all. To fall down on my knees and move my arms through them, as if I were swimming the breaststroke, with my face rubbing in their general warmth and softness, while their tiny bodies scurried gently across my arms, down my back and catching sometimes in the strands of my hair.

When I confided this to Herbert he said, 'Why don't you then? And you'll get what you deserve. They'll peck your eyes out and pull the cheeks off your face. You'll be lucky if they let you keep your skull.'

And so I contented myself with the occasional and single captive on the palm of my hand and the merest rub from the pad of my finger. I told myself this was because I would hurt them. But really I was afraid they might hurt me. I was afraid of being injured by something I loved so much. And so that's why I left them alone.

The chicks had only begun to make themselves at home when Mr Milinski came to take them away. And soon the barn was cleared of all fowl, right down to the fine black Minorca cock, that Aunt Greta had christened Masterson, after Uncle Henry. The perches had been pulled away and the dropping boards all scoured and put to other uses. There would never be dust baths again rising from the floor. The dust was all settled now, the barn an empty silent place. It would stay that way until Papa had organised himself properly with his new business. Then it would fill up again with automobiles and oily cans. The next time it played host to a venture, it would be as Papa's garage.

Aunt Greta didn't seem to mind the chicks being taken away, not like Danny and me. We cried and cried and chased after the truck through the yard and out to the street. With the cages they were locked inside wobbling away from us, we waved goodbye and goodbye and goodbye.

'Good luck and good riddance,' was all Aunt Greta had to say. 'And the next time I see any of you, I hope you'll be on a plate, roasted and well stuffed.'

Around the time that the chicks left, Benny and I left too. To live in Aunt Maude's house until such a time as we could afford a home of our own. And I wondered on that first drive out to Chapelizod if the chicks had felt like I did, moving through a strange landscape, powerless and alone. With my face pressed against a window pane, I watched the city turn scrawny and thin, till there was no more of it. And nothing for ages but grass and a river and the occasional run of stone brick houses. Then at last a village, where it was, I realised, the country – Aunt Maude lived in the country. But at least, I suppose we got to come back at the weekends. Whereas the chicks, so far as we knew, were never seen again.

Benny settled in at once, making friends with the boys in the village and wallowing in the luxury of Aunt Maude's home, behaving as though he were back in Jury's Hotel. (He even had the nerve to complain to me about the lack of an elevator.) Besides he was seldom in, always out somewhere, swinging out of trees or making a nuisance of himself some place or another. And coming home only for mealtimes or when he was too tired to do anything else but sleep.

But it was different for me. My cousin Patrice was an uneasy and cautious companion, preferring to sing than to speak, and Aunt Maude – whom I had always been led to believe was the soul of joy and gaiety – turned out to be far from my expectations.

Aunt Maude never did read Mama's letters. She played with them all right, organising them into bunches with thin ribbon and a crisp tissue wrapping on each one, so that they looked like a purchase from Mr Kalmer's shop on Cranberry Street, where Mama used to buy her cheese. She had them indexed too, into months and years. But she never did read them. I was glad too. That one last Christmas letter she received, the one we had posted just a few days before Mama had died, seemed to bring her enough sorrow as it was. When I asked her one time if I might read it, she refused, saying, 'It's a happy letter. That's all you need to know. Your mother was happy when she passed away.' But for a happy letter, I thought to myself, it sure did cause an awful lot of crying.

I didn't mind her refusing. I had my pick of the other letters (although she didn't know that). I spent a lot of time alone in her vast house and it hadn't taken me too long to find out its secrets, including where she had hidden Mama's letters. Aunt Maude was never too good at keeping secrets, unlike Mama. Had she lived, I suspect, I would never have got my hands on them. But Mama was dead, and so I took the letters, bunch by bunch to my room, where slowly I came to unravel the past.

I found out most things through those letters, about Aunt Greta and Aunt Maude, about Mama and Mr Pakenham. I might have found out a lot more but Aunt Maude had moved house by my second Christmas in Ireland, to a much smaller place off the South Circular Road. I couldn't search for the box with the letters there, too few rooms and not enough stairways. She would have heard me rummaging about and guessed what I was up to. So I just held on to the last few I had stolen and read them over and over. She never missed them. Or maybe she didn't care. By that time, she didn't care a whole lot about anything. Everything had been found out by then, everything had been unfolded: 'You can only take care of a secret,' she told me one time, 'until it ceases to become one. Then there is no reason to care any more.'

It was Lucia Carabini that led Mr Pakenham to us. Or rather to Aunt Maude. The grown-ups had taken so many precautions, schooling us, schooling each other. The one thing they had overlooked was Lucia. Lucia and her longing to be loved, and to love. Poor Lucia. And she knew nothing about it. Not a thing. Except that a man, after Mass one day, had climbed his way up the gallery steps to pay a compliment to her 'Ave Maria' and came back again many times, before he finally and shyly introduced himself. A man who smiled at her a lot, and held her hand on a walk by Whyte's Gate Road and took her on the penny ferry from the Strawberry Beds to Mill Lane. And told her that he loved her. And she decided somehow to believe him.

Her lover's name was Mr Pakenham. But he didn't call himself that. He called himself John Henry. If I had ever seen a photograph of Mr Pakenham I could have told her. But nobody ever showed me one. Nobody trusted me enough. And so bit by bit he found out who we really were. And bit by bit I found out who he really was: my Mama's husband.

From the garden through the French doors opened wide, I

saw Lucia one summer's day. Playing with Lottie's baby and bouncing him up first and laying him flat next. And all the time tickling and squeezing, saying over and over, 'I love you. I love you. I love you so much,' in a way that made me reluctant to come in from the garden. Too strong for a baby, I had thought, a stranger's baby: too much. But she kept right on saying it, as if she just couldn't stop and she dug her chin into his chest, nuzzling it until his baby laughter began to sound too big for his size. And then I saw her lift his arm and her head turn on it and her mouth open wide. And I heard myself shout out, '*Lucia*'. Then she stopped.

She was going to bite him, I was sure of that. She turned to me then, a frightened look on her face and shaking the two of us, both pretending to believe that I had wanted her for something else.

I had learnt from Aunt Greta's chicks that love needed some sort of control, some restraint. But Lucia didn't seem to know that. Her love was so great that a soft arm of baby fat had tempted her into a moment of insanity. When it came to love, there was the difference between us; she wasn't afraid. Afraid that something she loved too much might injure her.

And by the time Mr Pakenham had finished with Lucia, she was injured. He had left her as the chicks might have left me, with her eyes pecked out and the cheeks pulled away from her face. She should have been a little more afraid, I guess. It's always as well to be a little afraid, when it comes to these matters of love.

It was Lucia Carabini that led him to us but that only mattered when we were rich. Once we were poor, it didn't seem important any more. Aunt Maude lost her money in the 'crash' of October 1929. And Aunt Maude lost her second husband shortly after that. I guess most people thought her money and her husband disappearing so close to one another was no coincidence. But she didn't have to lose him. She chose to.

It was Lucia Carabini that caused Mr Pakenham to find us. It was me that caused Aunt Maude to lose Uncle Henry. And I was sorry until I realised that she wasn't. And then I wasn't sorry any more.

I could have blamed a lot of things, a lot of people besides, Aunt Greta, Aunt Maude, Mama's letters, for making me realise that things in the grown-up world are never as simple as they seem and are always ripe for manipulation. Or the house that allowed me too much time to be alone, to consider and devise, to look for things I should have been too busy to seek. I could have blamed all that too. Or Uncle Henry's shoes.

And Uncle Henry wore the most beautiful shoes. He had them sent from London, where they were made specially to fit and they were soft and tan and always gleaming. He had to have them made to fit because his feet were so long (not big, he would stress, but long). He had several pairs, all the same colour, which he used for day wear. In the evening he wore black ones and these, too, were of the same design. Although there was always the feeling that he might be adventurous elsewhere, he was not the most adventurous man when it came to footwear.

Sometimes, when the house was empty and Philomena was taking her nap in the kitchen and Patrice, in the drawing-room, was musically engrossed with Miss Bates and Lucia, I would sneak up to his closet and look at them, all lined up in a row with a wooden and spring contraption to hold their shape, so that they had a look about them as if they were appalled by something. The smell of Uncle Henry's feet, I used to suppose. I liked to try them on and flap about his room then and sometimes too I would put one of his tall silk hats on my head and watch myself in his long looking-glass, guessing what it must be like to live Uncle Henry's life. It was a way to amuse myself, for although this was a house with every comfort, it was awfully dull compared to Aunt Greta's. Hushed and orderly with a politeness about it that you could almost wade through.

Nobody came down before eight o' clock in the morning, and often, with the exception of Philomena, it was much later. I was always first to rise, wandering through the downstairs rooms passing the endless and often unused furniture and looking out on the enclosed and lonely garden with nothing in its solitude to keep me amused. Nothing moving unless the wind told it to, just lawns and trees and flowers that always stayed in the same position. I would go to the kitchen and fix myself some bread and jam and then back in the drawing-room, lie on a rug flicking through a picture book and longing for the weekend when Papa would come to collect me and take me to Aunt Greta's again. Where there was always something to do. Always people to see. And where there was always, of course, my cousin Herbert.

Sometimes I would hear the front door shiver and Uncle Henry's step come into the hall. He usually made his way softly up the stairs, but occasionally he came into the drawing-room, his beautiful shoes passing me by until they came to the drinks cabinet where they stopped for a while. Then I would study them carefully, from the corner of my eye. Sometimes they were dry with just a scuff of dust at the toe, sometimes they were wet, strings of dewy grass clinging to their soles. While he filled up a glass from a decanter, I would try to guess just where it was they had been. Then I would hear the sounds of Uncle Henry's drink coming into shape. A reluctant gurgle would come along first and then toc, the sound of an eggshell crack into the glass. And how loud its single fat glug pushing down Uncle Henry's throat. And how soft the little gasp he uttered when it did. I would watch the shoes pass by again, and hear his voice from way up there say, 'Good morning, my dear.'

'Good morning, Uncle Henry.'

And the shoes would be gone, always so soft, always so shining, always so long. I might not see him for days after that. A voice in another room, perhaps, or the destination of a freshly laundered shirt held out in Philomena's arms as she passed me by on the stairs. A name that was mentioned from time to time, on the telephone or in a discussion about the arrangements of a meal yet to be prepared. A figure seen from an upstairs window climb into or out of a motor car, a coat in the cloakroom: that was what Uncle Henry meant to me.

'A mystery man,' was what Aunt Greta called him. And I guess that was just about right.

Aunt Greta took a great interest in my second household: Aunt Maude and her clothes; Aunt Maude and her visitors; Aunt Maude and her telephone; and the general who, when and what time of it all. So I was always careful to take home for her all the details carefully arranged, layer by layer, like a box of sweetmeats or sugared candy.

And then come Saturday morning, when at last we were alone together, I would share them with her, one by one, while we did the weekend shopping, with the noises of the city around us, racing up and down a scale of their own. And not a bit like Patrice's scales either, which were tight and sweet and always the same. These were loose and fast. And much more beautiful.

And through the cries of the street sellers her questions would scurry down to me. Through the 'Spanished onions', the 'Rush bodaroes' and the 'sound tomaroes', chip by chip. It was only in the shops, where she was expected to be polite and where she was always careful not to 'let them know your business', that we might lose the thread for a little while. But once back outside again, we would resume, she would allow nothing to interfere with the conversation or its flow. And the barrow ladies would never dream of doing so. They always helped her out in that respect. Her hand would indicate what she wished to purchase ('What can I get you ma'am? These is it? A pound? A half? And how many, missus? A dozen? A half a dozen? Do you want some lovely Victorian plums? Are ye sure now?') All Aunt Greta had to do was nod or shake her head, the barrow lady would do the rest. I guess they knew as much about Aunt Maude as we did, by the time we had all our business done. By the time we were ready to move on to another barrow with the next question already on the air. Holding her hand while we hurried along, me breathlessly relaying the events of the past few days, I would sense the only real happiness I had known all that week, the only real companionship, Monday through to Friday.

And she may have given me the idea about Miss Bates. I couldn't say for certain but she was awfully keen to know everything about her. Was she pretty? Was she plump? Did Uncle Henry like her? How did I know? I hated to disappoint her with a dull or unsatisfactory answer. I could have made them up, I suppose, just to please her. But I wasn't a child who could lie too easily. Not about that sort of thing anyway. I always liked to be precise in my reportage, priding myself on the accuracy of my memory. And so sometimes, I helped things to happen, so that they could be true. And I guess that's just what I did, with regard to Miss Bates.

Miss Bates lived in Chapelizod village, in a cottage that seemed to grow like a wart out of the schoolyard gate. On a cut-off lane that strangers easily missed. Even the rain seemed to skip overhead, it was that narrow. And I don't know what made me call in that day or why I should have talked Patrice into coming with me, I think I only wanted to see what the inside was like. It was just to have a fine story really, a Hallowe'en gift, I guess, for my Aunt Greta.

It was the day after I had come back from spending the weekend in New Street, an empty Monday afternoon with luncheon just over and hours to go before the next meal would cut another slice away from the day. Patrice's music lesson had been cancelled and any prospect of my exploring the house along with it. And besides Aunt Maude had taken Benny into town and with Lucia on her afternoon off, I would have to spend the afternoon with my cousin. I had a letter to post to Adeline and I went to the kitchen to try to persuade Philomena to send us to the village for some errands. 'But we don't need anything,' she insisted. 'We get everything sent.' But after some pleading, she agreed to needing four ounces of butter. At least now, with two errands, there seemed to be some purpose to the afternoon.

As we walked down to the village, Patrice was humming by my side, pausing occasionally to greet anyone whose path crossed ours.

'Good afternoon, Mr Burslem.'

'Good afternoon, Patrice.'

'Good afternoon, Mrs Caird.'

'Good afternoon, Patrice. How is your mother?'

'She's well, thank you for asking.'

And here was the difference between running into people with Patrice and running into people when you were with Aunt Greta. Each time Aunt Greta greeted somebody, once they had passed by (and not always safely out of earshot either), she would have something to say: 'That's Mr Seezer, the pork butcher. Would you look at him, all done out like Mutt. And well he might be, the prices he's charging.'

Or: 'There's poor Mrs Ryan; her husband fecked off on her. Left her with six children and an ulcer ... She drinks, so I'm told.'

But Patrice never had anything to say. You could ask her all right: 'Patrice, who was that?'

But the most you could expect was a 'Oh, that's just Mrs Caird' type of reply, a mere confirmation of the name you'd just heard mentioned before she returned to that secret song that always seemed to need singing inside her.

After I had posted Adeline's letter, we went into O'Shaughnessy's shop ('Good afternoon, Mr O'Shaughnessy. Good afternoon, Patrice') and waited our turn to order the butter. There were three other people at the counter and they all fell silent when we came through, waiting for a moment before resuming their conversation, gently at first, then later with as much vigour as before. They took a long time, but I didn't mind; it was something to listen to, something to while away the time. Patrice stood as straight as a lamp-post in the centre of the shop, with her hands pressed into her sides, like a little soldier. In the meantime, I got busy with my surroundings: the women were leaning against a long mahogany counter; rows of drawers filled up the walls behind it, nutmegs, cloves, cinnamon, mace, each one with a badge of identification under its neat wooden lip. And I wished I were with Aunt Greta; I felt sure she would buy something from them. And then the drawers would be pulled open and I would be able to see what nutmegs, cinnamon and mace might look like and which way they were stored inside.

Overhead, giant tea canisters were brooding in the muted light and I thought about how sometimes, when the shopping was all done, Aunt Greta and I would go into a small café for a sugar bun and a pot of tea. And exchanging exhausted sighs and sympathetic glances with the other shoppers already seated inside, we would take our place, while the groceries rested at our sides. Bags and plenty of them.

I looked up at the ceiling. From the dark brown V-jointed gallows, copper snuff-scales hung diagonally down. There were hams and sides of bacon, and flypapers too, sharing that space. Convenient to the shopkeeper's hand there were other scales, much larger, with a polished brass pillar and a wide assortment of brass weights piled in a box. Along the sides there was a showstand for Jacobs biscuits with glass lids that lifted from the bottom. There was plenty in here to inspect and report, but somehow, when I thought of Aunt Greta, I didn't think they would quite do.

The women had almost finished their business when one of them said, 'Here, give us a try of that newfangled margarine, a quarter will do.'

'You won't like it,' the shopkeeper warned, laying it out like white muck on the paper. 'It's nothing like butter, nothing like the real thing at all.'

And then at last it was our turn to be served.

'Now, Miss Masterson, and what can I do for you?'

'Four ounces of butter, please.'

'And how is your mother?'

'She's well, thank you for asking.'

He looked at me. 'Who's your little friend?'

'Oh, just someone of Father's.'

And I thought to myself, here was another person who was much better at keeping secrets than Aunt Maude. You wouldn't catch Patrice leaving too many clues on the ground.

I watched the shopkeeper pick up two big wooden platters and dip them into water, then manipulating a portion of butter from a huge lump, he placed this offcut onto the scales with a

266

piece of greaseproof paper beneath. It didn't weigh enough and so he added an extra piece. Then he slapped the butter with the platters sending drops of water flying into the sifts of afternoon light. The butter was a regular shape now and that was it. That was all. The afternoon's activity was over. I looked back at the door through the hanks of hanging boots and the empty square outside with nothing to see, not a passer-by, not a motor car, nothing to report. And it came to me then. The idea about Miss Bates.

'Let's call on Miss Bates,' I suggested to Patrice when we came outside.

'Miss Bates? Whatever for?'

'Oh, because she asked me to,' I lied.

'When? When did she ask you?' Patrice sounded doubtful, but I pulled her by the arm, up the sneaky laneway and before she had time to think, I had knocked on the door of Miss Bates's cottage.

It took a long time for her to answer and Patrice was growing restless. 'I want to go home,' she said more than once. But I just pretended not to hear. It was cold in the laneway without the sun and Patrice said, 'I'm freezing. I want to go home.' I was just about to give in but then the door pulled open and I didn't have to.

'Oh hello, Miss Bates. We've come to visit,' I announced.

She was wearing a housecoat, her hand gripped at the top part and her bare knee poking through a slit near the end. She seemed very surprised to see us and not at all pleased. 'I'm afraid I'm not well,' she said, 'I was in bed.'

'Oh, I am sorry,' Patrice began. 'We had no idea . . . only Maudie told me.'

But then I heard myself say, 'We brought you a gift,' and after some hesitation, she reluctantly stepped aside.

There was no hallway in Miss Bates's cottage, no vestibule either; you just stepped right in and there you were, right inside her living-room, which was everything I expected it to be. How pleased, I thought, Aunt Greta would be, as I looked around with my greedy-gut eye.

A piano had the lion's share of the far wall and there was a table with a lace cloth, its polished rosewood showing through the flimsy loops like smooth brown skin. There were flowers in a vase and portraits of relatives arranged along the walls, there was a tiny stairwell that cut off the side of the room, and a velvet curtain covering it down to the ground. There was a black iron fireplace with ornaments crowded along its mantel and on the floor, was a fitted fleur-de-lis linoleum and a rug at the centre, with vinery pressed green and red and fringes spiking out from all the sides. And something else. There was something else on the floor. 'So, girls . . . ' I heard her say, 'and what gift have you brought me?'

I looked up from the rug, warning myself that I shouldn't look down again, no matter how strong the urge. Not the slightest peek. Not even that. 'Gift?' I said, 'Oh, yes. We brought you some butter. Fresh from O' Shaughnessy's shop.'

'Butter?' she laughed and I could see Patrice's face light up all over.

'Yes and none of that newfangled margarine either.'

'Butter? Well, thank you, I'm sure.'

Then I disobeyed myself and looked down on the floor again. I just couldn't seem to help it, couldn't pull my eyes back up, couldn't pull them away.

'We better be going,' I said. 'I'm so sorry you're not feeling well. Patrice, are you ready?'

But when I looked at my cousin, she too was staring at the

rug, with the fringes at the edges and vines pressed into a pattern. And the mark of a chair that had once stood there. And Uncle Henry's shoes.

When we got back to the house, Aunt Maude was in the hall. Removing her hat and coat she turned to smile at us. Her face was pale but it would get paler. 'Father's shoes are in Miss Bates's house,' I heard Patrice say. Her voice sounded a little surprised. Not in the least shocked, not at all.

The following Saturday, I walked hand-in-hand again with Aunt Greta down Francis Street. 'Now let me see . . . ' she began. 'We need curly kale for the colcannon, apples and nuts for the games. And flour. I need flour. Oh and I must go to the chemist; don't let me forget, whatever you do . . . How was your week?'

I looked up at the stone heads over the arches of the Iveagh market; one after the other they looked back down on me as we walked by on the opposite side of the street. Waiting. Waiting to hear what I would say. The last one wore a turban. He was staring particularly hard.

'It was all right, I guess.'

'All right?'

'Yes, all right.'

'I see.'

The street was busy with Saturday people, women with shopping bags stopping off at St. Nicholas's Church before they faced the day. A young boy was pushing a handcart and whistling to himself. The handcart was full of rags but they looked better than his clothes. His boots were too big for him, I thought. They slapped around his feet as if he were paddling in the sea.

'And have you had any visitors this week?'

'Ah ha,' I shook my head.

We went into Mushatts the chemist and Aunt Greta said to the assistant, 'An ounce of best gum arabic please.' And then she broke her rule about not letting them know your business and she turned to me, 'What? Not even Miss Bates?'

'No. Not even her.'

'She must be sick?'

'Yes,' I agreed, 'she must be.'

We walked back outside and took the corner into Thomas Street. A row of tables lined the sidewalk, all covered in coloured cloths and heavy with baskets of fruit and all sorts of seasonal treats, bright-skinned and dark. The women called out as we passed them by, 'Snap apples. Get your nuts and your snap apples. Can I get you some lovely snap apples ma'am?' A horse lifted his tail and large brown braids dropped out of his keyhole on to the street.

'Your hair is getting nice and long at last,' Aunt Greta said. 'We must get you some ribbon. Would you like that? Some new ribbon? I'll do it up nice for you.' And her hand lifted my hair at the back and weighed it gently before settling it back down onto my shoulders.

'Yes, Aunt Greta.'

We went into the butcher's shop then and she bought long sausages and two pounds of scrag end. She bought bacon pieces too and a lump of scarlet meat for Sunday. The butcher laid them out on reams of white paper and asked, 'Is this your helper?'

'Yes,' Aunt Greta smiled patting me on the back, 'this is my little helper.'

'Well, there's an extra sausage so, for her.'

He placed a package in my hand. It felt like a soft damp mess on my palm. We came out of the butchers and moved over to a barrow.

'A dull week so?' Aunt Greta said pointing at apples and holding her bag out while they plopped down inside. She held her hand out for the change and then let it slide back into her pocket purse. 'Yes, it was,' I apologised, slipping the bundle of meat into the top of her shopping-bag.

When we finished the errands and came back up along the street, our hands were full. I carried the flour and a bag of mixed nuts. Aunt Greta held everything else up high in her arms. We stopped just before the corner of Francis Street so that she could rearrange her load. She looked at me and said,

'And how is your Aunt Maude?'

'I don't know, I haven't really seen her.'

'Haven't seen her?'

'No.'

'Is she away then?'

'She hasn't been very well,' I said.

'Really? What's the matter with her?'

'I don't know.'

'Would it be the same thing that Miss Bates has?'

'I guess.'

As we turned the corner, I looked back across the road to John's Lane, running away from Thomas Street and down towards the river. And I knew it went a long way; I had walked that way before. But from here I couldn't see how. I couldn't see where it ended. It was like a shelf, a sudden drop. Everything seemed to have taken a dip, everything seemed to have fallen down. I watched a woman make her way along it until she came to the edge of the shelf. I watched her until I saw her disappear.

FIFTEEN

Her head was like the inside of Waterloo station. Every face she had ever known was there, every face she had ever glimpsed in passing on a city street, a blur on an old photograph from a childhood album or on the society pages of some forgotten newspaper. Rushing and pushing to get to an exit, too narrow to take all of them at once. And was there nobody willing to wait? Not one who would stand back just a little? Not one who could bring themselves to step aside and say, 'Please. I insist, after you . . . ' Her head was like the inside of Waterloo station. Waterloo station, just after the war.

There were decisions, too many decisions shoving each other out of the way. But in order to decide anything she would have to start thinking and she preferred to leave her thoughts alone. Let them be; let them wander. She could consider the topics but not their details. The crisis on Wall Street, Pakenham and Lucia, the children, the children. All this and Henry too. Henry and Miss Bates. Henry and whatever other name had sat with his on the same shared whisper over the years: 'Have you heard the latest? Henry Masterson and that . . . ?'. But what was it really but a tattle to delay until the lines of dinner conversation have all been cleared, the weather, the government, the price of china tea.

While in an anteroom, the bending of the port takes place, bleeding through muslin, drop by drop. Preparing itself for the trolley which eventually will be pushed through, into the crux of the matter, the separating of the sexes: so that sex may be discussed. And then along the table's left-hand side it will move, giving a little curtsy before each appreciative face. Glittering beneath its puckered glass, glittering as if it is adorned with jewels. ('Well, poor old Henry's got himself in a proper jam, and no mistake.'). Moving as a scandal moves, hand to hand. Poor old Henry.

And in another room again, the women will have their busy little say, seeing it from a woman's point of view – both women's point of view – with Henry the sandwich filling. The back of their silk-covered knees, their calves, their ankles crossing and uncrossing, chintz flowers and frills. And cigarettes . . . before a word can be uttered the cigarettes must glow.

('Well, who could ever have imagined? Such a mousy one too . . . The quiet ones . . . You have to . . . Whatever will she do. Poor old Maude.')

And they will bandy the possibilities, trying desperately not to gloat, trying desperately to cut that sound from their throats and replace it with sympathy. They sound so similar, gloating and sympathy. The practical Germans have a word for it. A word that means taking pleasure in other's misfortune. Malice and glee all in one word. (What is the word?) Cut from the same cloth, from the same cut-and-come-again cake. Malice and glee. They have waited so long for her to fall and watching now her head over her heels, her heels over her head, how will they feel? With her hair coming undone and tumbling in disarray and her choice of underwear now on display for all to see. How will they feel? And her face without its touch of rouge showing the marks of her forty years. Will it be the spectacle they had always hoped it would be? Or will it leave them wishing they had stayed at home? They will carry on watching to see how she might land. They will point out the places to each other; they will point out the places they would choose in her position. And they will stop only when the men come back in to interrupt them or until the voice of experience speaks out, in a way that makes silence fall among them: 'She will do what we have all done. She will pretend not to have noticed.'

Maude lifted her head from the pillow and kicked the counterpane she had earlier wrapped around them, off her feet and on to the floor. There were decisions to be made. But they could wait. Right now she had a game to play, a game of chess.

Against an unseen opponent, an unknown personality in the shadow facing hers, the opposing wills of two egos engaging with each other across the board. She would go back to the beginning; she would relearn. Her playing strength would have to be regained, move by move. She would have to remember things she had forgotten; she would have to remember that hers was a strategic game, not to move on impulse or simply because it was her turn to play. She would have to remember the most important rule of all: the play which is to take place in the middle game already exists in embryo after the opening move. This time she would refuse to allow herself to play like a master, when she had lost a master's ability.

Sometimes the sun shone; sometimes it didn't bother. Sometimes it was dark and later came the morning. But it made no difference to her, seated in the middle of the room, to where she had moved the table. Under the light of a single lamp – enough to see what she wanted to see – sixty-four squares and the pieces that would occupy them from time to time. Looking for holes. She was looking for holes. And creating them for herself sometimes. Just to be reminded. Of how easy they were to create.

She stayed at a game as long as she could, until she felt her eyes strain and blink and her judgement melt into black and white confusion, with the black always proving the stronger, spreading finally across the table, like an inkpot fallen over. Then she knew it was time to sleep.

Her dreams were clear. Each had a beginning, a middle, and an end. Events followed each other like little lambs in and out of situations until a predictable conclusion had been reached, dull enough to wake her. Each time she opened her eyes, she would go over them again until she felt alert enough to return to the table. Then she would play some more.

She had her longest sleep after the fifth game. She had a different dream. She dreamed of a man she knew only by sight. A short stocky man with thick curling hair and small hooded eyes that showed no expression. A man that she had never considered beyond the facts that he was not very attractive and not the type to be socially demanding. A simple word or two was all that would be necessary were she ever to find herself standing next to him in company. But she was in his company now.

She dreamed she was naked with him, him lying behind her and his tongue licking at the skin on her neck and peeling it off, layer by layer in his mouth. She dreamed her legs were tied back around his, they were trussed together on her bed. His hands were free and helped themselves, bite by bite to her flesh, selecting random pieces that came away in his hand, which he ate with considered greed, making a soft slurping noise in her ear. He was eating her off the bone. But there was no blood. She could smell herself as cooked meat. The smell of herself made her feel hungry. She dreamed it as a most pleasurable experience and when she woke before it had finished, she tried to bring him back again. She wanted to see his unattractive face; she wanted to kiss his hooded lids and hear herself tell him how much she loved him. She wanted him to finish what he had started, to know again the

275

gentle slurping of her flesh between his tongue and his lips, of her flesh melting between his teeth. But he was gone and all that she could hear now was the sound of a telephone ringing, like an aggrieved husband pleading for acknowledgement.

She got up and looked down at the board. She poured herself some cold tea, treating it as if it were only just made. A lump of sugar, a drop of milk. Nibbling at toast that crunched and crumbled dryly on her lips, she studied the game she had left behind. She saw her mistakes. They were many but they were nearly all of the same type. Each game had boiled back down to that, a repetition of similar mistakes.

The telephone fell silent again and she opened another game. But her head hurt too much and she had to stop. This time the squares stayed steady and clear; this time they refused to budge: they were no longer willing to help her sleep. She took a pill and woke in the middle of some night or it could have been the beginning of some morning. She was still wearing the dress she had on when Patrice had made the announcement concerning Henry's shoes.

She sat in a bath that was barely warm and waited for the light to declare its position. She washed her hair and clipped her toenails. By then the light had settled on the morning. Hoping it wasn't too early, she rang for Philomena. She remembered then how she had taken Philomena into her confidence, had given her a letter to hand to Henry. The letter had announced that she wished to be left alone and would he kindly stay in the back room until further notice. It had been an impersonal sort of a letter. Like a notice one might read pasted to the window of an empty shop:

This premises will stay closed until further notice.

But it had, in a postscript, informed him, that she knew about Miss Bates. In a hasty postscript, polite and to the point, giving it no more importance than any other domestic memo: (PS: Don't forget we're dining out tonight and your mother's birthday is on Tuesday next.)

He would be nervous, she knew. She had never seen him nervous and found herself speculating on its manifestation. But then reminders of the past two days came back to her, making an appearance like acts on a vaudeville show. And she lost interest in Henry's nervousness, now that she had other things to amuse her.

Philomena's face, that came first. The tears in her eyes when Maude had explained the situation. A series of intermittent taps on the door then followed. Philomena's voice, 'I'm leaving a tray, ma'am. Are you sure you're all right?'

And there had been other voices too. Henry's voice, pleading sometimes, another time a little on the angry side. And then this too had passed. No more taps, no more words. Although his step had appeared from time to time and hesitated outside before moving away again. Had he lost his voice, she wondered. Or could he simply think of nothing more to say? Was that the sound of Henry being nervous, silence?

And then? Then there had been telephone calls put through to her room. (They must have been urgent for Philomena to allow them.) Yes, indeed they were. All from that investment man. Person to person, from the United States. The first few had been very efficient, reassuring and businesslike, urging her to ignore any wild rumours she may have heard concerning the New York stock exchange. (Rumours? What rumours?) 'Yes, yes, all right.' The next few were a little different, asking her advice this time: should he offload or did she wish him to hold fast?

'Yes. Yes, whatever you like.'

The last one she could remember, was Mr – what's that his name was again? – crying. Why was he crying? She was the one who was supposed to be crying. 'We're finished,' he had said, 'ruined.'

'Oh well . . . these things happen, I suppose.'

There was a knock on the door and she said, 'Philomena?'

'Yes, it's me.'

'Come in.'

'I can't, ma'am; it's locked.'

Maude walked across the room and unlocked the door.

When Philomena came in she asked, 'Will I lock it again?'

'Oh no, Philomena, that's all right; there's no need now.'

She dropped her head towards her knees and unwrapped the towel from her hair, then she rubbed it gently from crown to nape, catching the longer strands between the nap of each corner and patting them gently between her hands.

'How are the children?'

'They've been asking after you, ma'am.'

'And?'

'I told them you weren't well. That you weren't to be disturbed.'

'And Mr Masterson?'

'He's been asking too. He's not up yet but he wanted me to find out what he should do about *Carmen* tonight?'

'*Carmen*? Oh yes, the opera. How like Henry not to forget the opera. You can tell him I'll be down at six.'

'Yes Ma'am. Are you all right?'

'Yes, Philomena, I'm all right now.'

She made a shawl of the towel and arranged her hair against it, Philomena handed her a comb.

'I went to see Miss Bates, you know.'

'Miss Bates? Oh you did not?'

'Yes, I remember now. I sent the children in for their tea and went back out again. I suppose I must have expected him to have still been there. He may have been, I suppose . . . Hiding upstairs. I wonder how he manages those stairs? They're so low and narrow. He must have to practically crawl on his knees to get up to her room. Anyway, I called in and asked her out straight.'

'And what did she say?'

'She denied it at first but then she started to cry. Everybody seemed to be crying – except me.'

'Oh, Mrs Masterson.'

'She sends her handwriting away for analysis, can you imagine? Sends it off to an advertisement in the newspaper, where a stranger looks at it and then tells her who she is. I wonder what they saw, in that neat little hand, in that tidy little signature?'

She started at the bottom of her hair, flicking at the knots until they loosened and finally relented. Then she traipsed the comb through each cleared section.

'Poor girl, I feel sorry for her really.'

'Sorry? Oh no, not sorry for *her*. She's nothing but a common prostitute.'

'Oh come on, Philomena, I'm sure he didn't pay her. The poor girl probably didn't even enjoy it that much. She probably just didn't know how to say no.'

Maude smiled at Philomena and touched her softly on the arm. 'Would you leave me now, Phil. I have some calls to make.'

'Calls?'

'Yes, I'd better telephone to America and my hairdresser, and then I'm going into town. Will you keep the children out of sight for one more day? Will you do that for me? Will you take them to Lottie's? I'll telephone her to expect them.'

'Yes, of course. But . . . '

'I'm not ready for them yet, you see. I won't be ready until tomorrow.'

Philomena nodded softly to herself and lifting a tray of old tea and toast crusts to her chest, moved reluctantly out of the room.

Maude watched her hair fall in chunks to the floor and listened to the scissors' slow reluctant crunch. The hairdresser was nervous and kept asking, 'Are you sure about this now, Mrs Masterson? Are you certain?' but Maude just smiled at the collection of hairgrips piled like a scrapheap on the counter before her. However had she managed to carry that lot about with her? However had it all stayed up so long, together? Her old hair was swept away under the nose of a brush; it gathered with the dust as it left her feet and by the time it reached the corner all its colour had drained away.

Her head was light now and she wanted to laugh. She refused to wear her hat. No, thank you, she would carry it in a bag by her side. How long was it since she had gone out without a hat? She couldn't recall.

The hairdresser held a hand-mirror up to the back of her head and asked her if she was pleased with the result. And through the mirror she replied. 'Oh, yes. Oh yes, indeed.' But she wasn't looking at herself at all. She had passed herself by to the wall behind her and the arrangement of filmstar heads, one over the other: Gloria Swanson, Norma Talmadge. And that one there? Mary Winter was it not? It teased the back of her neck as she walked across the marble floor of the bank. She could feel it move, tickle and scratch. It reminded her of the first time she had dared to wear a short skirt, the back of her knees and the hem bouncing off them, it was the same itch, just in a different place. She cleared her personal account and felt the wad of money like a *millefeuille* pastry in her hand. Then pulling one slice of it away, she slid it into an envelope that already held a letter addressed to John Henry. She turned into Westmoreland Street and started to walk.

John Henry shared a room with a stranger. In a house with rooms that were made to be shared by strangers. Lumped in together, like it or not. And a fanlight over the door with a child of Prague peeping out like an overdressed dwarf. The room-mate was a country man, with a gold ring on his lapel and a pleat between his eyebrows that gave him an anxious air. He opened the door to Maude on his way out to Mass. 'I'm his cousin,' Maude explained and he showed her the room at the top of the stairs. John Henry was out, he told her; you wouldn't know what time or when, but she could wait, if that's what she wanted.

There was a crucifix on the wall over each bed. There was a separate space on the table under the window for each man's shaving tackle. Out through the window was the Jesuit church with people queueing to get in and to get out again, in a steady stream. The queue going in was by far the longer. She waited for twenty minutes or so and it hadn't thinned at all. If anything it had thickened. She watched John Henry's room-mate inch his way up along it. He pulled the cap off his head when he reached the top, then he disappeared behind a pillar.

She decided to leave. She put the envelope beside the shaving tackle she presumed would be his, propping it up against a small marble bowl and a silver backed brush. She walked to the door and looked back to see how amenable it was. And just about to go out when it occurred to her . . . the name John Henry. She came back in and taking a pen from her handbag, struck out the first name and replaced it with T. Pakenham Esq. There now, she was beginning to learn, she had managed to avoid it: a repetition of a similar mistake. She hoped his room-mate was honest and wouldn't deprive him of his very last dividend and smiling to herself then, she closed the door behind her and came slowly back down the stairs.

She caught a cab back into town and asked it to leave her at the bottom of Grafton Street. A paper boy was ranting on the corner. She bought the latest editions and turned up Dawson Street to the Hibernian Hotel. She was ready now for her lunch.

She had onion soup, with a long curly name, but it was onion soup just the same. Her hunger had behaved itself well up till now but as soon as the smell of deep brown onions reached up to it from the table, it began to tremble through her. She burnt her bottom lip. She had stuffed white trout next, whose flesh disintegrated to the touch and fell in flakes through the prongs of her fork. She ate potatoes in large chunks, which gave more satisfaction, large enough to fill her mouth but not so large as to choke her. She took coffee at the table and a slab of New England pound cake. Then reluctantly, she opened the newspapers. The cake was solid and spiced, it filled her mouth up nicely, and she felt sad to realise that her meal would soon be over. She felt as though she could spend the rest of the day eating, and considered finishing this and then going on somewhere else for another full four-courser. But the newspaper kept insisting on telling her things, all about Wall Street, San Francisco and London too. It told her there had been a general crack of between five and forty points. It showed her columns of figures wearing strings of noughts around their necks like pearls. (After the first few noughts they ceased to make any sense and so she ignored them.) It tried to explain to her then, the stampede of mob psychology and why gilt-edged issues had been thrown recklessly overboard. It listed her own investments so that she could see how much she had lost. It tried to make her feel sorry for forlorn faces all over the financial world, waiting outside banks and investment houses for hours on end. But all that she could see was the Jesuit church on Gardiner Street and the stream of communicants bursting to get in. Everyone

282

wanted to salvage something, it seemed. Everyone had something to save. And so she was broke or near enough. This would mean she would have to start watching her money . . . she supposed.

She turned another page and felt her face move into a smile, the very thing. She would go shopping. There were one or two things to see to first. But after that? Why not? There was a sale on in Clery's. She could be thrifty and extravagant all at once.

In Clery's department store, she cut quite a dash, moving from counter to counter and buying gifts for anyone she could think of. The store was filled with onlookers, fingering hems and dotting perfume samples on to curious wrists, but she seemed to be the only one determined to buy. A sales assistant was assigned to accompany her on her tour, gathering parcels as they moved along and disappearing from time to time to deposit them in the delivery room. Then she would return, arms swinging free and ready to be reloaded. She bought a jumper suit of lido blue for Maudie and one just like it in clear scarlet for Patrice. She bought five navy blue overcoats for her five nephews. ('Bedrock quality, madam, five-guinea garments going for a song.') She laid them out along the counter from the large down to the small and closed the buttons on each one first. Then went back over them again, this time to run her fingers under each collar before lifting it and patting it back down into place. It was as though her nephews were already inside.

She bought a footstool for her brother, with a lid that lifted and a place to put a hot water jar inside. ('Just the thing, Madam, coming into winter, for a man with a tricky leg.') She bought several Oxford shirts in an assortment of sizes, to divide among all the males she knew. For Samuel, the boys and whoever else they would fit. They were striped in multicolour – blue, mauve, brown on white grounds. Each came with two collars to match.

She bought a gold pendant for Philomena and for Henry a Borsalino hat, dove-grey with a navy band. She bought him a selection of French cord silk ties too, with full wide ends in the latest semi-club style (which he would never wear, she knew, but bought them just the same). She couldn't quite make up her mind for Greta and finally decided to visit the drapery department. She would choose a cloth and Greta, whose taste was anyway impeccable, could decide on a style of her own. She would buy her something to match the cloth, a handbag maybe, or a pair of shoes.

Upstairs, she ran her fingers over the drapery bales, felts, longcloths, printed voiles. She removed her gloves to feel them better with her bare fingers, casements, poplins, art silk hoses. Finally she decided on a shantung silk. It was time Greta wore silk again. She had something for everyone now. But she had bought nothing for herself. So she ordered a half-yard of black gaberdine. More than enough to make a mourning band for the arm of her coat.

On her way back down the stairs she looked around for anyone she knew, thinking to herself what fun it would be to see if she was recognisable with her altered head. To see if anyone could tell her which star she had been based on, Gloria Swanson, Norma Talmadge or Mary Winter, was it not?

Her shopping was finished now and she folded the envelope of money over in two and inserted it into a smaller slit in the inside of her handbag. Each time she had made a purchase, she had taken the bundle of notes from the envelope and felt them thin out. And like a fat girl who suddenly finds herself losing weight, the thinner it got, the more thrilled she became. By the time she left the shop, she was ecstatic.

It was half past three in the afternoon by now. She could have tea, she supposed, or go home. She made her way up to the bridge and turning her head to check the traffic coming from the left, she saw the startled sign over the Corinthian Cinema burst into sudden light. *Girls Gone Wild* it said. How appropriate. She would go to the pictures.

She sat in the dark and lit a cigarette. There was a girl up on the screen smoking as well. 'A jazz-mad daughter,' an older man with a pencil moustache had just called her, shaking an exasperated finger and holding one hand on his hip. Her father, he was probably supposed to be. Maude sat back and thought of her busy day. She wondered what she had enjoyed the most. Was it having her hair cut? Eating her lunch? Then she decided that after all, it was placing her advertisements: telling a condensed version of her business to a stranger and having him read it back, across a mahogany counter. In a beautifully uninterested monotone pulled up through his nose, 'Right now, what have we got here? "Large house for sale, extensive grounds, Chapelizod area, apply box 441." All right?' "Roomed house wanted within 2d fare of city centre; apply box 442." – All right?' And finally, her favourite one of all: "Maude Masterson would like to announce a memorial service for her beloved sister Kate who passed from this world on 10 December 1928, to take place in St Laurence's church, Chapelizod, Saturday, 9 November 1929 at 11 a.m." – All right? Happy enough with them are we?' With telephone bells ringing out behind him and the background of pigeon-holed walls that her advertisements could now be slotted into. And everything poised to put her plans into action, everything ready to take them away. Yes, she had been happy with that.

Maude put out her cigarette and looked up at the screen again, but she grew tired of the jazz-mad daughter hopping in and out of motor cars and waving her hands about every time the scratchy sound of music came through. It was time to go.

She got up from her seat and edging her way along the row, half expecting the voice of the irate father to shout out after her, 'Come back here, young lady, I'm not through with you yet.' She turned her back to him then and gave her step to the guidance of a torchlight, thanking a woman whose face she couldn't see.

She wore a georgette gown, a sherry-coloured gown. She took her time, a careful dressing. She took her time, as though she really intended going to the opera, then sat before the mirror and waited for six o'clock to come. At ten to six she decided to go down. A drink, perhaps, to hold her steady? But coming down the stairs she realised she was steady as she ever was. A drink perhaps then, because she fancied the taste. Of sherry on her lips and a sherry-coloured gown swooning around her knees.

Henry was there already, his face jumped up when she walked into the room. She moved over towards him and raising herself up, kissed him softly on the cheek. 'Dear Henry,' she said.

He looked down at her and started to smile. 'Then, then you forgive me?'

'There is nothing to forgive.' She patted him gently on the arm and moved over to a sofa beside the wall. And dropping herself down on to it, she stretched her legs out, raising them a little at the heels. 'I can't begin to tell you what a busy day I've had.'

He poured a glass of sherry and brought it over to her. Then plucking his tails up, sat carefully by her side.

'I just want to tell you . . . '

Maude took a sip of the sherry and held it on her tongue. She raised her finger to Henry's lips. 'Shhh,' she said, and then swallowed it down.

'But I want to explain . . . '

'There's nothing to explain,' she said.

'You've had your hair cut.'

'Yes. Do you like it?'

'It's, well it's different. It makes you look younger.'

'Thank you. I put the house up for sale today.'

She waited for him to say something. She thought of examples of things he said when caught off guard. When the children defied him, or a member of his cast had disobeyed his wishes: 'I will not tolerate this contumacy,' she seemed to remember him saying one time. But she was never quite sure of what he meant by that. She took another sip of sherry and thought of things he might say when trying to guide somebody to his will while making it look as though it were for their own good. 'Nothing is denied to well directed labour; nothing is to be obtained without it.' Hadn't he said that once to Patrice when her piano practice was being neglected?

But she hadn't defied him. Nor was she in need of his direction. Nor had she neglected anything. She waited to see what he would say. But all he could come up with was: 'But I don't understand?'

'Well, my money is all gone, you know. I need the money, quite simply.'

'But where shall we go?'

'Not we, Henry. I've advertised for a small house. For Patrice and myself. Maudie and Benny, well, it's time they started to live with their father again. I know that's what he wants. I'll help him of course, if he'll allow me. But of course you know Samuel.'

'What are you saying?' Henry put his head into his hand and then stood up and walked across the room. After a moment he walked back to her again.

'You've had a shock,' he decided.

'Perhaps . . . I'm over that now.'

'Well, you're shocked then. You're shocked because I . . . but I promise you Maude, I swear to you . . .'

Maude put down her glass. 'Oh Henry, I'm not shocked.'

'Of course, you are. The idea of infidelity . . . you give it more importance than it warrants. I've wronged you, I know. I know how wrong I was but it doesn't merit this. Not this. To be thrown away, just discarded. There are plenty of people whom you respect and honour who have been infidels.'

'Infidels?' Maude laughed. 'Oh Henry, you have such a way with words.'

Henry took a seat at the opposite wall and she looked at his horrified face. She walked over to him and knelt at his side.

'Dear Henry, I am not shocked, I've always known what you were like. That appetite of yours. I never was naïve enough to suppose it was confined to my bed.'

'Now, you're being vulgar.'

'Vulgar? Oh Henry, you're a sketch.'

'Will you stop laughing? Will you please stop?'

'Yes, I'm sorry. But Henry, please don't suppose me to be such a prig. I know my friends are unfaithful; I know it's always been part of our world.'

'Yet you find it so unforgivable?'

'No Henry, I don't find it so unforgivable. I've had to forgive myself, you see.'

'Yourself? Don't be absurd.'

'Is it so absurd?'

'Are you asking me to believe that *you* . . .'

'I'm asking you to believe that I, too, have been an . . . an infidel, as you put it.'

'What? Are you telling me you've been unfaithful to me? Maude? Is that what you're telling me?'

'Calm down, Henry. Not to you. Never to you.'

Maude stood up and walked towards the door. 'It was to Pat, I'm afraid, shortly before he became ill.'

He thought for a moment and then continued, 'Before he . . . ? How long before?'

'What you really want to know is if Patrice . . . Was he Patrice's father? Well no, he wasn't; it was somebody else.'

'Somebody else? Somebody else? What somebody else, if you don't mind my – '

'It's nobody you'd be likely to know. I hardly knew him myself, if you must know.'

'Why? Why did you do it? I mean, how could you have done such a thing?'

'Because I wanted a child. I wanted a child so badly, I lost my reason, I suppose.'

'There are other ways.'

'Oh yes. I suppose. I could have advertised in the newspaper: "Respectable woman willing . . . " Or answered one. I thought about that once. There used to be such ads. Do you remember those? I do. One in particular: "Respectable Protestant woman wanted for baby girl. £20 to include layette and cot." I considered it but Pat . . . well it wasn't something I could have discussed with him.'

'Well, you could have told *me*. You could have told me before I married you.'

'Could I, Henry? I don't think so. I wanted to, of course. But . . . well, you were always so respectable, you see. I told myself it was before anything happened between you and me, that I hadn't wronged *you*. I told myself she could just as easily have been Pat's. I convinced myself. I convinced myself and then I almost came to believe it.'

'Well, you're a lovely family, I must say. Between yourself and your sister. A lovely lot indeed.'

'Yes . . . and it gets better than that, I'm afraid. You might as well know the worst: Greta's eldest and Patrice.'

'What about them?'

'They share the same father.'

'They *what*?'

'The same man.'

'My God. What did you do? Rent him out between you? Pick him out as if he were a hat?'

'It wasn't like that, Henry.'

'Well, what was it like? Tell me, because I would really like to know.'

'Henry, please. Lower your voice. The servants.'

'Damn lot I care about the servants. I'll go out and shout it out through the house if I so bloody-well wish.'

'Henry, listen to me. You must listen to me. Nobody knows. Not even Greta. She doesn't even know I met the man. Nobody knows, except you and I. I know I can trust you. I hope I can trust you. For the children's sake, if not for mine.'

Henry stood up, and walked to the fireplace. He stretched his arms out, laid his hands on the mantel and dropped his head between them.

'So you see, Henry, now you know. And even if I could forgive you – could you ever forgive me?'

'Why did you have to tell me? Why couldn't you just have kept it to yourself? You have had long enough. Why do this to me now?'

'I didn't have to tell you, Henry. I chose too. I wanted you to know that, that none of this is your fault.'

'Well, you're hardly in a bloody position to judge anyone, are you?'

'No, I don't suppose I am.'

'Get out,' he said. 'Just get out of my sight.'

Maude turned the handle of the door and opened it wide. She looked out onto the chequered hallway, square, black and white reaching out to every wall.

'Do you know, Henry, I never really liked this house. No, I can't say I ever did. I've so often looked up at that chandelier there and thought I might lose my head sometime, and swing from it like a baboon. It's always been too large for me. Always made me feel lost somehow. Like one tiny bead in a large box.'

She looked back into the room and saw Henry pour himself a drink. She watched him for a moment, lifting it to his lips, his eyes looking straight ahead at nothing. At least, *he* wasn't crying, she supposed.

Then she pulled the door quietly behind her and walked out into the hallway. Her feet followed behind each other, along the tiles of the floor. She looked down and noticed how neatly they were moving. Crossing it neatly on a clear diagonal line.

VI

THE DARK LANES: JUNE 1935

SIXTEEN

The two bicycles kept pace until they came to the High Road that skirted the strand. It had been pelting down all morning and now, as if they'd been waiting in shopways or shelters, the crowds re-emerged as suddenly as the sun. There were cars and bicycles on the roadway, families with picnic bags walking at the sides and jaunty sea-bathers with towels stuffed and rolled under their arms walking anywhere they liked. Herbert couldn't see George and for a while he was afraid he might have lost him altogether, in some short-cut up the green lanes of Clontarf. But then he saw him cut and duck between one car and another, before the next swerve of the road took him out of sight.

Herbert struggled to keep up. Rows of shops and painted seafront houses struggled past him in the opposite direction. There were churches lurking among them that stepped out unexpectedly just as he cycled by. There were colours and cubes, shadows and squares; there were skirt legs and trouser legs dog-trotting towards and then behind him like impressions on an early kinematic roll. Up front there was always the back of George's head, or the prospect of his head, zig, zag, zig – a rock-steady ball from behind and before the curves of the Clontarf road. The only stillness was on his right-hand side. The water and sky going nowhere at all. Perfectly still, perfectly vast.

When the boat club sprang out at him, he caught, across at the sea side, a glimpse of the breakwater. It seemed to retreat then for a moment until the road took a last upward sweep and it popped back out, Bullbridge and Bullwall: like a tongue rolled out full span from the tonsils. Herbert slowed up. It seemed very quiet along its causeway: nothing moving at all.

He noticed a slur in the traffic flow then, and the closer it got to the bridge entrance, the thicker it became. Until finally, just a little before the turn, it came to a complete standstill. Now only the pedestrians and a few determined cyclists were getting through. Something had happened.

Heads popped impatiently out of car windows and the cars themselves complained in low-noted calls like a herd of disgruntled cattle. But then from the distance behind came a more consistent call, a call from the city, confident and clean. And that shut them all up then. A corporation ambulance was pushing through.

Herbert got off his bicycle and pulled it alongside him. He came up beside the closed petals of onlookers blocking the mouth of the bridge. He stooped and stretched until he found a decent gap to peep through. Shoes, the soles of a man's shoes, heels to the ground and pointing upwards in surrender. He went to call ahead to George but George had passed the bottleneck by and was now a lone figure disappearing into the distance.

Herbert poked his head through the crowd. 'Who is it?' he asked a woman beside him.

'A poor man, God help him. It's a priest he wants be the look of him, not an ambulance.'

'His heart, I'd say,' another man said and then wisely mouthed, 'a coronoray.' Herbert nodded. He could hear someone at the centre shout at the crowd. 'Clear the way, would you? How do you expect the ambulance to get through?'

A small boy in front of him screeched and clapped. 'Is he dead? Is he dead?' and a woman dragged the child away by the arm.

Herbert stepped into the space they had vacated.

He could see a man lying on the ground now, muttering away to himself in a foreign tongue. A box lay by his side and the man was struggling to reach it.

'Give him a drink,' somebody suggested, and a small woman pulled a milk bottle from a bag she was carrying.

'Here, he can have a sup of milk.'

'Ah not milk, for God's sake,' somebody else chided. 'Water, water, it's a drop of water the man needs.' A bottle of water was produced. 'Or brandy, better still,' an old man decided. And for a moment there was silence as if to allow the brandy time to make itself known. When none was forthcoming the commentary resumed.

'He's a terrible high colour.'

'I wonder what's in his box?'

'Something good in anyway; he thinks he'll never get a hold of it.'

'Ah push it nearer to him; then the poor man can stop fretting.'

A man bent down and tried to lift the box. 'Jesus, Almighty,' he said. He looked at Herbert. 'Here – you're a fine strappin' lad.' Herbert dragged the box over to the man. He looked down at the full frightened face that managed somehow to look florid and grey at the one time. The man was dressed in an old-fashioned black suit with an old-fashioned collar which a busy-fingered woman had just finished unbuttoning. She held the bottle of water to his lips and with her other hand placed behind the poor man's head, tilted one towards the other. But her effort failed; the water fell straight back out and down on to the man's shirt.

'What's your name?' she asked the man kindly. Herbert heard the deep dry voice struggle with itself and then utter something. 'Al.' It sounded like Al.

'What's he saying? What did he say?'

'And where are you from, sir?' the woman continued, trying the water on him once again.

'Lucca,' the man answered, touching his box once more.

'He's from Lucan. The poor man. Lucan.' And a woman in the crowd declared. 'I know someone who lives out in Lucan.'

The ambulance call ceased and there was silence again. The stretcher came through and the crowd reluctantly stepped back. Herbert watched the stretcher settle beneath the man and the two bearers stoop and heave it from the ground.

'You'll be all right now, sir! Here's the ambulance men to mind you. You're not to be worryin' now; we have your box, the young lad'll put it in with you.' The woman held on to his hand, rising with it and patting it kindly all the way. 'You'll be all right now,' she said again.

Herbert lifted the box again and carried it over to the ambulance. The man raised himself a little and looking at Herbert said, 'You unnerstand, son? I . . . I . . . I don't want to *spettare* a . . . I mean to be, to be . . . encumbrance for anyone.' And then his head dropped lightly and turned away.

The last thing Herbert saw was the woman let go of the man's hand and cross herself, and through the open doors of the ambulance an attendant lean over to cover his face.

It took him a few minutes to catch up with George. It was past the Dollymount Hotel and George was leaning over the handlebars with a newspaper folded into a convenient size, studying the horses again.

George looked up. 'What kept you?'

'He died. A man . . . he's dead.'

George nodded and looked away.

Herbert looked back at the scene. He could see the motor cars one by one pop on to and over the bridge, and the boats in cosy flocks sidle out to sea. There were random dots of golfers out on the links. The Great Northern train cut along the coast. All was back to normal again: Whit Monday had been resumed.

'I think I'll go back home,' he said. George didn't ask him why.

'Suit yourself,' he shrugged, tucking the newspaper back into his pocket and turning his bicycle to take the last four miles to Baldoyle alone.

Herbert walked back in the direction of the city with his bicycle by his side. Now he could see the complexion of the houses, bright and flat, like the faces of unglazed sweets. And names the like of Seacrest, and Seaview and Strandside and Seaview again pinned to their pillars or front wall chests. How original, Herbert sneered to himself, turning away to look towards the sea.

The dark strand stretched swollen and uneven, fleshy-black like the belly of a sea lion. Any show of seawater was scant, scattered silk sheaths that had accidentally fallen. The tide was out, miles out. He could see the peg-legged bridge running a three-legged race to catch up with it. And he was glad that in his pocket he had no more than the price of a cup of tea. He was sick in his stomach. He couldn't have eaten a bite, even if he could have afforded one. He crossed over the road and leaned his bicycle up against the sea wall. He sat down then and with the toe of his boot flicking at loose pebbles that had come undone from the grey stone block, he thought about the previous Saturday. How different it had all been then. Last week at the Phoenix Park. Herbert remembered it now with sadness. Similar weather but with a kinder rain, no more than a drizzle to cool them down on their cycle up to Parkgate Street. They had stopped at Bart Tully's pub. From a background of dark wood and porter-bottle troops, Bart's face beamed out like a carriage lamp. He came from behind the bar to greet them with an outstretched arm and a laugh as pleased as punch could be. He poured them a pint glass of lemonade fizz and said, 'It'll be a pint of porter before we know it.' He asked them to stay and have a bit of dinner with him. And when George said no, they'd miss the first race, he grinned and said, 'Oh ho, just like his father, to the very hat of him.'

Herbert gulped on the lemonade, following its course downwards where it rolled like surf into empty corners. He folded his arms over his stomach as if it might cry out and betray its disappointment. With nothing inside it but a heel of fried bread and a cup of red-headed tea since early that morning. A bit of dinner? He wouldn't have minded. He wouldn't have minded at all.

But the sun had come up then as they cut through Chesterfield Avenue and yapped at the two of them all the way about everything the day might bring. George had said they would win a bucketful and go away for Whitsun, to a Great Northern Hotel or somewhere. Bundoran, or one of those fancy seaside towns. They could take Danny with them, if he was well enough to travel. And if he wasn't? Well they could pay for a consultant or at least a decent doctor, for a change. They would have a zotofoam bath, he insisted, and when Herbert had asked him what that was, he shrugged and said, 'Who cares? We'll have one anyway. We'll play golf too.'

'But we don't know how,' Herbert had laughed.

'We'll learn.'

And Herbert had believed him about that, if nothing else. George could learn anything once he put his mind to it. He didn't know anyone as clever as George. Already he knew as much as Samuel about cars, inside and out. Some day George said he would own his own garage, as soon as he had the hardihood to buy himself a motor car. He'd win the down payment, no sweat, he would. And Herbert wouldn't have been a bit surprised because he knew how to back winners too. Anyone would tell you that. When they got home Mother would be waiting, just like she did every Saturday, no longer pretending disapproval for George's gambling. She would take the money now and sigh, 'Oh thank you, George,' and touch him softly on the cheek. George would shrug her touch off, in a way that never made clear if he was pleased by it or not.

Last week had been the first time Herbert had accompanied his brother to the races and he had hardly known what to expect. But his studies were done now for the summer and he only had to wait to see if Aunt Maude would come up with the money for the university or not. Fifteen pounds would see him in and after that ten quid and ten shillings each half-year. She had been silent on the subject up to this and now that she was no longer rich Herbert worried that she might stay silent. But Mother had said Wall Street or no Wall Street, fifteen pounds to us was still like fifteen shillings to her and of course she would come up with it. But her lip was bitten as she spoke and she had looked across the room at George, adding, 'We'll get it somehow.'

Herbert's heart collapsed; she meant George would get it somehow. He felt it was too much to expect from George. It wasn't fair, his having to work all day and well into the summer evenings while Herbert sat on his backside shoving facts and figures inside himself like Billy Bunter eating cakes.

George hadn't looked too put-out by Mother's expectations last week on the way to the races. He was in the best of form, joking and laughing and calling out loudly to people he may or may not have known. He pulled his bike to the kerb near the Ashtown Gate to greet two go-boys who came up to his elbow.

They had the faces of old men and the mannerisms too. They should have been in the circus, Herbert thought to himself, with their bandy legs and their fuckin' this and fuckin' that, all over the place and not a care about people passing by, ladies even and ordinary women as well. 'He hasn't a fuckin' chance.'

'He won't be fuckin' bet. I'm fuckin' tellin' you now. I fuckin' am.'

And George asked one of them, 'How did you fare out after, last week?'

He replied, 'I lost me bollix,' and spat on the ground.

'Well, I hope you get them back today.' George laughed, before beckoning to Herbert that it was time to move on.

And it wasn't the fact of such language that made Herbert uneasy. He cursed himself from time to time, but always in appropriate company and always, while doing so, fully aware of his own daring. Whereas George was so careless about it all. As if it just didn't mean a thing. It had made Herbert feel nervous to realise that his brother at sixteen was already a man in size and demeanour, while he, a year older, still looked on things as a schoolboy would. He nodded a scarlet-faced farewell to the two grinning scuts and skulked off after George. And wondering to himself, if this was a selection of the company so far, what would he be letting himself in for, once they got inside?

But on the other side of the walls, his worries left him. A city from the past it was, fresh and bright. With grass as plush as velvet and trees as well groomed as its residents. And painted buildings along a stretch like grand Edwardian mansions. There were touches of the marketplace, too, with barrows of fruit and chocolate and ruddy-faced oul' ones full-throatedly expressing their wares. It had made him feel his hunger again. Although he was always hungry, he usually could ignore it, by-pass any sly reminder in a shop window or on the page of a book and in a moment leave its taunt behind him. But not this time. This time, he could feel a greed well up inside him and felt as though he could stick his face into one of those barrows like a pig at a trough.

'How much money did he give you?' he heard himself ask George. George looked at the fruit and said, 'Sorry, Herb, not enough.' And then he bought himself a race-card.

George took him as far as a clock near the parade ring then and told him he'd see him there after each race. 'But what'll I do?' Herbert asked him helplessly.

'Enjoy yourself,' George said. And then he was gone.

And Herbert did for the first hour or so, wandering through the afternoon, a stranger in this foreign city, familiarising himself with the course, sorting it out in his head. After a while he saw that it was divided in half. There was the front stage course, where all was easy, with the parade ring and the brass band playing and the women strolling in fancy hats and neat little costumes. There were various refreshment areas, tea and cream buns, or tiny brown burnt sausages served with thin triangled bread. And public bars and softer lounge bars, too, with a dressed-up barman rattling drinks and *frappé* ice together in silver shakers. There were horses to be paraded all shine and strut and jockeys at the centre in glossy coloured silks that astounded the eye. That was the front of the house.

Then there was the back stage where everything was frantic. The other side of the Edwardian mansions, which turned out to be lacking in a back wall and had, instead of rooms, steps tapering upwards full of anxious faces. And down on the ground, book-makers' pitches had brown bags of leather crouched beside each one, like a row of faithful dogs, fat and getting fatter by the second with the shove-and-push punters eager to feed them to the brim.

He spotted George now and then, once at the parade ring, once down at the railings that skirted the track. Another time talking to a well dressed man in a mauve silk shirt and a fashionable low-crowned bowler, with a woman by his side who laughed whenever George had a word to say.

After the fourth race, the novelty had begun to wear a little thin and he found himself back at the clock more often than not, to supervise the passage of time. It was warm and he was thirsty now, as well as hungry. He had seen all there was to see and was sorry he hadn't taken a book. He sat on a bench that encircled the trunk of a tree and looked up at the squiggles of leaves overhead. He thought about taking a snooze. But then he spotted Beatrix Bumbury.

She was leaning against an ivy-stuffed trellis and chatting to a couple of men standing by her side. Her fingers plucked leaves from the neat little patchwork of wood and rolled them gently first before flicking them carelessly to the ground. Like a film-star, she was, with her head turning to the right with a smile and then back to the left with another one. She wore a parchment crêpe dress and a hat to tone. A big picture hat it was, with her hair hidden by its wide sheltering brim. She had changed a lot since last he'd seen her at Aunt Maude's old house. But he had known her just the same. She had changed completely since their first meeting at Kingsbridge station, more than seven years before. That was when he had looked like a right sap in his knee breeches and roll-topped stockings. And she had been just a little girl then pretending to be a woman. She could stop pretending now.

Beatrix Bumbury; it had made him shake just to look at her, even from the distance. It made him feel shy all over and the blood burst up to his face. And the sort of tingle come into his legs that he sometimes felt in the dark. He hoped what usually happened then wouldn't happen now, and him without as much as a newspaper to cover the shame. He crossed his legs and leaned over a bit. No, it would be safe enough: he was much too nervous for that sort of thing.

He followed her to the ladies' room, keeping a good distance back and hanging about under the trees until he saw her come out again. She was wearing lipstick. He followed her again and saw her sit down on the same circular bench he had left just a few minutes before. The *exact* same bench. He felt overpowered by this latent intimacy. He cursed himself. Why had he not stayed where he was? How could he have been so stupid? But then realised had he been sitting there, she probably would have walked on by and he felt himself calm down a little. He watched her unravelling paper from a chocolate bar then, and not breaking pieces off as he would have expected, but eating it from the top, her finger gingerly tipping the corners of her mouth from time to time to clear off the crumbs, real or imagined. He followed her again and her hips had a sway to them, moving fully from side to side. Like the horses he had been watching earlier on.

She came back to the parade ring and picked a spot not too far away from George. A little bit behind and only a few spaces off. Herbert came up beside his brother and nudged him in the ribs. 'Do you know who's over there?' he whispered to him.

'Mmm?'

'Over there, to your right. Beatrix. Beatrix Bumbury. Look.'

George looked over for a second and said, 'Oh, right.'

Then he looked back down at his race-card.

Herbert tried to distract himself with the parade of horses, but they just reminded him of Beatrix now, their full slow walk and long carved legs. He glanced to the side. She was looking. She *was* looking. He glanced again. She was looking all right. But it wasn't at him. It was at George.

Afterwards they lay in the long grass with George reliving each race as if he hadn't been there at all. They ate until they were sick. They had a bag each they had bought from the dealers on the way out, apples and chocolate and pears as yet unripe which they ate anyway, right down to the hairy little heart of them. They passed each other swigs from a large bottle of lemonade. And George told jokes and funny stories till Herbert thought he would be sick from laughing as well as eating. Then George produced a five packet of Players and they smoked in silence until it was time to go. George stood up then and passed three notes to Herbert. Two ten-bob ones and a pound note too. 'Hide that,' he said.

'Why?'

'Because I'm sick to me bloody teeth giving him money to throw away on drink. We'll give it to Mother when he's not looking.'

'Will he not know?'

'No. I had a few bets on the sly. He'll be none the wiser. I'll give him what I have in me pocket. You just hold on to that and keep your mouth shut.'

They strolled back out on to Chesterfield Avenue and took a slow cycle home. Herbert wanted to talk about Beatrix Bumbury but each time he carefully introduced her George carelessly swept her away. He asked George what he thought of her and George just shrugged. 'But you must have noticed?'

'Not really.'

'Would you say she has the men all feeding out of her hand?'

George shrugged again. 'Who cares?'

'I think she has the eye for you,' Herbert said.

'I'm too young for her.'

'So? You don't look it.'

'Well, I wouldn't be bothered with her anyhow.'

Then Herbert confessed how he had followed her from the ladies' toilet and described how she had eaten the chocolate. And then how he had followed her again, all the way back to the parade ring, managing to keep up with her through the crowds. Never taking his eyes off her, not once. And George said: 'Well, you'd hardly lose her anyway, the size of her arse.' And Herbert nearly fell off his bicycle. But George just grinned. His mood was changing now that they were nearly home. He wanted to talk about other things besides Beatrix Bumbury. Father mostly or Danny's night-long cough. Which set a gloom on their journey home.

'Since Sam left, he's gone to hell. Gone to hell altogether. I should have gone with Sam. He wanted me to, you know. Could have made a few bob. Could have done all right for myself.'

'Why didn't you then?'

'How could I? Who'd look after Mr Cardshaw's motors? Who'd run the yard? And besides, they wouldn't have the room for me. I'd have nowhere to live. No I'll have to wait till I'm ready to make me mark. And then, *bang* I'm off.'

Herbert was shocked. He never imagined the house without George. It would be unthinkable having to live there and George somewhere else. And yet he could see by George's face that he would go, as soon as he could. Samuel's new house might be too small . . . but next time maybe. He'd be gone next chance.

'I hate his guts,' George said when they came out onto the quays. 'Let's not go home yet. Let's go to the pictures first?'

'Have we the money?'

'Of course we've the money.'

'All right, then, I don't mind.'

'Just remember, we only backed two winners. The second and the fifth.'

'But what if he asks me any questions?'

'He won't. He doesn't care about the races any more; it's only the money he's interested in now.'

'The second and the fifth,' Herbert repeated and then opened his mouth to mention Beatrix again. But George got in first:

'I'll never be like him when I'm grown. I'll kill myself first.'

'No, you won't.'

'Well, I'll kill him then. Stick his sparkly cane up his hole. That should suit him all right.'

Herbert smiled. 'Well, I'm going to be so unlike him,' he said, 'people will wonder if he's my real father.'

He laughed and looked over at George. But George had cycled ahead.

Just as he had cycled ahead today. Always on the move, was George. 'Glass arse,' was what Samuel called him, always slipping off. Always leading the way. Herbert looked out at the waterfront and watched the widgeon and the cormorant and the rest of the dark spindly waterfowl spiked along the seashore. And sorry now he hadn't gone along with his brother. Sorry most of all because in deserting him, he had left himself alone. And supposing he did go home? Mother would be at the hospital; Charlie would be in Aunt Maude's. That left only Father. Sitting in the saddle-bag chair and staring at the floor. And not a move out of him, except sometimes to lean his head in his hands. He had stopped going up to the hospital these past few days. He had even stopped going out to the pub. Silent now for more than a week. Not a word since that last Saturday night, when he had had so much to say.

He had been waiting in the yard when they got home after the pictures. Leaning against the wall and smoking a clumsy cigarette. He looked up when they came through and they could see at once that he was drunk.

'Well now, well,' he said, 'if it isn't Mr Punch and his Dog Toby.'

He held out his hand. 'You took your bloody time,' he snarled.

George got off his bicycle and left it on the ground. 'What are you worried about? The pubs are still open.'

Herbert had hung back while George walked past his father and into the kitchen. He guided the bicycles one at a time along the narrow alley made by Mr Cranshaw's motor car and the outside wall of the old henhouse. He arranged them carefully side by side and then made his way back to the house. There was no sign of Father. Herbert looked through the window and winced. Maudie was there, laying knives and forks daintily on the table. The kitchen was tidy in an unfamiliar way, in a way that wasn't Mother's. There were tea-cloths on a stool by the fire, folded and neatly stacked, and cups and porridge bowls rearranged along the dresser according to size and colour. She had obviously been making herself useful while waiting their return. 'Hello, Herbert,' Maudie smiled with her face blushing up to him. Herbert nodded and looked over at Mother.

Mother was nervous, standing by the stove, a cloth draped on the edge of a plate in each hand.

'I kept you some dinner,' she said, a little too brightly.

George sat down by the fire. 'I don't want any.'

'Mutton chops,' she continued as if she hadn't heard him, 'with bread sauce.'

'Where's Danny?' George asked her. 'I brought him a bar of chocolate.'

But Mother wasn't listening to him. She raised the plates in indication. 'Samuel sent them over with Maudie,' she smiled over at her niece. Maudie smiled back, confirming. 'Yes, there's two each. And I got a nice bit of cabbage from . . . '

'Where's Danny?' George asked again and Mother took a little breath.

'He's not here, pet. They took him . . . they took him to Peamount this morning. The doctor thought it would be for the best. Now it's nothing to worry about. He's going to be fine. He just needs treatment. A bit of a rest.'

'Peamount?' George said, 'But that's for – '

'No. No. Not necessarily. They just want to have a look at him, that's all. He'll only be gone for a week or two. Samuel is bringing me up to him in the morning. I'll give him the chocolate then.'

'Can I go with you?'

'We'll see.'

She laid the plates down on the table and looked over at the door. She lowered her voice. 'Don't pay any mind to your father. He's been up at the hospital all day. He's a bit upset.'

'Drunk, you mean,' George said.

Mother ignored the remark and looked over at Herbert. 'Are you not hungry?' she asked him.

Herbert shook his head. 'I'm full,' he said.

Then Father came in. 'Full, full – and what has you full, then?'

Herbert looked down at the ground, 'Nothing,' he muttered.

'Nothing has you full? Well that's a good trick. We'd all be doing well now, wouldn't we, if we could get full on nothing? And just as well, too, that's all you need . . . seeing as nothing is what you're bringing into this house.'

Maudie spoke up: 'I . . . I'd better be off now, Aunt Greta. Father will be expecting – '

'No, hold on, Maudie, one of the boys will see you home. George?' George didn't look up. 'Herbert? Herbert doesn't mind.'

'Well, if you're sure,' Maudie gushed, sitting herself down to wait.

Herbert looked over at his brother. George was staring into the fire as if it were lighting, with no particular expression on his face.

'Can't you eat the dinner your mother made for you?' Father said, 'Some of us had to go without this day. While you two gorged yourselves like pigs.'

George uncrossed his legs and leaned over closer to the fireplace. Mother turned to Father. 'Young Maudie is just off now,' she said with a warning note to her voice. But Father wasn't listening.

'Can't you eat the dinner your mother went to trouble over?'

'It's all right; it'll keep – ' Mother began.

'Will it keep? Will it?' He walked around the room, looking at each one of them as if he wanted someone to speak. But there was only silence.

The silence seemed to egg him on. The longer it continued, the louder he became.

'Will it keep now?' he roared, and then, leaning across the table, he pushed his forearm out and the plates slid off, one after the other, down on to the floor.

Mother was on her knees all at once and grabbing the bits of food from the floor. Herbert hated the way she was doing it and the lumps of bread sauce glued on to her fingertips. He hated Maudie being there too, the frightened look that had washed her face pale. And the skimpy little legs on her dangling between the loose hem of her coat and the upturn of her white cotton socks. What did she have to come here for? Why did she always have to be here? Listening to everything. Looking at them all. Looking at Mother shaming herself that way.

'Leave it,' Father said without looking down. 'Leave it, I said.'

George stood up, 'I'm going to bed.'

'Well, hold it now, just a second. Where's my money?'

'There isn't any.'

Herbert couldn't believe it. Father was worse than he ever had seen him, ready to give them both a hiding, and George wasn't even going to give him the money in his pocket.

'What do you mean: there isn't any?'

'What I said. We lost. Didn't back a winner all day.'

'You don't tell me now?'

'Ah, but I do.'

Herbert watched his father take a step towards George and without thinking he pulled the money he had been hiding out of his own pocket.

'Here,' he said, 'here's what we won. Two quid it is.'

He hurried across the room and laid the money on the table. His father said nothing. The only sounds in the room now were female sounds, of Mother's harsh sobbing and the lighter sniffle of Maudie trying to be brave.

Then at last Father spoke, but like a different man now. A touch of shame had quietened his voice. He was looking at Herbert. 'Here. Here's ten bob between you.'

Herbert looked over at George.

'What are you looking at him for? Take it. Take it, I said.'

But Herbert couldn't move. Couldn't bring himself to look directly at the ten-bob note wagging from Father's hand.

He kept his eye on the string of airing clothes above the stove, five black socks, one grey tweed, one Sunday shirt . . .

His father fell towards him and grabbed him by the arm. 'Take it, I'm telling you.' He raised his hand; he was going to hit him.

Herbert ducked, 'Father, please – ' he said.

'Father please? Father please?' He gave a little flighty laugh and looked over at his wife. 'Did you hear that, Mother? He's calling me Father! Isn't that a scream now?' He turned back to Herbert. 'Don't you call me Father. Don't you . . . Now take the money, you crossbred bastard, before I shove it down your throat.'

Herbert wasn't yet convinced of what exactly happened next. He heard his mother scream, that much was definite and then George . . . George, moving in from somewhere, pulled his father's hand away and dragged him up by the lapels of his jacket. 'You lay a hand on him and I swear I'll fuckin' kill you. I'll fuckin' . . . '

They stared at each other for what seemed like a long time. Then Charlie stumbled in from the bedroom, rubbing his eyes and crying. 'I want Danny,' he said. 'Where's Danny?'

Then George let go of Father's jacket.

He shoved him down into the saddle-bag chair and dragged the notes up from the table. He threw ten bob into Father's lap. 'I tell you what,' he said. 'You have the ten bob. We'll hold on to the rest.'

Herbert sat in a corner of the Dollymount Restaurant and nursed a cup of tea. Down to the dregs almost. Sooner or later he would have to make a move. He thought about following George out to Baldoyle, finishing his tea and then taking his time out; it would at least be a bit of company for George on the way back.

But then if George had won a few bob it might look mean. Might look as if he had just come along for the gorge-up afterwards. Not that he could eat it. Not that he could begin to taste it. The thought of food, even the thought of the amount that they had put away last Saturday. The memory of his own gluttony sickened him still. And besides he was tired. Too tired. He was tired of travelling.

All week, he felt as if he'd been at it, travelling nowhere on a train that was taking him there. And not even as a face at a window, no. Not that sort of passenger. But stretched out flat on top of its roof with his face pinned down and his hands clutching two steel braces to keep him from falling off. And only through tunnels or under dark bridges bearing particularly low. The crown of his head catching sometimes, no matter how flat he laid it. The crown of his head leaking a slow seep of blood. And any occasional spin of sunshine gone by the time he lifted it again to have a look. And hearing nothing but whispering sounds, coming loud and then soft and then going away again. Nothing had seemed real, nothing tasted of anything. Even this tea might be water, might be piss.

A stranger had died before his eyes; that was all he could vouch for with any certainty. A face that had been florid yet grey, the only real colours he had seen. Not the sky, not the boat sails, not the rows of pastel-coloured houses: they were all just postcard prints. They meant nothing to him. The stranger had left the only sure taste in his mouth, the taste of death. He stood up and knew now where he would go. Up to Peamount to see Danny. Before the taste had faded again.

SEVENTEEN

Greta was crying for all sorts of reasons. Her two older boys were dressed in mourning clothes she had borrowed from the canon. The sight of them, just two lads trying to be men, in borrowed clothes, trying to look as if they owned them. That nearly broke her heart. And the pillowcase then, with the three bread pans inside. Remembering, as she pulled it out of the hot press to make sandwiches for the mourners, how the body of a baby boy had been found in the canal the week before, stuffed into a pillowcase, just like this one. Could they not have left him in a doorway somewhere, or in the basket up in St James's hospital? The poor little mite, why drown him? What harm could he have possibly done? She pushed the knife through the flesh of the bread and watched it fall away from the loaf and keel over to one side. With her eyes full of tears for the baby in the pillowcase, she was cutting the bread as though she were half-blind. And yet there were the slices perfectly formed. Instinct, she supposed.

Behind her, neighbours were offering to look after things, to see to the men and see to the teas. Offering to handle her bread and poke at her sugar and squeeze into her scullery for a root in her press. But no, thank you, she kept on telling them, she preferred to keep occupied, do it herself. And besides, she couldn't help but notice the splint of black dirt under the fingernails of that Mrs McMunn one, now pointing at the cucumber. 'Wha's dha?' she asked, as if it were going to bite.

'Wha's dha'?' Greta pretended not to hear her.

They were all in to get their eyeful, most of them in anyway – though one or two – Mrs Punch and Mr West – had been kindness itself. But as for the rest? An opportunity to have a good gawk for themselves, to fill their mouths in more ways than one.

She pressed a plate down over another plate of sliced cucumber. She placed a brass weight on top of it and then moved on to separate another pair of plates she had pressed together earlier on. 'Wharra you doin' that for?' Mrs McMunn asked.

'To extract the indigestibility,' she said, just to annoy her.

Then as she listened to Mrs McMunn whisper to Ivy Burns, 'She cuts the bread terrible tin,' she slid cucumber rings off the knife and on to a row of sliced and buttered bread. She sprinkled a dusting of salt over first before closing them over with top sheets and then with a knife that was willing and long she pushed the heel of her hand down at every corner until the crusts broke away from the rest of the sandwiches. She threw the crusts into a bag beneath the table then, a crumb bag for the hens. But not her hens now. Now Mr Milinski's. A penny a bag he had paid Danny for the scraps. Every other day . . . he paid him . . . a penny in his hand, his little . . . She could see Mrs McMunn squinting after the crusts. Let her think she was throwing them out. Let her think it if she must.

Greta arranged the triangle shapes neatly around each other on a big platter that was only ever used for Christmas turkey or Easter, whenever she could afford a leg of lamb. She handed it carefully to young Maudie to offer the company about. Mrs McMunn's eyes were on everything she did. So she called Maudie back for a second and arranged a sprig of watercress in the centre of the bread. 'There now,' she said. 'I always say, a bit of a garnish makes all the difference.'

And then Mrs McMunn's voice nudged up behind her: 'Is it St. Patrick's Day or wha'?' to Ivy Burns and Rita Casey. And then repeating it when another neighbour walked in, 'I say, is it Paddy's Day or wha'?' nodding at the plate with the sprig of cress. 'I see the sambiches is wearin' their shamrock.'

Greta lifted the ham from the oven. It was nicely glazed now, with cloves punched on the corner of each scored square. It looked like a golden cushion. 'Now,' Greta sighed as she placed it before her. 'We'll leave that to settle.'

'Leave it to settle?' She could feel Mrs McMunn's glance cut behind her back to Mrs Burns. 'Settle wha'?'

She would have her jaw stiffened and her stupid little chin poked out in front and her ginger eyebrows lifted half-way up her forehead. She would have her face arranged to get her sarcasm across. Greta had had about enough of her.

'Yes,' she said, 'otherwise it will go all stringy. Now, why don't the two of you go out to the yard and get yourselves a bottle of stout and a pinch of snuff?'

Ivy Burns, who was anyway a bit simple, smiled gratefully, but Mrs McMunn, catching the snub, turned on her heel out through the doorway. 'I don't take snuff, actually.'

'Oh do you not? I always presumed . . . Now whatever put that into my head?'

Greta pulled bowls out of the press above her and filled them with pickles, then she whipped a drop of milk into a pot of Colman's mustard, to make it stretch. She arranged them to one side so that Maudie could take them to the outdoor table, where the ham would be served later on. Now what would she do? What would she do? Tea? Yes, she would make some more tea. She tested the kettle, it was full, and pushed it on to the gas ring at the back. Bread and butter. Yes, you can never have enough. The butter spread easily, the weather was so warm. She hoped it wouldn't melt away altogether, and the price of it.

Herbert came in to the scullery with a crate of stout pulling down on his arms. He hoisted it up on to the edge of the table, 'Bart Tully – ' he said.

'What about him?'

'He brought these over.'

'Hmm. As if there won't be enough drunkards about the place.'

'Mother, it was nice of him to bring them all the way over. To take the trouble.'

'Oh I'm sure it was. Did he walk, then?'

'No, Mother. He has his own motor car.'

'And well he might.'

Herbert swung the crate away from the table and, swaying under its weight, moved through the crowd and out into the yard. He pushed it under the makeshift table that George had constructed earlier on. It was well hidden now, from the sun and the hangers-on that would stay all night if they caught as much as a glimpse of it. Then he went back into the scullery.

'Are you all right, Mother?'

'I'm all right; I'm all right.'

'Mother, are you sure?'

'I'm busy Herbert, that's all I can tell you. And as long as I'm busy, I'm all right.'

Herbert nodded and went to go out.

'Where's your brother?'

'Where do you think?

'Oh for God's sake, not today.'

Herbert lowered his voice. 'He's only gone to the bookies, Mother, not the races. He'll be back shortly.'

'He could have given it a miss, just for one day. It wouldn't have killed him.'

'Ah sure let him, Mother. What difference does it make?'

'Difference? It makes a difference to me. Wasting his – '

'He paid for the funeral,' Herbert reminded her, then immediately regretted it.

'The heat is killing me,' she said to Maisie Punch, who was coming in to take Herbert's place in the doorway.

'Well, why don'tin you take off your coat?'

'Oh yes, I never thought of that,' and she handed her coat to Maisie's kind face, remembering that she, too, had had her sorrows. Her boy smashed flat by a Lipton's truck down on the quays a few years back. And her tears changed course for Maisie then, who patted her arm and said, 'Let it all out, Missus. You have to let it all out.'

Greta snapped the lid of the teapot closed and waited for it to draw. She dried a few cups and saucers and left them ready for use. She looked outside. They were spilling out from the kitchen into the yard, mourners and other stragglers, pressing their black shapes against the windows and flashing white handkerchiefs trimmed with black to mop at the sweat that had grown under their funeral hats. Teacups and bottled stout came in and out, carried by hands she couldn't always identify.

She wanted to see her boys. She couldn't see her boys; she wanted to see them all together. She stepped out into the kitchen and the voices turned down to a murmur. Spoiling their day. She was spoiling their day. She tapped Maudie on the arm. 'Where's Charlie?' she asked.

'He's out in the shed with Daddy and Benny. He was a bit upset. They're playing a game.'

Greta nodded. Where would she be without Samuel? Poor old Samuel, as good as gold. And him with no wife and two children to rear. Now they were Samuel's tears scalding her eyes, as she turned away from Maudie. 'Is George back yet?'

'Not yet.'

'Send him into me when you see him.'

'Yes, Aunt Greta.'

Greta went back into the scullery and blew her nose. She carved the first few slices off the ham, dusky pink and tight-fleshed with its trim of golden fat. There might even be a bit left for dinner tomorrow. A coddle, maybe? Had she any sausages? She would hold over a few slices anyway; then wait for about a half an hour and take the rest outside. Now. The tea. Who'd be wanting tea?

She glanced through the gap to the kitchen outside. The schoolmaster had nothing in his hand. Yes, the schoolmaster. He would be going away soon. He had told her so last night. 'I'm going away,' he had said, 'to the Turkish *Lycée* in Nicosia – that's in Cyprus. I'll be headmaster there in Nicosia. A TCD man preferred, that's what they said; English and games. You'll be able to have the house to yourself again.'

She would miss him. She would miss all the things that she hadn't done with him. Or the things that she had done with him inside her head. So many times. She had imagined the two of them together, so many different situations. Sunday afternoon cruises along the coast in the Royal Mail steamer. They always took seats in the saloon: four shillings, no expense spared. And afternoon tea then, her pouring for him, and him saying, 'What nice hands – so white . . . ' And later on, up to take the air on deck, their fingertips touching off each other on the balustrade, their eyes meeting across the stretch of Kingstown harbour or Dun Laoghaire or whatever you were supposed to call it now – like a watercolour painting between their gaze. And the Royal Hotel where later they would share a slice of Madeira cake off the same plate. And the salt on their lips and the wind on their cheeks. He would kiss her when no one was looking; he would kiss her and she would feel his face, chilled from the sea air, his lips flavoured salty, his mouth warm and moist. What would he think? If he knew how many times she had imagined them together walking down the crimson corridor of the Gaiety theatre, to a guinea box over the stage. And the sweet words she had given him to whisper in her ear (if only he knew). While the people in the parterre would look up at them and say to themselves, 'Now, there is a couple in love. They are in love.' And not fooled for a minute by her pretending to be composed, pretending to read the advertisements on the safety curtain below. With her heart pounding at the promises he was breathing softly on her neck. And her head held just so, to emphasise the slope from her chin to just beneath her shoulder, bare flesh indicating the way, pointing it out to him, the road he should take and what he might find there. Later, when they are alone together. And the silk on her dress rustling pale-green, to show off the flecks in her eyes. Just for him. Just for him. What would he think?

And how would he feel about the part she had given him to play in her secret world? Or if he knew that thoughts of them together were the only thing that had kept her going these last few years?

And now crossing the room to hand him a cup of tea and a sandwich she had saved for him, the triangles running around the rim of the saucer like points of a Christmas-tree star. What would he say if he knew? That right at this minute she would give anything to have a man to lie beside, a man to hold her and stroke her hair, a chest beneath her face that would soak off the tears she kept crying for other folk. 'A cup of tea, Mr Whyte?'

'Oh. Thank you, ma'am.'

'You're welcome, Mr Whyte.'

And now that he was going away, it seemed pointless to have him lying by her side in Nicosia, Cyprus. She needed a man she could imagine here with her. Here with her in Dublin. She needed a man.

And where was her husband? she wondered then, the one she was supposed to be needing. Drunk, you could bet on it. Drunk. She took a space beside old Mr Milinski, holding his hand while he wept silently down into his beard. 'Who now will gather my eggs?' he whispered to her. 'Who will I scold when they crack?'

Greta squeezed his hand but she didn't know who he was talking about. Not really. She knew it was her son. But already she couldn't remember his face. She could remember him as a small rosewood coffin and a shock of floral wreaths growing over its lid. And so who was this boy they called Daniel James? The boy the reverend had mentioned over and over throughout the service. Who was that boy who had drifted away from her mind? Who was he? She tried to call him back again but he wouldn't come in. That was Danny all over for you. Always scuttling off somewhere, always having to be called for his tea. 'Danny, Danny, come here when I call you. I know you can hear me . . . Come in here this minute, I said.' But he wouldn't come in. He wouldn't come in to her mind. Was he too shy? Because there was a man already there lying by her side, a shared pillow and a dark large head placed next to hers. 'Time is a great healer, Mr Milinski,' she heard herself say. 'He's with God, straight to the angels.' Reciting sentences that had earlier been recited to her. And Mr Milinski taking her comfort and prising with it the floodgates open, wept like a baby for anyone to see. Greta got up.

Mrs Gunne from behind a raised teacup was trying to catch her eye. But she had heard all she wanted to hear from Mrs Gunne.

322

She had heard all she wanted to hear from anyone. 'My poor Willy, I'll never forget. I know exactly how you feel, I too have had my heartache.' Why did they do that? Use the occasion to relive their own grief? Why could they not just step back for once and stop grabbing at hers?

There was a photograph hanging beside the door that led to the back stairs. Her four boys, her four stepping-stones. Taken when Maude had bought them all those navy-blue overcoats. She walked over and looked up at the photograph. There was Herbert looking pleased as could be. And George beside him, a little embarrassed, but the coat suited him well enough. She ran her eye down to the end of the line. There was Charlie, smiling obediently after the photographer's instructions. And between George and Charlie was . . . she couldn't see his face. She couldn't make it out. But his head was turned to a different angle from the rest of the boys. Out of step, so to speak. Looking away. As if he knew he would be going somewhere else. She couldn't see his face. There was a gap. His coat? Where was his good coat? Had he taken it off? She looked again and he had faded completely away. There was nothing, an empty space between her youngest son and her second eldest. Danny?

The curtain swayed and the schoolmaster walked through. She heard herself gasp and saw her hand fly up to her breast. 'Oh my goodness. You startled me.'

'He's upstairs,' the schoolmaster said. And for a minute she thought he meant Danny. That he had wandered up again, as he had often done before and that she would have to shout up at him. 'Danny, get down here now and don't have me to get up and get you.' But he meant her husband.

'Drunk, I suppose?'

The schoolmaster shrugged, 'I really don't know.'

The Reverend Tunks was getting ready to leave. He would want a last word. He would want to say, 'Have courage, have faith.' She would have to go up and get her husband. She would just have to hope he was in a fit state to come down.

The stairs were so dark, yet she knew they were trimmed with bright blue lino. Hadn't she bought it herself from the peddler at the door knowing it was a dark stairwell, knowing it well, bright blue to brighten it. Hadn't she planned it that way? The door at the top had a glass window but no light came through. She felt her way up, gliding her hand along the wall. When she got to the top she took a little rest. She opened the door and walked into the hall that was supposed to have been hers. Not this man's. This TCD man preferred. There were the drapes she had hung herself at each side of the archway, the amber-coloured drapes and the cord she had braided to keep them apart. The tassels were limp. They could do with a good cleaning. There was the hallstand with just two coats hung on, the schoolmaster's dust coat and his school coat as well. All those empty pegs . . . And only one umbrella, poking out from the side. There was the lampshade she had chosen herself. Look at the dirt of it, you could hardly see the orange trace she had bought to pick up the amber in the drapes. How many years ago? Was Danny born? Who? Danny. Was he born? Yes. An absolute disgrace, those drapes. She would have to get them sponged when he went to Nicosia. Nicosia, Cyprus.

The door to the side was the bedroom door. She opened it and stepped inside. This once was her room. For a very short time. There was the bed she had imagined herself on so many times. But not as her bed; she had forgotten it once was her bed. She couldn't now remember ever having slept in it. In her mind it was always the schoolmaster's bed. Since that day when she had burst in and caught him washing his neck, since that day when he had become hers in her inside world. His bare shoulders and broad back crouched over the wash stand. A towel tucked into the waist of his trousers to keep them from harm. His braces looped down over his hips.

'And just what do you mean by sending my son to the bookie's shop when he's supposed to be doing his lessons?'

He hadn't even covered himself while he ran through his careful explanation. What had he said? She couldn't remember; she could only recall the soapsuds on his chest and the water drops on his neck. Had it been obvious that she was staring?

The bed was unmade. There were two pillows moulded together into the shape of the schoolmaster's back and his head. He must have been sitting up reading. Or studying the horses, more like. She sat on the edge of the bed and felt the embroidered coverlet under her hand. A wedding present it had been. How fine at the time. Now baldy it was, the nap all worn and smooth. How had it got so smooth? She touched the hollow of the pillows and laid her head inside it for a minute. But she had to pull herself back up almost at once. Finding to her shame that she had been just about to fall asleep.

She walked back out into the hall. There was the cupboard where Danny used to hide. 'I'll skin you alive if you don't come out this instant. Do you hear me now?' She peered inside: so small, so dark. How had he not been afraid? How could he fit? But then she remembered he was only a child and always had the ability to fold himself into the most peculiar places. She heard a noise. Coming from the kitchen. Drunk, I suppose and the Reverend Tunks waiting to pay his last respects. Drunk. Shaming me in front of the whole street. Mrs Gunne. And Aunt Florence as well.

She opened the door and her husband was there, sitting with his back to her at the kitchen table. She looked around for the whiskey bottle, to see how far he'd gone through it. To get an idea of how bad he might be. But it wasn't on the table. It wasn't on the floor either; it was nowhere in sight. He was bent over the table. She couldn't bear to look at him yet. If he was absolutely stocious, she would just have to go back down alone, draw the reverend into a corner and say, 'He isn't feeling the best, I'm afraid . . . '

She walked over to the window and looked outside. There were cars in the yard and people leaning against them, sitting on their side runners or propped against their luggage holds. A few children were weaving around them playing games. There was a sound of conversation and laughter. Her absence had raised their spirits, it would seem. There was Maude talking to Aunt Florence, the crowns of their hats nodding politely to each other. And Patrice standing by her mother's side like a court attendant.

There was Beatrix Bumbury, bursting out of her dress, smiling and talking to all the men. But one eye straying over to the archway from time to time. Was she expecting someone? Who?

Greta sighed, 'This was supposed to have been my dining-room,' she said. 'My window. My view.'

She turned around and looked at her husband. He was holding something in his arms. Squeezing it tightly into his chest. She took a step towards him. He was holding Danny's overcoat. She thought for a terrible moment it was the boy himself. The same overcoat that had been missing from the photograph downstairs. She thought that he had plucked the child out of the picture and had taken him up here, where he had always liked to hide. 'What are you doing?' she whispered to him, 'what in the name of God?'

The tears were running down her husband's face. He took a moment to answer her. 'My boy,' he said, 'my beautiful boy.'

Greta ran out the front way. She slammed the schoolmaster's door behind her and ran up the street. When she got to the corner she ran back again. She put her hand to her face. She was expecting tears but there were none. She thought she might be sick, then that feeling too left her. Now she felt nothing. She stood at the steps of her house and looked up and down the street as if she were searching for something. She sat down on the steps then and tried to make herself think of anything. But nothing came into her mind. She held on to the railing, feeling its rust gnaw at her hand. It was hurting her, she knew, but she couldn't feel the pain. What would she do? What could she do? Where should she go?

She saw George then, coming back from the bookies, turning the corner, his hands in his pockets. He was looking down at the ground, walking away from her. 'George,' she tried to call him, but no voice came out. 'George,' she whispered and he turned suddenly around as if she had shouted out loud. He peered for a moment up the street and then recognised her. She watched him cross over the road and then he was standing over her, looking down.

'Mother?'

'Get Samuel,' she said. 'Get Samuel, son.'

George hurried away and disappeared around the side of the house. Samuel would be here soon, she told herself. Samuel would know what to do.

She watched the two of them come out together. Samuel and George, both hurrying along. George was nearly as tall as Samuel already. How could that be? He would pass him out soon if he didn't stop growing. He would pass them all out soon, now that he was almost a man. She saw Samuel stop and whisper something to George. He hesitated and then nodded slowly, going back the way they had come. Back under the archway and into the yard.

327

Samuel sat down beside her and, reaching over, prised her fingers away from the railing. He held her hand, rubbing the rust flecks away with his fingers.

'I can't remember him, Sam.'

'You will.'

'I can't remember him. Because he took him away. He took him from me, right from the start. It was to punish me. He took my son and now I can't even remember his face. He took him out of the photograph. I couldn't see him. He wasn't there. I can't remember what he was like. What was he like, Samuel? Tell me what was he like.'

Samuel let go of her hand and reached into his pocket for his tobacco pouch. He made a table of his knees closed in together. 'He was like you, Greta,' he said.

'Me?'

'He had your face. The same eyes. He had your smile.'

'Me?'

Samuel pulled the paper skins out and licked them together.

'He had George's sense of adventure.'

'Yes,' she agreed.

'He had Herbert's way of seeing things.'

'A worrier, you mean?'

'No. He didn't worry like Herbert does. He just had the same way of seeing things. The same kindness.'

Samuel plucked the cigarette into shape and placed it between his lips.

'And Charlie. He was brave like Charlie.'

'Yes,' she said, 'yes, he was brave, wasn't he?'

Samuel lit the cigarette and threw the match to the ground.

'But he was his father's son, Greta. You can't take that away from him. You can't begrudge him that.'

'The world is full of grousers, Samuel.'

'Yes, but you're not one of them, Greta.'

Samuel smoked his cigarette and took her hand again.

'There were good days too, Greta.'

'Good days, Sam?'

'Yes. Do you remember that day we all went to Wicklow? You and the kids in the sidecar and him driving the motorbike?'

'Yes. Yes I remember that day.'

'I drove behind you with Mr Carnshaw and his wife and Mr West and poor old Ivy. Do you remember?'

'Yes. Yes. I do.'

'All she kept saying, all the way down was: "Oh I wish I was in the sidecar with them. Look at the fun they're having in there."'

'Ivy . . . '

'We stopped outside a pub on the road into Arklow. We had a picnic. Mrs Carnshaw brought the cakes. You brought the ham and the bread. Ivy was supposed to have brought the fruit. She forgot the bananas.'

'Or pretended to have forgotten the bananas. If she ever had them at all.'

Samuel smiled, 'She kept on about them just the same: "I can't believe I'm after forgettin' them bananas . . . "'

Greta laughed. He had her to a tee.

'After the picnic, the men went inside for a pint.'

'And left us out in the sidecar.'

'Ah, but we took turns to bring you out glasses of sherry. And packets of arrowroot biscuits . . . '

'Yes, you did. The children ran around playing with a ball and Danny wouldn't stay with them.'

'Yes, that's right.'

'He wanted to be with his father.'

'He did,' Samuel agreed. 'Although he did try to send him back out. He kept on saying, "Go out now to your mother and bring her this packet of biscuits."'

'When we wanted to go to the toilet, the woman of the house, she sneaked us up the side stairs like thieves. She kept saying, "Shh, shhh." As if it wasn't her husband's pub. As if it wasn't her house. You'd think he was going to kill her if he found out. And Ivy got locked in the lavatory and had to bang the door down. The woman wasn't a bit pleased. And we were afraid to ask again. The next time Ivy wanted to go, she went in the bushes. We had more laughs! Poor Ivy.'

Samuel smiled. 'And do you remember when we all came back out again?'

Greta looked at Samuel. 'What happened then?' he asked.

'You all came out first: Mr West, you, and Mr Carnshaw . . . '

'Yes, and then?'

'Danny and his father.'

'And what did they do?'

'You announced them first; you had a hunting horn you'd found behind the bar, blasting it out across the field. And then they came running out of the pub. They sang and danced. He had taught him to dance.'

'What did they sing? Greta. Can you remember?'

'Yes, yes I can. It was "Yes We Have No Bananas."'

Samuel and Greta smiled at each other. Ivy's bananas. Samuel patted her softly on the knee. 'That was a good day, Greta. That was a day to remember.'

Greta looked away from Samuel, out in front of her at the empty street. She could see him now, her little boy. The hat that kept slipping down from his head, the cane that was nearly as big as himself. His little feet following the lead of his father, left and then to the right and then back again to face them. His little face, smiling, smiling. Over at her. He was doing it for her. She could see his face now. Yes, it was like hers. She could see his face. Samuel's arms came out to her then and she felt herself fall over into them. She had found an unlikely shoulder to pour her tears onto. But they were for herself this time. They were for herself. And the smile she had shared with her little boy.

EIGHTEEN

Where do they go when they all go away? The schoolmaster had gone to Cyprus. He sent a picture postcard of himself, sitting amongst a hundred brown-faced children at the Turkish *Lycée*, his own long face white and thin. He looked like Wallis Simpson, lantern jaw, lantern light, there amongst the brown round buds dressed in Eton collars, pretending to be English. Then he had gone away again, to Africa this time. Another picture postcard. His face looked even paler, in among more buds, as black as a stack of tinkers' pots. Dressed in cricket white, those were. The blacker the face the more English they pretended to be.

And Harvey the Jarvey, he'd gone too. To a lodge at the end of a gentleman's gate, five miles from Wicklow town. Free vegetables, free firesticks, eleven bob a week. From their hundred-acre forest and their fifty-acre kitchen garden. And out of their countless heads of moaning cattle, free milk, freshly squeezed. A cowhand he would be. What did he know about cows? Chuffed with himself he was, though. The thoughts of something for nothing. And what does he do now, five miles from anywhere? Does he sit alone in his scutty kitchen, the fire at full throttle even in summer? Burning the arse off himself, getting his value. A great bucket of boiled vegetables to stuff in his face, carrots and onions and whole heads of turnips?

George perched his foot on the luggage turn-up of the car. Tuesday night, the middle of it somewhere. He had fallen asleep to the sound of thundering hooves and a rearranged race running through his head. Then he had woken. Wide as the morning, no chance of regaining either the race or the sleep. He had come downstairs for a smoke but hated the sight of the kitchen with its clothes strung up over the stove: his father's underwear – long combinations. Hers – whatever you call those things. And the face on the firegrate, surly and grey: ashes to ashes powdering out to the floor. The table with Charlie's schoolbooks in a heap and its unwashed cups and half-cut loaf of bread. Typical that. Her complaining about the price of a fourpenny loaf and then leaving it out overnight. The smog of the room, the stuffy dry room with the sour taste of a dying fire breathing all over it made him feel sick. He could smoke outside. But the breeze said forget it, snuffing each match out and drafting sneers into his earhole. He would get into the car.

The bucket seat squeaked as he settled himself in. Clean as a whistle inside. He had cleaned it himself. Zek brass rub and saddlesoap and beeswax, this was the cloud he stooped his head in through. Not much more to do with only one car in the yard but clean the living daylights out of it. He pulled the leather strap and the door thudded him in. Nice and cosy in here. Away from the wind. The smoke struggled around him, pushing up against the windows, looking for an escape route. It couldn't find one and so settled down with George. And the Zek brass rub and the saddlesoap. And the beeswax with its sweet pissy smell. All of them in there. All together now. All nice and cosy.

The light from the street lamp flopped over the wall and rested on the bonnet, simpering in at him through the window of the car. No point in taking out his notebook so; he wouldn't be able to see a stim. 'You're as bad as your Aunt Kate,' his mother had jeered, 'with your lists and your scribbles and your God only knows.'

So the notebook had come everywhere with him after that. How else had she known? Obviously been sticking her beak in. He had a directory of horses, coded for his eyes only and thoughts on them and other things besides that came to him from time to time. He had a couple of poems written in too. He should have coded them too, while he was at it – saved himself the worry of her seeing them and thinking him soft. But then he realised: had she seen them, the whole world and Gareth Reilly would have been duly informed. He wouldn't have been too long about finding out either. The minute he set foot out on the street, 'Hey George, I believe you're writin' d'oul po-tree now.' She was a mouth, that's what she was.

He had his present dilemma laid out too. Belfast on one page. Crumlin on the other. The Belfast page was nearly full. Would she have guessed what was on his mind? She might have thought it was a poem:

> Union Castle Company. Fitter, could be. Mechanics fully fledged.
> Papers forged how much?
> Reconditioning ships called castles: Arundel, Windsor. Lodgings easy got.
> Mr Kippie (check spelling with Carnshaw).
> Aircraft works another option. An engine is an engine after all.

She would think it was a queer class of a poem. But it all made perfect sense to him.

The Crumlin page had nothing as yet. He would have to think about that soon, sort it out in his head and in the morning then, fill in the lines under the title. And side by side then study them:

Belfast on the left, Crumlin on the right. See which could give a better account of itself. Like studying form. What could be simpler? Herbert always said he could think about nothing but horses. But that wasn't true. All Herbert thought about in any case was women, his nose twitching at every bit of skirt that passed his way and his thoughts all sloppy and loose. But that wasn't how he thought about things. He thought about things the same way he thought about horses, carefully.

He finished his smoke and watched the breeze work itself up to a gale. A storm it looked like. He liked a good storm. He could stay where he was in a comfortable seat or he could go out and become part of it. Even with this wide screen and the blind angle reduced to its lowest, the view was in anyway limited. The walls were too high, the archway too narrow. A prison yard, that's what it was like. What would you see stirring from here, by the head of a street lamp? A daffodil peering over a fence. The odd flutter from an outhouse shutter. A waggle from a tuft of grass that had somehow managed to grow on the roof of the shed. A shudder from a slice of corrugated iron. That would be it. That would be your lot. He opened the door. But the wind slammed it back in his face. Sorry pal, private function.

He had a key. He could take the car out. Who'd be around at this hour of the night? Who'd ever find out? He could drive as well as anyone else. Samuel had said so himself. 'As far as I'm concerned,' he'd said, 'you're good enough to drive for the king. But you're not old enough yet to go out on your own.' Weren't those his words? Was it his fault he was too young and the city full of half-blind oulfellas peering over the wheels of their car? 'Oh Jaysus, what do I do next?' Was it his fault he was on his own? In the middle of the night. And the key burning a hole in his pocket. What about now? What about this very minute?

Out on the street, the lovely wide street, things had perked up considerably, stray litter passed him by, slipping the field. There was the butcher's car parked up the way. A snub-nose Peugeot, he'd tuned it himself. It sang like a bird now. A brown paper bag rose up airborne beside it. A bird. Richard Byrd made his first flight over the North Pole. And then Clarence Birdseye put a packet of frozen peas on sale. If he could see his notebook he could connect them all. Bird, Birdseye, Byrd. Richard Byrd peering down at Clarence's vegetables unrecognisable under the snow. 'Good Lord, old chap, look at those icebergs. They look like peas from all the way up here.'

They are, you fuckin' eejit.

He drove on, his hands placed carefully on the steering wheel at ten to two. Or ten past ten, whichever way you looked at your time. The car was motoring along nicely now, up towards Patrick's Park. From behind the railings he could see the trees rear. Wild to get out, they were, pulling against the bit. They shed bits of themselves, like leper scabs whistling through the gaps. It had better be a long storm so, if that was how they planned to escape. They'd never get anywhere that way. Bit by bit. Scab by scab. You were either out or you were in. You just had to find your exit. And one you could fit through, preferably.

Bart Tully had offered him fifty quid.

'You only have to say the word now; you only have to tip me the nod. You're an old head on young shoulders. I've always said it. A man before your time; it's not right. You take my advice, son, and go away, otherwise you'll be carrying their load for the rest of your life. And give up them oul' horses; they'll have you shagged. I've seen it before, I know what can happen. Now don't get me wrong . . . I don't mind givin' you the money. But – (he might have known there'd be a 'but') – to give yourself a real start. Not to flitter away on some oul' nag, mark you. No, I won't be skivvy to that . . . '

The 'but' had lashed out at him like a clip in the ear.

Buts were for the end of cigarettes. Coffin nails: that's what buts were. And he had felt resentful enough to decline. And who did he think he was, in anyway, with his: 'He wouldn't mind . . . '

Why should he mind? Wasn't it Aunt Kate's money that set him up in the first place? Samuel's by right. And besides when had he ever flittered away on some oul' nag? A typical comment from a typical pin-on-the-page sort of a punter who only ever rouses himself for Derby day. Or the National, if he was feeling frisky. As if he knew the first thing about horses. To flitter away . . . When had he ever left it to chance? And sorry then he'd confided in him at all, told him his plan. To go away. Make his own mark. To go away to Belfast.

He turned the wheel in his hand and steered the car into Dean Street. The best run he knew was the one through the park where the road never straightened, from Chapelizod gate up to Island-bridge. Like travelling on the back of a snake, it was. He liked to turn corners. He liked the spring of leaving the straight way into the curve. Until that became the straight. Another corner so.

He was in Pimlico now. He drew the car to the side of the road and shoved his weight full against the door. Now. Now he was out. There was the semicircle path where there was always a pitch-and-toss school. He walked around it; it seemed funny no one was there. There was always somebody there. He moved along the way.

His coat pushed him on, like a hand on his backside. Mr Milinski, the dirty old dog. Used to. But wouldn't try it now; he knows what he'd get. Keeps his hands to himself now, for wringing together, for chewing his nails. Maybe he'd just lost the inclination, too old. Too worried, more like. Too worried now about everything. That Hitler for a start. They stop people in the street in Germany, his cousin had written him. Stop and measure their noses to see if they're Jews. Herbert would be bollixed so, the snout on him. He lifted his hand to his own nose. Come to think of it . . . His own might outstretch the tape. Then he rubbed it as if it were itchy, embarrassed in front of himself, with his nonsense.

There was a light in a window. Somebody else? How dare they intrude. What were they doing up there, he wondered. The light blinked away, the window now black. Some pair at it, he supposed, getting their large bit. Bucking away. What must it be like? What way would you feel? What would you say? If you said anything at all. He listened to the wind. There was no other sound.

What sort of a noise would you make? Cats, Herbert had said. Women wail like cats. Men grunt like pigs. Weeeooooow, grunt, grunt. He'd read it in a book.

He had no one to ask. You couldn't ask Father. 'Here, listen, I was just wondering like . . . what sort of a sound do you make when you . . . ?' But they'd be past that sort of thing now; at their age, surely they'd have to be. The thoughts of them doing it were enough to turn your stomach. They probably wouldn't even remember, so long ago now. He couldn't ask Samuel either. He'd be too embarrassed to ask Samuel. Bart maybe. No, Bart would have a heart attack. Milinski, he'd be the very man. Although Bart was always thinking about it, you could tell: 'Have you got yourself a sweetieheart yet . . . kissie kissie behind the wall?' He could just see Bart wailing, 'Aaaaeeeeeoooo.' Wailing like a cat. He was always making little comments. But sly ones. Unlike Milinski. He'd dive straight in and say it. 'Take my advice; get yourself one from the girl's brigade. Good girls from the brigade, let me tell you. Onwards and upwards that's their motto. Upwards and on.'

He always said it twice, with his eyes slit knavish and narrow. And then he would poke his index finger through the buttonhole of his coat. And pushing it, in and out, in and out, with a grin on his face, lecherous Lucifer with a lump in his porridge. That's what they called him. Dirty old dog.

But he couldn't ask any of them, not really. He'd just have to wait and find out for himself. He'd have more of a chance finding out in Belfast than in Crumlin, that much was a certainty.

The Ruddys moved out there, a few weeks ago. He had met Shamey last week on Reginald Street, his little florin face purple from the cold. Sitting by the shrine spitting through the railings. 'Ah it's great, George, it is. We have our own jacks, we have. You must come out.'

'All the way out to Crumlin to go to the jacks? I'd never hold it in.'

Shamey had laughed. 'Ah, it's great George, it is.' But if it was so great, why did Shamey keep coming back?

Crumlin was a kip. Kippy Crumlin. Shamey called it Crumblin, which probably made a bit more sense. When Mother told him they'd be getting a house and all delighted with herself, she was. 'Wait'll I tell you: three bedrooms, one room for the toilet, another one for the bath, a gate and a garden. With a space for grass front and back. And . . . air. Fresh mountain air,' she had added then with her eyes growing sad. Probably thinking about Danny, she was; how it might have saved him, fresh mountain air, but too late now. Now Danny was gone. A year and a half gone.

But it hadn't thrilled him much. He had felt as if he'd been lassoed in at the arms. He felt like that statue in the middle of Reginald Street, caged in, no way out. Stuck in the centre of the road, with Shamey sitting outside slinging golliers in. That's how he had felt. And anyway how would he go to work every day?

How would he get into town? And all the way in every time he wanted to go to the races. Twice the journey there. Twice again back. And not even a bookie's shop to tide you over. You could bet on that.

He came into Meath Place and there was the playground. The playground didn't know it was empty. Didn't know it had the evening off. It carried on as if it was a busy day. Swinging and swonging worn-out noises. (These kids'd have you feckinwell jacked.) Ghosts maybe, of all the dead children. Was Danny there? Which swing was going the highest? He felt himself jump then, oh Jaysus. Two tins clattered by his feet. Nearly tripped him up. He looked down at the twine connecting them to each other. Stilts. Somebody had forgotten their stilts. Danny used to be a great man on the stilts. Two empty condensed milk tins, punch the holes in, loop in the twine and off he'd go. Perfect balance. He would have made a great little jockey. He walked back to the car.

Inside it now again, he waited for a while sitting perfectly still. He stared at the dashboard and sparred in his mind. Left, right, left. One, two, three, he knocked the thought out. Danny had left him. He had punched him away. He cleared his throat and his hands moved into place, ten to two and the car moved slowly off.

He was alone on the road to Crumlin now, just him and the car. And the sounds of the storm warning them off. But it could howl all it liked, he'd made up his mind. And besides he quite liked this feeling, this feeling that he was taking a short-cut through limbo. There were worse things to listen to than a few disgruntled souls. There were worse things to see.

All to himself. Alone in the world. If he went away he'd be going alone. Some people travelled in a gang. Like cows. Or Blueshirts. What would it be like to be part of a crowd? Not quite the same as being at a race meeting. That was more like being on a train journey, never alone but each had his own station, his own destination. Each went his own way at the end of the day. But to go with a crowd, one mind, one purpose, say, like that lot that went off to Spain? A thousand of them in the middle of the night, marching into Galway city. Singing and shouting while they waited for the boat. Off to fight for Franco. How did they know what he'd be like when they got there? Supposing he turned out to be worse than Hitler, measuring their noses and examining their nudgers for foreskin. Or Mussolini even. Banning betting. What sort of a bastard would do something like that? And eight-year-old boys up for military service. Imagine, Charlie in a uniform, a gun in his belt? How did they know what they were letting themselves in for? Or were they too busy singing to think that far ahead?

The road was straight for a very long time. Could he remember the turn? First there were street lights and random square lit windows. Then there was nothing, just shadows and wind. He left Dolphin's Barn behind and watched the trees on either side throw themselves about. He was in the wilds now all right, no turning back. He'd been to this part of the country before. Twice in his life. Once on a cycle, a long time ago. Herbert was with him but they'd only passed through. He couldn't remember much of it then, just any old country village, cowshite and cottages. The next time, more recent with Samuel, he was. They were selling a car to a doctor was it? Or a vet maybe? He had a black leather bag in any case. A few years going back now. They had driven around, him in the back, and the two men up front talking about cantilever springs and the side-valve engine. The doctor was just like Bart Tully chancing his arm with the horses, a collection of phrases and suitable questions borrowed from newspapers or dipped from other people's conversations. But you could tell, just the same, he didn't know the first thing about cars, except maybe that they moved. There was a dump, a stinking jagged dump. With scavengers picking at the city's waste. A stink place it was, old clothes and broken bottles. But after a while there had been fields, too, and it had all turned into a nice country drive in the end. They had stopped by a meadow, Samuel offering the driver's seat to the doctor. Behind the wheel, the doctor took charge, giving them a tour of the countryside with the car bouncing along under his clumsy hands.

He spoke like a teacher – an old woman teacher: 'Now this area here is known as the "Dark Lanes",' he said. 'It goes all the way up to the Tongue.' This had caught his attention; it was like something old Milinski would say.

Samuel, his arm resting along the back of the front seat, had rolled his eyes heavenward into the back, while he tried to draw the conversation back to the car. 'As I was saying . . . a lot of these light cars suffer from high speed complex. You know yourself . . .'

'Oh indeed and I do . . . '

After a time, they had come back into the village and stopped at a pub on a corner. 'Now, I tell you what you'll do,' said the doctor. 'You'll take yourself up to the Puzzle. You'll find a shop there; you can buy yourself some sweeties.' And he presented him with a shilling as if it were a pound. The two men went into the pub. He went for a walk.

What was it like? One long road, bending at the hips, a small school at each end, one for the Prods, one for the other crowd. A row of terraced cottages, the last one done up to the nines, with fancies and paintwork: a gingerbread house all blue and goo. He had stopped to look at it. It was summertime and people were sitting on kitchen chairs outside, kids in bare feet playing on the roadside. Older ones surrounding the car. 'Don't touch that now, I'm warning you,' he had said. (Or had he just meant to say it?) Shops. There were shops. A dull collection as he recalled. Yes, around the Puzzle, and the only puzzle he could see was why it was called that. Just a streel of shops off the main drag. Where was the puzzle in that? A bootmaker's shop with a few old rusty shoes sprawled in the window, a ladies' hairdressers with cardboard cut-out faces beaming out. *Maison* something or other, it was called. And a window ledge long as a bench curving around the outside of a newsagent's shop. There were a few culchies playing cards on it and two little girls reading comics, perched on the end. Around the corner was a lane and he followed noises he could recognise until half way up he had found a game of pitch-and-toss. He changed his money and joined the school. That was all he could remember. Next thing was Samuel standing behind him.

'So this is where you've been hiding yourself?' That was that then. That was all there was to consider about Crumlin. Kippy Crumlin.

He swung to the left and the car pushed along, cautiously, nervously, passing the ploughmen's huts and the tantrum of hedgerows flinging from the roots. He could hardly see in front of him now, so dark. And the whole countryside seized by St Vitus's dance. He could feel the wind pull and tug at the car. 'Get out here, ye bastard. I'll have you yet.' Like a mad dog it was, chasing its tail around the car. Looking for a fight.

He could feel the car labour against it. He leaned over the wheel and tried to judge the roadway but it felt as though he was moving in midair; he had no sense of the ground beneath him. He had no sense of the roadsides either. They had been whisked away and dragged off somewhere. Then he felt himself jerk against the steering wheel and thought for a moment he had driven off the lane. It was cut off. Cut off like a cliff and he had to pull the car to the side.

'Jesus Christ Almighty,' he heard his voice say. He offered himself a cigarette to calm his nerves.

His eye could see now. A long way ahead. His eyes could see forever. The wind snatched and slapped but nothing would move. The wind roared its head off. But there was nothing to blow. Only houses. Unwilling concrete, unwilling to budge.

He finished the cigarette and drove slowly along, stopping from time to time. It never let up. It never varied. He felt like a general inspecting the troops. Inspecting the whole bloody army. Line after line. House after house, identically turned out. Some were finished, others were at various stages of growth, long multiplication crawling all over what had once been the tillage fields. He drove around for a long time. And that's all there was. Houses. No shops, no schools. No parked cars. Just the endless line-up of ghostly troops, shoulder to shoulder calmly resisting any attack.

At last there was a break in the ranks and a country road stretched out long and wide before him. He could see something at the end of it. Something vast, marking the end of the passage. Like a huge hand held out: Halt. It was some sort of a building. He continued towards it until it was close enough to identify. They had built a new church. A Catholic church, a Catholic monstrosity: Ave Maria, me mother's on the game. He turned the car to the right.

He was in the village, a good way from the houses. It would be a long trek to buy a loaf of bread. The length of Thomas Street. You could add on James's Street too, if you'd been shoved into the far end of the bottle. He drove up and then down and then came back to the Puzzle. At least there were a few bits growing here. From behind and before cottages and larger houses too, bits of greenery. It was almost pleasing to the eye after all that concrete. It almost looked real. He stopped. The wind had thrown all the fat in the fire now, beating and bashing up the village street. Making one last stand. He would wait for it to blow itself out. It would mellow soon. It would tire itself out. Sooner or later, everything did.

He pushed his hands down into his pockets and crossed his legs. He looked up the street and remembered then another street, his own street, last Sunday afternoon. And how he had seen his mother and father walking together. She, in her Sunday shoes showing an inch or so the taller and cutting her stride to suit his bad leg. Not linking arms, nothing like that. But keeping pace with each other, just the same, their heads moving occasionally, as if they had just exchanged some remark. They might as well have been in the nip, walking up the road, the shock it had given him. He'd never seen them like that before. Together. It had made him see things in a different light. It had made him think.

What did they need him for now? Why should he stay? Hardly to protect them from Father. He was harmless enough now. Mister Mellow. Since Danny had died. It was as if Danny had left a bit of himself behind, left it inside his father. He still drank of course, but not as angrily. He still fell silent for days at a time but you wouldn't be afraid of him now. Not with Danny inside him, you wouldn't be.

So what else could they need him for? To bring home the corn? No. Herbert had a job now, a clerk in the civil service. Money coming in. And prospects up ahead. 'Oh the prospects, the prospects,' his mother always said, her face in full beam. As if it was a well-to-do family living down the street that had just invited them to tea. Besides he could still send his share down from Belfast. It would amount to a lot more than he was handing up here. And they wouldn't have to feed him. Wasn't she always complaining about that too? The amount he put away? Make you feel like a dog, eating under her calculating eye.

But they had always needed him. For something or other. Or had he just supposed they did? Had he taken it all on himself without invitation? Had he made them lazy? Unable to reach a decision, always ready to jump at the first option, to back the sure thing?

The lease on the house would be up next year. So what? How long was a lease? Guinness's had 9,000 years on St James's Gate. When would they start worrying about where to go next? 'Oh my God, what are we going to do? The lease is up in another 800 years? We better move to the scheme in Crumblin so. That's the only thing to do.'

His father didn't need him any more, not even to back horses; he had lost the taste for it. Backed like a slob now. And Herbert? Herbert would get himself a girl soon. He was always on the lookout. Him and his tongue. Did he still love Beatrix? Maybe, maybe not. She was in Belfast too. Aunt Maude had had a letter. Would that make Herbert jealous? 'I'm going to Belfast.'

'That's where Beatrix is, you bloody bastard.'

Herbert loved Beatrix and Maudie loved Herbert. You'd think they could come to some arrangement. Sort it out between themselves. But he didn't love anybody. Not anybody yet. Love was for people who had nothing better to think about. Nothing better to do with their time. Who did Beatrix love? Anybody who didn't fawn all over her. Until they did and then she'd probably lose interest. She fancied herself, that one. Full of herself, her.

He'd hardly run into her in Belfast, anyway. Belfast was a city, like Dublin. You could lose your neighbours there. Not like this hole, not like Crumlin. You wouldn't be able to breathe without them knowing: 'Here, did you hear that George fella, breathing last night?' 'No? Go away!' 'And again this morning, when he was writin' a pome. Breathin' again. The cheek of him. Imagine? And him eatin' his poor mother out of house and home . . . '

He looked out through each window of the car, turning himself from side to side until he had completed the rectangle. Two and a half thousand people they planned to move out here. Two and a half. And God knows how many more now that the hutches were up. All those kids squeezed into two parochial schools, built to suit a village of this size. Two and a half thousand. No cars, no bookies, no picture-house even, just a couple of window parlour shops to keep them amused. An extension of the city dump, that's all it was. And what would they do with themselves when the novelty wore off? What would they do when they'd all had their baths? And how many times in one day could you go to the jacks?

George sighed. He was beginning to feel tired now. He was beginning to feel the cold. The wind had dropped. He'd been right about that. And he had made up his mind. Fifty quid would give him a fair start in Belfast. Ten of that would buy him his papers. Forged of course. Not forged, no. Exaggerated. They would get him a job, a fully-fledged mechanic out of his time. He only had another eighteen months or so in anyway. And what difference now? He knew as much as any mechanic. He was almost eighteen years of age. He could get away with it. He could get a job. Mr Carnshaw said he could fix it up. With Mr Kippie (check spelling).

Yes, he would go . . . There was little enough for him in New Street. But here in Crumlin? There was nothing for him here.

And yet his decision didn't please him completely. Like placing your bet, wondering up to the last second, should you chance something else. You'd all your sums done, all angles covered. And yet . . . He got out of the car and looked at the headlamps, goggling out at him from the forehead of the car. He reached into his pocket and pulled out a coin. Yes, just in case, just in case, a second opinion, just to be sure.

On the bridge of his thumb and forefinger he balanced the coin. Two thousand five hundred. Two thousand, four hundred and ninety-nine? He stooped a little at the knees as if it weighed a stone and springing himself from the heels, filliped the coin into the night. He watched it disappear and waited for it to come back to him. It seemed too long a time. He thought he had lost it. It had been sucked up into the stratosphere and he would never see it again. Then he saw a sudden flick and turn and he watched it fall gently, tumbling down, head to harp, head to harp, out of the blackness, through the air and spinning into a shine as it skimmed through the car's yellow beams. His hand shot out and caught it before it hit the ground.

It felt like a live thing, beating in his fist; it felt like a pulse. He straightened himself up carefully as though he might disturb it. Then he slapped it on to the back of his other hand. He stood for a while, listening to the sound of the breeze pulling itself back into silence and wondered what the coin would tell him to do with his life. He waited a moment. Here it was. That last-minute urge. Swinging from side to side in his head: Heads or harp? Harps or head? A warm feeling was coming over him now. He smiled. It was a feeling he knew, a feeling that's how it would always be.